SPARK OF CHAOS

SABRINA FLYNN

SPARK OF CHAOS

BOOK ONE

SABRINA FLYNN

Published by Ink & Sea Publishing
www.sabrinaflynn.com

ISBN 978-1-955207-20-1
ebook ISBN 978-1-955207-21-8

Book 1 of Spark of Chaos
Book cover by Miblart

ALSO BY SABRINA FLYNN

Ravenwood Mysteries

From the Ashes

A Bitter Draught

Record of Blood

Conspiracy of Silence

The Devil's Teeth

Uncharted Waters

Where Cowards Tread

Beyond the Pale

A Grim Telling

Spark of Chaos

Flame of Ruin

God of Ash

Untold Tales: Prequel

Bedlam

Windwalker

www.sabrinaflynn.com

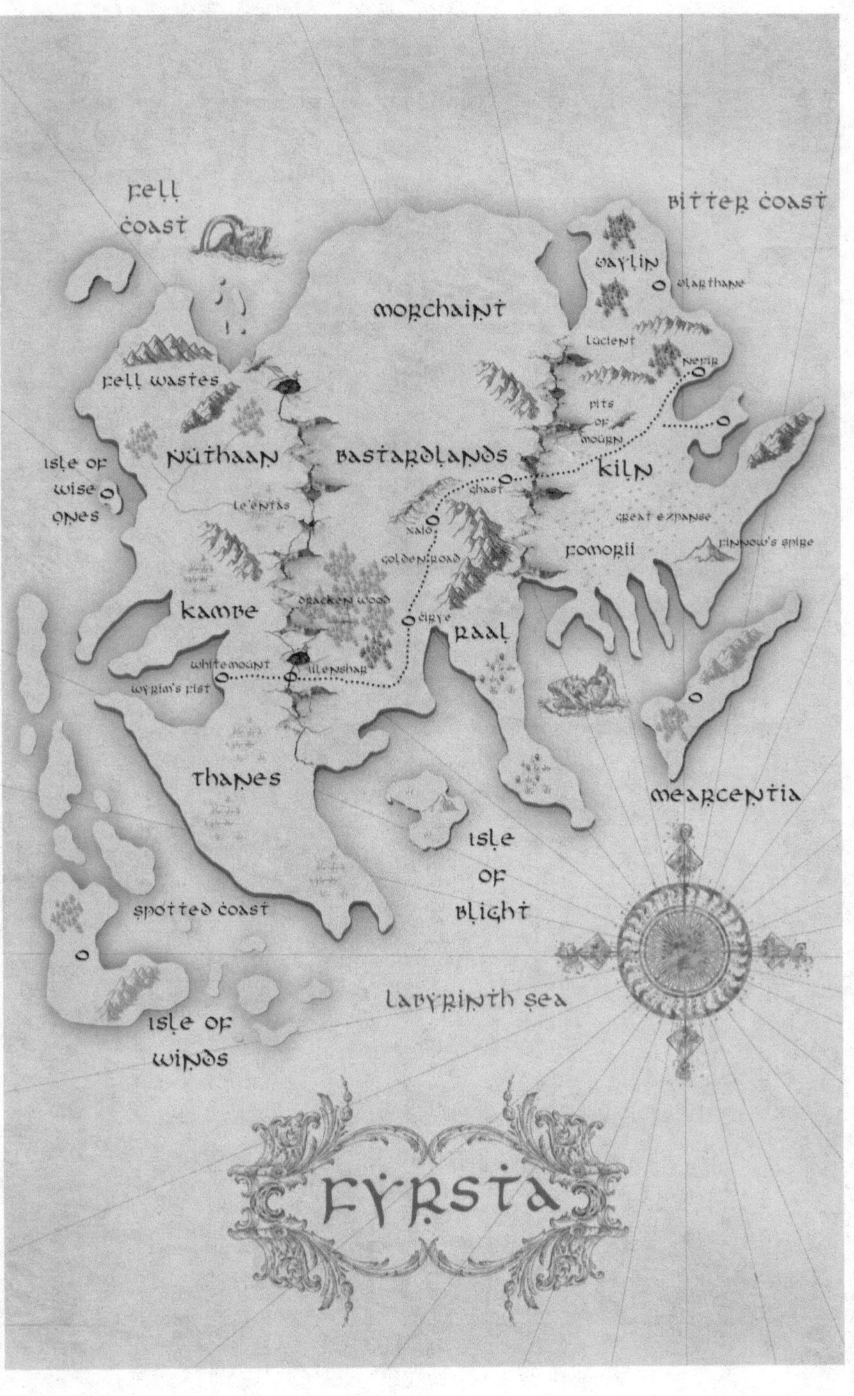

pell coast
Bitter coast
vaylin
olapthane
Morchaint
lucient
nepip
pell wastes
pits of mourn
Nüthaan
Bastardlands
Kiln
Isle of wise ones
chast
le'enfas
Naio
great expanse
Finnow's spire
Golden road
Fomorii
Kambe
Dracken wood
Cirye
Raal
Whitemount
lilenshar
Wyrim's fist
Thanes
Mearcentia
Isle of Blight
spotted coast
Labyrinth sea
Isle of winds
FYRSTA

"Every story has a beginning; the task is finding it."
—Galvier Longstride

PROLOGUE

TIME IS FICKLE, ever changing and flowing, ebbing like the sea, a vast ocean of moments brushing against the next. It slips between our fingers when we wish to hold it, yet clings when we seek to flee it. Time is a burden we cannot escape.

Our lives are swallowed in its dark waters, never to be remembered or recalled, fading like a whisper that never was. But once in a rare time, one moment brushes against the next and a spark flares to life that refuses to be forgotten.

This is the moment, the spark, and this is how the end begins for a shattered realm—with a small nymphling who was cold.

1998 A.S. (After the Shattering)

THE SLEEK HORSE cut through the night, racing over slick cobblestones with a fearlessness her rider did not share. Sleet battered him. It stung his cheeks and tugged on his cloak, threatening to rip him out of the saddle. He closed his eyes and offered a silent prayer to the Guardians for protection.

It was the Felling Wind, a storm brewed in the frigid mountains of the Fell Wastes. Every man, woman, and child had taken shelter from it —everyone save the rider.

Edmund Flaetfoot cursed his luck, the uneven roads, the biting wind, but most of all the fiendish force that had started a fire in the Royal Nursery.

Lightning lit up a ramshackle pleasure house. Edmund pulled sharply on the reins, and the horse skidded to a stop in the mud. He placed a calming hand on her neck, tugged his cloak back down, and squinted at a sign swaying on its chain.

The faded letters of *The Mermaid's Blush* were lost in the storm, but Edmund knew Whitemount like his own home, and this run-down hovel of red paint and gold-flecked balconies was his destination.

Why in the Nine Halls would the Emperor's Wise One favor so unsavory a place?

The common room was nearly empty of patrons, save for the truly immobile. He picked his way past snoring drunkards and equally soused whores, wrinkling his nose at the gaudy decor. Some optimistic soul had tried to spruce up the worst of the termite-ridden wood with a layer of gold paint and a dousing of cheap perfume to mask the under-lying stench of sweat, piss, and unwashed men.

Edmund stepped into the light of a spluttering candle. A haggard woman stirred in the corner to study the young man with her small, suspicious eyes. Her gaze shifted to the man's tunic and the Emperor's crest: a black sword and two blue crowns on a field of silver. Her face creased like old leather.

"Our dues are paid," she spat out.

"Where is the Wise One known as Oenghus Saevaldr?"

"Wise One?" the woman snorted. "Don't know about all that. Is the big oaf in trouble again?"

A brute with a crooked nose dragged himself out of his chair, planted his feet and crossed his arms to wait for orders.

"I have an urgent message for him—nothing more," Edmund replied quickly. It was common for officials like him to disappear in these dock districts, with no one the wiser for it.

"I'll give it to 'im once you've had a drink. Vigum, there will take yer coin." The woman jerked her head towards the guard.

Edmund's throat went dry, but he stiffened, remembering his orders. He did not have time for these games.

"In the name of Emperor Soataen Jaal III, take me to the Wise One or this hovel will be burnt to the ground!"

The woman looked him over while the guard chuckled. Edmund Flaetfoot resisted the urge to do what he did best: run.

After a few moments of consideration, she stood, spat at his feet, and tottered up the stairwell. With a sigh of relief, Edmund followed. Planks sagged and groaned in protest as they climbed. On the third floor landing, the woman stopped and waved him down a hallway.

"Oenghus' room is the last door there. Good luck wakin' 'im."

Edmund hurried past peeling walls, stained chairs, and the artwork of a drunken, one-armed sailor with a paintbrush. He rapped on the door three times, quick and authoritative, then waited, shifting from foot to foot. When no one answered, he began pounding on the door.

"Who in the Nine Halls is that?" a voice bellowed.

"I have an urgent message for you, m'lord," Edmund yelled.

A loud grumble answered, followed by sounds of rustling fabric, then approaching footsteps. The door opened a crack to reveal a sleepy-eyed woman with a heart-shaped face.

"Quiet down or you'll wake the whole house," she scolded as she ushered him inside.

Flames flickering in a small hearth illuminated a cluttered room, but not the common sort reserved for patrons who came and went by the hour.

The unclothed woman hurried back to a large bed. Edmund watched her slip under the covers, thinking the Wise One's tastes weren't so bad after all. A loud snore broke his reverie—the healer had fallen back asleep.

Edmund walked over to a massive pair of feet hanging over the end of the mattress. Those feet made him uneasy. This would not be the first lord he'd had to drag out of bed, but he was certainly the largest.

Edmund cleared his throat, loudly.

The Wise One's snoring cut off with a grunt, and he lowered the covers to study the intruder. "Well?"

"Lord Saevaldr... Wise One, I have urgent news. There's been a fire in the palace."

"Good thing it's raining," he growled, draping an arm over another woman in the creaking bed.

"M'lord," Edmund persisted. "Emperor Jaal requests your presence."

"Kiss my arse."

"The fire was in the nursery wing." His words were like a crossbow trigger.

The two women yelped in surprise as the Wise One threw off his blankets and surged out of bed. Before Edmund could run, a crushing hand grabbed him by the collar and yanked him off his feet. He stared into the baleful eyes of what could only be a Nuthaanian Berserker— over seven feet of fury, death, and carnage.

"Is Isiilde safe?" Oenghus demanded.

The young man spluttered in fear as his feet kicked uselessly in the air.

"Oen," a second woman interrupted. Her voice was ever so gentle. She slipped from the bed and wrapped herself in a blanket. She was lush with golden brown skin, and in that moment, hovering at the edges of his sight, she seemed a benevolent goddess. "Put him down and let him talk." She placed a hand on the powerful arm—an arm that was larger than her waist.

"Oh, aye, might be a good idea." Oenghus relaxed his grip, and Edmund fell to the floor, collapsing in a breathless heap. He scuttled away from the looming Nuthaanian until he was stopped short by the closed door.

"Spit it out, lad," Oenghus growled, black beard twitching with threat.

"I don't know the details, m'lord." Hasty words tumbled from his lips. "I heard there were injuries... and deaths. I don't know who, but His Majesty is furious."

The bull of a man grimly donned his clothes and tore from the room, his eyes as deadly as the storm.

A BATTLE RAGED above the sprawling palace of Whitemount. Wind and sleet dueled flame and smoke, engulfing the entire east wing with smoldering fury. Every able-bodied person in the palace strived to quench the unnatural blaze.

Oenghus Saevaldr raced towards the palace infirmary. He was a hard man to miss—a mountain that rivers flowed around—and the lords and soldiers of Kambe scattered like so many startled chickens at his approach.

He ducked beneath the infirmary door and surveyed the wounded. He counted nineteen people; nine were already dead, their charred bodies covered with white linen shrouds. Another five wounded appeared to be well on their way to the same end.

A woman pulled herself from the wounded. Short for a Nuthaanian, but every bit as sturdy, she barely came up to Oenghus' chest.

"Oen," she breathed in relief.

"The children, Morigan?"

"Aristarchus and Sarabian were both injured, but nothing serious." She glanced at the dying. "I can't say the same for their bodyguards."

"Isiilde?" Oenghus asked, bracing himself for the answer.

"I don't know," Morigan admitted. "The guards can't find her. I suspect she ran off, and it's a good thing because the Emperor is furious. His heirs nearly burned tonight."

"Isiilde is his daughter too," Oenghus snapped.

A guard by the door shifted with a jangle of armor. Morigan's eyes slid to the listening guard, and back to Oenghus. When she spoke, her voice was tight with control. "You should remind him of that, because he ordered his guards to throw her in a dungeon until she's old enough to sell."

Oenghus wanted to pummel the emperor. He clenched his fists, imagining flesh transforming to pulp beneath his blows.

"I'm sure she didn't mean to start the fire. But does she ever?" Morigan asked. "After the disaster with the gardens, the library, *and* the banquet—it's clear she's more dangerous than we imagined. But tossing a four-year-old nymphling into a dungeon..."

Oenghus knew that look in Morigan's eyes. He'd watched her wade into battle to heal the dying and kill enough men to cover a battlefield. Once the woman got something in her mind, there was no stopping her.

"The bastard is not putting her in a dungeon," Oenghus rumbled.

"He's the *Emperor*," Morigan reminded. "We can't fight the army he has. You need to think of something that doesn't involve bloodshed. Otherwise, your head will be on the chopping block."

"It's *my* head," Oenghus growled.

"So use it and stop thinking with your bollocks."

He bared his teeth and stalked out of the infirmary, growling at the guards as he passed. They reached for their swords, but he ignored the men.

Oenghus stepped outside into a chilling sleet. It nearly cooled his temper. Then his gaze fell on the army of bucket-wielding servants fighting a hopeless battle. Only Isiilde could have started a fire in this weather. The east wing looked like a bonfire at The Feast of Fools.

Where would the nymphling hide? Morigan was the first answer that came to mind. But not with guards in the infirmary. The kitchens and forges, then. But no—too many people.

The palace garden was Isiilde's favorite place to roam. The gate was usually locked, but Oenghus knew better. A fox had tunneled beneath the wall, a perfect fit for the nymphling.

With a glance over his shoulder, he pressed his hand against the garden gate, and uttered the Lore of Unlocking. The lock clicked, and he slipped into the walled garden.

The nymphling liked to play Raven and the Prey. She hid from everyone—save for a select few. But *he* knew every one of her hiding places.

Her favorite perch in an oak tree was empty. And her climbing rock wasn't sheltered enough, so he went straight to a fallen, hollowed out tree.

Oenghus crouched in front of the opening. "Isiilde?" he called.

No answer.

He found a small pebble in the mud and wove a rune of light around it. When the runes settled, he blew into the palm of his hand. A soft glow blossomed, and he tossed it into the hollow. A tiny form huddled in the center, sitting chest deep in a pool of muck and water.

She had stopped shivering.

He forced words past his lips. "Sprite," he called, reaching in, but he was too large, and she was too far away. "It's Oen, come out of there."

The nymphling did not move.

"Isiilde!"

When she did not stir, a rare panic clutched him. He squeezed himself farther inside, stretching his fingertips towards her. He brushed Isiilde's arm, and a little hand touched his own. Oenghus seized her hand and dragged her out.

"You'll have to find a better hiding place than that." He tried to keep his voice light as he gathered her up in his arms.

"I'm in trouble, Oen," Isiilde whispered.

"You're always in trouble. It's nothing to worry about now. We'll get you nice and warm first, all right?"

Isiilde did not answer. Her silence worried him—more than the chill of her skin. He quickly stripped off her soaking nightgown, tossed it aside, and tucked her beneath his shirt, against the heat of his skin and the rhythm of his heart. He wrapped his cloak tightly around them both, and hurried back to the palace, hoping no one would notice the tiny bundle.

The urge to walk out of the palace into Whitemount and head north until he reached Nuthaan was nearly overwhelming. But Morigan was right. He could not single-handedly protect a nymph from men and gods alike. Isiilde's best chance was in Kambe as the daughter of an emperor. But she'd burnt the emperor's last straw.

Halfway to his rooms, the nymphling started shivering, which eased a knot of worry between his shoulders. But as Oenghus rounded the last corner, that knot returned. The Guard Captain and a pair of guards lingered outside his rooms.

At his approach, the guards barred the door with a pair of crossed spears. But it was more symbol than threat. They all knew trying to stop a berserker was as useless as damming a river with two twigs. Oenghus scowled at the guards. They tried to take a step back, but were stopped by the stone wall at their backs.

Their captain stood his ground. He was built more like a keg than a Kamberian—short and muscular, with the temperament of a bear. "I have orders to find the nymphling and bring her to His Majesty at once," Darius said. "I know she's under your shirt."

"And do you know what his next order will be? To throw a child into a bloody dungeon. Are you willing to do that, Darius?"

"His Majesty's word is law," Darius stated.

Oenghus turned slightly, eyeing the captain. The guards tensed for a fight. But Morigan's words came to mind, and he summoned every bit of control he possessed. "All I ask is that you let me heal her. You can go get His bloody Majesty, but I will *not* hand this child over before she's healed. And we both know you'll need an army of reinforcements to stop me."

He wasn't called Grimstorm without reason.

"Fine," Darius relented. "But she can't leave my sight." He issued orders to his guards that sent one running down the corridor with a message for the Emperor.

Oenghus swatted the remaining guard's spear aside and barged into his chambers, leaving the door open for the captain to follow. He wrapped the nymphling in a blanket, set her on the hearthrug, and lit a fire.

Isiilde inched closer to the blaze. "I didn't mean to," she chattered.

Oenghus shrugged off his drenched cloak and scooped her up. Fire and the nymphling were never a good combination.

"I don't wanna go in a dunge'n, Oen," she pleaded, eyes filling with tears. "I was cold."

"You're not going to a dungeon, Sprite."

Oenghus sat in front of the hearth and began rubbing her hands and feet to restore warmth. Her curly red hair was plastered to her face, exposing the unmistakable ears of her race: a slender, sweeping elegance that rose to a sharp point above her head. The tips were currently wilted and alarmingly blue. Mud caked her face, her hair, and every exposed part of her body, save for the long tracks of tears on her cheeks.

Oenghus doubted Darius would defy his liege lord for the child in his arms. She was a faerie, a nymph, and by the decrees of the Blessed Order, she had no more rights than a dog.

Nymphs were born into slavery. Their rarity and allure made them both dangerous and highly sought after commodities. A single nymph was worth a king's ransom and a thousand wars had been fought over them.

A coughing fit interrupted her shivering, and when it finally let go, she collapsed into the cradle of his arm.

Oenghus slipped a hand over her stomach and placed the other across her forehead, linking him to both spirit and flesh. He murmured the Wise One's Lore, plunging into the nymphling with his mind's eye, leaving the physical realm behind, until only power and life pulsed hypnotically around him.

Using the Sylph's Gift to heal was dangerous; it was easy to lose one's self. But the same could be said of battle. He anchored himself with an intangible thread to find his way back, then focused on the nymphling's spirit.

Every spirit was unique. Some were vast and empty, others dark and cold, but Isiilde's was a bright flame. Only now, her flame was flickering. The slightest breeze would snuff out her life.

Oenghus shoved his fear aside. He carefully wrapped his power around the weak flame, fanning it with his own spirit, and opening himself to all her pain. He thought his heart would tear in two.

After the flame was steady, he pulled himself along the tether to his own body. Coming back was like plunging into icy water. It took a moment to regain his senses.

Isiilde was unconscious—a normal side effect after a healing. It allowed the body to mend.

Oenghus smoothed back her hair. The tips of her ears had returned to their natural shade. He grunted with relief, then placed her gently in an armchair and considered his options.

The nymphling's Fate, and his own for that matter, depended on Soataen's whims. The Emperor had always cultivated the good opinion of his people. He was known as a benevolent ruler, and his craving for popularity might be used against him. But if that failed, Oenghus would resort to what he knew best. And by the gods, there would be blood.

A commanding voice echoed in the hallway. Darius snapped to attention while Oenghus planted himself in front of the nymphling. The door opened and Emperor Soataen Jaal III strode through. His four bodyguards took up a defensive position at his side.

The Emperor of Kambe was once a handsome man, but grief had left its mark. After Isiilde's mother died, Soataen lost the will to live and the Keening was slowly dragging him towards death. His once flawless skin now sagged with age, and his golden hair had turned a dull grey. He still retained some of his gracefulness, but his muscles were weak and his bones ached.

And yet his subjects loved him more than ever—thanks to a few clever minstrels who had spun a nymph's death into a tragic love story.

Oenghus knew better; the stories were lies.

"Why isn't the nymphling in my dungeons, Captain?" Soataen asked, ignoring the giant looming in the room.

Oenghus was never one to be ignored, not even by royalty, so he spoke before Darius could shoulder the blame. "Your Imperial Majesty." He was careful to keep the disdain out of his tone. "Your *daughter* was near death when I found her. Although she's better, she's still weak. It'd be best to let her remain here with me."

"I don't care one whit for that nymphling, except for the gold she will fetch me."

"She'll fetch you nothing if she's dead."

Soataen arched an imperious brow. "Do you think me a fool, Wise One?"

"I don't think you've thought this through."

"Oh, I assure you, I have given this matter a great deal of thought.

That creature nearly killed my heirs. Nine of my subjects are dead because of that fiend curled safely in your chair. What of *their* families?"

"The laws of your land do not hold a child accountable for an accident."

"This matter is not up for debate," Soataen warned.

"A dungeon, no matter how comfortable, will kill her."

"You have served me well, but I am in no mood to be trifled with tonight. Step aside, Oenghus Saevaldr, or I will lay treason upon your head."

Soataen's word was law, and it snapped his bodyguards into action. Four hardened soldiers fanned out.

To the Void with diplomacy. It hadn't worked for him in the last nine-hundred and eighty-four years, so why the Void would it be any different now?

Oenghus pinned the emperor with a stare that had made men faint with fear. "Try it, you bastard."

Soataen bristled. "How dare you."

"I will not let you harm this child. You owe it to her mother," Oenghus growled. "You discarded the laws of your—"

"Enough!"

"—own land."

"Kill him."

"You abducted the nymph and raped her!" Oenghus roared, backing up as the guards approached.

Darius faltered at the accusation, but the bodyguards kept coming. Oenghus turned in time to catch a thrusting spear. He tore the weapon from the guard's hand and snapped it in half.

Oenghus roared, and the floor exploded with a crack of stone. Three guards were thrown back, landing in a heap of clattering armor. The fourth guard dove over the wave of debris. He landed, rolled, and came up swinging his sword. Oenghus caught the blade in his hand, letting the edge dig into his palm.

The guard's eyes widened.

Oenghus grabbed the guard's collar, yanked him forward, and drove his head into the man's face. Then he picked up the reeling soldier and chucked him into his fellows like a sack of grain.

"I will tear this palace down stone by stone, Soataen!" Oenghus bellowed, throwing his hands apart, reaching toward the walls as if he held them by invisible chains. At his thundering call, the walls shifted and cracked, pelting their heads with mortar and stone.

"She was a nymph. That's what they're good for," Soataen snarled.

The guards stumbled to their feet, preparing for another attack. But Darius stayed back.

"Think, Soataen," Oenghus hissed, unhooking his war hammer. "You're no fool. Why can't you escape the Keening? You haven't lost your will to live; you lost the *right* to live! It's not the Keening. You were cursed."

Soataen flinched with guilt.

The guards came at Oenghus in a rush. He drove his bulk into the closest before the man could finish his swing. Oenghus grabbed the stunned soldier's collar and spun him around. The guards scrambled to avoid their comrade, but one soldier's reaction was a split second late, and his blade plunged into the human shield.

"Enough!" Soataen snapped.

His guards retreated eagerly. Oenghus tossed their dying comrade at them with one heave of his powerful arm. He'd just been warming up.

"What would you have me do, Wise One? Shall I keep the nymphling in my palace and pray she doesn't burn down my kingdom? Or do you think her a tame, innocent little faerie who presents no threat to my subjects?"

"I'm not saying she isn't dangerous."

"If not a dungeon, then where do I keep her? Answer me that."

"Send her with me to the Isle."

"They won't take a nymph."

"I'll deal with the details." Even as he said the words, he wondered if he had a chance of persuading the Council of Nine to accept her.

"No, absolutely not," Soataen said, shaking his head. "The nymphling is worth far too much. You're nothing but a barbarian. How do I know you won't sell her, or take her for yourself when she comes of age? Your debts and fondness for women are well known in my court."

"How dare you question *my* honor, you bloody bastard!" Oenghus clenched his fists, swallowing an urge to toss the emperor out a window. "You forced yourself on Yasine. She trusted me, Soataen. Not you. I sat by her deathbed. I held her newborn when she had no strength. And now you question *my* intentions towards her daughter!"

"Leave. Now. And take that nymphling from my sight. When she comes of age, bring her back, or by the gods I will summon an Interrogator from Ghast for your torment," Soataen hissed. "Captain, I want them out of Kambe before the sun rises."

Oenghus wasn't about to argue over details. He hooked his war hammer on his belt, hastily threw his gear into a rucksack, and shrugged his cloak on before picking up the sleeping nymphling.

Without a backward glance, he strode from his chambers, severing his ties to Kambe. He left behind his books, his potions, and all his belongings, save the rucksack on his back and the combustible creature in his arms.

But as he hurried down the hallway, the Guard Captain fell in step at his side. "Is it true?"

"Ask his bloody bodyguards," Oenghus replied. "They dragged her back into his bedchamber when she tried to flee."

Oenghus could never forget that night.

"That's not what I was asking. She was a nymph, after all—laws don't apply to them. I didn't even know the creature had a name," Darius admitted. "Still, I wouldn't have thought it of His Majesty, especially with the songs they sing. Why didn't you say something?"

Oenghus sighed, feeling sick. "It's complicated. This isn't the way to the front gates."

"You'll need more supplies."

Oenghus nodded in gratitude. "One more thing. Tell Morigan I'm headed to the Isle. She'll worry otherwise."

"Consider it done," Darius said, then lowered his voice to a whisper. "Tell me... is it true His Majesty was cursed?"

"Aye."

"Why?"

Oenghus hesitated. He couldn't tell the truth, but he could tell something close to it. "Nymphs are favored by the Sylph. She cursed him for attacking one of her own."

Darius smoothed his mustaches. "I don't understand... nymphs aren't our equals."

"You're bloody right they aren't. They're something far above us, Captain. Don't forget that."

"If that were the case, the Blessed Order would honor them. Your claims don't make sense."

"They sure in the Void don't, but it's the truth."

"Oenghus." Darius gripped his arm and drew him to a halt. "The Blessed Order serves the Goddess. If nymphs are favored by the Sylph, then the Order wouldn't have decreed them property."

Oenghus glowered down at the man. "The Blessed Order doesn't serve the Sylph."

"But they serve the Guardians, who are servants of the Sylph."

"So the Guardians of Iilenshar claim."

"Careful, Oenghus," Darius warned, "comments like that border on heresy."

"Are you going to squeal to the first Inquisitor you find?"

"Of course not. But you've burned many bridges here tonight. You've made a powerful enemy in His Majesty, and there's no point in adding the Blessed Order to your list."

"The Blessed Order can rot," Oenghus snorted.

"You might say that now, but one day you could find yourself backed into a corner without an ally in sight."

Oenghus bared his teeth. "Then I'll turn around, lift my kilt and bend over real nice-like so they can all kiss my arse right before I drag the lot of them into the Pits o' Mourn."

"Spoken like a true Nuthaanian," Darius sighed.

"ARE WE GOING IN THERE, OEN?" a timid little voice whispered from his rucksack. He twisted his neck around to study the freckled face poking from beneath the flap.

"Keep your head down, Sprite," he growled for the hundredth time since arriving on the Isle of Wise Ones.

"It's very scary." The nymphling shivered before she ducked back into his rucksack, pulling the flap closed like a turtle hiding in its shell.

"This tower is the Spine. This is where the Archlord of the Isle lives." Oenghus squeezed his bulk between the shrubbery and scanned the strange stone.

"There's no door," Isiilde pointed out from her concealment.

"It's a secret one. Now hush," Oenghus said.

It wasn't just any secret door. It was an invisible rune. He placed his palm on the stone and slid it over the general area, where he vaguely remembered the door being hidden. A slight tremor in the stone brought him up short. He spread his fingers and murmured words that would awaken the stone's dormant power.

A cold, ancient weight embraced him, sucking him through the teleportation rune before spitting him out a heartbeat later.

A gasp rose from his rucksack, but he thought it more excitement than fear. Shaking the chill from his bones, he stepped into a thick sheet of cobwebs that stretched from one end of an empty alcove to the next.

"You have to be on your best behavior, Sprite," Oenghus instructed as he emerged from the alcove into an equally deserted hallway.

The nymphling poked her head from the rucksack with a curious tilt of her ears. "I'm always good," she said.

"Aye, that's what I'm afraid of."

Oenghus walked straight to an identical alcove at the far end of the corridor, and touched another mundane bit of stone. He summoned the Lore and a familiar chill tugged him through the stone.

Another empty corridor greeted him. But this passage was slightly different—there was a large, ornate door waiting at the end. A sign, he thought, that his former master and friend hadn't taken him off the guest list.

Oenghus stopped in front of the door and squared his shoulders. The next minutes were critical. He had to convince the Archlord to let Isiilde remain on the Isle. But the Archlord was immune to intimidation and threat. It was infuriating. And since Oenghus' powers of persuasion were sorely lacking, blunt honesty would have to do.

"Keep quiet," Oenghus murmured over his shoulder.

Obedient silence answered. He took a deep breath and pounded his fist against the wood. At his persistent knock, the door flew open. Isek Beirnuckle, advisor to the Archlord, stood at the threshold. Isek reminded him of a bald weasel that was always on the verge of running.

Isek jumped back in surprise. But his shock didn't last long. "By the Pits o' Mourn, I didn't expect to see you here," he said, offering a hand.

"Me either," Oenghus grunted, ducking through the doorway. "Looks like I'm still welcome." There was a question in his words, directed at the back of a tall, graceful man with pointed ears standing in front of a crystal window. Moonlight streamed through the crystal, illuminating his long white hair and a collection of artifacts, each a power in its own right.

The Archlord did not immediately stir. Instead, he continued his silent vigil, gaze fixed on the oval window that filled an entire wall. The window glowered down at the Isle and the ocean beyond like some monstrous, multi-faceted eye watching its surroundings.

Oenghus stepped into the center of the study, eyeing his former master. The Archlord had not changed over the centuries—he was in the prime of his life, as timeless as the crystal window. And he never quite seemed to be of this world. He was too graceful, too perfect and angular. From the point of his ears to his high cheekbones and tall, slender body.

Oenghus had always found his masculine beauty disconcerting. But then, that was an immortal elf for you.

The Archlord stirred from his contemplation. "Isek," he said without turning. "Leave us."

"Right, then," Isek muttered. "We'll have a drink later, Oen, and catch up on the past ten years, aye?"

"If you're buying."

"I'll have to if I want to find out what's so important." Isek bounced his gaze from the Archlord to Oenghus before leaving.

When the echoes of Isek's footsteps had faded, the Archlord turned to regard his visitor.

"Marsais."

"Oenghus." The corners of his long lips twitched in greeting.

"Are we good, then?" Oenghus asked.

His grey eyes glittered. "Were we ever not?"

Oenghus grunted. Marsais had probably forgotten their disagreement. Either way, Oenghus wasn't going to dredge up old arguments. "I take it you know why I'm here?"

"Hmm, I knew you were coming, but not why," Marsais mused, stroking his braided goatee. Brushing confusion aside, Marsais stepped forward with a sweep of his robes, stopping directly in front of his massive visitor. "It's good to see you, old friend."

"I might have missed you a bit too, ye ol' bastard." Oenghus tugged on his beard, and then threw awkwardness to the winds, pulling Marsais into a hug that threatened to break the man. "You haven't changed a bit."

"I wish I could say the same of you." Marsais stepped back to study his face. "Is that a bit of grey in your—" he cut off abruptly, glancing over Oenghus' shoulder. "Ah, that answers the why. I assume you know you have a stowaway peeking out of your rucksack?"

There was no hiding the nymphling now. Resigned, Oenghus unslung his pack and set it carefully down.

Isiilde untangled herself from the container and stood, gaping up at Marsais with wide, curious eyes. The timing could not have been worse, but books always made her sneeze, and the nymphling did just that, every sneeze accented with a burst of flame that puffed from her pointed ears.

Marsais blinked in surprise and batted at his robes where they had caught fire. Smoke trailed from the fabric.

As Marsais stooped to study the redhead, a knot settled between Oenghus' shoulders. He cleared his throat. "Sprite, this is the Archlord of the Isle."

"Oenghus," Marsais said slowly, transferring his gaze from faerie to man. "This isn't a sprite; she's a nymphling."

The knot between his shoulders tightened.

"Could I talk to you in private?"

"Hmm." Marsais gestured towards the far wall of the chamber. Oenghus picked up Isiilde and set her on a gleaming white rug in the center of the study.

"Stay here and don't move," he ordered. "And *no* singing." Oenghus turned to leave, but stopped short. "And don't touch anything either."

Isiilde tilted her head up at him. But instead of voicing her confusion, she obediently thrust her hands into her pockets.

Oenghus stepped off to the side, and Marsais wove an Orb of Silence to give them privacy from curious ears.

"Look, before you say anything, I brought her here because I didn't know what else to do with her."

"That certainly clears up everything."

"It's reason enough, you sarcastic bastard."

"I see your diplomacy hasn't improved."

Oenghus took a deep breath. He was trying to keep his temper in check, but Isiilde's life was in danger. They needed the Isle's protection.

Marsais held up a calming hand. "Oen, you look on the verge of flying into a berserker's rage. Just start at the beginning. Wherever that might be."

Oenghus started with the night of the fire. And Marsais began pacing, continuing throughout the narrative, then pausing when Oenghus explained how he'd smuggled Isiilde onto the island. Long minutes passed in silence.

"I can't grant her sanctuary," Marsais finally said. "The nymphling is Emperor Jaal's daughter. He is her rightful owner. You know as well as I that the Isle doesn't link itself with the kingdoms."

"I'm not asking for the Isle to sign a treaty with Kambe. I'm only asking for refuge," Oenghus said.

"You know the Nine won't see it like that."

"What about all the nobles training here? How is that any different?"

"Hmm, they aren't nymphs," Marsais pointed out. "Nobles rarely bring the Blessed Order's attention upon us, and a nymph would do just that. Our relations with the Order are strained at the best of times."

"How can you turn her away? The bastard was going to throw her in a dungeon. Look at her," he hissed, pointing at the tiny faerie who was currently studying them with large almond-shaped eyes that shone bright and fresh as spring. "Only a cold-hearted bastard would leave such an adorable thing out in the cold."

"You're forgetting that an adorable nymphling will mature into an intoxicating nymph in a few scant years," Marsais said, his voice hard and sharp as steel. "Nymphs don't mature at the same rate as humans. What will happen when she Awakens? Allow me to refresh your memory, since you seem to have forgotten that *minor* detail. Her blood will begin to stir and every man on this Isle will be drooling after her— including you and me.

"Blast it! We could very well be at each other's throats over this *adorable* creature. I can't believe you were foolish enough to involve yourself in this affair. You know as well as I that a nymph belongs with her kin, with her father, until she's of age. A nymph's family is immune to the creature's allure. You should never have taken her from Soataen— no matter what he planned!" Marsais said sharply, grey eyes turning to flint, challenging Oenghus to argue the obvious.

He turned his back on Marsais, tugging roughly on his beard. The words rang true, and that was the rub of it—a nymphling should stay with her kin until she's of age.

"Isiilde looks exactly like her mother," Oenghus whispered. "You know how Soataen always had a thing for redheads."

Marsais stared blankly at his back, then blinked as realization dawned. "Oh, by the gods, you bloody fool."

Oenghus turned to find Marsais massaging the bridge of his nose. "What in all the realms were you thinking when you bedded a nymph who belonged to the Emperor of Kambe, much less get her with child?"

"Not much thought was involved, trust me," Oenghus admitted. "I'd like to see how you would've fared, waking up with a nymph standing next to your bed. I'd wager not too well, 'specially considering your incident in Mearcentia. So don't get all high and mighty with me, you bloody bastard."

Marsais held up his hands in peace. "Point taken. Forgive me, it's just a bit of a shock, which is saying a lot for a seer." He turned to study Isiilde, who seemed entranced by the crystal window. "Does she know you're her real father?"

Oenghus jerked his head to the side.

"Let us assume for one moment that I can persuade the Nine to let her stay. Without revealing her... connection to you. What happens when she comes of age, Oenghus? What happens when her 'father' sells her?"

"I've thought a lot about it," Oenghus began, slowly. "We could make a run for it; I could keep her hidden for a time. But even I'm not fool enough to think I can protect her forever. Not alone. As much as I hate to admit it, a nymph with royal blood will have a better chance of being sold to someone who can protect her. And maybe care for her. If the lords of Mearcentia or even Kiln made a bid for her, then I think at least she'd be comfortable. It's probably her best chance."

The words left a foul taste in his mouth. But he had a promise to honor. He was bound by his word.

"That's wise of you. But will you be able to let her go, old friend?" Marsais asked, gently.

"I'm not the bloody seer."

"Well then, I'll grant your request. But..." Marsais held up a finger. "She'll not live within these walls."

Oenghus glowered. "She's not gonna bloody burn the stronghold down."

"Not for that." Marsais glanced at the nymphling. "Faerie don't tolerate stone well. I have a cottage by the seaside you can live in."

"Oh. Erm..." Oenghus tugged on his beard.

Marsais arched a brow, waiting.

"I don't suppose they've started growing strawberries on the island?"

"Strawberries?"

"You know, little red berr—"

"I know what they are. Why?"

"She's fond of them."

Marsais started to shake his head, but glanced at the faerie and found himself saying, "She'll have all the strawberries she can eat."

CHAPTER I

2011 A.S.

Thirteen Years Later

IN A CHAMBER SET high in a spire on a misty isle, a group of apprentices sat listening to a lecture on the realms beyond. The apprentices were evenly spaced, sitting on stone steps that pooled into an amphitheater's center. They dipped their quills into inkwells, wiped off the excess ink with harmonious precision, and put tips to paper like a hive of busy drones.

This perfect concert of flowing ink was broken by a pupil who never did anything dutifully. The source of discord came from the very back of the chamber, on the highest bench, where a nymph lay on her stomach.

She seemed a dream, a vision, and the only thread connecting her to reality was a cascade of vibrant red curls that pooled on the stone beneath her body.

Isiilde paused to study her work, quill poised while her feet kicked lazily in the air. Satisfied, she dipped her quill into an inkwell and stirred the black liquid with wonder before beginning anew.

"Isiilde!"

Isiilde looked up. Everyone was staring at her, but that was normal. "Yes, Wise One?" she asked.

Yasimina fixed her with a stare that would have made any other student uneasy. That look reminded Isiilde of an icy river—beautiful but cold.

"I do not tolerate singing during my lectures."

Isiilde blinked in surprise. Who would do that? Unfortunately, all eyes pointed back to her. "I'm sorry," she said, hastily. "I didn't realize I was singing. But I *was* paying attention."

Murmurs rippled around the amphitheater. Along with a single snort—Zianna relished the nymph's misfortunes.

Isiilde ignored the woman and stood. "I was drawing a picture of the realms and their interconnecting domains," she explained, passing her paper down the line for Yasimina to examine. Several overlapping circles filled the page, each labeled in flowing script. Their realm was called Fyrsta, and it sat like a bloated spider in the center of a spiraling web.

Zianna studied the drawing when it reached her hand. "I wasn't aware there were monkeys in the Spirit River."

The others laughed. They usually did. Zianna was quick-witted and beautiful, and people fell over themselves to please her. Isiilde had noticed that humans liked to follow each other. She found it puzzling. Unfortunately, Zianna disliked her, and the others went along with that too.

Isiilde didn't rise to the woman's bait. There was no point in arguing. No one but the gods knew who was in the Spirit River.

"This is an excellent representation, Isiilde," Yasimina noted. The class fell silent. The Wise One might be firm, but she was also fair. "It's obvious by the amount of detail in your drawing that you've already been lectured on the realms beyond. Perhaps you can answer my next question: why is Fyrsta commonly known as the Realm of Gods?"

Yasimina handed her drawing to the nearest student, and the apprentices leaned in close to make copies (minus the monkeys).

Isiilde made a mental note to ask Marsais about monkeys, then turned her mind to Yasimina's question. "Fyrsta is known as the Realm of Gods for three reasons," she began with a lilting voice that danced around the chamber. "The Sylph blessed Fyrsta and honored it by bestowing us with her Gift, the ability to channel her essence.

"Secondly, the people of Fyrsta are near to immortal. We live as long as we have the will, barring sickness or violence. And when we lose the will to live, the Keening takes us and we die. Then our spirits return to the ol' River, where we can be reborn again."

Isiilde wanted to point out that this supported her drawings of monkeys floating in the Spirit River. But she kept quiet, because everyone was staring, and she did not like being the center of attention —it was tiresome and it always made her want to disappear.

"The last reason is because the Sylph favored this realm above all others. The Goddess of All placed her daughters on Fyrsta, where they were to grow and live, until they were gifted to a god who found favor with the Sylph."

She liked this reason most of all.

"That's ridiculous!" Mindle Sorethumb hopped to his feet. Although the gnome was tall for his kind, he still was shorter than his seated associates.

"That is certainly cute, but it's a childish fantasy," Zianna cut in before Mindle could continue his tirade. "If it makes you feel better, please go on believing it. But how do you account for the numerous laws regarding your kind? If the Sylph favored nymphs, then they would hardly be bought and sold like horses—expensive horses, to be sure, but sold nonetheless." Zianna's lips curved with pleasure. She enjoyed reminding Isiilde of her impending enslavement.

Isiilde shrugged. "Ask the Archlord if you doubt me."

"I would love to. Unfortunately, the Archlord has been gone for some time and only a fool would take the word of a *nymph*." Zianna might as well have said filth for all the disgust in that single word.

"A fool answers, but a wise man questions," Isiilde replied, quoting her master.

"You are the fool, nymph," Lord Kulthin said. He was a formidable apprentice who alternated between leering and sneering at the nymph.

"Nymphs are not human," Kulthin continued. "They are property, deemed as such by the Blessed Order of Zahra, the Guardian Of All That Is Good." He touched fingertips reverently to lips. "The Guardians of

Iilenshar serve the Sylph. If the Sylph favored nymphs, then I would not be in the market for one."

Lord Kulthin leered so openly at Isiilde that it made her skin crawl. The ever tedious chorus of amusement rippled through the room.

"I keep forgetting you have to buy all your women, Kulthin." She knew the comment would earn her another reprimand. But she didn't care.

"How dare you talk to me in that manner, you insolent little—"

"Enough!" Yasimina snapped before he could finish the insult. "You'll both be reported to your masters."

Isiilde sat back down, idly wondering how long it would take the Archlord to sort through her letters of reprimand when he returned to the Isle. With as many as she had earned already, what was one more?

Yasimina picked up the lecture where she had left off, using Isiilde's drawing to illustrate the connections between known realms. Fyrsta was surrounded by Somnial's realm: the realm of dreams. The veils were thin between the two realms, and it was common for the inhabitants of Fyrsta to drift into Somnial's domain while they slept. All realms shared a foothold with the realm of dreams and all manner of creatures could be found there—so went the tale of Galvier Longstride, the wanderer whose feet never stopped moving.

Circling Fyrsta like four faithful moons were the realms of fire, water, wind, and earth: Fir ˇ dum, Aegir ˇ dum, Aesir ˇ dum, and Gol ˇ - dum. And from those four stretched countless realms, fanning out like a giant web, each sharing a juncture with the next.

Isiilde didn't care what the other apprentices thought—at least that's what she told herself. Pretending not to care was a lesson she'd learned early in life. They could ask the Archlord when he got back. That was, of course, *if* he returned.

She absently plucked at an ink stain on her skirt. Marsais had been gone for over six months, time enough for her to turn seventeen.

According to Isek Beirnuckle, Marsais had woken up one morning and left. No one knew where he'd gone, not even Oenghus. But the Order wasn't alarmed by his disappearance. Marsais disappeared every few years, leaving no word of when he planned to return. He'd done it often enough when she was younger, fading in and out of her life. Sometimes for years. But lately, his absence left a hole in her heart.

He hadn't even said goodbye.

An ocean breeze swept through the amphitheater, agitating burning torches. The flames wavered for a heartbeat before hissing back to life.

Isiilde's gaze was drawn like a moth to the nearest torch. The fire's hypnotic dance soothed her like an old friend. She longed to coax the flames to life, but she was forbidden to sing in the tower.

Isiilde had another day to suffer through until she could return to their cottage. She let her imagination drift, dreaming of Fir ˘ dum and its everlasting heat, a realm where the sky rained fire. It sounded like bliss. And if the secrets of the Gateways were ever rediscovered, she'd be the first to step through.

"Isiilde."

At the call of her name, she jerked in surprise. The chamber was empty, save for Yasimina and herself. She had missed the entire lecture.

"Sorry, Wise One, I meant to pay attention."

Yasimina dismissed her apology with a wave of a hand. "Your master instructs you well. Surprisingly so, given his... Well, yes, at any rate, I'm sure there was nothing new for you to learn."

Yasimina lifted the hem of her robes to climb the steps. Isiilde stood expectantly as the Wise One approached, marveling at the way the willowy woman moved, flowing like water over rocks. Yasimina always made her feel clumsy.

"I wished to have a word with you before you go to your next lesson with Mistress Thira."

Isiilde's heart sank. She had forgotten all about Thira's lesson. Worse, she would be late for the dreadful class.

"I should warn you—some knowledge is better left buried."

Isiilde stared up at the woman in confusion. "I don't understand."

"I don't doubt you for a moment. I'm sure the Archlord told you that nymphs are daughters of the Sylph, but it is unwise to call the teachings of the Blessed Order into question," Yasimina confided. "As Kulthin pointed out, the Order has the Guardians' backing, and your master has always shown a blatant disregard for the younger gods. Though he may be foolish or brave enough to challenge them, I would not be so quick to, especially when he's not here to support you."

The cool voice of reason left Isiilde even more confused. Unfortunately, Yasimina offered nothing more than that. The Wise One folded her hands inside her robes and continued up the stone steps without another word.

ISIILDE STUFFED her supplies inside her knapsack, and darted up the stairs, perplexed as ever. Why would an esteemed Order, whose sole purpose was to preserve knowledge, be so quick to dismiss the truth of a matter?

Isiilde did not have time to unravel three thousand years of history. She ran for all that she was worth.

The running nymph was hard to miss as she darted down the corridors, weaving in and out of people in near panic. She eventually skidded to a stop, and stared at an oak door that smelled of spoiled eggs and rotten fish. She wrinkled her nose. It was the door that led into the Alchemy workshop. But it might as well have been the Gates leading into the Nine Halls.

Panic threatened to overwhelm her, but she stood her ground, gathering what small shreds of courage she possessed. Nymphs were not known for their courage.

Taking a deep breath, she defied her very nature and ventured a peek into the workshop. But the door was yanked open, and a hand snaked forward to drag Isiilde into a predator's domain.

A thin vulture of a woman glared down at her with hateful eyes, while an orange puffball of a dog charged her. The dog snapped at Isiilde's heels. She closed her eyes, willing Thira and her loathsome familiar Crumpet away. But this tactic rarely worked.

"You're interrupting my lecture, nymph," Thira snapped. Crumpet's lips curled back, displaying a fang-filled maw. "Do you imagine that your time is more important than the rest of the apprentices combined?"

"I'm sorry, Wise One," she said with a gulp. "Yasimina asked to speak with me after her lecture."

Isiilde took a sudden interest in her boots. They were good, sturdy boots, and the leather fit like a glove, but they were of little help at the moment.

"I don't care if a pit fiend invaded the castle. I will not suffer any more of your excuses."

Isiilde nodded quickly in agreement, and turned to leave, but was stopped short by an iron hand curling over her shoulder. She stifled back a cry.

"I didn't dismiss you," Thira whispered in her ear, squeezing her shoulder so hard that she feared it would break.

Thira steered her to the back of the room. And as she was paraded past the other apprentices, she met Zianna's smirk with narrowed eyes.

"I have a use for you today," Thira said, sweeping her hand towards a tottering stack of cauldrons. "They're covered in last week's grime. I suggest you get on your knees and begin scrubbing."

"Ah, just where a nymph belongs," Kulthin quipped.

Isiilde suffered their gazes in silence. An insane, suicidal thought entered her head: to simply tell Thira Olander, the Mistress of Novices, *no*. It was a grand thought, a noble stand against tyranny, and it lasted a thrilling three seconds.

Thira spun on Kulthin, her fingers flashing in a complicated weave before a single, harsh word spat from her lips. The word echoed through the chamber with the finality of a sword thrust.

Lord Kulthin clutched at his throat, gagging in shock. Weaves of Silence were Thira's favorite disciplinary tool for minor infractions, and her weaves were legendary for being uncomfortable.

Marsais called them torture.

Every novice went pale and quickly faced forward in their chairs. They hunched over their notes in silence, ignoring the struggling lord.

The Vulture turned back to Isiilde. As thrilling as those three seconds of defiance had been, the thrill shattered under the woman's gaze.

Marsais had forbidden Thira from using weaves on the nymph. But he was gone, and his influence only stretched so far. Not wanting to test those boundaries, Isiilde snatched up a wire brush and bolted for the cauldrons.

The first cauldron smelled like a nest of squashed cockroaches. She tried not to gag. Three cauldrons later, Isiilde turned to the fourth. She crawled deeper inside the stinking pot to scrub the bottom and heard the tap of claws on stone.

Crumpet. A growl, a nip, then sharp teeth pierced her right boot, sinking into her calf. Isiilde bit back a cry and scuttled out of the cauldron to glare at the beast.

Crumpet snarled back in challenge.

She batted at the dog with her wash rag. "Don't you dare bite me again," she hissed in warning.

He danced backwards, away from her reach. Watching the fiend out of the corner of her eye, she returned to her work. But Crumpet attacked again, sinking his teeth into the tender flesh behind her knee.

Isiilde yelped in pain, and a nearby torch fluttered with a pop, sending a spark into the air. It drifted onto a precariously balanced cauldron, igniting some sticky mixture. A gout of flame surged into the air.

Isiilde jerked in surprise, knocking the stack of cauldrons and the flaming pot. It tumbled from the stack and landed on Crumpet, caging the beast in a burning kiln.

Canine screams filled the workshop. Heads turned, realization dawned, and Thira's eyes widened with horror. She rushed towards the screams, and Isiilde fled, leaving Crumpet to burn. The other apprentices were too shocked to grab the fleeing nymph.

Isiilde bolted out of the workshop and down corridors. With heart thumping and sides bursting, she took a shortcut through the gardens before barreling into the infirmary.

Oenghus was bent over a patient, and she darted to his side. "What's happened, Sprite?"

"Oen—" she panted.

"Did someone hurt you?" he demanded.

Isiilde pointed at the doors, trying to catch her breath.

Morigan Freyr hurried over. "What's the matter?"

Oenghus shrugged. Whatever the reason, they could both be sure of one thing—trouble usually followed the nymph.

"Just ease up and try to breathe," he urged, eyeing the doors. An instant later, trouble arrived, cradling a smoldering lump.

"I need a healer!" Thira croaked. She rushed over to Morigan and shoved her charred familiar into the healer's hands.

Morigan assessed the burns and passed the patient onto Oenghus. "He needs your skill."

"I'm not healing a bloody dog," Oenghus grumbled.

"That whelp of yours did this!" Thira screeched.

Isiilde darted behind her guardian. Oenghus took one look at the nymph and then his gaze drifted to the mangy rat of a dog. With a muttered curse, he took the thing in his hands and began uttering the Lore. His gaze became vacant as he set about mending the beast with an inner sight.

"I'll see you ousted for this, wretch." Thira reached for Isiilde, but Morigan grabbed the woman's wrist.

"Don't touch her," Morigan warned.

Thira froze at the look in the healer's eyes. Then she wrenched her hand free, and took a hasty step back. She might be the Mistress of Novices, but this was Morigan's domain. No one crossed her in the infirmary. Not even the Archlord.

"That creature set Crumpet on fire."

"I swear it was an accident," Isiilde said.

"You'd have to be mad for it not to be," Morigan muttered.

"By the gods, how can you believe that? How many times, Morigan? It's the same pathetic excuse. I have witnesses to her crime."

"There's no bloody crime," Oenghus growled, thrusting Crumpet at Thira. "Your canine bedfellow will be good as new after his fur grows back. Though personally, I think it's a better look for him. I always thought he was more rat than dog."

Thira glared. "I won't let this go unpunished."

"You will, or I'll toss that rat off the highest tower. Then you can try to kick my arse out."

"I'd see you in the arena before bothering with protocol."

"Don't tempt me, hag."

"Both of you stop it," Morigan ordered. "Thira, I'll ask you to take your leave and tend to your companion. He'll need rest and a warm place to recover. You should be grateful Oenghus was here, because no one else could've managed that healing."

Thira didn't back down for a tense minute. Then she turned and stalked out of the infirmary.

Oenghus fingered his beard as he eyed the door she'd slammed. "The woman has some bollocks. I'll give her that."

"What the Void happened?" Morigan asked.

"I don't know," Isiilde insisted. "Crumpet bit me twice," she pointed at her punctured boot and the back of her knee, "and then a spark from the torch fell in a cauldron, started a fire, and the cauldron fell on top of Crumpet."

Morigan sighed. "What's done is done."

"Bloody right," Oenghus grunted.

Isiilde looked up to her guardian. "I didn't mean to cause you more trouble."

"Haven't you ever heard, trouble follows a faerie?"

Morigan snorted. "That explains it. You must be a full-blooded faerie, Oen. You've caused me enough trouble for a lifetime."

Oenghus bared his teeth. "You love it, Mori."

"I love this child." Morigan planted a kiss on the nymph's head. "I tolerate you."

"I tolerate you, too, woman."

The two shared a look that encompassed a lifetime.

"See to her bites," Morigan said, turning to leave. "I'll come by the cottage to check on you both later. You're cooking."

"Hope you like sausage," he called to her back.

Morigan answered with a laugh.

CHAPTER 2

Isiilde melted into the coarse sand beneath her body. Her bones soaked in its heat, storing the memory of bliss for the long winter to come. She sighed, content, at peace, then opened her eyes to a blazing sun. It was in a rare mood today.

She stretched with languid pleasure and rose to her elbows, squinting at the sea. A small army of little lugsail fishing boats drifted offshore—their nets mostly ignored and rarely gathered up.

A throaty bark disturbed the ebbing tide. Isiilde turned to a herd of walruses who shared her beach. Two of the bulls were arguing over a swath of sand, uncaring that a mile of vacant beach stretched in either direction.

"Put some clothes on, Isiilde!" Another familiar bark interrupted her peace.

Isiilde rolled onto her stomach and squinted across the beach. Oenghus stood by the woodpile of their cottage, his hands planted on his kilted hips. But he wasn't alone—a tall, slim man stood in his shadow.

"Marsais," she breathed, hopping to her feet.

"Not without your bloody clothes!" Oenghus bellowed over the grassy dunes.

Isiilde found her wrap in a sandy heap. She wound it about her waist, tucked it in place, and darted towards the cottage.

The perfect day was now exquisite. If the Feast of Fools and the Sylph's Fortnight were put together, it wouldn't have excited her more. The Archlord of the Isle, her master and closest friend, had finally returned.

Her feet flew across the beach, over dunes, and through tall grass. She stopped in front of Marsais, near bursting with delight.

"Hello, Isiilde."

His words were as gracious and gentle as the sun's caress, and his smile warmed her from the inside out. She nearly hugged him, but caught herself. The Archlord held himself apart from others. But he stepped back and favored her with an elegant bow. Despite travel-worn clothes, he seemed a king at court.

Isiilde returned his bow with a bobbing curtsy. Questions warred on the tip of her tongue, but a swirl of emotion captured them.

"How many times have I told you to keep your blasted clothes on?" Oenghus asked.

His demand knocked her tongue loose. "No one else was on the beach."

"What do you call that fleet of fishing boats leering at you offshore?" Oenghus growled.

"They weren't leering—they're fishing." She narrowed her eyes at him. "Are we going to offer Marsais some food?"

"Not dressed like that. Get inside and put something presentable on. A loincloth doesn't count as clothing."

"I'm dressed the same as you," she pointed out.

"I'm not a bloody woman," he bit back.

"My hair is covering my breasts."

Oenghus' beard twitched dangerously. "I'll send him away."

Isiilde huffed at the giant. But her anger stilled when she looked at Marsais. His grey eyes danced with amusement, and she gave him a small smile before walking inside.

Her black cat, Mousebane, was curled on her bed. Taking care not to disturb his nap, she searched through the small chest at the foot of her bed. Isiilde swore under her breath. Everything she owned was for cold weather.

Mousebane cracked an irritated eye open.

"You should be outside, you lazy cat."

She finally settled on wrapping a cotton scarf around her breasts. It was only Marsais, and she didn't have a lot to cover. She threw a loaf of bread, a chunk of cheese, and the last of her strawberries into a basket before hurrying outside.

"...quiet for the most part. Everyone's high strung, especially along the Golden Road. The lack of an enemy has them nervous, so they've taken to fighting each other," Marsais was saying as he perched on the edge of a stump.

"The Ardmoor aren't even out and about?" Oenghus asked. He glanced at her with a look of disapproval as she emerged, but didn't order her back inside.

"Oh, there have been raids on the outlying settlements and towns, but nothing organized. Alrik seemed to think they were all on holiday," Marsais replied, wryly.

"Aye, well, Alrik's even more of a crazed bastard than you are."

"Oen." Isiilde shot him a glare before offering the basket to Marsais.

"Thank you, my dear."

"You can have some strawberries," she offered generously.

Marsais plucked a berry from the basket, looked up and froze. His grey eyes sharpened on her, and he seemed to see her for the first time. "You look different." He sounded puzzled by his own observation.

"I put a shirt on."

"Hmm."

She offered the basket to Oenghus, batting his hand away from her strawberries. "You take too many." Isiilde bullied Oenghus aside to sit, then turned her attention back to Marsais. "I turned seventeen while you were away."

Concern spread over his face. "When did that happen?"

"There are these things called years, which are made up of months. And each month is—"

"Isiilde," Oenghus growled.

While Marsais seemed interested in her explanation, she stopped all the same. "You've been gone forever, Marsais. Where did you go?"

"I went for a walk to stretch my legs."

"That must have been some walk. You've been gone for over six months."

"I have long legs," he quipped.

"Marsais."

"I travelled to Cirye to visit a friend by the name of Alrik."

"In the Bastardlands?" Her eyes widened. "Did Grawl and Reapers attack you? Isn't it dangerous beyond the Gates?"

"Who'd want to rob a scarecrow?" Oenghus said with a snort. "Even a Reaper wouldn't want to gnaw on his leathery hide."

"My greatest defense." Marsais flashed a grin.

"Starving yourself to death isn't much of a defense," Oenghus replied, eyeing him. "Did you forget to eat again?"

"I can never decide whose mothering is worse—yours or Isek's," Marsais mused.

With a snarl, Oenghus chucked a wood chip at Marsais, who caught it with trifling ease. He wove an enchantment that was too quick to follow and uncurled his long fingers to reveal a butterfly fanning its wings on his palm.

Isiilde nearly fell off her perch with delight. She watched it fly away and wondered how such a man occasionally got lost in his own tower.

"Did you cross the channel safely? Have you heard about the new dread pirate?" Isiilde asked around a mouthful of bread.

"Ah, yes, I think the bards have coined him the Bastard Prince."

"I like the ballads they sing about him," she admitted, and began to sing the latest drunken ditty about the dread pirate.

> "O'er the seas sails that fiercest of men,
> Hail the prince and his bastardly swagger!
>
> His eyes are asmolder,
> With the lust of a rover
> He'll take all your wives,
> With his cutlass and knives

While you're all out asea getting older!

O'er the seas sails that fiercest of men,
Hail the prince and his bastardly swagger!

His blade gleaming afire
He's as swift as a tiger,
To take off a head
His blade burning and red
Yet he's still the man we admire!"

"I think it's supposed to be sung a bit grittier, Sprite, by a room full of drunken louts."

"I was trying to sing like that," Isiilde said.

"My dear," Marsais sighed, opening his eyes, "your enchanting voice could make a curse sound like a Harper's melody. I have sorely missed the sound of it." At this unexpected compliment, the tips of her ears heated.

"Have you heard the rumors drifting around?" Oenghus asked, slipping his pipe from his belt.

"Probably not near as many as you have."

"They say he was the Widow's Recluse."

Marsais narrowed his eyes. "You're joking?"

"Who's that?" Isiilde asked.

Considering Marsais' reaction, she likely wouldn't want to know, but while nymphs were not known for their courage, they were known for their curiosity. Not asking would go against everything that she was.

"One of the Widow's Own," Marsais said, slipping into his role as her master. "He was a notorious assassin, second only to the Widow herself. Mention of his name made kings shudder. In some circles, it's rumored that he was the one who assassinated King Syre of Mearcentia, and the Viscount, Isiig Vauth of Vaylin. He is sometimes referred to as the King's Bane, or as the Widow's Bane, for defying the ancient guild and its mistress. He was hunted, and, as legend goes, killed by his own assassins."

Isiilde shivered.

Marsais noticed her fear and changed the subject. "Hmm, but enough about rumor. Has anything of note happened while I've been away?"

Oenghus shrugged, blowing out a harsh breath of smoke. "The usual bickering nonsense. Nothing Isek hasn't been able to handle—not that you handle much, anyway. But if I were you, I'd stay away a bit longer."

"Don't give him ideas, Oen."

"Trust me, the last thing I want him to do is leave again. I've had my hands full trying to keep your faerie arse out of trouble."

She bristled. "I haven't gotten into any trouble."

"Oh, really?" Oenghus asked. "I suppose last week's incident in the infirmary has already slipped your faerie mind, or the week before that, and do I dare mention the month before last?"

Isiilde pursed her lips in thought. Instead of answering, she rose to offer Marsais more strawberries. "Will you come to the festival tomorrow? There's a troupe from Xaio. Oen spent all his coin again, so he's taking me to sell his brew. If you come with us, you won't have to go back to the tower so soon."

"How could I possibly say no to such sound reasoning?"

"It's impossible," she agreed. "But Marsais?"

"Hmm?"

"If you're going to stay, I would appreciate it if you bathed first."

CHAPTER 3

Sunshine should never be wasted, so Isiilde returned to her beach while Marsais bathed. She hummed as she balanced across the slippery rocks to explore. A tiny crab skittered across the rocks, moving with a lopsided gait caused by one claw that was larger than its carapace. She watched it, captivated, until it crawled into a crevice.

Isiilde checked back on the cottage, and her ears perked up. Marsais strolled along the beach. She quickly hopped from rock to rock, and slipped, falling into the tide pool and splitting open a toe. She scrambled upright, climbing over the rocks to the safety of the sand.

Blood dripped from her big toe. The sight and smell of blood made her lightheaded. Her vision narrowed, the world tilted, and her eyes fluttered open to find Marsais dusting sand off her face with his sleeve. She was lying on her back.

His long hair shone in the sun, falling past his shoulders as he crouched at her side. "You fainted."

She groaned. "My toe is bleeding."

"Not an uncommon occurrence," he mused.

"For me, or in general?"

"Both."

Isiilde stuck her bloody toe in his face. "It hurts."

He studied the wound with grey eyes that always twinkled for her. They reminded her of stars.

"I'm no healer, but I believe you'll live." Marsais produced a pristine handkerchief and carefully wrapped it around her toe.

"Thank you," she whispered.

Marsais dropped his worn rucksack next to her and stretched on the sand, propping himself on his elbows to gaze at the sea. She wanted to reach across the leather pack and poke him to make sure he wasn't a dream.

"Do I pass inspection?"

Isiilde took her time looking him over. She had never seen hair so vibrant a white. It wasn't white from age and the Keening's touch, but possessed of an otherworldly glow, like the paintings of the Guardians. With his pointed ears and hair like freshly fallen snow, she wondered if faerie blood ran through his veins. He was the most beautiful man she'd ever seen.

His shirt was patched, and the laces of his collar hung in tatters, revealing a tanned throat. She leaned closer to sniff at him. The fishy odor was gone, leaving a whiff of soap that mingled with his familiar scent. He always made her think of a hot summer day.

"You smell much better," she said.

"I caught up on some interesting reading during my bath. I can't say I've ever been so entertained."

Isiilde's heart sank as he produced an impressive stack of letters, all stamped with the familiar sigil of the Wise Ones: an open palm bearing a watchful eye.

"You've been busy."

She was too busy poking at her toe to catch the quirk of his lips. "You don't have to read them," she finally said.

"You're right, I don't."

Satisfied, she stretched out beneath the sun. Ocean waves tugged her towards sleep as heat seeped into her bones. She drifted in a place without time. It was bliss.

Isiilde eventually stirred, stretched with pleasure, and opened her eyes. Marsais was still reading through her letters of misconduct.

"I missed you," she said.

"Apparently," he agreed, gesturing at the stack of letters. "I think I like this one best. Thira accused you of setting Crumpet on fire."

He arched a brow in question. But it didn't mean she had to answer.

"You didn't say goodbye."

"I can't stand goodbyes, most especially when you're concerned. Your tears are unbearable."

"Is that why you left, because of me?" Her whisper was as soft as a breeze.

Marsais looked up from the letters. "Of course not. Did you think that was the reason?"

"I thought, maybe," she admitted, tucking a tendril of hair behind her ear. "You were gone a long time."

"Just over six months."

"For a butterfly, that's an entire lifetime."

Marsais chuckled at her observation. "I suppose for a certain nymph it might have seemed longer."

"It was unbearable." Isiilde rolled onto her side to regard him.

"Oh come now, even I enjoy the occasional respite from myself." But Isiilde couldn't bring herself to smile at his jest—at least she thought he was jesting.

"Why did you leave?"

Marsais sighed and turned to watch the fishing boats drift by. Several sailed past when she realized he'd forgotten about her. Not uncommon. He was a seer, after all, and had visions of the future. But he never spoke of them.

"Marsais."

At the sound of her voice, Marsais glanced around in confusion. He didn't appear to know where he was until his gaze fell on her. This was also common.

"I don't know how you manage when you're by yourself."

"Ah, but it's always a surprise to discover where I've ended up," he said lightly. There was humor in his eyes, but only worry in her heart.

Marsais sobered. "To answer your question, I've always found it helpful to go for a walk when I feel the Keening creeping up on me."

Alarmed by his confession, she sat up and edged closer.

Marsais held up a halting hand. "The reason I went away was to escape the Keening's clutches. A long walk does wonders for one's perspective on life. Staying one step ahead of the Keening is how I've stayed in the prime of life all these years."

"Are you better now?"

"Yes," he assured. His smile chased her worries away. "Most immortals need to figure out something that works for them. Otherwise, they wouldn't survive. Oenghus is a perfect example; whenever life starts gnawing at him, he becomes violent."

"Is that why he's been getting into so many fights lately?"

"If the fights end in bloodshed, yes. Otherwise, it's just his normal amusement." Marsais dismissed the topic with a gesture. "Enough about me, what have you been up to besides..." he paused, narrowing his eyes at the topmost report. "...adding a jar of ash to a batch of water-breathing potions? Let me guess, everyone was coughing up dust for days?"

"They have no proof."

Isiilde had only been trying to make it smell better.

"Let's see, Eldred caught you dancing on top of the table in the council chamber."

"I was singing."

"Ah, yes, the acoustics are very good there—it's the dome shape." He sifted through the papers, muttering under his breath. "Hmm, *kiss my faerie arse, kiss my faerie arse*, and yet another reference to your backside. You know, my dear, when Oenghus tells someone to kiss his arse, it carries a bit more threat. I'd use that one sparingly if I were you, because one day someone might try to take you up on the offer."

She frowned.

"Here's one that's suggestive. It seems that a batch of chocolate sweets shipped from Xaio and intended for Taal Greysparrow went missing. Oh, and imagine this—the very next day you handed in an unfinished assignment smudged with chocolate."

"I didn't want Zianna to get fat."

"How thoughtful of you." His brows furrowed when he caught sight of the next report. "You ditched your guards. *Again.* And Ielequithe finally found you hiding on the roof of the soldiers' bathhouse—"

"I was playing Raven and the Prey with Thedus. It took him a long time to find me. Your army is very fit."

Marsais chose not to comment.

"You wove a grease enchantment on Tulipin?"

"That's a false account," she defended, laughing in memory. "I wove an air rune in the middle of a corridor that he happened to be floating through. Then I wove a grease enchantment into the rune of air. He hit the slippery air and rebounded off the walls a few times before he reined in his levitation weave."

"Ingenious; I'll let it slide. And excuse the pun."

Isiilde thought Marsais would appreciate her experiments.

"Hmm, here's one from you. You broke the warding on my vault, riffled through my coffers, and began fiddling with various artifacts of power."

"Isek made me write it. He said the ward and the artifacts were dangerous, but I think he was just angry I broke your ward so easily."

"Well, my dear, the artifacts are dangerous, but you're still here and there's little point in hoping you learned something from your burglary."

"I didn't take anything," she said, but her nose began to itch with guilt, and she quickly amended her statement. "Well, I would have taken one item, but Isek made me put it back."

"Put what back?"

"There were two silver flagons with runes etched all over them—a complicated weave I didn't understand. One of them had a big metal cork in the top that was attached to a chain. I wanted to find out what was inside. Do you know?"

Isiilde didn't mention that she'd been poised to open that flagon when Isek discovered her.

"I don't know what's inside, but it would be very unwise to open them." He straightened the stack of letters into a tidy pile, and sat up, fixing her with a grave eye. "Oenghus mentioned you've been skipping lectures."

"He *told* on me?"

"He mentioned it because he's worried about you. He said all of this started after Caitlyn Whitehand paid her annual visit."

She wrinkled her nose. Every year, Emperor Soataen Jaal III sent his royal physician to examine Isiilde. But it wasn't her health he was concerned about. When Isiilde came of age, the emperor intended to sell her, and virgins always fetched a higher price.

Isiilde loathed the woman's yearly examinations, both for what they represented and the way they made her feel—like a prize horse with an excellent set of teeth. Worse, the woman had cold hands.

"She seemed surprised I hadn't come of age yet."

"You'd think they'd notice you aren't human."

Isiilde snorted. "They don't let me forget it, Marsais."

"And yet everyone holds you to human standards."

"If I were human, I wouldn't be auctioned off to the highest bidder."

"True, but as a human princess, you would've been handed off to some lord in a trade agreement at sixteen."

Isiilde shivered.

"I'm sure that knowledge doesn't lessen the sting," Marsais murmured. "Did you make ample use of my study after the examination?"

His study had a wonderful crystal window that directed the tiniest amount of sunlight onto a thick, warm rug. Isiilde spent most of her afternoons in the private chamber. It was the only place she felt safe.

"It's not the same without you," she admitted, tracing the flowing lines of a fire rune into the sand.

"I wouldn't think it mattered since I usually vacate my study. I dare not disturb a sun-bathing nymph."

"But I know you're close by," she said, leaning back to examine her rune. The lines wavered for a moment and she blinked. But when she opened her eyes, the rune was as inert as the sand. It left her feeling empty and adrift, and she turned to Marsais, searching for a haven. He was watching her, eyes wide and a little wary.

"Where did you learn that rune?"

The nymph tilted her head in confusion. "You taught it to me."

"Not that rune. I've never seen its like before."

"It's a fire rune. I just added a few lines to make it prettier." It was explanation enough for anything she might do. She skipped onto another topic. "Sarabian visited for a week while you were gone. She's so beautiful."

"Not an uncommon thing with womanly creatures," he pointed out, shifting with her mood instead of pressing her further on the rune. "How is your sister?"

"My father," Isiilde said with distaste, "has given her charge of the southern regions. She has her very own castle and an army. She came with a company of bodyguards. I think one of them guards her at night, too. I spied them kissing. He's handsome, but I don't think she loves him."

"Why is that?"

"He seems less than intelligent, but maybe my sister prefers that. I would at least want a man who could best me at King's Folly."

"Considering your skill at the game, you'll be hard pressed to find anyone."

Isiilde beamed at his compliment. The complex game of runes had always made sense to her, even as a nymphling. But her swell of elation ebbed as another more sobering thought struck her.

"I won't have much choice in the matter." Never one to dwell on depressing matters, she quickly changed the subject. "Ari is patrolling the borders of the Fell Wastes. He commands the army, and Sara worries about him. Although she's had her share of danger. When she sailed along the southern coast, just north of the Isle of Winds, the Bastard Prince had the bollocks to waylay her entire fleet and request a private audience with her."

"Did she accept?"

"Sara dined with him on her galleon under a flag of parley. She said he was the most dangerous man she'd ever met—like a dragon who'd been trapped in a man's body. His name is Hsien, and his slightest movement set her bodyguards on edge, but to my sister..." A sumptuous smile curved her lips. "...he was an absolute gentleman and the most charming man she'd ever come across."

"Definitely dangerous," Marsais agreed.

"Perhaps when I'm sold, he'll waylay my escort and come for me."

"By the gods, I'd forgotten the fanciful imaginings of innocent young women," Marsais drawled. "I wouldn't wish pirates on you. They aren't near as charming without a fleet of soldiers with you."

"And what should I imagine?" Isiilde snapped, narrowing her eyes. "How wonderful it will be when I'm sold to the highest bidder? I suppose I'll get to see something of the realm on my way to his bed." She hopped to her feet and stalked down the beach.

"Isiilde!" Marsais called to her back, but she ignored him. He rubbed the bridge of his nose before climbing to his feet to follow. He caught up to her in no time. "Forgive me, my dear. I didn't mean to upset you."

"It's not you, Marsais. Oen was right. I was fine until Caitlyn came, and then Sara arrived, but then she left, and after... with you gone..." Isiilde trailed off, wiping her tears roughly away.

A wave crashed on shore, crawling towards their feet, and she let the freezing water rise around her ankles. It stung her wounded toe and made her feet ache.

"I've had ample time to think of my future. As far as I can tell, it all ends the same. I snuck into one of the restricted libraries to read about nymphs. There weren't even any pictures. Just a lot of foul rulings by the Blessed Order, and none of them ended happily for my kind. I wish I hadn't read about it."

"I see," Marsais said. And he did, far more than she realized. "You've changed—grown in my absence."

Isiilde glanced down at her body as she puzzled over his statement. She seemed no taller.

The nymph tilted her head up in question. "You haven't shrunk, have you?"

"Your awareness," he clarified.

"Are you making fun of me?"

"I would never."

"Awareness of what?"

"Nymphs live in the moment. They seldom ponder their past or consider their future—or their present, for that matter."

"At least I'm safe for another year."

"Hmm, so is that why?"

"Why what?"

"Even for a faerie, this is an impressive stack of mischief," Marsais said, holding up her letters of misconduct.

Isiilde glared at the letters, hoping they'd catch on fire. "I don't know what's wrong with me. Since that cold-fingered hag left, I haven't been able to do anything right. My legs have been itchy."

Marsais pursed his lips. "You're going to have to explain that one."

She gestured impatiently towards the ocean. "This is an island, Marsais! Oen has taken me everywhere, even to the Alderwood. It was cold. Everywhere is cold, except for your study, and with you gone I haven't even felt like going there. I think I replaced one dungeon for a slightly bigger one. I know I should be thankful, but—" She fell silent when she thought about all the trouble her presence had caused Marsais over the years.

It had been difficult to persuade the Nine to let a nymph live on the Isle. He'd thrown his power and authority at the council, and only then had they relented. To say nothing of Marsais' recent decision to take her on as his apprentice. His choice had caused a stir in the Order's ranks.

Isiilde was openly despised by most Wise Ones. Others viewed her as a fascinating oddity. Nymphs were rarely seen; their owners kept them secluded. And so she was like some rare breed of animal that could hold a conversation.

"But that's how you feel," Marsais said softly.

Isiilde nodded, feeling foolish. "Will you promise not to leave again?" she asked suddenly, full of hope and yearning.

"I can't make that promise, Isiilde." Her heart twisted. "But I have something that might cheer you up."

Isiilde followed him to his rucksack and waited while he searched it. His entire arm disappeared inside. All his bags were enchanted. Years before, Isiilde had crawled in the pack to explore its spacious weave, but found herself in the dark with no obvious way out. Luckily, Oen had walked in as her foot disappeared and rescued her.

"For you," Marsais said, handing her a heavy velvet pouch.

Her world brightened at the simple pleasure of a present. "You thought of me while you were gone?"

"Of course."

She accepted the pouch and sat down, holding it with reverence.

Marsais crouched beside her. "It's a fine pouch, but you may want to look inside."

She opened it to find a flawless, palm-sized orb. Flowing runes decorated its vibrant blue surface like a sea of rippling waves. One rune caught her eye. "What's this one?"

"Memory," he said. "Weave that rune over the top of the orb to activate the enchantment."

Isiilde did so, and the orb's surface began to swirl like a whirlpool. She gazed into its depths and was soon lost in a vision.

She stood on a hilltop overlooking a bay that stretched to a distant horizon. A city hugged the bay's shoreline, and ships of every kind dotted crystal waters: Mearcentian trade galleons and swift clipper ships bearing the white flag of the Isle of Winds, and sluggish warships moving among them like titans. A bright white palace with spiraling towers crowned the highest hill—Whitemount, the power and throne of Kambe.

"To change the memory, simply touch another rune." His voice drifted to her ears through the vision.

Isiilde focused on the feel of the orb in her hand, which brought her back to the present. She touched a random rune, and another vision swirled into focus, intensifying until a tusked mammoth lumbered into view, stopping to graze on the swaying grass of a vast plain.

She marveled at its size, then reluctantly pulled away and looked at Marsais through a sheen of tears.

"I thought you might be getting restless. I'd like to take you off this island—" Emotion cracked his voice. "But I can't. This is the best I could do. Whenever I saw something I thought you might like I saved the memory—my memories."

"It's beautiful. Thank you." Her whispered words seemed inadequate. No one had ever put so much thought into something for her.

Isiilde reached for his hand, but he quickly stood.

"I've always thought a gift should do its receiver justice. But for you, everything falls miserably short."

Marsais had always remained physically distant. Never embracing her, never taking her hand. But there was so much warmth in his words. It left her confused.

"Now then," Marsais said, rubbing his nimble hands together. "I wonder what should be done with a certain nymph for her various acts of misconduct."

"You could rub her feet."

The edges of his lips twitched. "Hmm, somehow, I don't think that would satisfy Thira's anger."

Isiilde blew out a breath. She'd nearly forgotten about that.

"Answer me this—did you intend to harm Crumpet?"

"Lord Kulthin made a rude comment," Isiilde said, attempting to distract him.

Marsais snorted. "Kulthin is an egotistical bastard. He's too proud to admit that a nymph took a jab at him—an accurate one, I might add. Now back to Thira. She is a formidable woman, and her charges against you aren't light."

"Are you asking as my master, as the Archlord, or as my friend?"

"Hmm, what an intriguing question. One that I freely admit has aroused my curiosity—not a common occurrence, that."

"Except when you're with me," Isiilde pointed out.

Marsais couldn't argue with that. He held up a finger and continued in a stern voice that he only summoned for the gravest of matters. "First, as the Archlord."

Isiilde bowed her head with respect. "I did not do it on purpose, Archlord," she said, trying not to laugh.

He flashed a grin in return. "Now, as your master."

"Crumpet attacked me. I gave him ample warning, but I still didn't do it on purpose."

"And your friend?" This was a careful question.

"I don't know what happened, Marsais," she admitted. "I swear it on whatever you hold sacred. I just wanted the dog to leave me alone. The next thing I knew, he was on fire. I didn't feel very bad though—if that matters."

"Hmm." Marsais gazed out to sea in thought. "I was asking for my own curiosity. I doubt Thira will care whether it was an accident or whether you'd been plotting the attack for a month. But as your Archlord, master, and most especially your friend—I'm happy to hear it wasn't intentional."

"What's going to happen?"

"Unfortunately, since I'm both your master and Archlord, I'll have to punish you."

Isiilde quickly scooted backwards when he started rifling through his rucksack.

"Oh, by the gods, have I ever hurt you?"

"I've never set Crumpet on fire before."

"An excellent point." As he searched the contents of his pack, he mumbled his thoughts aloud. "Hmm, let me see... What's a suitable punishment for a faerie... no strawberries?" She squeaked in dismay. "Waking up at the crack of dawn, perhaps?" He looked up in question and quickly shook his head. "No, no, that's far too lenient."

"Lenient... that's torture, Marsais!" Isiilde spluttered.

"Ah! I have the perfect punishment."

Marsais ignored her smoldering gaze and plucked a crystal lens from the extra-dimensional pocket, and held it to the sunlight. After careful study, he polished it on a relatively clean section of his shirt. "We will sit here and swelter in the sun until you've burned every one of these reports—using this lens."

Isiilde narrowed her eyes.

To demonstrate, Marsais plucked a letter off the stack and laid it on the sand. He positioned the lens above the paper, and caught the sunlight, directing a scorching ray towards the vulnerable print. A trailing wisp of smoke rose into the air, searing a hole through the letter. A ring of fire spread to its edges.

Her heart quickened. "Isn't this supposed to be my punishment?"

Marsais handed the lens to her, and they watched the flames curl along the pages in silence for a time.

"This is pure torture," she purred.

"I'm practically a vile slave master," Marsais agreed. "I'll make sure Thira knows how you suffered."

"Terribly."

When the letters had all been consumed, Marsais added kindling and Oenghus joined them, bringing food and ale. Darkness fell, and a lilting song drifted from Isiilde's lips. She danced around the blaze, urging it to reach as high as it dared, to lick the heavens and set the stars alight.

The fire caressed her body as she twirled around its roar. And for a little while at least, the nymph forgot who she was and what she was. She was alone with her flame, in a realm woven from her voice, a place of wild freedom.

When her body shook with exhaustion, she stilled. The world sighed; the dream faded. And the nymph was still bound by her Fate.

CHAPTER 4

A GUST of sharp wind swept up the hillside and buffeted their wagon as they navigated the final, snaking road to Drivel. The city hadn't changed. It still huddled in its cove, safe from the turbulent seas of the Fell Coast.

Isiilde tugged her cloak firmly about her and leaned into Marsais, trying to focus on the gulls that circled over the harbor while he worked the brake and kept a tight rein on the horses.

"You look worried, my dear."

"Aren't you?" she asked.

"Aye, he's worried what's gonna happen when he tips over my barrels of brew. Ease up on the bloody brake before you snap it," Oenghus warned.

With those ominous words, the wagon lurched, and Isiilde grabbed onto Marsais' arm for support.

"By the Pits o' Mourn," Oenghus swore. "It looks like every bugger on the Isle has come today."

Curiosity won over fear, and she cracked an eye open. A long line of travelers stretched along the road, waiting to pass through the gates.

When Marsais eased the wagon to a stop at the back of the line, Isiilde stood to look past the gates to the festivities beyond.

"Why are they stopping everyone?" she asked.

Several travelers in line turned to gawk at the nymph. When she noticed, she quickly sat back down.

"They're probably confiscating weapons," Oenghus said.

He unclasped the long folds of his kilt from around his shoulder and gathered the billowing cloth. Then tucked the folds into his belt to conceal the war hammer hanging from its belt hook.

"I don't think that will work," she said.

"No, but this will." He pulled out a heavy jug from the wagon bed, and set it by her feet.

"Isn't bribery illegal?"

"Who said I was offering bribes?"

"The guards might. Then you'll be thrown into the lockup *again.*"

Oenghus shrugged. "It's not so bad, Sprite. They know they can't really keep me locked up if I don't want to be in there. We have an agreement of sorts. I stay in their jail to make them look good, and in exchange I get free room and board. It's rowdier than a pleasure house in there."

"Do the guards dress up in corsets, or do you?" Isiilde quipped.

Marsais laughed.

"By the gods, girl, what's got into you?" Oenghus demanded, returning her glare.

"I had to spend four days with Rashk when you were thrown in jail for disorderly conduct two months back—I still don't know what you did. And now I find out you enjoyed it."

"I thought you liked Rashk."

"I never had to watch her eat before." Isiilde's stomach lurched at the memory. "I thought the little piglet in her garden pen was a pet. I didn't know she was going to eat it while it was still twitching." She wrinkled her nose, wishing she hadn't eaten earlier.

Oenghus chewed thoughtfully on his pipe. "Would it help if I told you they tortured me?"

"No, but it would help if I told Marsais that Isek had to borrow coin from his coffers to bail you out of prison three different times." Isiilde smiled sweetly at her guardian. "It would also help if Marsais knew you owed him thirty gold crowns for the bail and a hundred and fifty for the tavern you ruined."

"But you wouldn't tell him, right?"

"I wouldn't dream of it, Oen."

"Hmm, interest on a hundred and eighty crowns—that's a fair profit for not doing much," Marsais mused.

"You flea-bitten scoundrel," Oenghus growled. "Only a backbiting bastard would charge a friend interest."

"I wasn't planning on it until you called me a scoundrel," Marsais pointed out.

Oenghus replied with a crude gesture. "You'll notice, Sprite, that *backbiting*, *flea-bitten*, and *bastard* don't offend him."

"So what *did* you do to offend the good and proper folk of Drivel this time?" Marsais asked.

Oenghus scratched his beard, glancing at Isiilde. "I'll tell you later."

Before Isiilde could press him, a flash of gold caught her eye. Two paladins, wearing gleaming mail and golden tunics, stood just inside the city gates, inspecting the crowd.

She quickly pulled her cowl over her ears.

The Blessed Order of Zahra made Isiilde uneasy. She was a nymph, after all. But she wasn't the only one who disliked the paladins.

The Blessed Order maintained a large garrison on the island. And while they patrolled the channel and helped defend against raiding Wedamen, they also ruthlessly stamped out any practices they deemed unholy. That, and they were a general pain in the arse.

"No weapons. No brawling. State your name," a guard called out hoarsely as they pulled up to the gatehouse.

Oenghus gave his name to the guard, and a second one started a routine stroll around their wagon.

"I got this one, corporal," a voice called from the guardhouse. A moment later, the captain on watch emerged. "Been a while, Oenghus."

He clasped the captain's forearm in greeting. "Aye, Jamus, good to see you. How's your family getting on?"

Oenghus and the captain began conversing. From the snippets Isiilde overheard, she gathered that Oenghus had healed one of his children.

When the second guard finished his circuit of the wagon, he paused by the seat, glancing up to peek under Isiilde's cowl.

Marsais nodded down at the guard. But the guard didn't spare him a glance. His eyes were fixed on the nymph.

Isiilde shifted in her seat. Worry soon turned to discomfort when the corporal stepped up to see what held his comrade's attention. He stared, too.

"Your captain knows my friend," Marsais said. "Surely there's nothing more for you to do here. Perhaps you should keep the line moving, corporal."

"I'd shut your trap unless you want trouble," the guard warned.

Marsais toyed with the reins in his hands. They were elegant and expressive hands, and Isiilde knew by the way his long fingers twitched that he was on the verge of a weave.

The Archlord of the Isle was known as a recluse, the crimson robes of his office more recognizable than his face.

"Get down from there, lass, so we can search you for weapons," the corporal ordered. The oaf moved towards Isiilde with a strange look in his eyes.

"I have a gift for you, Jamus," Oenghus said, casually reaching for the jug at Isiilde's feet. As Oenghus brushed past the oaf, the guard doubled over with a grunt, clutching his gut.

Isiilde blinked in surprise. Had he hit the guard?

"Your men should be more careful." Oenghus shoved the groaning man towards his superior before handing the captain his gift.

"Aye, the blasted fools are always comin' in drunk. You take care, and I hope to see you in the jailhouse this eve. You're a bloody bad gambler when you're drunk."

Oenghus grinned and gave Gungnir a slap on the flank. The wagon rolled into Drivel with a lurch.

THE MAIN ROAD was clogged with people, and their wagon made slow progress through the city. As the wagon creaked slowly down Sparrow

Road, Isiilde watched the people from her high vantage point. The crowd looked like a sea of bobbing heads decorated with flowers and ribbons.

Hundreds of voices mingled together. Minstrels, jugglers, and acrobats vied for coin. And groups of sailors, soused from the night before, staggered down streets singing and brawling. And although city guards were on patrol, they seemed more interested in women than in breaking up fights.

Rough-looking men eyed the kegs on their wagon, but one look at Oenghus changed their minds.

"Oen!" several women called.

They waved from the balcony of a pleasure house.

"We haven't seen you in months!" a busty blonde hollered down. Her breasts were spilling out of her bodice. "You'll pay us a visit, won't you?"

"I've been busy, lass," Oenghus called up with a grin.

"Aye, so I heard, you lovable brute," the blonde said, as the other women on the balcony giggled.

"How's your girls?"

"Missin' you," she replied. "Promise you'll come by?"

"I have a delivery to make, Maira."

"Come by after, then. We want to thank you properly."

"There's no need for thanks. I was happy to help."

"I won't take no. And make sure you bring your friend there!"

Several women wolf-whistled down at Marsais, who was eyeing the garishly painted building.

"I'll see what I can do," Oenghus promised.

Isiilde considered Marsais for a moment. "Do you visit pleasure houses?"

Marsais arched a brow in return. Before she could ask another question, he looked to Oenghus. "What thanks do they owe you?"

"They had a bad fever outbreak a couple months back, so I brewed up some potions and sat with the worst of them until it burnt out."

Oenghus rarely demanded payment for his healing, except for the wealthy.

Isiilde noticed a woman selling honey-roasted peanuts. Suddenly ravenous, she stood up, wondering if she could squeeze through the pressing crowd.

"A beauty like you should be enjoying the festivities, love," a slurred voice tore her attention away from food. Two men stared up at her in a daze.

"We'll escort you around," the taller of the two hiccuped, while the shorter offered her a rose.

Before she could accept the flower, Oenghus brought their heads together with a resounding smack. They crumpled to the cobblestones.

"Drunken louts," Oenghus muttered. "Put your hood up, Sprite."

"Why did you do that?" she demanded. "I don't think they meant any harm."

Oenghus snorted. "My arse they didn't."

Isiilde pulled up her hood and turned in the wagon seat, searching for the pair. But instead of the men, she spotted two paladins. They were pushing their way through the crowd towards the wagon. Although their visors obscured their faces, she thought they were the same pair from the gate.

She spun back around. Maybe they hadn't seen her.

Marsais directed the horses into the wealthier districts of Drivel. These streets were less chaotic than the main road. Isiilde glanced over her shoulder. The paladins were still there.

They turned into a narrow lane that led to the stables of the finest inn on the Isle—the Glass Goblet. It was a three-story building of smooth river rock and polished oak, rich with the scents of wealth. As Marsais pulled into the courtyard, a stableman came out to assist with the horses.

The paladins marched into the courtyard, too.

"Bollocks," Oenghus growled. He leaned casually against the wagon, puffing away on his pipe as he watched them approach. "Can I help you two?"

One paladin removed a visored helmet, revealing a stern-faced woman with raven hair shorn short. "State your business," she demanded.

"We're delivering some brew," Oenghus said casually. But everything about him intimidated, from his sheer size to his baleful eyes and rumbling voice. His mere presence was an offense.

The second paladin ordered Isiilde to remove her hood. She looked at her guardian. Oenghus' beard twitched, but he gave her a slight nod, so she lowered her hood.

The stableman gaped, and the visored paladin stiffened in alarm.

"*That* is a nymph," the raven-haired woman stated.

"Aye, what of it?"

"Who's her owner?" The woman glanced between Marsais and Oenghus.

"I'm her guardian," Oenghus replied.

"And you are?" The woman arched a brow.

He took a slow drag from his pipe before answering. "Oenghus Saevaldr."

"Sir, he's the one who—"

"I was cleared of those charges by the Knight Captain himself," he cut in.

"You can't bring a nymph here." The statement made Isiilde's heart sink.

"She's been to Drivel before."

"Not on my watch," the woman said. "I'll be lenient and let you deliver your goods before escorting you out." There was a clear warning in her words. It was within their right to seize Oenghus' shipment and escort him and Isiilde directly out of town.

"I'll worry about her safety," Oenghus rumbled.

"I don't care about the creature's safety. I'm concerned about the trouble that their kind cause. This isn't up to debate. You can do this the easy way or the hard way, Saevaldr."

"With all due respect, Holy One," Marsais said softly. "I do not recall any law that prohibits a nymph from appearing in public."

"We are the law," the woman snapped. The pair gripped their sword hilts. "Now do as you're told."

"Since we've broken no laws, I'd say you're getting ahead of your-selves," Marsais reasoned.

"And what is your name, so I can charge you with the contempt of a paladin?"

"I specifically stated that I was speaking with respect," Marsais replied.

"Your name, fool!" The visored paladin drew his sword with a scrape of steel.

Isiilde turned to Marsais in fear, and his arm came protectively around her shoulders.

"I'm Marsais," he replied. "And unless you're accusing us of consorting with Voidspawn, then *I* am the law on this island."

"Now you're claiming to be the Archlord?" the woman asked with the sort of disbelief reserved for the truly insane.

"I'm not claiming," Marsais said, raising his left hand. A runic eye flared to life on his palm.

The paladins stiffened in shock.

"This nymph is my apprentice, and I'll vouch for her. I suggest you let us go about our business. The Knight Captain won't appreciate you harassing me."

The visored paladin pointed at Oenghus with his sword. "This man is armed. Weapons are forbidden inside city limits today."

"I'm the Archlord's personal bodyguard. You can't tell me the count is walking around with an unarmed escort."

"We will report this to the High Inquisitor," the woman threatened.

"Hmm, please do, it will save me the trouble of informing him that I've returned."

The paladins weren't happy, but the Archlord's runic eye was indisputable. They sheathed their weapons and marched off without another word.

"And that's why it's good to be Archlord," Oenghus muttered, gesturing crudely at their backs.

"Must you antagonize them?"

"I *was* being diplomatic," Oenghus defended. "More so than you, ya sparkly left-handed bastard." The rest of his insults trailed off as he stomped to the back door of the Glass Goblet.

"You're safe, Isiilde," Marsais said, softly.

She looked up from his shoulder, her heart thundering against his ribs. He stared down into her eyes for several heartbeats, then his arm fell away.

"Sorry," she whispered, pulling back.

"It's all right. The paladins were being rude." He seemed about to add something more; instead, he quickly secured the reins and hopped off the wagon. "By the gods, I've forgotten how torturous these things are."

Marsais grimaced as he stretched. Everything about him was long and agile, and he moved with effortless grace. He was built for speed; not for riding.

"I've heard the Mystics use flying carpets in Kiln. You should get a carpet."

"I have one."

"You do?"

"Yes, it warms my floor."

"Marsais," she warned.

"I'm serious. You can make anything fly. It doesn't have to be an expensive carpet. It simply takes concentration."

Isiilde wrinkled her nose at the word. Concentrating was far too much work, in her humble opinion.

"Take this gentleman here." Marsais gestured towards the stablehand, who shifted from foot to foot. "If we had him lie down, then we could just as easily sit on him and fly as we could on a carpet."

"Could you teach me?"

"Hmm, I don't think Oenghus would react well if he came out and saw you sitting on that fellow."

"You're right—he'd tear off his head." She frowned, but quickly brightened. "You could turn him into a carpet and then we could try."

The stablehand bolted. Isiilde controlled her laughter long enough for him to skid around a corner.

"Perhaps we'll start with something smaller," Marsais mused. His nimble fingers moved swiftly. Then with a gesture and a quiet command, he lifted her off the ground.

Shock replaced her helpless laughter. Isiilde floated off the wagon seat and was gently pulled towards Marsais by an unseen weave.

"You always hide your runes from me," she accused.

"Only the ones that have ill occurrences when done improperly."

She arched a brow at him. "And how often do I perform a weave improperly?"

"An excellent point," he conceded. "But a Weave of Flying requires a certain amount of control."

"Oh, never mind then." Self-control was another ability that escaped her.

"I thought you'd understand. Without control, the most desirable outcome would send you careening off into the sky." That didn't sound so bad. "Which Oen wouldn't be happy with," he added, noting her thoughtful interest. "At worst—too heavy a hand would crush you."

"That sounds painful."

"Messy would be a better description."

"So what will you teach me?" She knew him well. At his beckoning gesture, she drifted closer to touch lightly upon the ground.

"Levitation." A dozen wonderful things she could accomplish with that weave flashed through her mind. Although flying would be far more useful, she'd take what she could get.

"Do you remember the feather rune that I taught you?"

"It tickles when I weave it."

"Really?" Marsais' brows shot up in surprise.

"It doesn't tickle you?"

"Hmm, no, but I'm not a nymph."

"Are you otherwise ticklish?" she asked.

"Yes."

She opened her mouth.

"No," he interrupted. "I'm not going to tell you where."

"Why?"

Marsais took a hasty step backwards. "Because."

"That's not an answer, Marsais."

"Questions hardly require an answer, only a reply, and that, my dear, was a reply."

She lost her train of thought when Oenghus ducked under the doorway, stepping outside. He was trailed by the owner of the Goblet and two strong men. The group walked over to the wagon, where Oenghus poured a sample of his ale for the finely dressed proprietor, Haimon

Goodfellow, who took as much pride in his oiled mustaches as he did with his inn.

The innkeeper took a swig and gave a satisfied sigh as a trail of smoke wafted from his lips. Oenghus Saevaldr's ale was renowned throughout the Isle, Nuthaan, and Kambe. The trip to the gullet was smooth, and the delayed bite was memorable, causing the drinker to exhale a puff of smoke a few seconds after swallowing the red liquid. Hence the name, Dragon's Breath Ale.

"I think that's better than your last batch." Haimon plopped a heavy pouch into Oenghus' hand. "I had a merchant from Mearcentia buy two barrels of it. You know, you could be a rich man if you put more work into it."

"That's far more commitment than I'm after," Oenghus grunted.

As the two laborers began unloading the wagon, Isiilde turned to Marsais to find him besotted with a rosebush. She checked the bush, but it was empty aside from roses.

"Marsais?"

"Hmm?" he replied, distantly.

Isiilde repeated his name again, this time louder. He snapped out of his trance, casting about in confusion. Finally, his grey eyes sharpened on her. "Oh, hello, my dear. What were we talking about?"

"You were about to tell me where you are ticklish."

He stroked his goatee in consideration. "I think not."

This did absolutely nothing to satisfy her curiosity. She lunged for a spot under his ribs, but Marsais was quicker. He skipped to the side and held up a halting hand.

"If I tell you it's considerably lower, will you leave it at that?"

Isiilde tried to keep from grinning, but her attempt failed. "Do you get tickled often?"

"I believe you've managed to sidetrack us again."

"I have a knack for that."

"You have no idea," Marsais said, snatching a pebble from the ground. "Now then, pay attention. To levitate, you must weave a feather rune around the desired object, and then layer an air and spirit rune overtop. Do you know why both air and spirit are needed?"

Isiilde considered his question as she watched the laborers hoisting heavy barrels onto their shoulders. They were bare-chested with a sheen of sweat on their skin, and wore clinging trousers. She liked the way they moved.

When the men disappeared into a nearby cellar, she turned back to Marsais. A shadow of worry flickered across his eyes.

She raised a shoulder. "They're very fit."

"Hmm."

To show him she'd been paying attention, Isiilde answered his question with the first thought that popped into her mind. "An air and spirit rune creates wind, and a feather will fall if there's no wind."

He gave a slight nod of approval. Her guess had been correct.

"This is where concentration comes into play, because wind must be a constant if you are trying to keep your object in the air."

"Is that why Master Tulipin is always so absentminded?" The gnome Wise One levitated everywhere—come to think of it, Isiilde had never seen his feet touch the ground.

"Actually, he's just like that. Would you like to watch the weave?"

Isiilde focused on the pebble in his hand. She loved to watch Marsais trace runes, because the Gift was his art. He caressed it to life, never clumsy or harsh, but always shaping its power with an ease that left her breathless.

The Weave of Levitating was easy enough to follow. When the pebble was floating, she invoked the Lore, feeling a rush of energy flow around her that tugged at her mind and spirit like a river's current. She quickly traced the runes, and a heartbeat later, another pebble floated off the ground to join the first.

The weave lasted until a bright bumblebee bobbed past her ear to land on a rose petal. The nymph beamed and hurried over to watch the fuzzy bug. Her pebble fell to the ground, entirely forgotten.

"That was... better," Marsais said.

"Oh!" Isiilde gave him a sheepish smile. "It was?"

"You kept the pebble in the air for nearly five seconds, my dear. Your attention span has moved up an entire second. By a nymph's standard, that's monumental."

Isiilde brightened at his compliment.

"But I think it'd be exceedingly unwise to try levitating yourself until you can sustain the weave for a full ten seconds."

"How about six?" she bartered.

"Fine. But only if I'm around. *And* watching," he quickly added.

Isiilde could live with those terms. Although she doubted she would attempt the weave again—those five seconds had been exhausting.

WITHOUT THE WAGON, they made good time through the city, the crowds parting for Oenghus like water flowing around a crag. Men avoided the berserker, while women stepped aside to admire his stride.

Isiilde stayed by his side, and Marsais brooded some paces behind, staring at his boots.

She eyed the keg on Oenghus' shoulder. "I thought you and Sir Goodfellow had an agreement to sell your ale only to the Goblet?"

"Aye, we do, but this isn't my Dragon's Ale," he said around his pipe. "It's for Brinehilde at the orphanage. A drop of this will keep the little ones warm through the winter."

"Did you save some for me?" she asked.

"You'd drink the whole barrel and still manage to be cold."

She couldn't argue with that.

There was little rhyme or reason to the streets of Drivel. Taverns, shops, and houses had sprouted like weeds along the slice of coastland, and the roads had been left to fend for themselves.

Isiilde and Marsais followed Oenghus through the maze of streets to the fishing district, which was crammed with shacks along the mudflats. The dwellings were drab and faded, colored only by the droppings of seagulls that circled overhead. The place reeked of rotting fish, and filth and stagnant water mingled freely with mud beneath rotting planks.

Isiilde covered her nose with a handkerchief and tried not to dwell on what they were walking through. The trenches along the muck-laden road smelled like cesspits.

"What in the Void is that fool Count doing with his taxes?" Marsais muttered under his breath.

"I hear the bastard erected a statue of himself instead of fixing the roads between here and Coven," Oenghus said.

"Count Regald claims it's the Order's responsibility to fix the roads. But since we provide this island with protection, I think it's only fair that he sees to the upkeep of the roads."

"Exactly. It's not like he has to fund an army. He's just a greedy bastard living off his father's legacy."

"You know, I'm not quite sure if it's greed or pure laziness. If greedy, he'd be looking to increase his wealth. But since becoming lord mayor, he just sits in his manor collecting taxes. It's slothful."

"That sounds familiar. Although I'd interject 'Archlord' and 'tower' in there."

"Hmm, that's an awfully big word for a barbarian."

Oenghus ignored the jab. "You should lend him Isek Beirnuckle for a month. Your assistant would have this whole Isle looking like a Mearcentian trade port."

"Oh, by the gods, no! I'd be forced to deal with every petty squabble and irksome question that came along."

"If you don't like it, then why are you Archlord?" Isiilde asked.

"Aye, Marsais, tell her why you're Archlord."

"Because Isek likes to know what's going on," Marsais answered.

"Like a squirrel hoards nuts," Oenghus grunted.

"You see, Isek is a ravenous collector of information. This addiction of his drove him to cast my name as Archlord, without my knowledge. What's it been—eighty, or is it a hundred years already?"

Oenghus shrugged. "I stopped keeping track of years."

Isiilde cocked her head in thought. "So... you didn't want to be Archlord, but Isek did, so he'd know everything an Archlord knows?"

"Precisely."

"Why didn't he just cast his own name?"

"Because my friend has a rather nefarious reputation and prefers to lurk in the shadows. As he put it to me so many years ago, a seer born before the Shattering sounds better as Archlord than a former spy."

"And you get your own tower," she pointed out.

"Exactly." Marsais looked pleased.

"And since Isek is a cowardly bastard, whenever something dangerous comes along, he throws it on Marsais."

"And then I throw it on Oen," Marsais returned.

"So everyone's happy, Sprite."

"Then what do you *do*, exactly?" Isiilde asked.

"Entertain you."

Three brown-skinned children charged out of an alley. When the trio spotted Oenghus, they raced towards him, shouting excited greetings.

"How's your mum doing with the wee ones?" Oenghus asked, when they had calmed down enough to stand still. They craned their necks, grinning up at their giant friend.

"Well enough, sir," they answered as one. The three boys were filthy, but their eyes were bright and alive.

Oenghus snorted and reached into his pouch before dropping three gold crowns into the tallest boy's hands. "You give that to your mum, Zoshi, or I'll come after the lot of you."

The three boys stared wide-eyed at the gold. Overcome with emotion, the smallest stepped forward and hugged Oenghus' leg.

"Bah, Tuck," Oenghus grumbled even as he reached down to pat the boy on the back. "Go on, get out of here and find some trouble."

As the trio scattered, Oenghus tugged a braid in his beard and turned to Marsais. "The problem is, Scarecrow, most of the people in this quarter are squatters. Take those three runts: their father died at sea, leaving their mother pregnant with twins. Now she's an honorable lass who scrapes by. But if Count Regald put in proper roads and drains, they'd be run out with nothing but the rags on their backs. It's mostly sailors' women and their bastards—a good many who've never seen their fathers. Best to leave it as it is. There's no other place for them to go."

"You expect this sort of thing in the Bastardlands, but not on the Isle. I don't remember it being this bad."

"It's gotten worse in the last few years," Oenghus admitted.

"Hmm, remind me to have a word with Count Regald," Marsais said, sounding distant. He was watching a drunken sailor stagger down a narrow lane.

He fell silent. Then stopped walking. And even after the drunk had disappeared down an alley, he continued to stare.

Isiilde stopped to stare with him.

"Don't bother, Sprite. I doubt even the gods know what he bloody sees."

Marsais shuddered and finally tore his eyes from the lane.

"What were you looking at?" Isiilde asked.

"Was I looking at something?"

"You were looking at a drunken sailor," she reminded him.

"Ah, well then, I guess that answers your question."

CHAPTER 5

Oenghus pounded on the front door of the orphanage. It was the only one in Drivel. And the only stone manor in the dock district. Brinehilde watched over the children and tended a shrine dedicated to the Sylph. The shrine was in the courtyard, next to a small pond and sheltered by an ancient oak.

The Sylph's shrines were always outside. And while they lacked the formality of the Blessed Order, Oenghus had told Isiilde that what mattered most to the Goddess of All was how people lived their lives, not the temples where they worshipped.

"Before I forget." Oenghus dropped fifteen silver coins and an entire gold crown into her hand. "You should be able to get a dress with that, right?"

"Yes, thank you." She tucked the coins safely into her own purse.

The metal slat slid back on the door, and a suspicious green eye studied the three visitors. "Why, if it isn't a bloody Saevaldr!" a booming voice echoed from within.

The door opened, revealing a square-jawed Nuthaanian woman who was as tall as Marsais and as sturdy as Oenghus. A chubby-cheeked infant sat on her hip, happily tugging her long red braid.

"Where've ya been, you bastard?" She threw an arm around Oenghus and planted a kiss on his lips, before motioning them through the door.

"The usual," Oenghus answered.

"Don't think I haven't heard about *that* incident," Brinehilde said. "Thought you'd still be locked up. Wipe your feet, you big oaf!"

Oenghus quickly obeyed, then set down his keg.

Brinehilde's eyes widened. "Is that your cold ward potion?"

"Aye, the best I could brew."

"The Sylph bless you."

"This is for the children." Oenghus handed her half of his recent earnings, then unhooked the flagon that was swinging from his belt. "And this is for you."

"Oh, curse you, Oen." Considering the tears shimmering in her eyes, it wasn't a very sincere threat. "Here, lass, hold the wee one so I can give this lout a proper thanks." Brinehilde dumped the infant into Isiilde's arms. He was every bit as heavy as he appeared.

Having seen several women kiss Oenghus before, Isiilde ignored the pair and began bouncing the child while humming a tune. Babies always went straight for her ears, as this one did now, but she didn't mind, especially when he started drooling with delight.

"I think he has your nose, Marsais," Isiilde said.

"The poor boy. He won't grow into it for near a century." Marsais leaned down to study the chubby face. The baby quickly abandoned her ear, grabbing Marsais' hair and shoving a fistful into its mouth.

The baby looked into Marsais' eyes, and froze, transfixed by what he saw. Drool dripped around a chubby fist.

"Human infants have a remarkable ability to see past illusion," Marsais muttered.

Isiilde narrowed her eyes at her master. And nearly kicked herself. That explained why he looked more ragged than the day before—he'd woven an illusion weave around his hair to dampen the glow.

Brinehilde broke away from Oenghus. "Where's my manners? Isiilde..." The priestess faltered as she looked at the nymph for the first time.

Isiilde froze. Had she done something wrong?

"By the Sylph," Brinehilde breathed. "You're a proper woman now. And beautiful at that. But I'm sure you hear it enough, so I won't fill your head any more than it already is."

Actually, she rarely received compliments. Oenghus was more likely to call her 'sprite' or 'carrot top', and, as far as she could tell, Marsais wouldn't notice if the Sylph herself sauntered naked through a room.

Brinehilde brushed her lips across the nymph's forehead in greeting and blessing.

"Your friend here looks like he could use a warm meal." Brinehilde jerked her chin towards Marsais. With his patched clothes and illusion weave, he looked like a vagabond. "I have warm stew..." she trailed off, warily watching the stranger stare at the ceiling, entranced by the rafters.

"This is Marsais," Isiilde offered.

"Is he... a bit touched in the head, then?"

Oenghus boomed a laugh. "He's the bloody Archlord, Hilde."

"That's nothing to jest about," Brinehilde said, slapping his chest so hard it echoed in the room.

Isiilde started to correct the priestess, but Oenghus shrugged and took the baby from her and tossed it in the air. It squealed with delight.

"Who's this wee one?"

"He was dropped off on my doorstep yesterday. Likely another whore's son. I'm fairly sure he's not yours, because he's not near pig-headed enough."

Oenghus snorted.

"Isiilde, why don't you name him? I haven't gotten around to it yet. Being named by one of the Sylph's own daughters will bring him good luck."

It appeared Brinehilde shared Marsais' views on nymphs. Surely she'd know who the Sylph favored. So why did the Blessed Order treat her kind like animals? The question gnawed at her.

"How about it, Sprite?"

"Oh." She turned her mind to the naming. "What about Galvier? He seems adventurous already."

Galvier Longstride was a legendary traveler, who was said to have walked the realms twice over because his feet never stopped moving. His stories entertained taverns and royal courts alike. But she doubted they were true. How could the man sleep if he never stopped moving?

"That's a fine name," Oenghus said, spinning the boy around to the mutual delight of both. "Makes me want another one."

"Well, you can have this one if you like, because this realm doesn't need another Saevaldr."

"You're just jealous because you haven't had one of mine yet."

"I got a brood enough without your mule-brained offspring running around. How Morigan ever took Oaths with you, I'll never know."

"Our daughter, Kari, is the Clans Head of Nuthaan."

Brinehilde snorted. "That's Morigan's influence; not yours." She turned suddenly grave. "Say, Oen—I know you're here for the festival, but could you look at one of my girls?"

"You know you don't have to ask. What's the matter with her?" Oenghus asked, as Galvier tried to eat one of his braids.

"I just found her a few days ago. I wouldn't put her past ten. Drunk of a father whorin' her out. Some swine roughed her up real good." Oenghus growled, and Galvier cackled with delight at the sound.

"I already took care of the swine. Then paid the father a visit," Brinehilde said, cracking her scarred knuckles. "But the girl's already got the Keening, and now a fever to boot. So I doubt it'll be a quick healing."

Oenghus frowned, glancing at Isiilde.

"It's all right, Oen," she said, smiling through her disappointment. She'd been looking forward to the festival for months. "I can watch Galvier while you help her."

Marsais stopped his restless pacing. He stared blankly at the others until his mind caught up with their conversation. "I could escort you."

"You wouldn't mind?" Isiilde asked.

"I'd be more apt to ask that of you."

"Of course I wouldn't mind."

Marsais gave her an elegant bow, and offered his arm. She favored him with a smile that she reserved for him alone.

"You must really trust the fellow," Brinehilde remarked, eyeing Marsais as if she were sizing him up for a coffin.

"Hilde, I told you—he's the bloody Archlord."

It took a few moments before recognition shone in her eyes. "By the gods, he is, isn't he? I'm daft enough to miss Zemoch's bollocks today! I've only seen you from a distance and never had the chance to give you proper thanks for all this." She gestured towards the walls.

Marsais tensed—he'd watched her thank Oenghus already. "Seeing my old manor put to good use is thanks enough, my lady," he hastened to say.

"Aye, Hilde, a Nuthaanian woman would break him."

"Apparently." Brinehilde looked Marsais over with a critical eye. "Don't they feed you in that tower?"

"Oenghus eats it all," Marsais quipped.

Brinehilde slapped Oenghus's stomach with a hearty laugh. "He's a typical berserker. What you need is a good woman to fatten you up."

"Hmm, he takes all of those, too."

"I'm not even going to get into that," Brinehilde said, turning a baleful eye on Oenghus, who'd conveniently turned his attention to Galvier. "All the same, it's a pleasure to finally meet you, Archlord."

"Likewise, and please, it's just Marsais."

"You drop that 'my lady' nonsense, too," she ordered. "And if you see any of my brood running around, tell them to behave. I'm sure I'll have to fetch a few of them from the jailhouse before the day is done. I'd be watchin' over the little bastards myself, but someone had to stay with the poor girl."

"You're the only one here?" Oenghus asked.

"Aye, what of it?"

"Maybe I'll stick around to help you look after the wee one."

"I could use the help, but I'll warn you, there's a lot to be done."

"I'm up for it."

"I'll work ya hard, you brute."

Oenghus seemed pleased by the threat.

Isiilde tilted her head to the side. He wasn't near as eager to work around their cottage.

She opened her coin purse, plucking out the gold crown. "Here, Brinehilde, this is for Galvier. I think he'll need it more than me."

"Bless your heart," the priestess said, crushing the nymph to her breast.

Isiilde spluttered helplessly. She gulped in air when she was free, and quickly grabbed Marsais' arm lest the woman thank her again.

CHAPTER 6

"I didn't know you owned the manor," Isiilde said as they left the orphanage, walking arm in arm.

"You never asked."

"Do you own that shack over there?"

"Hmm, no."

"What about that one?" Isiilde pointed to a hut. When he shook his head, she tried another.

"I believe I have gotten your point," he said dryly.

"Are you sure? Because I could keep this up all day."

"Of that, I have no doubt." His grey eyes danced with amusement. "I used to live there before I became Archlord. I never could stand the constant interruptions of castle life."

"By yourself?"

"A few friends, such as Oenghus, stayed there when they visited." He stroked his goatee in thought. "Truth be told, I was never there much myself. Allowing it to be used as an orphanage is hardly a sacrifice on my part."

"All the same, I think it's noble of you."

"Coming from your lips, I'll take that as one of the highest compliments I've ever received."

Isiilde blushed. "You're welcome."

Feeling content with life, she began to hum. And soon the melody became a soft and quiet song. Her lilting voice mingled with the air, transforming their dreary surroundings into a shimmering dream.

But her words faded when they turned onto the main road. The crowds were thick, flowing like a river towards the parade grounds. Marsais eased Isiilde into the pulsing streams of celebration, and they were pulled along in its currents.

"Do you want to go anywhere?" Isiilde asked, surveying a display of silver charms. The man in the booth was claiming the trinkets warded off Voidspawn. She had her doubts.

"Just one place."

"Where?"

"I don't know, but I'm sure you'll find it."

There were too many distractions to question him further. Besides, Marsais was probably right—she would eventually get to wherever he was going. In the meantime, Isiilde followed her nose.

After buying a basket of food, they found an empty spot under a moss-covered oak to eat. They had a view of a puppet show across the way—the epic battle between Zahra the Righteous and Dagenir the Betrayer. The sinister Dagenir had a mouthful of fangs and curled horns, while Zahra was radiant in a pristine white and golden robe.

They hit each other over the head with wooden swords in a foppish battle for the Orb: a large ball covered in glitter and flaking gold paint.

Children squealed with delight.

Dagenir whacked Zahra over the head, and the audience shouted their disapproval. A red stain blossomed on Zahra's snowy hair, and the wounded puppet slumped. Slowly, Dagenir crept ever closer to the unguarded Orb.

The jeering from the crowd intensified.

"No wonder the populace is clueless." Marsais gestured towards the show with his turkey leg. "Performances like this both amaze and appall me. The past is never so simple."

The puppet Zahra stirred, then leapt to its feet. The audience shouted encouragement.

"Zahra and Dagenir never battled over the Orb?"

"Oh, they did," he said grimly. "But good and evil are not always so clear cut. The past is written by the victor. History is subjective. And the farther we distance ourselves from a point in time, the more it blurs, until fact becomes fiction. Things were much more complicated than this mockery."

"Perhaps you should stage a puppet show," she suggested.

"A splendid idea! The crowd will have a good laugh when the Blessed Order comes to hang, draw and quarter me," Marsais said, before sinking his teeth into turkey flesh.

There was both sorrow and amusement in his voice.

"Marsais?"

"Hmm."

"Humans are confusing."

"A wise assessment, my dear." He regarded her out of the corner of his eye. "My keen perceptions whisper that you have a question for me."

"I don't understand—" Isiilde was at a loss. She was trying to put her feelings into words, but it was difficult, so she ate a strawberry. That helped. Since it seemed like a good place to begin, Isiilde told Marsais about Yasimina's warning—not to repeat his words about nymphs being favored by the Sylph.

"Ah, I believe you're perplexed by the age-old question of *why*," he said, smiling with gentle understanding. "Your research regarding nymphs uncovered their mistreatment, but not the reason for it."

"Yes, that's what I don't understand. The Blessed Order worships the Guardians of Iilenshar, who claim allegiance to the Sylph. So why do they mistreat faerie? Why do people cower from knowledge? Aren't the Wise Ones supposed to 'protect the past to safeguard the future'?"

It was the motto of the Order. The words were etched into the top of the table in the council chamber.

"I'm afraid there is no simple answer to your question."

"I asked Oen why nymphs were mistreated, and he told me that humans were a bunch of thick-headed idiots."

"Blunt and to the point, as always. But if I were to put a single word to it, I'd say it's a matter of convenience."

Puppet Dagenir whacked the golden ball of glitter with his sword, and it burst apart, hurling rock candy into the audience. Children scrambled for the sweets.

Marsais jerked like he'd been hit. He put a hand to his forehead, in obvious pain, his breath ragged.

She touched his shoulder. "Marsais? Are you all right?"

His eyes focused on her, and she held his gaze until his breathing calmed. Slowly, he returned from whatever nightmare he'd remembered.

Marsais had lived through the Shattering. It had broken the land and nearly snuffed out all life. What horrors did he carry?

Isiilde kept her hand on his shoulder until he offered a small smile and drew away from her touch. "I'm fine. Thank you." He swallowed, turning his back on the puppet show.

"Convenience?" she asked, nudging him back on topic.

"Yes," he sighed, looking tired.

To give him time, she sampled her custard tart, and moaned with pleasure. "You have to try this." Isiilde thrust the tart at his mouth. He took a bite, and although he wasn't quite as expressive as she'd been, some light returned to his eyes.

"History is a tapestry," he said between mouthfuls. "Every thread affects the next. So, in order to understand why nymphs are mistreated, you need to understand the past. But you can't just pluck at a single thread; first, you have to unravel all the other threads. Everything is connected."

Shouts of *Thief!* rippled through the crowd. And every eye looked at a boy racing away from two angry men.

Isiilde checked her own purse. It was gone. "Blast!"

"I wouldn't worry." Marsais withdrew her purse from his cloak, dangling it in front of her nose. "If I could snatch it, then someone else would." The pouch disappeared back into his cloak for safekeeping.

"Thank you, Marsais."

"I've never been thanked so nicely for picking a pocket."

She gave him the last of the tart.

"Everything is connected," she reminded.

"Hmm, where to start with why faerie are hated..." He scratched at his chest in thought. "Long before the Shattering there was one race that stood above the others—the Lindale, called elves by people now. About my height, same ears as mine, and as beautiful as you."

Isiilde blushed at his compliment.

"They may have been shaped with Fyrsta. I don't know if that's true, but they *were* the first to watch over the nymphs. They were the original druids, or Eldritch. But after a time, some of the faerie rebelled against their nature and became a twisted race now known as the Fey. This sowed the first seeds of hatred and distrust."

Isiilde had heard tales of the first Fey, Pyrderi Har'Feydd. She'd thought them bedtime stories to frighten children into obedience.

"Later, unrelated to the Fey, most of the druids swore allegiance to one of theirs who lusted after power—Ramashan. He opened a Gateway to the Nine Halls."

"Why would the druids side with him?"

"Humans procreate at an alarming rate. Their numbers were growing, and so was their insatiable need to expand borders. Ramashan offered the druids a haven. Reason aside, the consequences were devastating. Thinking he could control forces beyond his power to fight the humans, he created an artifact that opened a Gateway to the Nine Halls. Fiendish hordes poured into Fyrsta.

"It was a grim time. The Fey and their twisted Fomorri creations were wreaking havoc, and now fiends were loose in Fyrsta. The Void spread like a plague and the Sylph's power was waning. In desperation, she gave an artifact of immense power to the Keeper and his Guardians —the Orb. It held the very essence of life, the root of her power. She hoped it would stop the Void."

"But she's a Goddess—the Goddess of All Realms." There was more question than statement in her words.

"The gods are not perfect," he confided. "Nor all-powerful. Do not repeat my words to anyone, or we'll both be swinging from the gallows. The Guardians of Iilenshar *and* Morchaint are worshipped as gods, but they were once ordinary faerie. Chaim and Zahra are elven—of the Lindale race.

"The only thing that separates a common man from a god is knowledge. Consider our floating colleague Tulipin. If he floated into a remote village, a primitive tribe would very likely mistake him for a god."

"Yasimina told me that you show a blatant disregard for the younger gods. Is that true?"

"I don't worship them and—" Marsais paused, holding up a finger to emphasize his next point. "And *there* lies the root of confusion."

A fiddler began playing an energetic tune, driving the crowd to dance. The nymph forgot everything for a moment as she watched their complicated jigs, listened to their laughter, and basked in their joy until a voice inserted itself into her reverie.

"Am I boring you?" The voice brought her back to the present. She returned her attention to familiar grey eyes that were patiently inquiring.

"You never bore me," she said. "But so much happiness should not be wasted."

"I do agree." Marsais smiled. "Shall we continue another day?"

"No, please go on. It was a small diversion and nothing more."

"Diversions make life palatable. Now then, where was I?" Marsais mused, as he stole a bite from her honey roll. "Ah, yes... Evil spread, distrust and suspicion were rampant, and lines were drawn between races. The situation was ripe for chaos, which fell from the vine when the Orb shattered. I can assure you, candy did not shoot out of the Orb when it broke.

"Powerful forces with no direction, no conduit for control, were unleashed. Even the Gift, when it's used in error, will cause an ill occurrence. But the effects of the shattered Orb were not limited to a few feet. A shock wave of raw power swept through the realm and beyond. Fyrsta was devastated. Civilization as we knew it was brought to its knees, and afterwards... it was ground into dust.

"Dagenir and Zahra absorbed most of the Orb's power, but their bodies couldn't contain it. They had to pass the power on to the few Guardians who still lived, or be destroyed along with everyone else.

"Sides were drawn. And Dagenir and Zahra continued to fight at a time when mankind should have been licking its wounds. War blazed and life was reduced to surviving at any cost. It was a time of horror— death was a mercy.

"Just when life was on the verge of annihilation, the Keeper returned and erected the Gates with the last of his power, trapping

Dagenir and the Guardians of Morchaint in the area we now know as the Bastardlands. Civilization began to rebuild, but instead of a civilization built by the hands of faerie, it was one built by humans, gnomes, and dwarves.

"Kambe and Kiln rose from the ashes. Kings perched on thrones once again, and that was when nymphs reappeared. Out of all men, the druids fared best because they were already in hiding, having been hunted for the sins of their kin. They were at home in the wilds, but as civilization spread, the druids were rediscovered.

"The so-called wise, this Order included, remembered the druids' involvement with Ramashan. They saw the druids as a threat. And even though most of the druids who had sided with Ramashan had already been killed or Blighted, kingdoms began hunting them.

"The witch hunt served a purpose. You see, after the Shattering, women were in short supply, so the druids were hunted down like animals, and their nymphs taken. But here comes an unforeseen problem—a man is possessive enough when it comes to a human woman. Nymphs are quite another matter. The hunters began fighting each other. Entire tribes, clans, armies, and kin slaughtered each other over possession of a single nymph.

"The newly formed Blessed Order recognized the danger that nymphs presented to civilizations. So, with Iilenshar's support, they seized every nymph they could find, intending to protect them from harm. But nymphs were never meant to bond with human males."

"They weren't?"

Marsais shook his head. "They're faerie—their blood is ancient. Humans born after the Shattering are too young for faerie. From what I've observed, faerie have an intoxicating effect on humans, especially nymphs. It has something to do with a nymph's scent—it's like a potent drug. And humans, even when sober, aren't known for their self-control."

"I'm not either," she muttered. "So it is true? Men *can't* control themselves around a nymph."

"They *could* if they wanted to. But it's convenient to use that excuse —like a brute who beats his Oathbound claiming she's displeased him. It takes away accountability and shifts false blame to the woman. I suspect that nymphs reveal the true nature of a person, stripping away the lies and masks that humans cloak themselves in."

"I think the ancient faerie had a point—humans *aren't* trustworthy. Except you, of course."

There was a question in her words: Are *you* human? Marsais could pass for a Kamberian, but there was something more to him—an elegant beauty of sharp angles and a gracefulness that made everyone else seem clumsy.

He answered with a secretive smile.

"You said the paladins wanted to protect nymphs. What happened?"

"They *began* with noble intentions, but it didn't take long before the paladins started taking the nymphs for themselves by force."

There was a raw edge to his voice.

"The Blessed Order strictly forbids rape—it's a death sentence. They couldn't ignore their own laws; that would have weakened the very foundation of the Order. So Damien Caal, one of the first paladins to dedicate his sword to Zahra, declared them property. Nymphs became creatures without rights. The declaration was readily accepted, especially when the wars over nymphs stopped. A single man, under the Blessed Order's Law, could challenge a nymph's current owner to a duel to the death for possession. Only the most formidable men could hope to possess a nymph.

"Now we come to my answer to your question of why people hide the past. In this case, it has to do with what the Guardians have become. Even the Guardians of Morchaint, though considered evil in these lands, are thought of as gods."

"But you said the Guardians are faerie—Yvesa, the Guardian of Peace, is a sprite. Why would they allow faerie to be mistreated?"

"A ruler has little control over his subjects," Marsais explained. "Take the temples dedicated to the Guardian of Love. Asmara is known as the Ever-child, because she hasn't aged a day in mind or form since the Shattering. She's a five-year-old little girl. But her temples are nothing more than exceptionally exquisite pleasure houses. The virgin priestesses who offer themselves for temple service don't remain virgins for long."

"Really?" This surprised her. It was said that boundless blessings were bestowed on a family if their daughter was chosen for temple service. She wondered if daughters knew what their service entailed.

"Yes, and I can assure you that Asmara has nothing to do with her temples, nor does she have any influence over her devotees, because where there is a desire in the masses... you can't stop it, especially when it involves their gods.

"To openly admit that nymphs are the Sylph's favored daughters would call into question the foundations of the Blessed Order and the very nature of the Guardians. The Order serves its purpose as peace-keepers, corruption notwithstanding, and above all, its devotees bring order to chaos, stamping out Voidspawn and fiends wherever they appear. From the majority's point of view, the Order fights for justice. You just happen to see it from a different, more personal perspective."

"That's why it's convenient," she whispered, turning to watch the twirling dancers. Despite the festivities, she felt very much alone.

"Unfortunately," Marsais sighed. "Most nymphs aren't as outspoken as you—to be more precise, I have never met another nymph like you. For the vast majority, it's convenient to overlook the rights of an inno-cent creature who knows no better, in the name of peace."

"I still don't understand. How can they claim to serve the Sylph?"

"Because they're a bunch of thick-headed idiots."

Isiilde laughed at his perfect imitation of her guardian.

His eyes danced. "Come, my dear, let us be diverted."

EAGER TO FIND the Xaionian troupe, she dragged Marsais through the dancers, continuing their exploration until she was distracted by a fiddler. He played a jig for a monkey in a red vest.

"If I could be any animal, I'd choose to be a monkey. What about you?"

"Hmm, what do you think I'd like to be?"

"A goose."

"Is my singing that bad?"

"I read they fly the farthest every year. If you were a goose, then you wouldn't get restless," she pointed out.

"I doubt I could ever settle on just one animal. I'd have to try them all before choosing."

"Even a vulture?" She wrinkled her nose.

"Vultures are not hunted—not so bad, that. It'd be a fairly safe form to assume." He stroked his goatee. "On second thought, if I were a vulture, I'd have to compete with Thira."

Isiilde's laughter danced with the fiddler's jig. The air was charged with her joy. Smiles brightened and cares fell away, forgotten in the dreamy haze of her voice.

But the nymph was oblivious to her persuasion. As she moved out of earshot, a ripple followed. People shook themselves, waking from a dream. And with a pang of sorrow, they found the world a darker place.

"Do you want to go to the tourney?" she asked.

Oenghus usually dragged her to every tournament on the Isle. Tournament rules called for first blood. But duels to the death were not uncommon.

"I've seen more than enough men knocking their heads together in my lifetime."

"They make me sick to watch," she admitted.

"I know. You're a nymph. Violence goes against your very nature."

When Marsais spoke about nymphs, she never felt inferior.

"Can I change my nature? You said the faerie did—the Fey."

She felt Marsais go tense under her arm. But he kept his voice light. "An interesting question. Do you want to?"

Isiilde fell silent with thought as they strolled through the festival. "I don't know," she finally admitted.

"Then I doubt you will."

Her ears straightened when she saw a familiar face in a canopied pavilion. It was a shop that sold weapons and armor forged by master crafters of the Order. But Sir Helwick, a famed swordsmith, wasn't the one who had caught her eye; it was a young, bronzed man with broad shoulders who held her attention.

The moment they stepped under the awning, Sir Helwick recognized Marsais and hurried over to greet him.

"It's an honor, Archlord," Helwick said, clasping Marsais' hand with a brief bow of his head. He was a short, bald man with the physique of a keg and a strut of a bulldog, whose handshake made Marsais grimace in pain. "I didn't know you were back."

"I returned yesterday."

Whatever else they might have said was lost to the nymph's ears. She wandered off towards a certain young man with black hair, soft eyes, and a sincere smile. He sensed the nymph's approach, and his conversation with a customer stuttered to a halt.

Isiilde poked at a visored helm. The young man quickly excused himself from his customer to join her, bowing deeply.

"Hello, Coyle," she greeted with a smile and a curtsy. "I almost didn't recognize you with your shirt on."

Whenever Oenghus worked in the forges, he took her along. The forge was the only place in the castle where she could breathe life into her flame. For the apprentices, her presence meant a break from the bellows. She was popular at the forge.

"It's been near a month, m'lady. We've all missed you—well, I've missed you especially," Coyle corrected, rubbing his neck. The movement caused the muscles of his arms and shoulders to flex, rippling beneath a cotton shirt that strained to fit across his chiseled chest.

"Oen and I haven't been to the castle much of late."

"Yes, I heard about that. Truth be told, I wish you'd killed the little mutt. You should've heard the cheer that went up in the forges when we heard what happened."

"Really?"

"There's not a soldier or servant who doesn't despise that runt of a dog. I think he's bitten just about everyone in the castle." Coyle suddenly glanced around the pavilion with concern. "You're not here by yourself, are you?"

"Of course not. Marsais is with me."

"The Archlord?" Coyle stammered, running a hand through his hair in an attempt to smooth the unruly mass.

"Didn't you know he was my master?"

"Of course, but I didn't know he attended festivals."

The odd ideas people had about Marsais never ceased to puzzle her.

"Have you seen the performers from Xiao?" she asked.

"I'm not free until sunset, and they're charging a crown just to get into that part of the festival."

"An entire gold crown?"

"It's mostly for the wealthy, not for the likes of me. One day I'll have coin to spare, but not anytime soon," Coyle said, with a proud tilt of his square chin. This reminded him of his current duties. He glanced towards the patron he'd abandoned, looking suddenly embarrassed. "Speaking of which, I better get back to work. You don't think—that is, would you like to have lunch with me sometime, m'lady? When you visit the forge again."

"I'd like that."

"You would?"

"Why wouldn't I?"

"You're just so... and I'm just an apprentice," Coyle stammered, awkwardly.

"So am I." She smiled, then turned serious. "But only if you agree to stop calling me m'lady."

"As you wish, Isiilde," he said with a broad smile.

Coyle looked as though he might float off the ground at any moment, but he did something else even more surprising. Before she could react, he seized her hand, bowed over it, and pressed his lips against her skin.

When Coyle straightened, he found the Archlord of the Isle standing at the nymph's side. His eyes were like steel. And Coyle felt exposed under that piercing gaze.

"Archlord," Coyle gulped. He hastily let go of her hand, and bowed like a peasant before his king.

"Marsais, this is Coyle. He's a friend of mine, a talented swordsmith apprenticed to Sir Helwick."

Coyle straightened, but he had turned an ashen color and seemed nervous. Isiilde never understood why people seemed uncomfortable around Marsais.

"That's high praise. Helwick's not the most lenient of masters."

"I do my best, Archlord. It's a true honor to meet you, sir."

Marsais inclined his head politely.

"I best be getting back to work, sir." Coyle offered a hasty bow to them both.

"Don't forget about our lunch," Isiilde reminded him as he turned to leave.

"How could I, m'lady?"

Isiilde smiled, and Coyle stumbled over his own feet, nearly toppling a rack of weapons. She slipped her hand through Marsais' offered arm, and the two continued on their way, but she stole a peek back at Coyle.

"Did you leave something?" Marsais asked, following her gaze.

"No," she admitted, studying the chiseled apprentice from behind. "Coyle is nice to look at, though."

"I'll have to take your word on that."

"You don't think he's handsome?"

"It's not something I generally notice," he confided.

"Oh."

They continued walking as she chewed on her lip. Marsais watched her out of the corner of his eye, wondering what in all the realms she was going to ask next. A distraction rescued him from further questions.

Fluttering sails of crimson and gold had caught her eye—a silk wall of color encircled the Xaionian pavilions. Snaking dragons curled on the billowing cloth, frozen in battle against other fearsome creatures of legend.

Isiilde stopped to gawk at a glittering phoenix emblazoned on one panel. Its wings glowed with fire rippling in the breeze. "I take my choice back. I'd rather be a phoenix."

"I didn't know we could pick any creature," he mused. "In that case, I'll be an Assumer."

"I've never heard of them. What are they?"

"They're chameleons, shape-shifters, who assume any shape they desire. Since they can mimic any creature or person, you may have met one and simply not realized it."

"You could already be one, and I wouldn't know it." She studied him with suspicion.

"A possibility," he admitted. "But you'll never know."

"I'm sure there's a way to tell," she mused, as they strolled along the silk wall towards the entrance.

Two acrobats silently detached themselves from the flowing artistry. Isiilde tensed with surprise, but Marsais seemed untroubled by their presence as they tumbled over to block the entrance.

One was a man and the other a woman. Both wore sweeping masks of pristine feathers and outfits of gauzy fabric. Their garments were scant, revealing naked flesh covered with tattoos. The pair were living canvases.

The man's taut stomach was decorated with a fiendish mouth full of fangs. It looked real.

The explosion of shapes and images covering skin made her queasy, and she tore her gaze from the tattoos.

The male acrobat held up his hands in front of her—they were empty. Quick as a viper, he plucked a gold crown from her ear. The gold coin disappeared with a flourish and he bowed, sweeping his arm towards the entrance to indicate that she could enter without charge.

The costumed woman held out her hand to Marsais, palm up, silently demanding payment. He gave her a crown and the two acrobats back flipped to land beside the silken tapestries, drawing them aside and granting passage.

On the other side, another realm greeted them, an exotic place where the fantastical thrived, ripped from renderings of Somnial's Court and brought to life. Scantily clad acrobats, wearing bizarre costumes that merged beast and man, mingled and performed in the crowds.

Performers wearing hooked masks strolled through the masses on stilts, like grim birds of ill omen looking for their next meal. Gnomish acrobats used them as traveling props, clambering up and down the looming birds of prey, leaping over one head to land on the shoulders of the next.

Everyone wore masks, even the visitors. Faces were obscured by fanciful creations of feathers and twisted visages of horror. It was a feast of bizarre beauty.

Her head spun.

She stopped in front of a silver statue, marveling over the lifelike rendering of a man poised for battle: muscles straining, arm raised to strike, body caught in disrupted motion.

The statue's lips curled, revealing white teeth, and she nearly fell backwards in shock. He reached behind his shield with small, jerking movements, pausing between each new pose. Slowly, his hand emerged, revealing a butterfly mask.

When the performer tried to place the mask on her head, Marsais grabbed his wrist in a vise-like grip.

"She won't be needing that."

The silver man's eyes flashed. He dropped his act, and with a whirl of motion, sprang backwards, disappearing into the crowd.

"Why was he going to give me a mask?"

"Wearing a mask here means you've left all restraint behind. You hadn't wondered why they let you in for free?"

"Well, no, not really," she admitted.

"Beauty and innocence are never turned away from a Xaionian festival."

"But why?"

"You haven't noticed?" Noting her confusion, he gestured towards the crowd with a sweep of his hand. She turned her attention to the masked attendees. "The inordinate amount of indiscreet activities."

It took a while for his words to sink in, and when they did, she studied her surroundings with new eyes. How had she missed it before? People *were* carefree and ribald.

"There's a lot to look at," she defended, feeling her cheeks heat, and then quickly cast about for something suitably distracting. "Like those."

Isiilde pointed up at the glowing orbs floating overhead like giant, translucent bubbles with fireflies dancing inside. "They must be beautiful at night."

"We'll be leaving before nightfall."

"Must we?"

"Xaio is a land of pleasures. Festivities become even less restrained at nightfall."

They stopped to let a gnome, who was riding a tiger, pass. Impulsively, she reached out to pet the massive feline. It growled with a swipe of claws, but found only air as Marsais yanked her back with blinding speed. The tiger looked as surprised as she.

Gnome and tiger took one look at Marsais, and quickly trotted away.

"As long as you have the coin for it, anything goes in Xaio," Marsais continued as if nothing had occurred. "And if you don't have the coin, then you have little choice in the matter." She could tell by his tone that he cared little for the culture and questioned him further on it. "I've never condoned the slavery of anything—be it man or beast."

"They keep slaves?"

"Most kingdoms do. But Xaio takes slavery to an excess, as they do everything else, which reminds me of something that I'm sure you'll like..." Marsais searched over a sea of heads until he spotted what he desired—a wonderland of edible delights.

CHAPTER 7

Dusk came swiftly. And in the last hour, Isiilde finally came across something that gave her pause. She froze, her teeth poised to sink into a caramel-coated apple, transfixed by the vacant area before her. Looking around at the evenly spaced pavilions, she found the irregular void an odd sight.

Marsais selected a chocolate from her basket. "Fascinating... an empty spot."

Isiilde realized she was drooling and quickly finished her bite. "It doesn't seem right."

"And why is that?"

"It doesn't *feel* empty." The words sounded foolish to her own ears. But everyone was avoiding the space.

"Have more confidence in your instincts."

His deft fingers flashed with movement before he swept a hand over her eyes. The weave tickled her skin, and she laughed in response, but her delight ended a moment later when a drab, grey pavilion shimmered into existence.

"You've found what I was looking for." Marsais popped a piece of chocolate into his mouth, which was followed by an appreciative grunt. "The Xaionian lifestyle does have its advantages."

"Marsais?"

"Hmm."

"Why would a shop be hidden?"

"Why do you think?"

They started walking towards the entrance, but she felt a strange desire to avoid the tent. The area was warded, she realized.

Isiilde pondered his question for a moment. "So ordinary people won't find it. They only want those with an arcane sight to enter, such as Wise Ones."

"Precisely."

"I should've known you'd want to go to the most interesting shop."

"I find every shop interesting when you're exploring it. I thought that poor clothing merchant was going to have a heart attack when you insisted on trying on half the garments in his shop."

"If he didn't charge such outrageous prices, I would have liked that green cloak," she admitted.

The tent was far larger on the inside than out. An entire bazaar sprawled inside, where anything and everything that might interest a Wise One could be found. Instead of having the temporary feel of a cloth pavilion, it felt solid.

Guards posted at the entryway ordered everyone to remove their masks as they entered. She took a cue from Marsais and pulled her cowl down, concealing her features.

Many people from the tower would recognize the Archlord, vagabond or no, and she doubted he wanted to deal with his fellow Wise Ones just yet. She certainly didn't want to be recognized. It'd been over a week since her incident with Crumpet and she hadn't been back to the castle since, nor had Oenghus, for that matter. It was highly unlikely that everyone would be as understanding as Coyle.

Translucent orbs full of fireflies drifted in the air, but their brilliance was magnified in the darkness of the tent, casting an ominous glow over the bazaar. And while the festival outside had had a blithe atmosphere, in here things were intense, with an undercurrent of powerful forces seething below the surface of her awareness.

When she asked Marsais about the change, he bent to whisper in her ear as he explained that Xaio was not restricted by the Blessed

Order's laws. There were few boundaries to their practices, which was part of the reason that the tent was obscured. They didn't want the paladins sniffing around their wares.

The unknown put her on edge, and she stuck close to Marsais as they strolled through the shadowed tent. She could feel the tension in his body—he was brimming with awareness. He didn't like this place either. But he seemed to be looking for something, or someone.

Isiilde was studying a jar of dragon egg fragments at an apothecary when she heard Zianna's voice. She cringed. How could she have missed the curvaceous apprentice who was stuffed into a satin dress of periwinkle blue? The edges of her bodice were trimmed with intricate lace, which put her bosom on full display.

Zianna's master, Taal Greysparrow, wore a matching waistcoat and breeches that were snuggly tailored to his chiseled form. When it came to choosing an apprentice, Taal had a penchant for beauty over skill. Every apprentice he'd trained in the last two hundred years ended up sharing his bed—not that the women seemed to mind.

Isiilde muttered an oath under her breath and stood on her toes, searching for Marsais in the busy shop. She spotted his tattered grey cloak in the crowd, where he was conversing with an ill-mannered shopkeeper. She started towards him, but someone chose that inopportune time to open a jar of grave ash. A fit of sneezing overtook her, accompanied by three bursts of flame puffing from her ears.

"Isiilde," Zianna said, loudly. "Why, if it isn't everyone's favorite *nymph*." Every pair of eyes locked on the redhead. "We've all missed you this past week." Zianna detached herself from Taal's arm, leaning in to kiss the air over Isiilde's cheeks.

"You have?" she asked, wanting more than anything to believe the woman.

"Of course. Lectures are so dull when you're not around. It's been quiet without you—almost peaceful."

Most of the onlookers had moved on, but a few eyes lingered on the faerie.

"You're looking lovely today, Isiilde," Taal said, greeting her with a bow, which she returned with a bobbing curtsy.

"What was that assistant telling us about faeries?" Zianna inquired, ever so sweetly.

Taal seemed hesitant to answer, so his apprentice answered for him. "See that jar of Wisp wings over there? It fetches a small fortune. Anything from a faerie is particularly potent in a potion. Your race is highly sought after as a resource for potion ingredients. I wonder what an entire nymph would fetch?"

Zianna wrapped an arm around Isiilde's shoulders, and turned her towards the counter, catching the assistant's eye. "Tell me, what potions are being made out of nymphs?"

Isiilde jerked away from the woman.

"A single strand of hair makes a powerful love potion." The tattooed Xaionian fixed a hungry gaze on the nymph, studying her exposed features with the same fascination that people reserved for oddities at a performance.

"Really, a love potion? How quaint," Zianna purred.

"There's nothing trivial about it, m'lady. A single strand of her hair would fetch ten crown and if she be a virgin, then a hundred."

Isiilde paled at his words.

"Of course you're a virgin. Aren't you, dear? Or Oenghus' head would be on a pike." Zianna laughed at her own observation. "You could start selling yourself a piece at a time, Isiilde. I think that's splendid news, don't you, Taal?"

Isiilde swallowed down a lump in her throat. Taal frowned, and then his eyes widened when a vagabond stepped beside Isiilde. It took a long moment for Zianna to recognize him.

Isiilde wiped away a tear that had escaped.

"Please don't let me interrupt your conversation."

"I wouldn't dream of wasting your time with trivial matters, Archlord." Zianna offered Marsais a hand and a curtsy. The angle put her attributes fully on display for his perusal.

Marsais stared at her hand as if it were Blighted. Without missing a beat, she straightened and offered a charming smile.

"I wasn't aware you were back, Archlord. You look like you just got off the boat," Taal said, diffusing the awkward moment.

"Oh, I got off ages ago," Marsais muttered.

Zianna ignored his vague remark. "Did you have a pleasant trip?"

As much as the woman made her life unpleasant, Isiilde was ever in awe of the way she carried herself. The suggestive eyes and coy smile that she directed at Marsais were impressive. As was the subtle way she put her attributes in full view, so that any man bending to kiss her hand would be hard-pressed to miss her plunging neckline.

"Not until I arrived on a small beach yesterday," Marsais said, slipping Isiilde's arm through his. "Would you excuse us?"

Taal gave a slight bow. As Marsais turned to leave, a man screamed. Startled, Isiilde turned to find the assistant curled at her feet. He clutched his hand in agony—a hand as black and cracked as a charred log.

Marsais glanced down at the man. "Stealing is illegal, sir."

"What'd you do!" the man screeched.

"Did I do something?" Marsais glanced around in surprise.

A ring of customers formed around the scene, calls of alarm rippled through the tent, and the guards soon appeared, pushing through the crowd.

"I only wanted a strand!"

Isiilde scuttled behind Marsais, all too aware of the audience and their stares.

"You admit to attempted theft?" Marsais asked.

"She's only a nymph," the assistant snarled.

"Did you do this?" A guard, encased in armor modeled after a scorpion, stepped forward. The guard only came to Marsais' chin, and he tried to make up the difference with a threatening posture.

"I was conversing with this couple. My back was to the fellow. Had I done something, it would have been quite a feat, wouldn't you agree? Perhaps it was divine intervention."

The guard turned to Taal for confirmation.

"It's true. When it happened, he was conversing with my apprentice," Taal said with an uneasy glance at Marsais.

"This could become rather troublesome," Marsais said. "Where nymphs are involved, paladins must be too. I'm sure they'd love an excuse to search this pavilion."

This reasoning, along with the assistant's confession, quickly settled the issue.

"Move along then," the guard ordered. "All of you get moving. There's nothing more to see."

"This thief might benefit from serving a month of penance at a temple dedicated to Chaim. It may help his ailment." And with that, Marsais led her away.

"Oh, come now," he sighed. "If you cry, I'll be forced to sing."

Isiilde laughed through her fear. "It's too late for that," she said, dabbing at tears with his offered handkerchief.

True to his word, he cleared his throat and launched into his favorite ballad about the Mule King. But Marsais couldn't hold a tune to save his life. Patrons glared at the madman and he paid them no mind.

Eventually, her tears turned to laughter. "For the love of all that is good, Marsais, please stop now," she begged.

His eyes slid over to her, and the edge of his mouth quirked. Much to her relief, he stopped singing.

Isiilde glanced over her shoulder. "What did you do to that man?" she whispered in his ear.

"It was just a trick. An illusion that will wear off in a month, whether or not he does penance at a temple."

"But he was in pain... wasn't he?"

Marsais tapped his head in answer. "Pain often lives in the mind as much as in the body—sometimes more."

"Not for a nymph. My toe still hurts."

"Ah, but—" He held up a finger. "Did you feel the sting in your toe when my singing held you so captivated?"

"I was being distracted by a more acute pain in my ears."

"Listening to Zianna *is* rather tiresome," he replied, eyes twinkling along with her laughter. "Come, my dear, there's someone I'd like you to meet. I assure you he won't be so rude—well, not intentionally."

MARSAIS LED her through the crowd until they came to a garbage heap. Why there was a pile of junk inside a bazaar, she did not know. A soused dwarf was rummaging through the pile like a deranged badger.

"Did you lose something again, old friend?"

The dwarf spun around, clutching his heart. "Blast it!" He searched through his pockets in a panic until he pulled out a pair of spectacles. "Well, bust me britches! If it isn't my favorite crazed seer—this calls for a drink."

"A lady is present," Marsais pointed out.

The dwarf squinted at the nymph, then lifted his spectacles to get a better look.

"Allow me to present Witman, the self-proclaimed Wondrous."

Isiilde blinked when she heard the name. She wouldn't have believed it if Marsais hadn't said so. Witman the Wondrous was *the* legendary enchanter, known throughout Fyrsta and beyond.

Witman smoothed the sparse strands of hair that remained on his head.

"Witman, may I introduce Isiilde Jaal'Yasine, an extraordinarily gifted apprentice."

Isiilde curtsied in greeting.

Witman looked from her to Marsais, his mouth hanging slightly ajar in shock. "A nymph Wise One?"

Marsais nodded in reply, and Witman shook himself like a wet animal. "Oh, my—I need a drink, lady or no." He turned towards his junk pile, attacking it with renewed ferocity.

"Maybe it's in your pocket?" She pointed at a squarish outline on his bright green waistcoat, which was covered with little yellow flowers and dubious stains.

Witman patted at his pockets. Finally, he tugged a battered flask free with a triumphant cry. "You're a sharp one. Course you'd have to be with that madcap," he said, before taking a long swig from the flask. "Oh, how rude, how rude." He straightened his waistcoat and motioned them forward. "Come into my shop, please, come in. I don't want them staring."

He led them behind a little wall of junk, and once inside, he sat down on a barrel. Isiilde bit her tongue as she sat on a nearby crate. It would be rude to laugh at his shop.

"I'm surprised you aren't in Iilenshar," Marsais said, settling himself on a pile of sacks before stretching out his long legs.

"Bah! I'm not their personal enchanter. The Guardians can kiss my arse." Witman spat, shifted uncomfortably, and glanced towards the shadows. "You think they heard that?"

"Hmm, always possible, I suppose."

"I was joking," Witman sputtered, taking another swig to clear his head.

"Is that who's watching you?" Isiilde asked.

"No, lass, it's those vile sneaky little gnomes and those wretched paladins, and..." he licked his lips and leaned closer with the air of a conspirator, "... *Others.*"

"Others is a fairly broad term," she pointed out.

"Exactly!" The dwarf bounded to his feet, knocking over a barrel of fish heads in his excitement.

Marsais suddenly found an earth-shattering portent to study in the slimy pile.

"See, he knows," Witman said, stabbing a finger at the seer. "*They* trick him all the time, picking at his brain like leeches!"

Isiilde wrinkled her nose. "I don't like leeches."

"Smart girl." Witman gave a nod of approval. "But don't fret. I'm working on something that will keep *them* at bay."

"What is it?"

"Shh, not too loud," he said, his bloodshot eyes darting from one corner to the next.

Marsais snapped out of his momentary lapse, and glanced around with confusion. "Why are we whispering?" he whispered.

"The leeches," she answered.

"Blast!" Marsais surged to his feet, batting at his clothes. "I hate leeches."

"Smart lad," Witman grunted.

After Marsais checked under his shirt, he looked sharply at Witman. "What in the Nine Halls are you drinking?"

"*Nothing.*" The dwarf clutched his flask to his chest.

"Hmm."

"Nothing the Archlord of a law-abiding Isle needs to know about." Witman quickly gulped down the liquid until his flask was dry.

"Ah, well, should I come back then?"

"Do I owe you coin?" Witman demanded.

"No."

"Did you commission me for an item?"

"No, I came to show you something."

"Save it for the ladies." Witman chortled, drooling on his grey beard.

"Save what?" Isiilde asked, but no one offered her an answer.

"Could we step into your workshop?"

"Keep it down, you bag of bones. If you're going to go blabberin' all my secrets, I'm thinking I might just deny you the honor." Witman crossed his arms.

"That would be unfortunate, as the matter is rather important."

"Can't be all that."

Marsais looked down at the stubborn enchanter. After a brief internal debate, he reached into his belt pouch and withdrew three smooth discs. The discs were pearlescent, perfectly round, and utterly flat.

Witman narrowed his eyes. Then they widened. "By the Keeper's moon," he breathed.

"What are they?" Isiilde asked.

"Mere trinkets from the Bastardlands," Marsais murmured, folding his fingers around the discs before she could investigate.

Whether the trinkets were simply payment or a matter of great import, Isiilde did not know, but they sparked a flurry of activity. Witman riffled through his pockets, muttering under his breath as he searched for only the gods knew what. Apparently Marsais knew what, because he began sifting through the dwarf's pile of junk.

Isiilde watched the two absentminded men. "Do you misplace your workshop often, sir?"

"No, come to think of it, I don't," Witman said, smoothing two remaining strands of hair on the top of his head. "*They* must've took it. Blast them all to the Pits, they took it!"

"They did *not* take it," Marsais replied with patient exasperation.

"Take what?"

"A piece of chalk." His reply did little to clarify things.

"Shh!" For a moment, she feared Witman would charge Marsais.

"You mean this chalk?" It lay in the dirt by her foot, and she picked it up, showing it to the enraged enchanter.

"Aha!" Witman did not charge Marsais; he charged her.

Faced with a barreling dwarf, she abandoned the chalk, throwing herself off the crate. Witman crashed into the crate, bounced away, and dove for the piece of chalk.

"That's it—I need an apprentice. Can I have yours, laddie?"

"You most certainly cannot," Marsais said. He ran his eyes over her, searching for injury, but didn't offer a hand to help her up.

Come to think of it, she could not recall a single instance, in the thirteen years she'd known him, when he had so much as brushed her skin. The thought startled her.

Maybe nymphs had some kind of infectious disease, she thought glumly.

"I'm rather partial to this one." He returned her look of confusion with a twitch of his lips.

"Oh." Witman abandoned his bright idea as fast as it had come. "I doubt another would do."

"Very doubtful," Marsais agreed.

The dwarf disappeared behind a curtain, which blocked an unremarkable segment of the pavilion wall.

Marsais stroked his braid as he gazed at the dingy cloth. "I think it wise if you wait out here, my dear. You'll be safe in his shop."

Isiilde looked around his 'shop'. "Are these all illusions?" she asked.

"Would you believe me if I told you the fish heads were actually gems?"

She sniffed at the slimy pile. "Not really."

"Good, because they're not." Marsais gave her a lopsided grin. "Remember, Isiilde, you're faerie. *Always* trust your instincts."

With that, he disappeared behind the curtain. She counted to five, then hurried over to peek behind the tattered thing. Only they were both gone. She poked at the pavilion wall behind the curtain, looked under the tent and out towards the fairgrounds, and finally gave up, seething with frustration.

Isiilde plopped down on a crate to glare at the threadbare barrier. Perhaps some type of rune or spoken word was required to activate an unknown enchantment? She attempted several words, speaking the Lore softly into the clutter. Nothing happened.

Her attention wavered as she looked up at the floating lights overhead.

Isiilde had no way of knowing if Marsais was watching, so she assumed he was, which gave her leave to practice her levitation weave. If she stayed in the middle of the garbage heap, she wouldn't be leaving Witman's shop.

Without further thought, she invoked the Lore, her fingers weaving the runes with quick confidence. A bubble drifted overhead, and she shot upwards.

Isiilde gasped in shock, nearly losing concentration: the source of light wasn't fireflies, or even flames of everlight bouncing inside the orbs; rather, it was tiny, shimmering Wisps. The naked faerie women zipped around like trapped birds, eyes wide and terrified, as they threw themselves against the walls of their glass cages.

Horror erased thought. Gravity yanked her downwards. Frantic, she grabbed for the nearest thing—a floating orb. Nymph and orb fell onto the pile of fish heads. But the orb of Wisps rolled from her hands and cracked open on the edge of a crate.

The Wisps soared into the air with a gleeful flutter of wings, racing to free their captive kin. As quickly as it took her ears to wilt, another glass prison was shattered, and the escaped prisoners fanned out to free the rest.

Shouts of warning rose over the hum of bartering voices as enraged faerie zipped through the bazaar, wreaking havoc on their captors. Stands toppled, precious vials shattered, and caged animals were loosed from confinement.

As the beasts ran rampant, the Wisps turned their attentions to the armored guards, swarming them with homicidal fury. Between the swarm of wings, the beasts, and the panicked crowds, the guards were quickly overcome.

Isiilde wrestled herself free of the slimy pile of fish, gagging with revulsion, and searched for something to clean herself with. It was only after she'd finished wiping her hands on a tattered grey cloak that she realized it was Marsais. He was wearing the cloak.

"Hmm, someone freed the enslaved Wisps. How thoughtful of them."

Something crashed above, wood splintered, and half of the roof caved in. Isiilde cringed at the resulting screams.

"It was an accident," she whispered.

"Of course it was. I doubt you meant to fall onto a pile of rotting fish." Marsais swept some orb fragments into a pile of garbage with a casual foot.

Isiilde climbed to her feet. "Marsais?"

"Hmm."

"Have I mentioned how much I missed you?" she asked.

"Probably not as much as I missed you," he admitted to her ears alone.

"You did?"

His grey eyes shone with warmth. "Very much, my dear. Who else could entertain me so?"

CHAPTER 8

Fog rolled over the land like a slow-moving wave, crashing upon the populace and drowning the sun, tucking darkness firmly into place. It was beneath this chilling cloak of blindness that Isiilde and Marsais returned to the orphanage, seeking warmth and food.

There were over a hundred children in Brinehilde's care. And while the older ones helped with the younger, the orphanage held firmly to the Nuthaanian philosophy of child-rearing: the strongest survived. Brinehilde tried to keep weapons to a minimum, though.

And so Oenghus spent the evening being attacked by a swarm of screaming children attempting to wrestle him to the ground. Isiilde wasn't sure who was enjoying the battle more: her guardian or the children.

As Oenghus struggled with the pint-sized warriors, Marsais escorted Isiilde through his old manor. The building was rife with secret passages and hidden rooms. And as they sifted through his belongings in one forgotten room, she found a little music box. It had a forest of trees carved onto its birch top.

Isiilde opened the box, and a melody leapt into the room. There was a folded piece of parchment inside. Curious, she removed it. A keen-eyed woman with sharp ears looked out from the timeworn sketch.

At the sound of the music, Marsais stilled and closed his eyes.

"It's one of your sketches. Who is she?"

Marsais did not answer. He gently took the parchment from her hand and tucked it back into the box, shutting the lid. With reverent care, he wrapped the box in an old shirt, and placed the bundle in his rucksack.

Isiilde no longer wondered who the woman was.

Later on in the evening, Brinehilde asked Isiilde to calm the children. Her lulling melody drifted through the halls, and the children stumbled off to find their beds.

A blanket of peace settled over the sleeping children. But a rare restlessness kept Isiilde awake. Her stomach ached. She felt strange and unsettled, so she left the warmth of her little room to find Marsais.

Brinehilde was in the kitchens, conversing with one of the older girls as they baked bread. When Isiilde mentioned her ailment, the priestess sent her off with a mug of warm milk.

Isiilde couldn't find Marsais, but she found Oenghus sitting beneath an oak tree on the bank of a pond. The heady scent of tobacco filled the air. Oenghus leaned against the tree, sucking lazily on the long stem of his pipe.

Fog clung to the ground. Its chill knocked her teeth together. She hurried over to her guardian and snuggled beside him for warmth. He draped an arm over her shoulders, tucking her in close.

She watched the fog curl over the pond for a time, then glanced up at Oenghus. His eyes were dim with sadness.

"Are you all right, Oen?" she asked.

"I'm fine, Sprite. I was just thinking," he said lightly, but it was forced. "How 'bout you?"

"Cold," she sighed, sipping her milk. "And my stomach hurts."

"Teach you to eat a basket of chocolates."

"Marsais ate just as many. Do you know where he is?"

"He went back to the tower."

"In the dark?"

"He likes to walk."

"Will he be all right?" The thought of him traveling alone at night sent her heart racing.

Oenghus chuckled, low and rumbling as a bear. "Don't worry about the Scarecrow. He can manage just fine by himself."

"I'm not so sure about that," she murmured, prodding a stick on the ground with her boot.

"He has a lot on his mind."

"Like you?" she asked.

"Aye."

"The sick girl... is she going to be all right?"

Three glowing Wisps appeared, fluttering through the dense fog, dancing lightly over the pond. Thanks to Isiilde, the tiny winged faerie were all over the Isle.

"I think she will be... with time." He took a long drag from his pipe before letting a line of smoke drift from his lips.

A Wisp darted over to Isiilde, hovering in front of her face. The tiny woman leaned forward, kissing her on the tip of her freckled nose. The whispering touch tingled her toes. The Wisp zipped to the side, landing on Oenghus' shoulder to flutter happily in his ear.

Isiilde sat up to study the tiny woman. "I think she likes you—they all do," she noted as the other two zipped over to play in his hair.

"It's 'cause I'm warm." One wisp sprinkled glittering dust over the bowl of his pipe. The embers died, leaving him grumbling.

"Did you have a good day with Brinehilde and Galvier?"

"Aye."

"I like her, Oen. You should ask her to take an Oath with you."

"I'd never ask her to leave here, because she wouldn't. And I'm too stubborn to stay in one spot," he admitted. "But it's nice to have a kinswoman around to polish off a jug."

He'd polished off plenty of jugs with Morigan. But then they'd taken Oaths together. An Oath tied a couple together for an agreed amount of time. Twenty years was common, while binding each other for life was rare.

But from what Isiilde had gathered, Nuthaanians were odd—the women took multiple Oathbounds at the same time. Often swapping their men for a night, or inviting others to join.

Kamberians thought they were heathens. Isiilde did not know what to think.

"Do you miss your home in Nuthaan?" she asked. As long as Oenghus remained her guardian, he was as trapped on the Isle as she.

"I'll get back there, eventually."

A wisp disappeared down his shirt front, and he squirmed, chuckling despite himself. With more care than most would credit a berserker, he loosened his laces and gently plucked the scowling Wisp out before letting her go.

"I wouldn't mind seeing my brood, though. You haven't seen a clan gathering 'til you've seen the Saevaldrs together."

"I'd love to meet them all," she said with feeling. But her excitement died when she realized it was never going to happen. Nymphs weren't allowed to travel where they pleased. She'd barely gotten into the festival.

Oenghus sniffed and hugged her closer.

"Tell me about my mother," she whispered against his chest.

"You look just like her, Sprite. Her eyes were like emeralds and her hair was brilliant as fire." Isiilde had heard these words a hundred times, and she could hear them a hundred more. "I've never seen anyone more beautiful. Your mother could make a man weep just by looking at her. Although she was a bit taller than you, and she wasn't near as mischievous—not a whipcord lookin' for trouble like you." He smiled, ruffling her hair.

"Did she look more like Zianna?"

"That ungainly thing has nothing on your mother. Everything about her was perfect. She was gentle and kind, and spent most of her time in the gardens."

"The one I burned down," she said in dismay.

"Things grow back. She would've understood."

A sudden thought occurred to Isiilde. The nymphs she'd read about were all forced to bond with the men who took them, but the bards sang of the emperor's love for her mother, and hers for him.

"Was my mother happy with the emperor—my father? Did she love him?" Isiilde had never asked this question before, and the brooding silence that answered twisted her insides.

"I must know the truth, Oen. Please."

"No," he said, harshly. "Your mother wasn't happy with him—not at all. She didn't love him, nor did he love her. He took her because of his own selfish desire."

Isiilde scrubbed tears from her cheeks. It had been a dim hope—a naïve dream—amidst the cruelty against her kind. The thought that one nymph had found love meant that perhaps, one day, she would too.

"Did you love her?" she asked, searching his face.

His sapphire eyes glistened with unshed tears in the dark. "With all my heart. I still do—I always will."

"Then she was happy because you were her friend," Isiilde said, laying her head back on his chest.

Oenghus said nothing more; he did not trust himself to speak.

"I wish you were my father," she whispered.

The silence deepened, the great heart beating beneath her ear quickened, and a shudder swept through his body. When he bent to kiss her forehead, cold tears dripped onto her skin.

CHAPTER 9

Oenghus and Isiilde left for home the next day. Her stomach was still unsettled, and she swore off chocolates for the rest of her life.

Despite the poor roads, they made good time with their empty wagon. Although the dreary landscape went by at a swifter pace, the journey seemed much longer, because she half expected to find Marsais lying unconscious in a ditch, or worse, dead. Bandits were always a threat.

To distract herself from worry, she told Oenghus about her day at the festival. But she was utterly unprepared for her guardian's reaction.

"You will not have lunch with that swine." Oenghus bit the words out with barely restrained fury.

"Coyle's not a swine—he's a man," she pointed out.

"Exactly!"

"I thought you liked Coyle?"

"Aye, until I find out he had the gall to ask you for lunch."

"And what's the matter with that?" Isiilde demanded, leaning to the side, distancing herself from him on the cramped wagon seat. "Why can't I have friends?"

"It's not friendship that's on his mind. Trust me," he grumbled, tugging on his beard in irritation.

"How do you know?"

"Because I'm a bloody man. I forbid you from seeing him."

Her chin tilted proudly. "I will see him if I like."

"You will not, Isiilde Jaal'Yasine. I'm your guardian, and you'll do as I say." It was never a good sign when he used her full name. "I'm dead well serious. If I catch you near that lad, I'll make him wish he never looked at you. I won't hear another word against it."

Isiilde bristled at his ultimatum. She turned away from Oenghus, staring straight ahead in tight-lipped fury. If he didn't want her talking back, then she wouldn't talk at all.

The silence deepened, with only the creak of the wagon and the ocean breeze to interrupt the chasm between them. They passed three lonely cottages before Oenghus finally took a deep, calming breath.

"Look, Isiilde, you can't go fooling around with the lads. I gave an oath to the emperor to keep your honor intact. If you go fooling around, it's not just my head on a block—you'll be sold first chance. And it might not be to one of the larger kingdoms."

It didn't matter which kingdom bought her. She'd still be sold as a slave.

"I just want to have lunch with him. I don't want to... bed him. Am I not allowed to have friends?"

"Not if they piss standin' up," he replied. "And don't think I haven't noticed you eyeing him up at the forge, so don't talk to me about friendship. I don't catch you staring at the other lads like that."

Isiilde stared at Oenghus in confusion. She looked at Coyle because he was nice to look at; she hadn't thought of anything beyond that. But it was pointless to argue. She'd have better luck arguing with a rock.

"You can't see him again." His final words echoed like the trapdoor of a gallows.

Isiilde bit her lip in frustration. And despite his attempts to coerce her into conversation, she kept her eyes firmly ahead. He finally gave up trying to make amends, and they spent the rest of the journey ignoring each other.

Isiilde struggled to make sense of his anger. She'd tried to make friends with other women, but for some odd reason, flaming sneezes unnerved them. It didn't help that she was the youngest apprentice on the Isle. Even Zianna, for all her pettiness, was double her age.

Most men just gawked at her. They rarely uttered a word in greeting. And the few Wise Ones who actually conversed with her were usually peppering her with questions, trying to dissect every detail of her life for research.

Coyle was different, though. He talked with her like another human —not a big-eared faerie of a lesser species who only belonged in a bedchamber.

When Oenghus pulled the horses to a stop in front of their cottage, Isiilde climbed off the wagon seat and stormed into the house, slamming the door in defiance.

Mousebane cracked open an irritated eye from the bed. The hearth was cold, but she didn't care. She slipped out of her clothes, tugged on warm leggings and a nightgown, and crawled beneath the covers. The cat flicked its ears, but forgave her, slinking under the covers to settle against her body.

Humans made absolutely no sense. She wished Marsais was here. But he wasn't, so she wallowed under the covers in misery.

Sometime later, Oenghus brought her a warm dinner and started the fire, chasing back the creeping chill. It promised to be another frigid night.

"I'm sorry, Sprite." He settled on the edge of her bed. "I know it's not fair, but such is life."

"I don't understand why you won't let me see him. Coyle isn't like the others—he's kind." Her voice was muffled by a cocoon of feathers.

"Because he's a man and you're a nymph. Even if you were free to do what you want, it wouldn't be a good idea." Oenghus sighed. "Believe it or not, this is for your own protection."

"Yes, Marsais explained it to me. Nymphs are intoxicating to human males. We're like a drug. It's not my fault they can't bloody well control themselves."

Oenghus grunted. "Not just with nymphs. Though I get drunk all the time and I don't go around attacking women."

"Then why do others?"

"Some people believe they have the right to do whatever they wish. Especially to people they consider beneath them."

"Coyle isn't like that."

"Maybe not," he admitted. "But I'm trying to protect you. I've seen good men—" He cut off, his voice raw. She peeked from under her blanket. His hands were curled into fists, knuckles white. "I'm not doing this to be cruel. Just trust me, all right?"

"I don't have much choice, do I?" she growled.

Oenghus looked at her with so much grief in his eyes that her heart ached. "I'm sorry. But I swore an oath." He stood abruptly, and left.

Isiilde awoke before midday. A warm ball of purring fur snuggled against her aching stomach. The heat felt good. But an uncomfortable wetness intruded.

It wouldn't be the first time Mousebane had fallen into a trough, then crawled into her bed.

She lifted the covers, preparing to scold the cat; instead, her breath caught in her throat. Blood stained her nightgown and sheets.

Her heart raced.

Had Mousebane brought in a mouse or gotten into a fight? Hope flared, then died when she checked herself over. She'd come of age. She'd be sold to a man who only wanted a nymph in his bed.

Isiilde fled the bed and stains that marked the end of her freedom. She paced from hearth to window, her panic increasing with every senseless footstep.

A desperate plan took shape. Isiilde shooed the cat off her bed and gathered the soiled bedclothes. Her plan was simple; she would not tell anyone. Caitlyn Whitehand wasn't due back for nearly another year, which was plenty of time to plan her escape—to leave everyone she loved.

Tears rolled down her cheeks. The walls closed in, slowly suffocating her beneath the thatched roof and cold stone. Her room seemed a cage.

The fire in the smoldering hearth answered her silent plea, surging towards her, as fiercely as a mother to her young, with a rush of air and sweet release.

The cottage shuddered with dread.

Time meandered as orange coils of heat swept slowly over the entranced nymph. Timber cracked and windows split. Flame filled her ears, stole her breath, and somewhere a cat screamed.

She felt strangely detached from her cold body.

Isiilde gazed from a high perch, watching the red flame devour her nightgown, licking at her naked flesh. Then the world shifted, and she fell off her perch. She looked down at her chest, where a jagged piece of timber protruded from her body.

A moment later, timbers groaned overhead; something crashed, toppled, and the cottage came tumbling down.

CHAPTER 10

OENGHUS SWORE under his breath as he heaved another stone onto a wall. Rocks were the only natural resource on the Isle. It made farming a nightmare. It was a good thing he wasn't a farmer, because he would have made a piss poor one.

Gungnir and Sleipnir raised their heads, gazing at a distant point across the fields. Oenghus turned to see what had caught their attention. A familiar form walked through the high grass.

Grunting, he set another stone in place. He'd spent enough time with Marsais to know when the man was agitated. His long stride tore through the grass, and when he arrived, he paced on the other side of the wall.

"That bad?" Oenghus spared his friend a sidelong glance. It looked like Isek had attacked Marsais with scissors and a razor, because he was clean shaven, except for his braided goatee. The vagabond had been transformed into a respectable Archlord.

"By the gods, don't even ask," Marsais growled. "I should've never come back."

"The throne suits you—when you're in the mood."

"Which is never," Marsais snapped, plucking irritably at his high collar. "Though occasionally, ruling has its benefits. The matter involving a certain nymph and the attempted murder of a dog has been cleared up."

Oenghus nodded in gratitude. "Whatever you had to do, I'm indebted to you."

"Oh, come now." Marsais dismissed the debt with a wave of his hand. "You'll always be indebted to me, old friend, and I to you, so stop counting. Besides, I'd miss her terribly. Fortunately, that dog is disliked by everyone. Most were amused by the whole affair. And since no one could explain how she'd orchestrated the bizarre chain of events, there wasn't any proof that it was intentional."

"What about Thira?" Oenghus spat her name from his lips. "She's not one to let things drop."

"Thira's one redeeming quality has always been her cold-hearted logic. I simply reasoned that since nymphs aren't human, bringing charges against a nymph for attacking a dog would demand that we hold a trial for every wolf who's ever killed a rabbit. Thira argued that a nymph shouldn't be here in the first place. I pointed out that if Isiilde was not allowed in the tower, then neither should Crumpet. She had no further comment on the matter."

Oenghus' eyes flashed with appreciation.

A gust of wind swept over the fields from the ocean, bending the tall grass with its restless touch. "You'd think winter was already here," Marsais said with a shiver.

"If you're bloody cold, then give me a hand."

"Hmm, as tempting as that is, I think I'll suffer through."

"Dandy," Oenghus muttered, grabbing a toppled stone from the earth. He heaved it back to its place on the wall.

"Is Carrothead still trying to get at the mare across the way?"

Oenghus ground his teeth together. Isiilde had renamed the horses. "It's Gungnir, and yes, he won't admit he's gelded." He suspected the beast would kick at the fences, even if there weren't a mare on the other side.

He continued his work, waiting for his friend to start venting. It didn't take long.

"Do you know what those fools in the Circle did?" Marsais asked.

Oenghus knew; he held a seat on the council. But Marsais answered his own question, before he could point that out. "The Nine sent another scouting party into the Dracken Wood."

"I voted against it—not that it mattered."

"Good scouts don't come easily. This will make fifteen whom we've lost to that cursed wood. One might think they'd get it through their thick skulls that some things are better left alone," Marsais said, rubbing at his chest.

Oenghus eyed Marsais. "Do you know what's in the wood?" he asked slowly.

A shadow flickered across his eyes.

Oenghus jabbed a finger at the man. "Look here, Scarecrow, if you bloody well know, why don't you just tell them and be done with it?"

"There are terrors in these realms that would make a god weep with fear. I pray every day that they remain shrouded in the shadows where they dwell. Some things are best left unknown." His voice was low and uneasy.

There were few things in the realms that terrified Marsais. And Oenghus knew enough to leave it alone. When the Scarecrow got that look in his eyes, it usually meant trouble of the worst kind.

"Hmm, speaking of which, Aislinn is petitioning to send a scouting party to the Isle of Blight. She's even volunteered to lead the expedition herself."

"Aislinn proposed the expedition last month and Isek flat out refused," Oenghus said, amused. The woman couldn't even travel to Drivel without an armed escort.

"And that's exactly the issue. All the requests and complaints that Isek has handled over the past six months are being brought up again in hopes that I will rule differently. I'll be sitting on that cursed throne for the next month."

"If I have to hear you complain about that bloody chair one more time, I'm going to have Isek put a frilly cushion on it for your bony arse."

"Hmm, I already tried. He claimed a cushion wasn't befitting an Archlord."

Oenghus threw his head back and laughed, startling the horses. "He grooms you, dresses you, brings you your bloody meals, and orders you around like he's your Oathbound. You'd be better off just finding a good woman. At least you'd be warm at night."

"You know I barely sleep," Marsais muttered, gazing at the ocean.

"Aye, well maybe that's the problem." Oenghus leaned against the stone wall with a sigh and fished his pipe out of his pouch.

Marsais had always been a recluse. It wasn't easy having friends when you were a seer.

"You didn't shake the Keening, did you?"

Marsais' silence was answer enough.

"Tell you what. We'll go back to Drivel, and take Maira up on her offer. We'll find you a few busty lasses and get you drunk out of your wits."

"Ah, the answer to every Nuthaanian's ailment. I sincerely doubt I'll find a good woman in a whorehouse, although you seem to find an ample supply."

"You might be right, probably wouldn't work for you with your tastes. Why'd you come back, then?"

Six months was a short time for Marsais to be away. It wasn't surprising to discover he hadn't shaken the tempting whisper of Death's embrace.

"The farther I went, the worse it became," Marsais answered, scratching at his chest. "My visions followed me with a vengeance."

"They've been bad?"

"When are they not?"

Oenghus had learned long ago not to ask for details. He didn't want to know what tomorrow would bring.

"Is Isiilde still sleeping?" Marsais squinted through the mist, over the fields, and towards the cottage. "I have another audience this afternoon, but I thought she might be in the mood for a lesson."

"She'll be in a foul mood, is what she'll be."

"I certainly hope I'm not the cause," Marsais said.

Oenghus tugged on his beard.

"What'd you do now?"

"I told her to stay away from Helwick's apprentice."

"I swear, I only turned my back on her for a few minutes, and the next thing I know some young man was kissing her hand. For what it's worth, he seemed respectful."

"That's the bloody problem." Oenghus sighed and sat on top of the stone wall. "He's a good lad, with more of a head on his shoulders than I ever had. I'd be thrilled if one of my other daughters had sense enough to find someone like him. By the gods, Scarecrow, you should've met some of the louts my daughters have dragged home."

"She's an unawakened nymph—too innocent for the idea to even occur to her, which is why you did what you had to."

"Aye, but I can't stop thinkin' that she's never going to be with a man she loves, or wants for that matter." He blew out a puff of smoke. "You remember what you were doing at seventeen?"

"Hmm, you're asking a man who forgot his own name for centuries. But I can guess what *you* were up to. Fighting, carousing, and— Oenghus!" His grey eyes widened with horror.

Oenghus followed his gaze to the source of his distress.

The two men reacted in the same instant, racing towards the cottage, which was being consumed by a dark cloud of billowing black smoke. They were halfway across the field when the fire surged, ripping through the roof. Timber groaned, splintered, and the cottage crumbled.

"Isiilde!" Oenghus bellowed, outdistancing Marsais.

Fire curled along the ground and shot up into the air with an unnatural ferocity that could only come from his daughter.

The barn was ablaze; the flames would find his distillery.

Oenghus vaulted over the garden fence, and the combustible compounds in the barn ignited. The shock wave caught him in midair and, like a child's doll, slammed him to the ground. He shook off the blast and surged to his feet, ignoring the wooden shards embedded in his flesh.

Oenghus reached the cottage door as Marsais' chanting voice filled the air. A blink later, a storm swirled to life, beating back the flames. He kicked in the door, and flames roared out. He twisted to the side.

Marsais thrust his hands towards the cottage and a gust of woven hail pelted the blaze. Oenghus followed on the storm's heels, wading through the flaming wreckage, searching for his daughter.

"Isiilde!" he coughed, squinting through the smoke. He fought his way into her room, or rather, what was left of it. The summoned storm had doused the blaze, leaving a smoldering maze of timber and stone. He searched through the wreckage in desperation.

A shock of red hair poked up from the rubble.

"Marsais, get in here!" Oenghus heaved the timber and debris to the side, revealing more of his daughter with every shifting piece. The timbers were still hot, burning his hands as he frantically worked to free her.

Marsais scrambled over the timbers to crouch beside her, pressing his fingers against her neck. "She's alive—for now, but she's pinned."

Oenghus grunted, dragging another heavy piece of timber off the pile and tossing it aside. He surveyed the remaining rubble, and then got into position, gripping a thick beam beneath the tangle of wood.

"Ready?"

Marsais nodded.

Oenghus lifted the timber with a surge of power, and Marsais dragged her out. When she was clear, Oenghus released his burden. It fell with a thud.

Marsais gathered Isiilde in his arms and carried her outside, where he laid her on a dry patch of earth near the garden wall.

Oenghus knelt by her side. Her clothes had been burned off, yet her flesh was unharmed by the fire's touch. A jagged piece of wood protruded from her chest. Blood seeped from the wound, carving paths through the ash that had settled on her skin. It was far too close to her lung for his liking.

The stake would have to stay for now; he'd have to wait until she was stronger. Once he pulled it out, the wound would need cleaning before it could mend. He finished his assessment in a blink of an eye, resting one massive hand on her forehead and the other on her stomach, linking spirit and body to his own. The Lore sprang to his lips as he directed the Gift into his daughter, mending her broken ribs and bolstering her strength.

It was all he could do for her now.

Oenghus returned to the present. Grim and silent, he stood to summon the horses. Marsais gently wrapped Isiilde in his cloak, taking care not to jostle her. He stood with her in his arms, and waited for Oenghus to swing onto a horse's bare back. After he'd passed her up, he vaulted atop the other horse.

Together, they spurred their mounts towards the castle. And Oenghus muttered a silent prayer to the Sylph, wondering what in all the realms he was going to do with his combustible daughter.

CHAPTER 11

Isiilde floated in a vast, uncharted sea. Pain lay on the horizon, but familiar voices kept it at bay. Eventually, as her fever burned out and pain lost its bite, she surfaced, opening her eyes.

Morigan was sitting by her bedside. "Don't try to talk, Isiilde. You've been mostly unconscious for four days."

The healer slipped a hand behind her neck and pressed a cup to her lips. A few sips, that was all, before Morigan pulled the cup away, leaving her wanting more.

"You can drink again in a few minutes."

Isiilde tried to sit up, but pain nearly pushed her back into darkness. She had to leave this island. *Now*.

"Calm down, child," Morigan said, smoothing back her hair. "The roof collapse broke four of your ribs. A length of wood impaled you here." She pointed to a large patch of salve-covered flesh. "We healed most of the damage, but you've been fighting a fever. Oen and me had a time of it, so the bruising will just have to mend on its own."

"Where's Oen?" Isiilde whispered.

Morigan studied her. "Resting. I finally chased him away."

"Who's been tending to me?" Isiilde asked, dreading the answer.

"Just me and Greta. I trust her."

And Isiilde trusted Morigan—she was the closest person Isiilde had to a mother.

"Does Oen know I've come of age?"

"I don't think so."

"Please don't tell anyone," she begged, tears leaking from her eyes.

Morigan wiped her tears. "Hush, now. I won't tell a soul."

"I don't want to be sold," she whispered.

"I doubt Oen will let it come to that."

"But he's bound by honor."

"He is," Morigan admitted. "But it's foolish to keep secrets from him."

"He'll have no choice."

Morigan smiled down at her. That smile was filled with grief and sadness, and wisdom. "There is always a choice, Isiilde. And sometimes, patience is the best one. Know when to wait, when to draw back your bow, and when to loose the arrow. Do you understand?"

"I can't shoot a bow."

Morigan sighed. She and Oenghus had tried to teach Isiilde to use a blade (like any good Nuthaanian child), or even shoot a bow, but weapons made the nymph ill—violence went against her very nature.

"I'm telling you to wait—to see what happens. It's no reason to try to end your life."

"I wasn't trying to."

"Then what happened?"

"I was scared—nothing more. I don't want to be sold. I don't know what happened." It was the truth, and it was all she had.

"It's your choice what you tell him, but Isiilde..." Morigan sighed. "You destroyed Oen's distillery and if you give him the same excuse you always give him, then it's only going to make things worse."

"I'm not going to lie to him. He can lock me in a dungeon if he likes, but I won't tell him." Her battered body trembled with conviction.

"Oh, child, it won't come to that," Morigan whispered, bending forward to kiss her forehead. "Oen loves you with all his heart. And I love you, too. All you need to worry about right now is regaining your strength."

Isiilde awoke to more pain. And a bouquet of wildflowers by her bedside. The Orb of Memories sat beside it. There wasn't a scratch on its rune-etched surface.

She was enduring a tasteless gruel being shoveled into her mouth when the door opened, and Oenghus ducked beneath the lintel. "You're looking brighter, Sprite." He smiled down at her. "I'll take over, Greta, thank you."

The attendant nodded, handed him the bowl of broth and left. Even before he sat on the chair, she spotted the look in his eyes. Here it comes, she thought.

"What happened?"

"I don't know, Oen."

"You're a poor liar. You always have been."

The silence deepened. His eyes sharpened, and she shifted beneath his gaze. Finally, he spoke, and she was able to breathe again. "I'm not going to get upset if you tell me the truth—no matter what it might be —but I bloody well want the *truth*."

"The room caught on fire... it just exploded. I wasn't even singing to it."

"A few smoldering coals just exploded?"

Isiilde did not like his low, rumbling tone. Oenghus Saevaldr meant business when he was quiet.

"That's always your excuse, girl. The nursery, the gardens, the banquet, Miera Malzeen—"

"That wasn't my fault," Isiilde defended. "Mistress Malzeen was the teacher, and *she* Linked with me. She was the one in control."

Over two years had passed since the accident, and she still felt a queasy twist of remorse. The practice of Linking was a routine matter, where one acted as a vessel for the Gift while the other controlled the weave. It was supposed to be a safe way for a novice to sense the Gift for the first time. Only with Isiilde things had gone terribly wrong. Miera Malzeen had lit up like a torch. No one could explain how it happened, and no one had attempted to Link with Isiilde since, not even Marsais.

"Aye, well, I'll give you that," Oenghus grunted. "But there's still the library, Flappers, *Crumpet*, and that's not even counting the charred objects I've found lying around our cottage over the years."

"I didn't know you were keeping count."

"Isiilde, I'm not gonna take that bloody excuse again. It's time you start owning up to the mess you cause, faerie or no."

"Yes, sir."

Oenghus blinked in surprise. He seemed confused, even a little worried by her easy surrender. "So, out with it, what happened?"

Isiilde would not lie to him. She never had. So she pressed her lips together and counted the grey hairs in his beard. What used to be black was now streaked with grey.

Oenghus ground his teeth.

Why would his hair go grey now—more than eight hundred years into his life?

He was the first to break their silent battle of wills. "You want to know what I think happened?"

Isiilde nodded eagerly, because she really didn't know.

"I think you were angry with me and you did this out of spite."

Isiilde's mouth fell open in shock. Did he think so poorly of her? But she'd backed herself into a corner, and there was no escaping now. "If you say so," she whispered.

"Ah, bollocks." He shot to his feet and turned his back to her. Ten deep breaths later, he turned back around. "When you're mended, you'll help me rebuild the cottage—stone by bloody stone. I don't want to hear a word of complaint either. That clear?"

"Yes, sir."

"That's it? No argument?"

She tilted her head, confused. "You just said I shouldn't complain— did you want me to?"

Oenghus tugged on his beard, and grumbled something rude under his breath about daughters.

"I'm sorry about your distillery and workshop." All of his equipment for brewing and his stock of potions had been stored in the barn.

Oenghus shrugged, settling on the edge of her bed. "They can be replaced. You can't, so I'm glad you're all right."

"Is Mousebane—" she started to ask, but Oenghus was already shaking his head.

"Marsais went back to look for him. There's nothing left 'cept the horses."

"The sheep?"

"They were in the barn."

Isiilde felt sick. "What are we going to do, Oen?"

Without his distillery and workshop, he had no way to earn coin unless he started charging for healing. To say nothing of their lack of housing.

"Don't worry about it. Marsais already offered us a place in his tower until we can rebuild."

"Where is he?"

"He's trying to keep your faerie arse in this Order."

CHAPTER 12

Isiilde was huddled against the side of a shop watching a building across the road, or rather those coming out of it. *Isadora's Closet* was the only pleasure house on the East side of Coven. Day and night, it was always busy.

Despite her concealing cloak, people stared at her as they passed. Her red hair attracted notice, even under a hood. Or maybe it was the cloak itself? It was warm and fine, and therefore expensive—a gift from Marsais after she'd burned down the cottage.

It seemed a lifetime ago. But at other times, she still felt the flame roiling over her body.

Isiilde pushed it from her mind, focusing on her current troubles. She touched a rune-etched flagon concealed beneath her cloak.

There was no going back now.

But by the Jack of Fools, what could be taking him so long?

Doubt wiggled its way into her thoughts. She'd watched Marsais enter the pleasure house while she was tinkering with a Gnomish Crystal in the Spine. But maybe he'd slipped out of the building?

The sun was high behind the clouds; she couldn't wait any longer.

Tightening her grip on the empty flagon, she strode across the muddy street to *Isadora's Closet,* and charged the doors.

ONCE INSIDE, her resolve faltered. The common room was choked with patrons and she was jostled away from the door like a twig caught in a river.

The air was thick with pipe smoke; the floor covered in nutshells, and the tavern pulsed with the beat of bawdy songs.

Isiilde froze in midstep. A pale woman stood on a table. She wore strands of silk over a body that glowed with ethereal light. Men elbowed each other to get near her. One caught the woman's eye, and he eagerly opened his mouth. She put her toes between his lips and poured a shimmering red liquor down her leg. The man drank eagerly, licking every last drop from her skin.

Two brawling sailors careened into Isiilde, knocking her over. She scrambled to her feet and ducked through the crowd, searching for a way out. But no door was in sight.

A press of bodies pushed her towards the long bar. Then the crowd shifted, and a gap opened up. She darted through and stumbled through an archway.

A haze of smoke hung in this new room, and moaning shapes moved in the murky air. Gradually, her eyes adjusted. Patrons lay on cushions in a tangle of limbs and bodies.

"Pull your hood up and get out of here, girl," a voice hissed in her ear.

Isiilde jerked in surprise. A massive shape with two pale blue eyes filled her vision. For a startling moment she feared it was Oenghus, but where her protector was dark and stormy, this man was fair and calm with a shock of blond hair and a neatly trimmed beard.

"This is no place for you. If you're lookin' for work, then take my advice and find another profession."

Isiilde took a hasty step back. His words registered, and she quickly did as he suggested, tugging her hood up.

"I'm looking for a man," she said, glancing uneasily at the men in the room. A few had surfaced from their pleasures and were staring at her.

An iron hand locked on her shoulder, but before she could squirm away, the hand steered her down an empty hallway. A memory surfaced. Oenghus had mentioned a Nuthaanian who worked as a guard in Coven. His name was Breeman.

"It's not a place to find a man, either. Trust me."

A man came to leer at her from a doorway, but Breeman growled him away.

"No—" Her mind felt muddled. "I need Marsais." It was all she could manage to say.

"Don't know him." Breeman produced a vial from his trouser pocket and waved it under her nose. Her head instantly cleared.

"I need to speak with the Archlord. I know he's here."

"The Archlord doesn't entertain visitors, not even women. So scat, before you get yourself into trouble."

"But—"

"No one disturbs the Archlord," Breeman rumbled.

"—I'm his apprentice," she finished.

Breeman rubbed his chin. "You're his apprentice?"

She nodded in answer.

"Lucky bastard," he muttered.

"It's important that I see him at once," she said. Her eyes were wide and pleading.

Nuthaanians were ever susceptible to a woman in distress. "Fine, but if he doesn't know you, you'll pay, girl."

Isiilde recognized an empty threat when she heard one.

"Come on, then."

Breeman led her down a narrow stairwell. It led to a chamber with curtained alcoves and a tall apparatus bubbling in the center. Tubes snaked out from it, each leading to an alcove.

Candles flickered in the darkness, and the air was heavy with exotic scents. She could see bodies moving sluggishly through the threadbare curtains. Soft cries and low groans throbbed in the air.

Isiilde glanced nervously towards her guide, feeling a sudden urge to bolt. But Breeman paid her no mind as he stopped in front of an alcove.

"Marsais," he murmured, pulling the edge of the curtain back and making sure to block her view. "Sorry to interrupt, but there's a young woman to see you—"

"I do not, have not, nor will I ever require company, Breeman," a familiar voice cut in. It was definitely Marsais, only... distant sounding.

"—says she's your apprentice," Breeman finished.

A stretch of silence followed as she stood by, nervously wringing the neck of the flagon. Perhaps she should leave—

"And what does this apprentice of mine look like?" Marsais finally asked.

"Scared out of her wits, with a shock of red hair and eyes like a gem-filled sea."

Isiilde froze.

"Send her in," Marsais ordered.

Breeman stepped aside, sweeping the curtain open for her. "You lucked out, girl," he murmured as she ducked inside.

A faint Rune of Light glowed on the stone wall. Isiilde waited for her eyes to adjust, and as they did, she spotted Marsais. He sprawled on a bed of cushions, wearing nothing but his small clothes. He was murmuring in the dark, his voice soft and troubled. His white hair glowed beneath the light, spilling over the faded cushions. He held a pipe of sorts in his right hand—a sleek wooden mouthpiece connected to the tube from the bubbling contraption in the center of the room.

Marsais took a long draught from the pipe. When he exhaled, a stream of flowery smoke swirled from his lips, and his hand fell to his side.

Isiilde sucked in a sharp breath. A raw scar marred his flesh. It was wide and jagged, slashing across his torso from shoulder to rib. Was this what he was always rubbing at beneath his shirt? Although he'd done that for as long as she could remember, the injury was fresh—a terrible wound barely healed.

She'd always thought it was a habit born from irritation. But then she'd never seen him disrobed before. He was long and lean, and muscular. Small wonder he was so quick.

His sharp features twisted with pain, the pipe rolled from his fingers, and his eyes snapped open. But they were not his own. Eyes white as a snowstorm stared blindly into the darkness. He gripped the cushions, fingers clawing at the fabric. Every muscle in his body tensed as if he were fighting an unseen foe. Then a painful moan tore from his throat.

The sound twisted her heart. Impulsively, she leaned in close to touch the scar on his chest. His skin was warm, and she savored the life beating beneath her fingertips. Her touch drifted down his chest, tracing the hard lines of wiry muscle, and then to the thin line of hair below his navel that plunged beneath his cotton drawers.

Marsais bolted upright.

She jumped back, but he paid her no mind as he continued forward, doubling over to clutch his head. He strained to catch his breath like a man who'd been running for hours. He was shivering and covered in cold sweat.

It was an intimate thing to witness. Unsure what to do, she stood her ground, neither moving towards him nor away.

When the tremors eased, Marsais studied her through a tangle of white hair. His eyes had returned to their normal grey.

"Hmm." He swept his hair back, then eased against the wall for support. "Sit down and give me a moment."

Isiilde sat on the edge of the lumpy bed, studying the forgotten pipe on the floor. Silence stretched between them. But the chamber was far from quiet—moans and hushed voices echoed in the dim.

She did not look at him. As lenient and relaxed as Marsais was, Isiilde realized she'd just overstepped some unknown boundary.

Perhaps caressing his naked flesh had been a bad idea. But not much thought had been involved. She sighed. As Morigan was fond of saying, what's done is done.

Isiilde untied her cloak, and let it slide off her shoulders, careful to keep the flagon concealed beneath the folds in her lap. She sniffed curiously at the air. Beneath the sweat, salt, and sickly sweet aroma of pipe smoke lay a kind of heavy musk that she could not place. It made her uncomfortable. A sudden desire to leave this place prompted her to breach the silence.

"Are you all right, Marsais?" she asked, turning towards him.

He dismissed her question with a wave of his hand. His eyes were closed, his head supported by the stone at his back.

Isiilde watched the prominent Adam's apple of his throat move as he swallowed. Her gaze lingered there. She ached to touch him again, to trace her fingers down his throat. But before her desire gave way to impulse, Marsais took a deep, steadying breath, and opened his eyes.

"Now then, my dear, you may speak, though I'm not sure my muddled brain is prepared. Hmm, perhaps it's better off muddled," he mused, gazing wistfully at the discarded pipe.

"Why would a man want a woman to put her foot in his mouth?" This was not what she'd meant to say, nor perhaps the best way to start a conversation.

"By the gods," Marsais groaned, reaching up to massage his temples. "Would you hand me that pipe?"

Isiilde did as he requested and tried to sniff it when it passed through her hands, but he deftly snatched it away before she could inhale. He stuck the mouthpiece between his lips, sucking in a bubbling draught. The tension in his neck and shoulders faded.

"You'll have to ask Oenghus, and *if* he tells you to ask me, then, and only then will I answer." He sounded intoxicated, or maybe drugged.

"If I ask Oen, he'll know I was here."

"Which brings us to an excellent point. If Oenghus finds out you're here with me, he'll have my head," he said calmly, pausing to suck on his pipe. "So I ask, though I am loath to hear the answer, why have you come?"

"I don't know why he'd have your head. It's not as if you brought me here. What is in the pipe?" she asked, reaching for it.

Marsais clutched the pipe protectively to his chest. "Actually, I *have* brought you here, for it is I who am here, and I whom you seek." His words hung heavy in the air with the weight of his gaze. "And this, my dear, is no place for a lady, most especially for a young lady of inno-cence, and even more so for a nymph."

Marsais leaned forward, the muscles of his jaw clenching as his eyes pierced her.

Isiilde casually looked elsewhere, avoiding his gaze.

"It's fortunate you ran into Breeman. He's a good man—a rare thing —which brings me back to my original question from which you so delicately steered us." He did not smoke his pipe, but waited, pinning her with steely eyes.

Most found his gaze unnerving, but she knew him well enough to know if she waited long enough, he might become sidetracked. Unfortunately, he seemed to be in one of his more lucid moods.

Isiilde took a deep breath, then produced the flagon, yanking the cork out with a dramatic flair.

Marsais jumped to his feet, fingers poised to begin a weave. After a few tense heartbeats, he relaxed and snatched the flagon from her hand to study its markings. Whatever he was searching for, he must have found it, because he shuddered with relief.

"Let me piece this together," he said, plucking the cork from her fingers and jamming it back into the top. "You opened it!" He gave a sharp bark of laughter. "My genius amazes me."

He favored her with a lopsided grin, tossed the flagon up in the air, sending it end over end, and deftly caught it by the narrow neck. "And since you are still here and I don't hear any screams of terror, I'd wager the flagon you opened was the one on the left?"

Isiilde nodded.

"I thought I asked you not to open the flagons stored in my vault?"

"You said it'd be unwise," she corrected.

"Hah! A loophole akin to a gaping hole to a faerie."

"I'm sorry, Marsais. I couldn't resist. Honestly, I tried, but I couldn't stop thinking about what was inside. And then when I opened it, something sprang out—an ugly creature that looked like a monkey with bat wings, a barbed tail, and a large mouth. It got away before I could catch it."

"Sounds like an Imp. A rather devilish Imp."

"I didn't know what else to do, so I thought it best to find you, but you were in here for so long." This last confession pushed her over the brink.

"Oh, don't start crying. You'll chase all the customers away. Everything will be fine, my dear."

Marsais reached towards her cheek, but caught himself at the last moment, lowering his hand. He bent to open his rucksack on the floor.

Isiilde hadn't noticed the awkward gesture. She wiped her eyes on a sleeve and blinked at his back as he searched through his pack. A myriad of violent scars crisscrossed the skin. They were old lashings, faded compared to the wound on his chest.

Sympathy overwhelmed her. She touched his scarred flesh with a soft, trailing caress.

Marsais tensed, then shot to his feet, breaking contact.

"Forgive me, I—" she began, thinking she'd angered him, but when he turned his head to gaze at her, she couldn't read the look in his eyes.

Marsais clenched his jaw. "Why don't you wait outside the curtain and let me get dressed, hmm?" His voice was hoarse with control.

More confused than ever, she nodded and did as he asked. Clothing rustled, and then he emerged, wearing tailored trousers and a simple shirt beneath his grey cloak. Marsais produced two vials from his pack, holding them out for her inspection.

"Choose one."

Isiilde uncorked each in turn, sniffing warily at the contents. The first smelled of wood, and the other of ash. She chose the ashy one. He nodded in satisfaction and guzzled the first vial—the one she hadn't chosen.

He shivered as if he'd been doused with cold water. "Good thing you chose correctly." The other vial vanished inside his pack.

"But I didn't—"

"Did I say I'd drink the one you picked?" He arched a brow to emphasize his point, and she clicked her mouth shut.

Marsais led her up and out a back door, which spilled them into an empty alleyway behind the pleasure house. She took his offered arm, biting back a swell of questions as they wound their way through the midday bustle.

Although she attracted stares, no one noticed the Archlord of the Isle without his crimson robes. There were benefits to being a recluse.

A question was on the tip of her tongue when he froze in midstep.

"The cottage," he realized.

Fire spouted from her ears in surprise.

Marsais absently patted out the flames on his shirt. "That's why you burned it down. You came of age and were frightened."

How could he know?

"Did Morigan tell you?" she whispered, numb with shock. And then a sudden, irrational thought burst into her mind. "Has the emperor already sold me?"

"No, my dear, not to my knowledge," Marsais said gently, but her tears continued to fall, and he felt just as helpless.

He said no more until they reached the edge of town, where he stopped beneath the limbs of a twisted old oak—away from prying eyes and curious ears.

"Isiilde," he said, offering her a pristine handkerchief. "You're nearly eighteen, but I'm sure we can fool Caitlyn Whitehand into believing you're not of age for another few years. Some nymphs don't come of age until they're nearly a hundred."

"Really?"

Marsais shrugged. "I don't know. I can't remember. But it seems reasonable considering your age—humans come of age much earlier, which is why they breed like rabbits." He grimaced, but she wasn't sure if his distaste was due to the infestation of humans or rabbits. "Besides, I was alive before the Shattering; people generally believe whatever story I weave."

"I think you overestimate your influence."

"It's still worth a try. I *can* be persuasive."

"When you remember what you're arguing about," she pointed out.

"But this would be an argument of the heart rather than the mind. My heart doesn't forget."

"That you remember."

He gave her a look. "I'm writing you up for that."

Isiilde snorted. "Please do, *master*. If you remember."

"Har, har," Marsais said dryly, then paused. "What were we talking about?"

"You lying about me coming of age."

"Right. Hmm, it helps that you're so..." He gestured towards her, searching for the proper word. "...slight," he settled uncomfortably.

Isiilde seethed at him.

Marsais pretended not to notice. But as she was forming a scathing retort, he turned away, distracted by a rustle in the leaves of the tree.

Isiilde sighed, following his gaze. There was nothing of interest at all in the branches.

"How odd—of course not!" Marsais snapped at the tree. "Do you mind, old one? I'm speaking with my apprentice."

Isiilde forgot her irritation, glancing from Marsais to the tree, and back again.

"We're terribly sorry. She's under quite a strain, you see—" He cut off mid-sentence as if the tree had made a rude remark. With a click, he shut his mouth and motioned her to follow, turning his back on the oak.

Isiilde twisted around to look at the tree.

"Don't provoke him," he hissed.

"Provoke who?"

"That rude old fellow."

Marsais launched himself up the steep road leading to the Wise One's stronghold. His legs were long, with a stride to match. She was forced to run, and then, halfway up the hillside, he stopped so suddenly that she ran into him.

"Marsais?"

"Ah, my dear," he said in greeting. "Why are you out in this foul weather?"

"We were talking about..." she hesitated, gesturing helplessly. "Coming of age," she finally managed.

"Oh." Marsais frowned in thought. "We should talk about that."

"I know how the female body works," she defended. "Morigan told me."

"Did she tell you about a nymph's Awakening?"

"Erm... no."

"Did Oenghus?" he asked hopefully.

"Just tell me."

He sighed. "Nymphs don't come of age like humans—they Awaken. It happened three months ago, didn't it?"

"I didn't burn down the cottage on purpose. I swear, I just panicked. Oenghus gave his word that he'd return me to Kambe. I couldn't tell anyone."

"I do understand," he said, gently.

She looked up into his grey eyes, soft with kindness, and felt the burden of her secret lifting at long last.

"Now, on to other matters, which require a blunt tongue, as wary as I am to delve into this subject."

"Which is?"

"I knew you came of age the moment you touched my back."

"I touched more than your back," she admitted.

"Ah."

"You're as fit as a duelist, Marsais."

He paused, his lips parted, mind seeming to go blank. "Thank you," he finally said.

"I didn't mean to anger you—"

"Anger is far, far, *far* from the word I would use." He waited until realization dawned in her eyes. "You must be careful. A single touch from an Awakened nymph has the same effect as drinking an entire bottle of Primrose wine."

Isiilde crossed her arms. "Have you drunk an entire bottle of Primrose wine before?"

That couldn't be healthy.

"When you touched my back, it certainly felt like that."

"Really?"

"Hmm."

Isiilde shivered, feeling exposed on the hillside.

"I don't mean to scare you, but a loss of innocence can be a brutal thing—far more brutal than the knowledge of it. You shouldn't have gone in there. I don't have much faith in human males—they're bad enough when they're cloaked in lies."

"But Marsais," she said, softly. "I wouldn't have gone inside for any other man."

He looked into her eyes. And for a moment, time seemed to stop, and she felt like she was falling upwards.

Marsais took a hasty step back. "It was unwise of you to go into town alone—let alone a pleasure house. Your safety is far more important than anything contained in a flagon. Please promise me you won't leave the castle grounds unescorted by myself or Oenghus, for *any* reason."

Isiilde pursed her lips. "I can't promise."

"And why is that?"

"I'm going to leave the Isle. I don't want to be sold."

"Neither would I. Where are you planning to go?"

"I haven't quite worked out the details," she admitted, feeling her cheeks heat. "I, erm, was in your vault..."

He arched a brow.

"Stealing, I suppose. Well, more like borrowing, really. I'll need coin to leave the Isle, to find passage on a ship. But I'll pay you back one day."

Marsais sighed, turning to the sea. He seemed at a loss, and some minutes passed before he spoke again. "I've always been an ardent supporter of running away from most situations. But Isiilde... Fyrsta is a brutal place. This Isle is sheltered in comparison. I'd hoped that teaching you to use the Gift would give you the means to defend yourself, but we've run out of time. There are few options left to you."

"I hate being a nymph, Marsais."

His only reply was to offer his arm, and they headed towards the looming castle.

"You do realize that if any other novice, apprentice, or Wise One had broken into my vault and opened a warded flagon, then she would have been ousted from the Isle without question."

Isiilde clicked her mouth shut.

"Which brings up an interesting point. If you weren't a faerie, you would not, I hope, be foolish enough to open it in the first place."

Isiilde frowned at the back-handed compliment.

"Besides, have you ever considered that being human, or even stuck in my boots, might be a worse fate? I'm a firm believer in taking what you get, and praying you don't get any more of it."

His gaze snapped towards the wind-bent grass, past the smoking chimneys of Coven, and out to sea. Isiilde followed his gaze.

A gust of wind nearly knocked her over. She moved to the other side of Marsais, letting his body buffer the wind. Sea mist settled on his face as he pointed his nose like a weather vane towards the horizon.

As far as she could tell, there wasn't anything out there.

"As the seas churn, its turmoil has spread," he murmured.

She had no idea what that meant.

"Blast it!" Marsais ran towards the castle.

Isiilde gawked for a moment. Stifling her irritation, she bolted after him. He was tall and quick, and she was having trouble keeping up. But eventually he slowed. When she reached him, she doubled over, panting.

"Hmm?"

"What is it?" she wheezed.

"What is what?"

"You were saying something about the sea, and then you saw something—"

"Did I?" He seemed intrigued.

"Didn't you?"

"I don't know. You say I did, and I dare not argue with a nymph."

"But—"

"Never mind." He waved an impatient hand. "If we linger in this cold any longer, the tips of your ears will freeze and crack off."

Isiilde snorted so loudly that a spout of flame shot out of her ears.

A group of Wise Ones bickered in front of the Storm Gate—the main entrance into the keep. The massive doors were made of witchwood, bound with Kilnish steel, and covered in warding runes.

Isiilde loved unraveling wards of protection. The more complex, the more tempting. But Oenghus had forbidden her to touch the gate.

Four guardian statues flanked the wide stone steps. Carved from obsidian, they were statues of champions long dead. Their shadows stretched across the courtyard.

To avoid the arguing Wise Ones, Marsais took the long way around to the Spine. He stopped by an overgrown hedge at its base, and Isiilde was on the verge of telling him he was in the wrong spot, when she recognized the posture of a man about to empty his bladder.

Marsais *would* piss on a legendary tower.

She looked up to its top, and swayed, feeling dizzy. The pinnacle was so high she felt like she was falling.

Hengist Heartfang, first Archlord of the Isle, had raised the spire straight from the seabed. It was a solid, twisting stretch of pale grey. Harsh winds had polished the rock to a glassy sheen, and veins of quartz swirled up its length, pulsing with light as the sun touched them.

Every Archlord in the Isle's history had lived in the Spine. Oenghus had said it was to make up for other shortcomings. Marsais only laughed. Three years later, she'd finally understood the crude jest.

Brooding clouds swirled overhead, and a single drop of rain hit her face. It was followed by a deluge. Isiilde sneezed. And by the time she'd stopped spouting flame, her hair was soaked and her teeth were chattering.

"Don't stand there glaring," Marsais said, brushing past her. "You didn't have to wait for me." He placed a hand on a hidden rune and activated its power.

After years spent on the Isle, using Runes of Teleportation was a familiar routine, but she still marveled. When Marsais removed his hand, he stepped to the side, motioning her through.

A single step took her from the Spine's base to the floor below the tower's peak. Isiilde ducked under the ever-present cobwebs, and tore off her soaked cloak.

"I hate the rain." It always made her sneeze. And she did so again.

Marsais strode down the empty corridor. But he didn't go to his study; he went to a library. Dusty tomes lined the walls like skulls in a catacomb, with only a single, round window to light the eerie crypt.

Isiilde stood in the doorway as Marsais searched the shelves. The other Wise Ones didn't like the combustible nymph around their books.

"Are you looking for the Imp in here?" she finally asked.

"Imp!" His face appeared from behind a shelf. "Where?"

"Perhaps not here, but certainly somewhere."

"Everything is somewhere, and that could be anywhere."

Isiilde tilted her head.

Marsais tracked a muddy trail across a rug to the center of the room. He turned in a circle, then stopped to stare out the window. "The Shadows of Dawn," he breathed. "We stand at a crossroads."

Isiilde edged into the forbidden library. As she passed the threshold, she half expected to trip off a Ward of Alarm or alert a squad of guards. Nothing happened.

Bolstered by her anticlimactic entrance, she ventured in farther. The window seemed to captivate him.

"What do you see?" she whispered.

He jerked in alarm. "Ah, Isiilde. What brings you here?"

"You."

"Then what am I doing here?"

"Don't you remember the warded flagon I opened? You were looking for the Imp."

"That was ages ago," he murmured.

"No, Marsais. It was today."

He stared, confused. Then his gaze traveled back to the window.

Marsais could be absentminded, but this was something more. Worried, she took his hand. He looked down at her, startled. But his confusion cleared.

"Oh, yes, of course," he whispered. "How foolish of me." He delicately extracted his hand from hers. "Now then, where am I... Aha, yes, I remember!"

Marsais launched himself at a sliding ladder attached to the shelves. Momentum carried him to the end of the bookshelf. He climbed to its top, ran a questing finger along spines, then plucked a book from the shelves.

Marsais dropped to the floor, landed lightly, and dumped a heavy tome in her arms. Then he hurried out, leaving her to stumble after him with her burden.

Isek Beirnuckle rounded a corner, and Marsais drew up short. He cast about for a place to hide in the barren corridor. But Isek had already spotted him.

Isek took a patient breath. "Marsais, the Circle of Nine need to speak with you." And his eyes said he'd wasted half the day looking for him.

"Here are the reports from the outlying scouts and a message with the emperor's seal." Isek placed a slim cylinder on top of the stack he'd handed Marsais. "And this is something I think you should read before you meet with the Circle."

"Hmm." Marsais tucked the cylinder into a pocket, and the two walked down the hallway.

"Marsais?" She felt foolish for bothering him.

He turned at her call.

"What about the... *monkey*?" she stressed.

"Everything you need is in that book. I'm sure you'll have no problem trapping him again." He turned to go, but caught himself. "A moment, Isek."

Marsais drew her away from his impatient assistant, and leaned in close. "Think about what we discussed. And by the gods, let me know when you plan to run away."

"It's not really running away if I tell you beforehand," she whispered.

"No, it isn't," he agreed. "But I should like to say goodbye."

"I promise then. But swear to do the same for me."

"Upon my honor," he said, placing a hand over his heart.

"Good."

CHAPTER 13

Isiilde studied a sketching of ten different containers covered with faded runes. The book *Binding and Baiting* was written in a pompous hand, though dubious stains (likely blood) marred its pages. From what she'd read, the escaped imp was a lesser fiend from the Nine Halls.

Splendid, she thought with a sigh. She'd already burned down their cottage, and now she'd loosed a fiend in the castle.

Isiilde missed their cottage by the seaside. Their rooms in the Spine did not feel like home. The earth was far below, and the stones were lifeless. A fire in the nearby hearth offered some comfort, but she did not like being alone in their new chambers.

Another thing I've ruined.

Isiilde rubbed at the pain lurking below her collarbone as she squinted at the faded runes in the picture. A thought struck her: Marsais had stowed the flagon in his rucksack. How was she going to catch the imp without a trap?

Isiilde sprang to her feet, nearly tripping over her skirts as she ran out the front door.

If she were lucky (which she usually was), Marsais would have left his rucksack in the Archlord's preparation chamber, which led directly to the Hall of Judgment where the Circle assembled.

She pressed her hand against a column, activating an invisible rune. A heartbeat later, she emerged on the other side, listening for approaching footsteps.

By order of some Wise One or another, she wasn't supposed to enter the outer sanctum of the Hall of Judgment. But how could she possibly resist the chamber? Marble glittered like freshly fallen snow, and supporting columns swirled with veins of molten silver.

A weave gone awry swirled at the pinnacle of the domed ceiling, some forty feet in the air. It was an everlasting testament to the Wise One who'd failed: Lispen the Louse, as he was called. A Wise One who wove a Gateway to prove he could and was never seen again.

It is never wise to try when using the Gift. So went the sage saying.

Isiilde circled around the edge of the chamber, keeping a wary eye on the unstable portal. What runes, she wondered, had Lispen used?

Isiilde hurried to an unremarkable marble wall and activated a hidden rune known as the Eye of the Archlord. It was reserved for the Archlord's use, but Marsais had granted her access.

A tall, square panel of stone pulsed to life, and she edged it open, slipping inside the Archlord's preparation room.

The chamber was small, but elegantly garbed with plush chairs, a gilded mirror, and a wardrobe. According to Oenghus, the previous Archlord had been a peacock. But then he also said that of Marsais.

A familiar rucksack and a tattered grey cloak had been dumped on a padded bench. Isiilde stepped across the room, and paused, glancing into a full-length mirror. She turned to the glass to study the faerie who stared back.

Who was she that kings would wage war over?

She was delicate and weak, too slender, and her hair was too bright. She was a study in disproportion, with large eyes and a wide mouth.

Isiilde sighed at her sweeping ears. To her, they looked like horns.

Her thoughts snapped back into focus. She hurried over to Marsais' rucksack, untied the flap, and poked at the ominous opening. It might be warded.

Marsais liked wards, placing them on random things whenever he was restless, drunk, or bored. But she wasn't sure how one would go about warding a bag.

She peered inside, wrinkling her nose at a sharp, bitter scent. Did he have a skunk in there?

Isiilde held the bag at arm's length and shook it roughly, to see if the olfactory offense would charge out. That was the problem with enchanted bags containing pockets of space—a tiger could fit inside.

"One never knows what one might find," Marsais had once remarked, and then claimed he'd once found a dragon hiding in a sock (Oenghus said it was a large lizard).

Nothing fell out.

Isiilde blew out a breath. Closing her eyes, she thrust her hand inside. Images of spiders and large, thrashing monsters played havoc with her imagination. She brushed something slippery, and quickly moved to the bag's other side, pulling out a variety of oddly shaped vials, a sketchbook full of drawings, and finally, the rune-etched flagon.

She held her prize up to the light to inspect the twisting runes on its silver surface. But in its reflection, she spotted a Bowl of Scrying.

Nymphs live from moment to moment. And in that moment, she forgot about the flagon and went straight for the pedestal.

WITH A MURMUR, Isiilde traced an air rune over milky water. The water swirled, and the fog cleared, giving her a bird's-eye view of the Circle of Nine.

They sat at a massive round table: Shimei, an ebony-skinned lord from Kiln; Eiji, a spiky-haired gnome from Xaio; Eldred Runewise, a dwarf from the Bastardlands; Tulipin, the levitating gnome; Tharios of Ghast, raven-haired and impeccably dressed; N'Jalss, a Rahuatl male with black lips and pointed teeth; Yasmina, Oenghus, and finally Marsais.

Marsais sat quietly as the others debated. His long, white hair gleamed against his crimson robes, and the stiff collar and clinging sleeves made him look severe.

He also looked tired.

The Circle of Nine were arguing about the Thanes in the south. A fractured kingdom of warring clans was uniting under a man named Lachlan.

"Unification of the southern Thanes would bring stability to a war-ravaged land," Yasimina said. "Don't my people deserve that?"

It sounded reasonable to Isiilde, but half the council disagreed, including Oenghus. It was rumored Lachlan had ties with the kingdom of Vaylin.

"Lachlan has ties with everyone," Tharios pointed out. "And he's the first Thane to seek peace." Tharios was smooth and cultured, and well respected in the Order.

"The ports could open up again. They'd no longer be a haven for pirates. Think of the stability this would bring to the trade routes along the coast," Eiji said.

"You're looking to fatten your purse, and nothing more. That new dread pirate is wreaking havoc on your affairs," Eldred growled at the gnome.

"Trade routes and stability. Bah!" Shimei spat. "We will see what happens to stability when Vaylin gains a foothold in the West. Kambe is weak and undisciplined. Their warriors have never faced a Vaylinish legion."

"You wouldn't oppose his offer if Lachlan had ties with Kiln!" Yasimina snapped.

Marsais gestured for silence, and all eyes were drawn to him. "Oenghus, you've been oddly silent. I would hear your thoughts."

"I agree with Shimei," said Oenghus. "There's a lot more than rumors floating around about his ties with Vaylin. And then there's that fool prophecy down in the South—"

"It is not foolish," Yasimina interrupted. "Lachlan will unite my lands. More than half of the Thanes have already laid their swords at his feet."

"Aye, well, it smells bad," Oenghus grunted. "I'd like to find out where a young upstart hero got the coin to equip an army of this magnitude. That's not a man looking for peace. He's looking to expand his borders. I won't throw our Order in with his lot. But I don't think we should interfere, either."

"So you propose we sit and wait like a lazy hunter for his prey to come?" N'Jalss sneered at Oenghus, black lips curling back.

"I don't shift my colors," Oenghus rumbled.

Marsais quickly intervened before these honor-sensitive men challenged each other to a duel. "Let's not forget the purpose of this Order: to gather knowledge. We do not meddle in the affairs of kingdoms."

"We don't meddle?" Tharios asked, dryly. "When have we not meddled? Have you already forgotten the request from Emperor Jaal to help capture this *Bastard Prince*? How can we aid Kambe, but turn our backs on a divided kingdom in dire need of guidance?"

Isiilde sighed with relief. So the scroll bearing her father's seal had not been about her, but a request for help.

"This is different. Kambe serves the Guardians," Oenghus said.

"The *Guardians*," N'Jalss hissed. "Your gods—your gods who have not held a Council of Kings for nearly a hundred years."

"How dare you mock the Guardians, you Rahuatl savage!" Tulipin wheezed with outrage.

"At least I'm not a boot-licking pup," N'Jalss hissed back.

"Please, please, gentlemen," Tharios soothed. "Now is not the time for petty squabbles. Look past your prejudices and motives and ask yourselves what is best for this Order?"

Silence followed as tempers cooled.

"There is merit to N'Jalss' words," Tharios continued. "The Guardians have been absent from our lives. We've only had whispers from Iilenshar, and the borders of Morchaint have been strangely quiet. This lull in the Everwar is a sign to build our strength and numbers by uniting the lands against the Void. This Order is stagnate. The Blood-magi are growing in numbers, and what do we do? We bicker and argue."

"It is true. We have grown weak," Shimei agreed.

"We've strayed from the point," Yasimina pointed out.

"When do we not?" Marsais mused. "Cast your say."

Four Wise Ones cast their support for whatever Lachlan's proposal was. The remaining four, including Oenghus, were opposed. And here came the reason for a Circle of Nine—a decision was always reached.

The final say fell on the Archlord's shoulders.

"I won't support this," Marsais said.

N'Jalss hissed in contempt, the ritual scars of his face twisting.

"Then may I make another proposal?" Tharios waited for Marsais' nod of permission. "I propose we send an emissary to the South to observe this Thane. As Tulipin pointed out, we shouldn't close the doors entirely."

This proposal passed unanimously.

Isiilde drew back from the bowl. She felt small and confused. So much anger and fighting. And this from people on the same side.

Marsais was right—her life on the Isle *was* sheltered. But she couldn't worry about distant kingdoms; she had troubles enough of her own. She'd loosed a fiend on the isle, and she had to stop it.

As Isiilde flitted from one teleportation rune to the next to avoid guards, she studied the runes on the flagon.

The runes were deceptively simple. This was the work of Marsais. She was certain of it. That meant it was complex.

Marsais didn't weave crude enchantments; he wove masterpieces that defied logic.

Isiilde paused in an empty storage room to upend the flagon. She gave it a little shake, but nothing fell out. Searching the floor, she picked up a pebble and dropped it into the small opening.

Silence. She gave the flagon another shake, but there was no answering rattle.

Knowing Marsais, the flagon was like his rucksack, with a pocket of space. But the neck of the flagon was long and narrow, bulging out only at the base—how had he fit the imp through the opening? She could only stick two fingers down the flagon's throat.

With a sigh, she checked the corridor outside and darted to the next teleportation rune before a guard patrol made their rounds. She knew their rotation schedules by heart.

A curtain wall on the edge of a cliff connected the Spine to the main Keep. When the weather was calm, she preferred to walk along the ramparts for the ocean view. But not in this storm, so she took the warmer route—a long hallway called the King's Walk.

A row of statues stood in alcoves—rulers of legend who had shaped the face of Fyrsta. She knew them all by name. Isiilde stopped in front of her favorite statue and smiled at the woman's serene face. Her name was Lith, the first queen of Kambe, a faerie.

"I've made a mess of things again," she confessed.

The statue looked down in sympathy.

Isiilde sat at the woman's feet, and leaned against her legs. "I don't suppose you know how this works?" She turned the flagon around in her hands. "Or, barring that, have you seen a flying imp?"

No answer.

As Marsais had said, everything is somewhere, and that could be anywhere. She didn't even know if the imp was still in the castle.

An idea sparked: the flagon might need activating like the Orb of Memory. Isiilde traced several runes over its top, and when that failed, tried touching each rune. But there was no change.

A faint sound tore her attention from the flagon. Her heart skipped a beat; she was not alone—a man stood over her. Neither young nor old, he was soaked to the bone and water puddled around his bare feet. His tattered brown hair was plastered to sunburnt skin, and he wore torn, mud-caked trousers. His chest was bare.

Alarm turned to joy. "Hello, Thedus," she greeted. "You've been walking outside again, haven't you? Not a good day for that."

Thedus didn't reply. He never did. As far as she knew, he was mute. Touched in the head, people claimed. The other Wise Ones were afraid of him. Even Thira. And nearly everyone had warned her away from the wandering madman. But she found his company soothing.

His milky, half-blind eyes drifted slowly over to the statue of the faerie queen.

Isiilde stood to admire the statue, too. "She's beautiful, isn't she?"

She took his silence for agreement.

"Thedus, if I tell you something, do you promise not to tell anyone? I opened this warded flagon, and accidentally let an imp loose in the tower—a winged fiend. I have to trap him in here, but I don't know how. Do you?"

Thedus didn't move for a full five minutes. Then, like the creaking of a rising drawbridge, he touched her arm, his fingertips trailing down her forearm. When he came to her hand, he picked it up, turned her palm face up and pressed something cold into her skin, curling her fingers around the small gift.

Isiilde stared in shock. This was more response than she'd ever received before.

Thedus let her hand fall, then turned and shuffled down the hallway towards the Spine like a Forsaken spirit.

Isiilde narrowed her eyes down at his gift. It was a molar covered in blood.

It took energy to wield the Gift, so Wise Ones had ravenous appetites. Isiilde hoped imps did, too, because she was hungry. And she might as well start looking somewhere.

A few Wise Ones had toyed with Runes of Sustenance, but that research was dropped after a string of lethal poisonings. Summoning food proved dangerous, too. So the stronghold had several mundane kitchens. She headed to the largest.

Isiilde froze in the archway. It looked like a tornado had ripped through the kitchen. A slop of food covered the ceiling, walls, tables, and floor. Pots were askew, utensils littered the floor, and flour dusted the kitchen staff and guards, giving them the appearance of apparitions. They were frantically battling several fires.

The head cook, known as the Ogre, was standing toe-to-toe with Thira, bellowing and shaking a meaty fist beneath her hooked nose.

"You should've seen it earlier," a voice murmured over her shoulder.

She took a quick step forward, whirling around to find a clean-shaven man with slightly pointed ears smiling down at her. It was Stievin, one of the Ogre's assistant cooks.

"What happened?" she asked.

"*Something* is loose in the castle. It swept through here like a banshee, then was gone as quick as it came."

Isiilde quickly hid the flagon in a fold of her skirt.

"Someone thought it was an imp or a cinder cat. I tried to catch it, but it's a slippery thing." He ran a hand through his sandy hair, trying to tame the unruly mass. "I suppose you were hoping for some food, m'lady?"

"It doesn't look like there's much left."

"Anything at all is possible for you. Hold on a minute, and I'll see what I can do." With a flash of white teeth, he plunged into the chaos.

Isiilde pressed herself against a wall, keeping a wary eye on Thira. The last thing she needed was to draw her attention—the Vulture would blame the entire mess on her.

But it was her fault. Though Stievin did say it *might* have been a cinder cat.

Stievin returned, bearing a tray of food. "As promised," he said, lifting the lid with a flourish.

Her mouth started watering.

"Thank you," she said, accepting the tray. His fingers brushed the back of her hands.

"There's not a scrap of meat on the plate."

Isiilde smiled. "Everyone always forgets that I get sick on it." Meat was like poison to a nymph.

"I'm not everyone," Stievin said. "I'd never cause you harm."

Stievin towered over her, and his eyes had always reminded her of chocolate. But just now, his gaze was making her uneasy.

"Speaking of harm," he continued. "With that thing on the loose, I should escort you home."

"Erm… no. Thank you. I'm sure you have a lot of work to do. I'm due back for my lessons." Isiilde bobbed a curtsy and hurried away with her tray.

CHAPTER 14

THE LANKY WISE One shifted in his chair, plucking at his robes with disinterest. The Circle was arguing again over which spy to send to the Thanes.

It didn't matter who they sent. Marsais knew Tharios already had his own spies in place. He was a seer, after all. And it was difficult to fake interest when he knew the ending. Or at least the gist of it.

Why pretend?

He studied the weft of his robes, mulling over the significance of its color. Was the crimson a reminder of the blood that stained an Archlord's hands, or was it intended to conceal?

There would be blood in the South and beyond, a great swath of it as vibrantly dark as the folds of his cloth. All paths led to war. But the misty parts lay in getting there.

Ice formed on the table, creaking as it covered its top.

Marsais leaned forward.

The ground trembled and a blast of icy air cracked the stone into frozen chunks. He looked from the broken table to the ceiling, where a blizzard churned overhead.

"That's not good," he mused.

"Beg your pardon, Archlord?" Eldred asked. But the howling blizzard snatched his words away.

"Marsais," a voice finally cut through the noise.

The blizzard vanished, replaced by two baleful eyes. Oenghus glowered across the table at him. It was undamaged. The storm had been another vision.

"Hmm?" he asked.

The Circle of Nine stared at him like he was mad.

"What does the weather have to do with this?" Shimei asked.

"With what?" Marsais always answered a question with a question when lost.

"The scouts we're sending," Tharios explained.

"I'm sure they'll be well suited to the task," Marsais said. He waited, hoping he'd recall their conversation, but vagueness seemed to satisfy the Circle.

Conversation resumed. And Marsais looked back at the round table.

We protect the past to safeguard the future. The words were etched into stone. But what had knowledge of past mistakes ever accomplished? How many times had history repeated itself?

There would always be those who craved power—like Tharios. He was an easy one to plot; his course was set. But how far would he travel down that path? What would satisfy his thirst?

There lay the problem with the pathways of time: choice. It created a vast sea of possibilities.

Marsais slouched in his chair. The scroll that was tucked beneath his wide sash dug into his ribs like a jab to his heart. There were variants and unknowns, and then there was a certain nymph. The problem with Isiilde was she never knew what she was going to do, so how could he foresee her future with any accuracy?

Chaos spun around her like a whirlwind. Trying to chart her path made his head spin—countless crossroads, intersections, byways, and shortcuts lay at the nymph's feet. And when she started on one path, she often skipped to another, tearing a new path through time.

Marsais blinked, and time rushed forward. The chairs around the table were empty, except for one. Oenghus was staring at him across the expanse of stone.

"They cast their say and called it a day," Oenghus said.

"Hmm, what did I vote?"

"You waved your hand, so they took it as a yes—not that you seemed to care," Oenghus grunted. "You doing all right?"

Marsais shrugged. "There's no simple answer, because if I say *yes*, you will accuse me of lying. And if I answer *no*, you will fuss over me like an old woman. A bit of a conundrum for such a mundane question."

"And if you keep avoiding my question, I'll make bloody well sure you're not all right," Oenghus growled.

"Ever thoughtful, Oen." Marsais stood to stretch. When he'd worked out the kinks in his muscles, he began pacing in thought. "To answer your question... Honestly, I am not well," he finally said, stopping beside his friend.

Marsais wove an Orb of Silence, with a thread of darkness in the enchantment. He couldn't risk spies. Not for this. When the weave had pulsed to life, he tossed a scroll onto the table as if it carried Blight. "From Isiilde's *father*."

Oenghus picked up the letter. The same hands that had wielded a war hammer against hordes of Wedamen now trembled.

"She's not of age yet!" Oenghus roared, surging to his feet. His chair fell over, and he kicked it out of the Orb of Silence as he raged. "Why send emissaries to inspect her if she's not a woman yet? The Pits o' Mourn would be too good a place for that sheep-buggering louse. Curse the bastard. I should have ripped him apart when I had the chance. And to the Pits with the consequences!"

The berserker cast about for something to hit.

Marsais took a calculated step back. "Isiilde *is* of age."

"No." Oenghus shook his head. "She can't be—not yet."

"Isiilde came of age three months ago. The morning she burned down the cottage. She panicked, and lost control."

Oenghus glared, then his shoulders sagged. "By the gods, why didn't she just tell me?"

"Because she knew you were honor-bound to tell the emperor."

"Bollocks," Oenghus snorted. "Why in the bloody Pits did she tell you?"

"She didn't. I only just found out before I came to the council. She took my hand in the library." Marsais lied, but only partially. "You know how careful I am with her, Oen. I was lost in a vision when she touched me."

The memory of her touch shuddered through his body. Hours had passed, yet he still felt her caress.

"Not only is she Awakened, but her blood has begun to stir. I doubt I'm the only man to notice."

"Already?" Oenghus asked. "This soon after... You're sure?"

"You know how... intoxicating nymphs are." Marsais perched on an armrest. "She can't remain unbound for much longer, my friend. You knew this day would come. We both did."

"Not this quick," Oenghus grunted. The braids in his black beard twitched and his fists curled. He turned away, fighting down a swell of emotion. "You say she didn't tell anyone?" There was grit and pain in his voice. "That means there's a spy in the tower, or the bastard would sell her before it's proper."

"I imagine Soataen has several spies on the Isle," Marsais said. "But she's nearly eighteen, Oen. By human standards, that's perfectly acceptable. He's not breaking any laws. Most rulers shove their spare sixteen-year-old daughters into the arms of strangers for profit or alliance."

"Are you siding with that bastard?"

"Of course not. Just because something is common, it doesn't make it right. I'm simply pointing out that he's well within his rights—from his point of view. He could have sold her off at sixteen."

A long stretch of silence followed. Finally, Oenghus stirred. "I can't allow this, Scarecrow."

"Hmm, and here we come back to our conversation of thirteen years past. The question I posed to you—the question to which I already knew the answer. Will you be able to let her go?"

"Curse it!" Oenghus flexed his arms. "It's not as if it's an arrangement between two nobles. She'll be sold as a slave. She won't even have the status of a concubine or fifth Oathbound. Even whores have more choice than she'll have."

"Do you think this is any easier for me?" Marsais cut through the echo of rage. "There isn't a soul I care for more. But what is left for her? By your own words, this is the best chance she has. What you hoped for has happened. Emissaries are being sent from Kiln, Mearcentia, and Xaio—the wealthiest and most powerful kingdoms of the realm. Has anything changed in this realm since you brought a nymphling to my tower some thirteen years back?"

"There's more at stake than you know."

Marsais nearly missed the half-muttered remark. "What exactly is at stake, Oen?"

The berserker ignored his question. "You're being stubborn 'bout all this. Have you had visions about her?"

"I have," Marsais whispered, closing his eyes. "They haven't been... encouraging. The sooner she's bonded, the better."

"What have you seen?" Oenghus loomed like a thundercloud.

"It's complicated," he admitted. "Most of her paths are unbearable. I dare not speak them aloud." His voice faltered. "Mearcentia would be best for her, but somehow her Fate is intertwined with events brewing in the South. I'm trying to sort them out, but it's like navigating the Labyrinth of Pillars at high tide with a leaky hull. That faerie you call a daughter is the most perplexing woman I've come across for over a millennium."

"I'd expect no less," Oenghus muttered. "I suppose there's no use telling her until they arrive. Why spoil the time she has left?"

Marsais said nothing more; he didn't trust himself to speak.

CHAPTER 15

"Psst."

Coyle looked up from the sharpening stone. It rolled to a stop when he saw the nymph. Her face peeked from around a corner of a side building.

Coyle glanced over his shoulder at his master, who was busy at the anvil. "What are you doing here, Isiilde?"

She held up a basket. "You wanted to have lunch."

Coyle hurried over. "I'm supposed to be working."

"And I'm not supposed to be here," she said with a shrug.

Her green eyes danced with mischief. How could he resist those eyes?

"Here, hold this." Coyle handed her the sword. But the moment it touched her hand, she let go and it fell to the dirt.

Coyle darted back to retrieve his shirt from a post. He shrugged it on and smoothed back his unruly hair. When he returned, he found Isiilde staring down at the sword as if it were tainted. "Is something the matter?" he asked with concern.

"I don't like swords."

"Why not?" he asked.

The nymph lifted a shoulder as she led him behind the building to a spot between a wall and shrubbery. Apprentices used the spot to sneak in a nap.

Coyle cleaned the dirt off the blade with his shirt. He gave it a twirl, testing the balance. "There's an art to swordsmithing."

"It's used to kill," she pointed out.

"But it's beautiful, like you." He gave her a lopsided smile and was pleased when her freckles turn pink.

Isiilde sat in the grass, opening her basket and handing him a cucumber sandwich. Coyle settled beside her with the sword balanced across his thighs. Half the sandwich was gone in a single bite.

"It's the steel, I think. It doesn't burn."

"But it melts," he said around a mouthful.

"I have more in here."

"Anything with meat?"

She wrinkled her nose. "No. It's like poison to me."

"Really?"

She nodded. "Same with steel, I suppose. It's like... dead fire."

Coyle chuckled. "Fire isn't alive."

"Yes, it is."

Coyle couldn't tell if she was joking, but he didn't want to argue with her, so he changed the subject.

"There's a lot of work that goes into this—take this style of forging," he held up the sword, "It's called pattern welding. It's forged from different pieces of metal. Hardened steel on the outside of the blade, and softer steel in the center. The center is made from several strands which are twisted and hammered into a pattern. We take them all, and forge weld them together and hammer it into shape. And see, we clip a V in the tip, and take the hardened edges and weld them to a point. Then we acid etch it, and the patterns of the different types of steel show up."

Coyle was excited now. He loved steel. Warming to the subject, he went on to explain all the different techniques of swordsmithing. There were a lot.

Three sandwiches in, and he finally stopped, a blush spreading over his cheeks. "Watch this..." He breathed on the blade, and a spiraling dragon appeared to climb from the hilt. It vanished with his breath.

"It is pretty," she admitted.

"And swords aren't just used to kill; they're used to defend, too."

"True. Oenghus carries his war hammer when he expects trouble. He was armed with more when we traveled to the Alderwood."

Coyle nearly choked on a grape. "You've traveled there?"

Isiilde tilted her head. "Haven't you?"

"It's too dangerous."

"I suppose..."

"I make swords, but I'm no swordsman." He frowned at the blade, and with a sigh, laid it back on his knees.

"If you want to go, I'm sure Marsais would take me. You could happen to meet us on the road."

"Are you mad?"

"Not yet."

Coyle stared at her, confused.

Isiilde hugged her knees, resting her chin on their tops. "If you could travel anywhere, where would you go?"

"Honestly? I like it here. The island is my home. The mainland is too dangerous. Look at all the trouble that imp has been causing. Have you seen it yet?"

"Hmm," she replied. "You don't happen to know where it is, do you?" There was hope in her voice.

"It came by here... we swatted it into a lit kiln."

Her ears perked. "Did you kill it?"

"You'd think." Coyle sighed. "The fiend was burnt to a crisp—a charred, blackened thing. And when we were celebrating, it hopped up, and tried to claw Hamish's eyes out."

Isiilde cringed. "Would you let me know if you spot it again?"

"I'll try. Not sure there will be time, though. He's a quick one."

And tricky, she thought grimly. Isiilde didn't want to dwell on the imp overly long, so she steered him onto other topics. "So, barring danger, where would you like to travel?"

Isiilde watched him chew. He had a strong jaw, a large mouth, and the appetite of a Wise One. "I've thought of traveling to the south side."

She brightened. "To the Spotted Coast?"

"No, to the south side of the island."

"Oh."

"What about you?" he asked.

"To the Spotted Coast. I hear it's always hot. There's no snow or ice."

"Sounds miserable."

"You don't like hot weather?"

Coyle shook his head. "It makes forging difficult. The weather here is perfect for forging. I can't imagine working in the heat and dealing with the forges. Besides, there are pirates."

"Speaking of pirates... Does your forge get shipments of things? Materials for forging."

"We do. Things like exotic woods and raw metals that can't be found here."

"Do you know any of the merchant captains?"

Coyle nodded. "I sometimes pick up the order for Master Helwick."

"Could you help me arrange passage on a ship? I have coin to pay."

Coyle rubbed the back of his neck. "Why do you want to leave?"

"I'm going to be sold, Coyle. To the highest bidder."

He frowned at the sword in his lap. "But you're a princess. I mean... it can't be that bad."

She stared at him.

"What I mean..." he hesitated, shifting. "Look, I'm practically enslaved as an apprentice. It's not all bad. I have work, and food, and a roof over my head. Maybe one day... I'll be a master blade smith. But that won't be for a long while. It will be years before I can even think of having the freedom to do what I please—years of hard work. Even this lunch here... I could get in trouble for taking a break. You won't even need to work."

Isiilde felt suddenly sick.

Coyle leaned forward and put his hand over hers. "Look, I'm sorry. It's just rough out there. I'm thankful for what I have."

It was a curious sensation, his hand over hers. His touch was not unwelcome, but she had no desire to explore the shape of his hand, to press her palm against his, and linger in the moment. He drew away.

"Will you help me?" she asked softly.

"I can give you a name. But that's all. I'm sorry."

A name would have to do. After he told her to try the captain of the

Swallow, she took out her pouch of stones for King's Folly. "Do you play?" she asked.

"The lord's game?"

She started laying out the rune etched stones in a swirling pattern.

"I never have time for games," he admitted. "But I've played some."

"That's all right, I'll go easy on you."

He frowned down at the stones. "Isiilde..."

"Hmm?"

"If I help you find a ship... would you do something for me?"

She paused and looked at him. "What?"

"There's, uhm... a legend about a certain type of steel. It would help me out—in my apprenticeship. I might even advance."

"I'd love to help you, Coyle."

Coyle took a deep breath. "The legend says that the piss of a virgin nymph will imbue steel with..."

Isiilde scooped up her stones, and left.

CHAPTER 16

THE HIGH-PITCHED VOICE of Tulipin Tuddleberry grated on her ears. She usually enjoyed the levitating gnome's lectures. But not today.

Virgin piss.

"Isiilde Jaal'Yasine!" She snapped to attention.

Master Tulipin hovered over her. "What does a monkey with wings have to do with the founding of the Blessed Order?"

Every pair of eyes in the lecture hall focused on her.

"I'm sure the Order has to slay imps all the time," she answered.

"Bah, imps." Tulipin rolled his eyes. "Nothing but rats. Do you think the paladins have nothing better to do with their time than waste it on vermin?"

"They do seem to be busy torturing people and running down faerie," she agreed, without thinking.

Tulipin's eyes bulged. "I'll not tolerate disrespect for the paladins. Leave. Now. And don't return until you've written a report on the *entire* history of the Blessed Order."

In the sea of disapproving faces, Zianna's eyes flashed with delight. Isiilde stuffed her scrolls in her bag, and rushed past the pair of guards by the door.

How could she write the history of the Blessed Order when she wasn't allowed in the libraries? And what was the point? It wasn't as if she had a future as a Wise One. Not like Coyle had a future as a blade-smith. At least he was working towards something.

Isiilde pressed her lips together as two whispering servants passed her in the hallway. She felt eyes on her back, and she wanted to turn around and shout at them to stop staring.

It had been two days of havoc since she'd released the imp, and she was no closer to capturing it. Others had tried, like the smithies, and failed.

Thira had already come accusing. And Oenghus had nearly come to blows with the woman. But in this one instance, Thira's accusations were correct—it *was* Isiilde's fault.

It seemed everyone in the castle had seen the fiend somewhere or another. Except Isiilde. She'd been searching the stronghold for two days.

Marsais had been no help at all. He'd barely said two words since he dumped *Baiting and Binding* into her arms.

Baiting.

Every kitchen had been ransacked by the imp. Maybe it was after food?

The thought made her stomach grumble. Yes, the kitchens were a good place to start today.

Guards were posted at the kitchen entrance. They stiffened at her approach, warily watching her. Isiilde often wondered what orders the Guard Captain had given the guards. Were they supposed to protect her, or protect others *from* her?

Neither one of the women returned her smile. They never did.

Order had been restored to the main kitchen. The aromas of sweet bread, pastries, honey-smeared loaves, and freshly baked pies filled the air.

She stopped in front of a table laden with pies, her mouth watering. What would attract the imp?

"Back for more, m'lady?" a voice asked.

She turned to find Stievin standing at her shoulder. Exhaustion shadowed his eyes.

"Most people, nymphs included, have to eat daily," she pointed out. "And this kitchen has the best food."

The ovens made the kitchens swelter. Sweat glistened on his throat and the skin at his open collar. She felt suddenly hot. And focused on the ovens instead.

"It's a competition," he said, flashing a grin. "Only the best work here. What is tempting your palate today, m'lady?"

"Could I bother you for another plate? And one for Oenghus as well?"

"It's no bother at all. We have strawberries today that will make your mouth water." Stievin practically caressed the last two words with his voice.

"I do love strawberries," she admitted.

"I know."

Isiilde tilted her head in thought. "There's hardly any sunlight on the Isle, and yet there are always strawberries—even at our cottage. Where do they all come from?"

"Regular shipments from the South," Stievin explained. "The Archlord charters a swift ship to import them regularly."

"Why would he do that?" she asked.

Stievin lifted a shoulder. "Maybe he likes strawberries, too." He favored her with another smile before wading into the kitchens.

As Stievin departed, Isiilde studied him, admiring how his trousers hugged his backside. Her breath quickened, and her heart fluttered strangely. She felt dizzy.

The fires in the ovens roared to life, spitting out heat. Servants leapt back, others ducked, more screamed, and a few failed to dodge the bursts of fire.

For the second time in two days, the kitchen was thrown into chaos. The staff hurried to douse the flames and the guards bolted from their posts, rushing inside with drawn swords.

They thought it was the fiend again.

Isiilde squeezed her eyes shut, afraid to move—afraid of the heat stirring in her veins. The charred corpse of Miera Malzeen flashed in her mind's eye, and she fled the kitchens.

On the other side of the archway, she slumped against a wall, turning her back on the frenzy of activity.

A Wise One has control, she repeated over and over in her mind. But the more she fought for control, the more panicked she became, until she could hardly draw breath.

The corridor spun. She slumped against a wall, pressing her forehead to the stone. *What was happening?* She felt trapped.

"Aren't you supposed to be at Tulipin's lecture?"

Head pressed to the stone, she rolled her eyes towards the voice. Marsais. He stood beside her, a hand on her back, his grey eyes filled with concern.

"What's wrong?"

"I do not feel well."

It felt like her heart was trying to climb out of her throat. When she tried to straighten from the wall, the corridor shifted violently beneath her feet.

Marsais caught her around the waist. "Isiilde. Look at me." She met his eyes and they drew her in, away from the crushing stone and stifling fear. "Everything will be all right," he said gently.

Isiilde was dimly aware of approaching footsteps. Marsais stiffened, his hands tightening around her waist as he focused on a point over her shoulder.

"Take my arm," he ordered. She did as he asked, leaning against him for support.

"Archlord." Stievin stopped in the corridor, bowing easily despite the heavy tray in his hands.

"Cook's Steward Stievin," Marsais stated.

"I was just preparing a tray for Lady Isiilde and Master Oenghus. I managed to get your strawberries before the commotion," Stievin added, glancing at her.

"Hmm." Marsais was staring at the cook as if he'd sprouted wings.

Stievin shifted uncomfortably. "Do you require food as well, Archlord?"

"Food? No. I've just come from the kitchens." With this odd remark, he took the tray from Stievin, balancing it on one hand.

Marsais stared at the cook. The intensity in that gaze made Stievin take a step back. He hastily bowed, and hurried away with a murmured 'Archlord.'

"WHERE ARE WE GOING?" she whispered, after Marsais had missed the turn that led to the infirmary.

"Hmm?"

She sighed at his answer. It didn't matter where they went, as long as he stayed with her.

As they walked, she calmed. Her breath returned, but the wash of emotion had left her exhausted, so she clung to his arm.

"I thought we might take the shortcut through the gardens," he said at length.

"Isn't it still raining?"

Marsais shrugged. "Perhaps."

As it turned out, it wasn't raining. It was storming. Sheets of icy water pounded the earth.

"I don't have a cloak, Marsais," she said, squinting through a narrow arrow loop.

In answer, he unwound his arm from hers. The Lore sprang to his lips, a soft whisper drowned out by the heavy beat of raindrops. He traced a series of quick runes over the tray in his hand. When he had completed the weave, he tugged on invisible strands and the tray rose from his fingertips, floating solidly in midair.

Marsais swung off his cloak and draped it over her shoulders.

"But you'll get wet," she protested.

"That is generally what happens when one goes out in such weather." He sniffed at his robes. "Besides, I think I've forgotten to bathe."

Isiilde cringed as he threw the door open. A sheet of chilling water pelted her, and she leaned into Marsais, using him as a buffer against the wind. With the tray drifting obediently in their wake, he hurled them into the storm.

It was wet, cold, and for once, she didn't mind. With every step through the garden, her head cleared and a weight of stone lifted from her chest. Isiilde took a deep breath. It felt like her first in two days.

Marsais led her beneath the broad limbs of a pine grove. Soft moss clung to their trunks, clothing them in a garment of lush green. Gentle raindrops slipped through the protective canopy above, falling softly to the earth.

Marsais let the tray drift to the ground, and then helped her sit beside a tree. She rested against its softness, breathing in scents of rebirth and gentle decay, listening to the pulse of the earth—one beat drifting to the next, calming her fluttering heart, until the worries of the day had faded into memory.

Senses renewed, curiosity restored, she opened her eyes to discover that she had been abandoned. Marsais stood some distance away on the unsheltered path, his shoulders thrown back and face raised to the storm. He swayed like a reed in the wind.

Water ran in rivulets down his hair and face, and he glistened beautifully in the rain. The sight brought a smile to her lips. Nature suited him. He seemed more vibrant. Alive. Enchanting even.

Greatly cheered, she plucked the cover off the tray to survey the feast before applying herself to a selection of its delicacies. Halfway through a honey-smeared bun, Marsais returned—soaked to the bone.

"I don't think that counts as a bath," she said, licking her sticky fingers.

"You sound like my mother." Marsais shook himself off, sending a spray of droplets her way. He ignored her glare and squeezed out the excess water from his hair and robes.

"If you forgot to bathe, then I'm sure you've forgotten to eat as well." She pointed at the food she had set aside for him. "You can have some strawberries, too. Stievin gave me more than enough." Her words brought Marsais up short, caught midway in wringing out his braided goatee.

"Are you feeling better?" he asked.

"Much better. I'm not really sure what happened. I..." She trailed off, unable to explain what she did not understand.

"We forget that we haven't always lived under these stone monstrosities of mortar and timber. In times past, in those long-forgotten days, people slept beneath a blanket of stars on a soft mattress of moss and earth."

Marsais settled beside her, leaning his back against the tree.

"It sounds wet."

"A little fresh air will do wonders for the mind and body, especially for a faerie, even if it's wet," he said, tossing a strawberry into his mouth, stem and all. (He seemed not to notice, so she didn't bother pointing it out.) She eyed a strawberry tart sitting innocently on the tray. After a brief internal debate, she broke it in half to share.

"Marsais?"

"Isiilde?"

She ignored the mirth in his eyes. "Who was your mother, and where were you born?" The question embarrassed her. Not because she'd asked, but because she'd never considered that Marsais started life much the same as everyone else.

"My mother," he began between mouthfuls, "was a woman."

Isiilde inhaled her tart, then collapsed in helpless laughter.

"I gathered that much," she finally managed, recovering her breath, along with a small measure of composure.

"I'm trying to remember," he grumbled, stroking his goatee.

Isiilde let him think. She finished her tart and started on a baked apple.

Finally, he elaborated, "My mother was a beautiful woman, although that's not especially rare. Hmm, most creatures of womanly nature are. She was a druid who was Oathbound to the king of the land. I suppose she was a queen of sorts."

"Your father was a king and your mother a druid?" Her eyes went wide. She forgot about her apple, and it fell. Marsais snatched it from the air.

"I believe I just said that," he remarked, stealing a bite. As Marsais had told her at the festival so long ago, druids were once respected, but now their names were whispered like a curse, and they were as reviled as Voidspawn and Wedamen barbarians, or Vaylinish scum.

"So you are an elf—a faerie." She eyed his pointed ears. She'd always assumed he was Kamberian, but the tips were finer than most.

He seemed to read her thoughts. "Kamberians are descendants of elven and human unions—something that was frowned upon before the Shattering. There isn't much faerie blood in them these days."

"But you are one?"

"My blood is ancient," he said, quietly. "I'm one of the last of my kind."

"There are others? Who?"

"The Guardians. And a handful of others. Not many Lindale are left."

"Oh." She eyed his white hair in thought. "Your mother... Did she side with Ramashan, too?"

"Not all the druids aided Ramashan when he opened a Gateway to the Nine Halls. Time has a way of muddling things, and people like to group the druids together."

Isiilde noted that he hadn't answered her question. She didn't press him.

"It's convenient," she said.

"Precisely."

"Were you a king?"

"Before the Shattering."

Marsais rarely talked about the cataclysmic event, at least not in any detail. But he'd lived through that horrible time more than two thousand years past. Thinking about his age always gave her a headache, especially now—when he was leaning casually against a tree, one long leg bent, an elbow resting on his knee.

Shouldn't he be distant and reserved? Instead, his eyes creased when he laughed, and she savored the slight upturn of his lips when he found something amusing.

Immortals should not be so... So many words swirled in her heart. All of them good. Marsais was as solid and welcoming as the tree at her back.

But his eyes were filled with mist. Her question had sparked some long-buried memory.

"Where was your kingdom?" she asked softly.

"It's long faded, my dear. Most of my kingdom was destroyed during the Shattering, swallowed up by the chasms that split the realm. Half lies at the bottom of the Eastern Gap, and the other sits along a river in Vaylin that once flowed into the seas of the Bitter Coast. It was a beautiful land, thick with redwood groves, and ferns taller than me. We were simple people who lived along the rivers: fishermen and trappers who worshipped the spirits that shared our lands. There's nothing left of them."

"You are here, and I'm glad of it."

Sympathy moved her, compassion commanded, and desire demanded that she breach the space. The nymph reached out to him, running her fingertips along the back of his elegant hand, wishing she could take his pain away. His skin was warm, inviting, and the feel of him melted her insides.

Marsais sucked in a sharp breath. His hand quivered beneath her touch and then he snatched it away, rising to his feet with an abruptness that startled her.

"Oen's food will get cold," he said hoarsely. He levitated the tray from the ground with a sharp gesture. His reaction wounded her, and she stared at his boots, feeling at a loss, wondering why he would react so strongly to her touch. If she had angered him, why didn't he say so?

"Are you staying here?" he asked, keeping his eyes on the path ahead.

In reply, she climbed to her feet, pulling down the cowl of her borrowed cloak. Marsais didn't offer his arm, but took off down the path with long strides, leaving her to hurry in his wake.

THEY WALKED clear across the garden courtyard. And when they arrived at a side door, he opened it for her.

Isiilde hurried inside. Ever optimistic, she pretended that the awkward moment had never occurred.

"Marsais?"

"Hmm." He slowed his pace, matching her stride so they might walk side by side.

"How did you make the tray float? It looked different from the Weave of Levitation that you showed me, but I missed most of the runes."

Marsais stopped, surprised by her interest. "Splendid, this will be your lesson for today." He changed their course, heading to a cushioned bench in an alcove, then dipped two fingers beneath his wide sash and brought out a gold crown.

"Do you recall the feather rune?"

Isiilde nodded, hanging her cloak on a nearby sconce.

"Good. One rune that I failed to show you is the binding rune. I levitated the tray and then bound it to me, much like one leads a horse." His fingers moved with graceful confidence as he traced the binding rune, leaving a gossamer outline floating in the air.

It always helped her to imagine the rune mark as something else, and this one reminded her of a knotted rope, which made perfect sense (as usual).

"You must be careful when you bind a rune to an object. This particular one is very gentle, but if I used a stronger bind on a feather rune, then it would crush the feather, which could backfire and result in an ill occurrence." There was a warning in his words, but Isiilde's quick mind had already leapt ahead with understanding.

She plucked the coin from his fingers, and uttered the Lore as her fingers flashed, weaving the feather rune deftly around the coin. The Lore's guttural tones grated on her delicate ears, but the discordant tune did not stop her from wading into the surging currents of power.

The binding rune was a complicated mark, and the weave took some concentrated effort on her part. When she was satisfied with her efforts, she let her voice fade, and felt the wash of power perish with it.

There was always danger when one used the Gift. Many found it difficult to drag themselves from the strong currents of energy. The promise of power, Marsais had once explained, was a deadly lure. But in greediness, some waded in deeper and deeper, drawing more of the Gift than they could handle, until it was impossible to return to their bodies. But Isiilde was never tempted by the Gift—it paled in comparison to the siren call of her fire.

As the last command left her lips, she let go of the coin and proudly watched it float in the air, bound to her fingertips by an invisible thread.

"Perfect as always."

"Not quite." She gave him a secretive glance and then began to sing.

This was what her blood yearned for—not the harsh language of the Wise Ones that bullied the streams of power, but her pure, flowing voice melding flawlessly with the Gift.

The nymph's voice was a gentle breeze, an intimate whisper, tickling the ears of all who breathed. There was no place for crude words on her tongue; thought and emotion mingled to form sound.

She sang to the flickering torches set along the wall, luring a tendril of flame to her outstretched palm as one might coax a sparrow with seed.

The nymph's blood stirred, hot and vibrant in her veins as she watched the flame's seductive dance. And with her voice, she won its devotion.

Sensitive to her whims, the flame sprang eagerly from her palm to hover in the air beside the coin. She stirred her finger in its blazing heat, and it danced around the suspended coin for her delight, creating a halo of fire around a circle of gold.

The flaming torches surged, crackling for her attention. With a call of her voice, she allowed her subjects to join in the spinning dance. The gold was surrounded by a cage of fire, rolling one over the other.

The lonely coin was helpless. The flame's intensity melted its metal. Liquid gold swirled with fire, and Isiilde gasped with pleasure—a sound more suited to a bedchamber.

The intimate merging aroused her desire, feeding her passion, and therefore her fire. Her voice rose with intensity, fevered and hurried. Every torch in the corridor leapt to her whim, merging to create a swirling ball of flame that entranced her with its complexities.

Another voice interrupted her melody, overshadowing her song with harsh, discordant tones. As quickly as she had formed it, Marsais wove a bind to her creation and plucked it from her control. She felt like a mother whose child had just been snatched from her arms.

Her emerald eyes blazed and her song changed to fury.

The fire in the torches leapt to her defense, hurling towards this new, unwanted master. But Marsais was prepared, and with a quick flash of his deft hands, her fire dispersed, sending a shower of harmless sparks scattering against the stone.

All that was left of the coin swirled to the ground—a mere splash of color.

Isiilde cried out, collapsing to the stone in a quivering heap. Her lungs constricted with terror, leaving her struggling to draw breath. Every inch of her body ached, her skin sizzled with heat, and she thought her heart would burst.

"*Isiilde*," Marsais' commanding voice broke through her panic. "Look at me. You *must* calm down." But fire blinded her, and the memory of its seductive roar consumed her, leaving her body unsatisfied and aching for more.

Marsais cursed under his breath, grabbed the wet cloak from the sconce, and draped it over her back. Steam hissed into the air as moisture touched her flesh, cooling her skin and leaving her shivering on the floor. She was dimly aware of Marsais kneeling beside her to loosen the laces of her bodice. When the confining garment was undone, her breath came easier.

"What's happening to me?" She looked to the grey eyes so close to her own, and they softened. A hand reached out to comfort her, but his touch fell short, brushing the air over her cheek instead.

"I'd say you owe me a gold crown."

Isiilde let out a shuddering breath, and promptly passed out.

CHAPTER 17

The gentle patter of rain sang softly in her ears, pulling her from darkness into a hazy in-between. Hushed conversations lingered at the edge. A hand rested on her forehead, and she cracked her eyes open.

Morigan smiled down at her. "Have a drink."

Isiilde scooted upright against a pillow and drank. It tasted of lemon, spice, and honey.

"I've had several children. But I've never had one who attracts trouble like you. That's saying a lot."

"At least I keep things interesting."

Morigan laughed. "Oh, child, you have no idea."

"What happened to me?"

Her memories seemed a dream. Fire, heat, and fear.

Morigan sighed. "I'm not sure anyone knows. Marsais carried you in. You were cold as snow, and just as pale. I've never seen him so frantic; it takes a lot to fluster that one. Which reminds me, I'd best get Oen and send word to Marsais. We've all been worried about you." Morigan kissed her on the forehead, and left.

Isiilde sighed. She was in the infirmary. Again. And judging by the darkness, night had fallen.

It wasn't long before Oenghus ducked through the door. He made the room feel cramped and overcrowded.

Isiilde steeled herself for another lecture.

"How are you feeling?" He sat on the edge of the bed to feel her forehead.

"Exhausted."

"Drink up the rest of that."

"Do you know what happened to me, Oen?"

"I don't know," he grunted, tugging on his braided beard. "And neither does Marsais. If you were a horse, I'd say that someone tried to run you to death."

"I sometimes wonder if you are trying to work me to death."

"Bah, you know what I mean. Least I know you're all right if you can be cheeky." Isiilde poked the back of his hand, and the two shared a smile before he continued. "Marsais said you lost control."

"I know I always say this... but I didn't mean to," she said with a sigh.

He silenced her with a shake of his head. "There's no harm done. I'm worried about you, is all. You... you should have told me you came of age."

The blood drained from her face. And Oenghus leaned closer.

"I'm not gonna tell Soataen. I'm a barbarian, remember? We're as dishonorable as they come, so I can break my word when it pleases me."

"You're the most honorable man I know."

"Well, you don't know very many." Oenghus snorted, but the swarthy slice of skin above his beard darkened, and he shifted, averting his eyes.

"Please, Oen, don't let him sell me," she whispered. He did not answer, only leaned forward to kiss her forehead. The tears that fell on her face were not her own.

CHAPTER 18

A PALE SUN greeted Isiilde the following day. The shutters had been wedged open, inviting crisp air into her room. A soft breeze rustled the leaves, tugging them gently from their summer perches, before hurling them towards the sea.

Isiilde could taste the salt in the air and hear the plaintive calls of seagulls over the lull of the surf far below.

Oenghus came in carrying a tray. "Figured you'd be awake. You never could sleep past lunch."

Isiilde sat up when he set the tray down. She was ravenous. "You look exhausted, Oen," she said around a mouthful of food.

"Aye, we've had a lot of injuries."

"What happened?"

"That blasted imp happened."

Isiilde nearly choked on a piece of bread.

"Mostly minor injuries: broken bones, blows to the head, and a lot of people who had their teeth ripped out while they slept." He scratched at his beard in bewilderment. "But last night, the fiend weakened the chains to the portcullis and timed it so the gate fell on a guard. Not much left of the poor bastard." A knot twisted in her stomach. "Oh, don't worry, Sprite, it's only an imp—more pest than threat."

"It killed someone," she squeaked.

"So do ladders and slippery stairs. Besides, I've warded this room, so it won't be bothering you."

"Hasn't anyone tried catching him?"

"Every blasted Wise One in the castle. But their traps have caused just as many injuries as the imp's trickery. He's a slippery little fiend and the strange thing is… half the people claim they've killed him already." Oenghus shrugged, and he thought no more of it, tapping a thick stack of scrolls on a bedside table. "Since you'll be resting for another day—" She started to protest, but he cut her off. "You might as well get busy writing the history of the bloody Blessed Order."

Isiilde ground her teeth together. "I have other things to do, Oen."

"Like what? Sleep? Eat strawberries?"

She stayed silent.

"Tulipin came floating down this morning to chew me out for your behavior."

"But—"

"You're not going to weasel your way out of this one."

Before he could surrender to her pleading eyes, Oenghus stalked out of the room. He forgot to duck beneath the doorway and smacked his head on the lintel. It left a dent in the wood.

Isiilde climbed out of bed and slammed the door shut on his heels. She slipped out of her nightgown, tossed it on the floor, and sprawled on top of the bed to let the sun soothe her agitation.

Fine, she'd write the report. And then catch the imp. She glanced at the stack of scrolls and decided reading them would take too long. So she wrote her own report. From what she'd read and heard—from a nymph's perspective.

By the time she finished, the sun was falling. After closing the shutters on the creeping chill, she crawled beneath a blanket. The sheepskin felt divine against her body.

Marsais had not come to visit.

Isiilde sighed at the thought of him. What had happened to her?

Someone knocked so hard that mortar crumbled to the floor. Oenghus. When he stepped inside, he looked exhausted.

"I finished a while ago," she told him.

"Thank you." His soft reply confused her. "Do you want to sleep here or in your own bed? I, for one, would like to get out of this damn place."

She hopped from beneath the covers, gathering her things.

"Blast it, girl!" he growled. "You're too old to be bounding around naked."

"Hardly, Oen," she defended. "Remember, I'm a nymph—not a girl. Here, hold these." She stuffed her papers into his arms and picked up her clothes.

It was a long way back to the Spine. And her exhaustion returned. Oenghus slowed his pace, offering his arm for support.

She was focusing on the scuffing of her slippers when a blur of movement sped across the corridor ahead. It zipped into a temple.

"Oen," she hissed.

"I see it," he said, stalking toward the corner.

Isiilde peeked around his bulk at a hallway. A pair of gilded doors waited at its end. One door was cracked open. It led into a golden temple dedicated to Zahra, the Guardian of Righteousness. Her heart fluttered with excitement, but mostly fear.

Oenghus motioned her to stay, then moved down the hallway towards the shrine. He eased the door open and stepped inside.

Long moments passed—moments that Isiilde spent chewing nervously on her lip. What if the imp snuck past Oenghus and darted out here?

Isiilde eyed the lonely corridors. Perhaps she should run for help? Oenghus was formidable, but he wasn't invincible.

Concern overcame fear. Isiilde darted towards the doors, slipping inside the torch-lit chamber. And instantly regretted it. Gripped with fear, she pressed her back against the door. It moved, and clicked shut.

Oenghus glanced over his shoulder. She gave him a little wave, and he muttered something under his breath.

The chamber was long, with evenly spaced columns. Deep pools of shadow drowned the flickering torchlight set in alcoves. A painting hung in each alcove, depicting the gleaming goddess and her fearless struggle against the Void. The Dark One's own eyes seemed to gleam from the shadows while Zahra's radiant gaze burst with light. Zahra was encased in golden plate mail, white hair billowing behind her, as radiantly fearsome as the shadowed figure she fought.

With barely a sound, Isiilde darted down the chamber towards Oenghus. She stuck close to his back. And every time she stepped into a pool of shadow, she squeezed her eyes shut.

During one moment of blackness, Oenghus stopped. Isiilde collided with him, but he steadied her with a hand. Stuck between terror and curiosity, she clutched the back of his shirt, glancing from shadow to shadow.

She didn't have the rune-etched flagon with her. Damn.

Oenghus moved under an arch that led into a horseshoe-shaped prayer room. Warm candles lined the tiled walls, illuminating a fountain in the center. A golden statue of Zahra knelt by the edge of the shallow basin.

A clawed monkey's paw curled over the goddess' shoulder, and Isiilde bit back a scream. A heartbeat later, she heard an odd chattering. Then the fiend climbed on top of Zahra's head. It looked like a greasy monkey with big leathery wings, except its fingers and toes ended in curving claws. Its lashing tail was barbed and its mouth wide, with an odd assortment of mismatched teeth.

The imp danced on top of Zahra's head, teeth chattering in what she realized was a song.

Oenghus invoked the Lore under his breath. His fingers moved at his side, tracing an unknown combination of runes.

The imp froze on the statue's head, and began pissing into the sacred fountain. The stench of its urine made her gag.

Oenghus thrust his hand towards the creature, and a crackling chain of lightning burst from his fingertips. The bolt blew Zahra's head to pieces.

The imp launched into the air with a wild flapping of wings, but not before the charge of energy hit the spray of urine. It screeched, bouncing off the walls in agony.

"Bollocks!" Oenghus ran into the chamber, hurling another bolt. But the imp spiraled under the wave of crackling energy.

The charge punched through the wall. Jagged shards of stone and tile rained onto the floor as the imp shot through the air, its deadly tail slashing over her hair.

Isiilde spun. A bristling hound materialized in the imp's wake. It charged her with gleaming eyes and a pelt of deadly spikes standing on end.

Oenghus shoved her to the side, rushing forward to meet the giant hound. She poked her head around the corner in time to see the hound leap for Oenghus' throat. Her scream pierced the chaos. But the hound never connected with his throat. It passed right through him.

Oenghus ignored the hound and kept running. He thrust out a hand, hurling an enchantment towards the exit. And before the imp could scamper out, a sealing rune flared to life on the double doors.

The fiendish hound skidded on the polished floor, snarling its frustration, until its cold eyes locked on her.

"Oen!" Isiilde screamed.

But it wasn't the berserker who responded to her call—the torches surged, flaring to her defense, leaping gleefully towards the hound. Fire passed right through, creating a storm of embers that greedily licked at the oil paintings.

"It's not real," he bellowed.

The hound might not be, but her fear was.

In a blind panic, she bolted down the main chamber with the beast breathing down her neck. Isiilde tripped on her skirts, falling to the stone as the hound leapt. Pain split her chin and torches flared at her cry. She squeezed her eyes shut. But death never came.

Isiilde risked a peek at the snarling beast on her back. A mouthful of fangs lunged towards her face, passing right through flesh and bone, leaving her terror-filled body unharmed.

An illusion conjured by the imp, and nothing more. Feeling foolish, she wiped the blood from her chin and climbed back to her feet. For principle's sake, she kicked the apparition, but her foot passed right through, and she nearly slipped in the blood on the floor.

The imp flapped back down the burning hall towards the prayer room, zipping past her with a lash of its razor tail. Oenghus barreled after it, chucking his knife at the fiend. The hilt slammed into the imp's head, sending it spiraling through the air. The imp hit what remained of Zahra's statue, bounced off, and fell into the sacred pool.

Oenghus threw another crackling bolt into the basin, agitating the water to life. But he misjudged the power of his weave. The delicate fountain exploded.

The imp twitched, screeching in pain as its body convulsed like a fish on shore, flopping pathetically in the sizzling puddle of water.

Isiilde covered her ears, watching the fiend's convulsions. Eventually, the charge sputtered out, and the imp went limp.

Isiilde wrinkled her nose at the overcooked fiend.

Oenghus walked over to the little carcass and kicked it, sending it flying into the decapitated statue. "Bloody bastard."

"Is it dead?"

"It better be." He glanced at her, his eyes widening in alarm. "Let me see that." He lowered himself to one knee and lifted her chin to examine the gash. "I thought I told you to stay outside."

"I misinterpreted your gesture," she explained.

Oenghus snorted, wiped his hand carelessly on his kilt, and stomped over to the dead imp. He snatched it up by its tail and tucked it under his belt so its head dangled towards the ground.

"You've made a mess, Oen," Isiilde pointed out. Zahra's serene head lay some distance from her body. "I don't think Zahra and the Sylph will be happy with you."

"She's never happy with me," he muttered. "And you're not one to be talking, Sprite." He gestured toward the smoke-filled chamber and its burning paintings, canvases curling as fire licked at their oiled flesh.

"They look better on fire."

Oenghus chuckled. "I suppose we'd better find someone to clean up this mess."

But someone had already heard the commotion and smelled the smoke. Clerics and acolytes came rushing into the temple. The clerics sent their acolytes for buckets, then turned on Oenghus.

He ignored their wrath, pushing his way through with the imp thumping against his thigh. Isiilde followed on his heels, poking miserably at her chin.

Without warning, the imp sprang back to life. With a flash of teeth and claws, it attacked his leg. He bellowed, ripping the thing off and slamming it against the stone. The imp bounced, then flapped, taking to the air with a squeal of delight.

They watched its flight in gaping silence.

"I thought it was dead," she finally whispered when it had flown out of sight.

"It was."

"You're bleeding, Oen."

He grumbled like an irritated bear.

CHAPTER 19

Determined to catch the imp, Isiilde dressed in shirt and trousers, and tamed her hair into two tight braids. She threw *Binding and Baiting* into her leather knapsack, along with the rune-etched flagon and her report.

She found Oenghus in his workshop. He was puffing away on his pipe as he watched a foul smelling concoction boil in a glass tube that sat on a heating stone.

"Good morning, Oen."

He smiled around the stem of his pipe. "You look mischievous."

"The sun is out."

"Let me see that cut of yours." Oenghus eyed her chin, then reached for a jar to slap some salve on it.

"I don't know why you just don't heal it."

"Your body will forget how to heal itself if you rely on the Gift. And it might teach you to bloody listen to me. Where are you off to?"

"The usual," she said vaguely.

"Be careful. And don't leave the castle." Oenghus tugged on his beard. "And if you see that blasted imp—run."

Liquid boiled over the top of the glass vial. Oenghus snatched it off the stone with a curse and set it carefully in a rack of similar tubes. "Do you have your dagger with you?"

"I hate carrying it."

"You should always have a blade."

"But you told me to stay away from sharp objects. Remember, I keep cutting myself."

"That was years ago," he growled. "And what I said hardly matters when I turn around and give you a blade, now does it? Better to have one than not. Trust me."

Despite her aversion to steel, she fetched her dagger, then headed for Tulipin's tower.

Thedus was sitting in the doorway of Tulipin's workshop when she arrived. He was stark naked, sunburnt, and was worrying at the doorpost with raw fingertips, dropping the pilfered wood into a tiny mound at his feet.

Tulipin hovered beside him, prodding him with a stout staff. "I swear I'll summon the Archlord if you don't move!"

Thedus didn't move. He was too focused on his rhythmic scraping.

"Good morning," Isiilde said.

Thedus stopped long enough to look up at the nymph and blink once, then he returned to his curious task. Tulipin glanced at her with a look of irritation.

"I'm sorry about the other day, Master Tulipin," she said, handing over her paper.

Surprise flashed across his face, because every Wise One knew that the nymph never completed an assignment. "I'll look this over."

Isiilde felt eyes on her. Another gnome stood inside the cluttered workshop: Eiji. The spiky-haired gnome was only three feet tall, but her calculating gaze was unnerving, as were the brace of throwing knives, dark leathers, and the short sword strapped to her back.

Eiji was studying her like an oddity in a cage—as if the woman were appraising her value. Eiji didn't return her smile of greeting. Isiilde quickly left. But the encounter had shaken her for reasons she didn't understand.

Marsais always told her to trust her instincts, but it'd be nice if she understood why they were telling her to do something.

Isiilde sang softly as she walked through the maze of stone passages, attracting attention wherever she went. Heads turned to watch her swaying form, caught up in the vision drifting across their path.

One passing apprentice tripped over his own robes. And a Wise One dropped his books on the freshly scrubbed floor.

Isiilde was oblivious to it all. She was focused on finding the imp—that was her largest obstacle. How could she try to bind it to the flagon if she couldn't *find* it?

Perhaps the fiend liked music. It'd been singing in the shrine. She switched her tune to the chattering of its song and quickly placed the melody: The Bastard Prince of the Seas.

Good gods, the imp liked pirates. She hoped it liked meat, too.

Isiilde walked past a pair of guards posted at the kitchen entrance, and searched for Stievin. He was hard to miss. He stood a head taller than most, and whereas everyone else was covered in flour and grease, he was always spotless.

Stievin was waiting for her with a tray. "I missed you yesterday," he said, gazing at her like a parched man craving water.

"I wasn't feeling well."

"If I'd known, I would have called. Are you feeling better?"

"More than better."

"I have a present for you." He opened the covered platter and picked out a plump strawberry. "I handpicked it especially for you."

Isiilde took it from his hand, and bit into the succulent berry. It made her moan.

The platter in Stievin's hand quivered slightly.

"What happened to your chin?" His fingertips brushed the cut, trailing lightly down her throat.

Startled, Isiilde took a step back. "The imp attacked me and Oenghus... Thank you, Stievin. I have to get to my lessons." She turned to go, but was stopped by a hand on her shoulder.

"Let me carry the tray for you," Stievin said, more a command than an offer.

"No need."

Even as she tried to escape his persistent grip, her fingers flashed, deftly weaving a feather rune around the tray. With a tugging gesture, she bound the tray to herself, and it floated from Stievin's hand, startling him.

Isiilde shook off his hand and hurried away. When she passed the guards at their post, she glanced over her shoulder. But Stievin was lost in the flurry of cooks, kitchen maids, and spit boys.

With every step, the thunder in her ears faded, until at last her heart quieted. But his touch still crawled down her throat like a creeping insect.

He was only concerned about your wound, she told herself. Her overreaction was foolish. She'd known the man for most of her life—even considered him a friend.

She glanced at the tray, and cursed—she'd forgotten to ask for meat.

THERE WAS one place she hadn't searched for the imp—the throne room. It was on the ground floor of the Spine, below the middle levels that housed the archives and an army of scribes. There were other chambers dedicated to other pursuits, but everyone just hurried back and forth from chamber to chamber, passing scrolls and reports from hand to hand.

It seemed a grandly dull game.

Above the archives was the rookery. Birds came and went, carrying messages to and from scouts and armies who didn't staff a Whisperer. The weaving of messages into the wind took talent, and not every Wise One could manage the weave. So great hawks, owls, and dull-eyed pigeons shared the Archlord's lofty perch.

The handler never let her near his birds. He claimed she made them nervous.

The three top levels of the Spine were used solely by the Archlord. Stairwells stopped at what many believed was the topmost level, a beautiful chamber ringed by natural stone pillars that created an open-aired terrace.

The only way to reach the pinnacle was by teleportation runes that bore the Archlord's runic eye. And to her knowledge, the only people allowed access were Isek, Morigan, Oenghus, and herself.

Since the sun was shining, she walked to the Spine by the curtain wall. She stopped to lean over the wall, and watch waves crash against the cliff face far below.

Could the imp be nesting in a cave in the cliff? The thought sparked an idea: she could levitate down to look.

A hand seized her belt, just as she started to weave. Isiilde dropped the weave and spun, ready to scold the intruder.

"I know that look, foolish fire imp."

"I am not an imp, Rashk," Isiilde said, crossing her arms. "I'm a nymph."

"So you say, but I begin to wonder." Rashk leaned casually against the battlements. The Rahuatl's bronze skin gleamed in the sun. The light emphasized her ritual scarring and the ceremonial needles of ivory poking through her exposed skin. She wore her sunbathing outfit, a sparse loincloth and little more.

"If I were a fire imp, I'd fly away from here."

"True," Rashk said, giving one of Isiilde's braids a tug—a rare gesture for the otherwise unaffectionate woman. Rashk glanced at the floating tray behind her and arched a hairless brow that had been imbedded with ivory studs. "You go to your master?"

"If I can find him."

"He is in audience and smells restless," the woman warned, studying her claws. "I have heard of your hunt with Grimstorm. Tell him to bite its head off next time. Mice play dead and so do imps."

Isiilde tucked that bit of information away, but she didn't think she'd try it when she caught the fiend.

Rashk's dark eyes narrowed. She touched Isiilde's cheek with one cool claw, running the flat of the little blade down her skin.

"You smell different, child." Rashk bared a row of pointed teeth. "Your scent is ripe."

Isiilde frowned. "What does that mean? Is it bad?"

Sometimes the Rahuatl language didn't translate well, but that was true of their entire culture.

Rashk cocked her head. "For you—maybe. Keep your claws on today and stay close to Grimstorm. But if you want my advice, stay closer to your master."

"I planned as much."

"When next we meet, I hope your teeth are sharpened." Rashk chortled softly at this last.

Isiilde pressed her palm against the woman's in the Ritual of Farewell, and headed inside. She skipped lightly down a winding stairwell, appreciating the echo of her singing in the spiraling emptiness, until she pushed through a concealed door into the Grand Entrance Hall.

The domed ceiling had been enchanted with a myriad of constellations to mirror the cycle of moons—a successful use of the Gift, unlike Lispen's unstable portal in the adjoining chamber.

Steeling herself, she walked towards the throne room, which was flanked by two statues that dominated the end of the hall. The guardian hounds sat patiently at their post. Their stone forms rippled with coiled muscle.

Isiilde shied from their gleaming eyes and grinning maws. Their expressions were comical, yet bordered on terrifying, like a jester with a painted face and plastered smile.

The twin doors they guarded were imposing: two solid barriers of titan metal, smooth as glass and nearly seamless, unadorned save for a circle of runes—a warning rather than a ward, to all those entering with ill intent.

Faced with the giant hounds, the warning runes on the doors were troubling, but none of the Wise Ones really knew what would trigger the hounds, or if they would awaken at all. 'Ill intent' was a vague phrase.

And as Oenghus had confided, everyone and their mother wanted to ring the Archlord's neck, so whatever the hounds guarded, it wasn't the bloody Archlord.

Wise Ones were not very knowledgeable when it came to their own stronghold.

Beyond the doors was a place of emptiness.

Isiilde nudged the titan doors open, and slipped through the crack, stepping into a dimensionless universe of obsidian—all polished darkness and glossy reflection. Then she ran, keeping her eyes downcast, focusing on the tips of her boots.

Shadows drifted in the stone's reflection, like bodies trapped beneath a frozen lake, features blurred and twisted in eternal agony.

The chamber felt wrong. Everything about it pricked and needled her senses, screaming at her to flee. And she was not alone in her fear. The Wise Ones did not speak of the chamber, refusing to put a name to what was better forgotten. It was like a dirty little secret, rotting in the center of the Spine.

Marsais usually escorted her through the Nameless. She'd asked him about it once. He'd fallen silent and gone still. Then confided in a whisper that she was wise to fear it. He never spoke of it again.

Relief washed over her when she stepped into the throne room. It was a columned monstrosity, its ceiling lost in shadow.

Isiilde focused on the weak light that shone from stained glass windows high on the walls. The stone mirrored the exterior of the Spine. Veins of gleaming quartz spiraled up the forest of monolithic columns; each pillar a masterpiece of brilliance.

The cavernous hall would have been beautiful if not for the ring of faces chiseled around the base of each column. The sculptor had taken exquisite care to carve ears, eyes, and mouths for his creations, but later, in some moment of madness, someone had come along and desecrated the stone faces. Their eyes had been gouged out, their ears lopped off, and their mouths hacked clean of lips.

Isiilde feared those faces, not for their ghastly appearance, but for the methodical way in which their disfigurement had been carried out.

Two men conversed at the end of the vast hall. And as she tiptoed from pillar to pillar, searching for the imp, their echoing voices took shape—one belonged to Marsais, and the other to Tharios.

"I've read all of your reports on Lachlan," Marsais was saying. "But I will not yield on this matter. You know my reasons."

Making sure her floating tray was out of sight, she crouched behind a pillar and poked her head around to survey the dais.

"Unfortunately, reason and your name are rarely found in the same sentence," Tharios said. "No one has ever known your reasons, Archlord.

You let your whims guide you, steering this Order haphazardly, with no clear path for the rest of us to follow."

Isiilde glared at Tharios, disliking his tone. It was the same one that Zianna used with her.

There was something about him that grated. His raven hair gleamed in the shadows and his pale face was as smooth as alabaster. He wore a high-collared robe of misty silk that showed off a lean physique. Handsome, yes, but... wrong.

Tharios was like a painting that was beautiful at first glance, but the more one stared, the more disturbing the image became.

"I refuse to be goaded in the direction you're aiming," Marsais said. He sat on an obsidian throne that contrasted sharply with his crimson robes. His long white hair gleamed in shadow, while his eyes were steel. High cheekbones had been honed by salt and sea, and his power drew her in rather than repelled.

"My apologies," Tharios said. "I am simply frustrated by your decision—many of us are."

"If enough of you were frustrated, then I would have been overruled at council."

"But you could influence them."

"I certainly could if I were not suspicious of Lachlan's motives," Marsais agreed.

"I fail to see what Lachlan has done to warrant such suspicion. He's a reasonable man. A cultured man, with a clear vision of unity for his people. He seeks our support, because in us he sees a like-minded ally. Throughout history, our Order has stood for the very things that he values: to rule through wisdom, not by force."

Isiilde didn't understand the issue either. The South was fragmented, full of warring Thanes and petty land disputes.

Surely stability would bring peace?

Marsais chuckled softly. Something flashed in the dim light, drawing her gaze to the end of his long goatee, where three pierced coins were woven into his braid. Their musical clinking seemed to mimic his amusement.

Isiilde had never seen him wear the coins before.

"Hmm, perhaps you should spend more time perusing our

libraries," Marsais mused. "Allow me to give you a brief lesson in history. You see, every man starts off much the same as this Lachlan. Every king begins with good intentions in his own mind, before the lure of power begins calling to him in the night."

Marsais leaned back, resting his elbows on the armrest to steeple his fingers.

"His eyes are enticed by a river, a single mile beyond the borders of his kingdom, so what does the king do? Simple really, he seizes it for his people, in the name of good. Then his ego swells, and with his brains between his legs he charges heedlessly onward, taking what is not even needed, until he finds himself in his dead neighbor's bed, mounting another man's queen. What does history whisper to us from the past?"

Not waiting for an answer, Marsais pressed relentlessly on. "The king's eyes drift again, this time to the next border, and he continues the vicious cycle, unquenchable and pointless. I will not tie the Isle to a path with no end."

"Yet you tie us to *Kambe*," Tharios replied. "What has Kambe ever done for us? *We* advise them, *we* aide them, *we* fight their petty skirmishes."

"What would Lachlan do for us? Or should I ask, what would this man do for you, Tharios?" It was nearly a purr.

"You would ask that of me?" Tharios laughed. "Such a question from a man who has the emperor's nymph stowed away in his chambers is a bit hypocritical, wouldn't you say? Rather obvious benefits, that."

"I'll warn you once and then no more—leave my apprentice out of this or I shall take it personally." Although Marsais' tone was quiet, his words carried as much threat as any roar from Oenghus.

"I only bring the whispers and rumors into the open. Nothing more. If not on everyone's tongue, then it's in their thoughts."

"Rumors regarding my apprentice may stay in their thoughts. I'll not have them spoken of in my presence."

"Even you cannot deny my words have merit. Appearances can be as damaging as truth, and it appears to the majority that we are tied with Kambe."

"We are tied with all kingdoms who oppose the Void."

"Which Lachlan opposes as well," Tharios said, taking a step towards the throne.

"Does he?"

"Beyond a doubt."

"I certainly have mine," Marsais replied dryly.

"Certainly he has his own schemes—every ruler must. No one faults them for it, but in *this* instance, our Order has something to gain."

"Trouble?"

"Respect," Tharios hissed. "It's time we remind the lands of who we are. Not servants of Kambe, or anyone else. Don't you see—we've fallen behind. There's no power to be found in the dusty tomes of the past. The Bloodmagi, the Mystics, by the gods, even the barbarian Shamans have unlocked secrets that our Lore cannot touch."

"I was present for the council and heard your argument the first time."

"This Order has done nothing but waver since you took the throne. And now you pass up your only chance for redemption."

Isiilde gasped at the blatant insult. She quickly pressed a hand over her lips.

"Hmm, I wasn't aware I was in need of redemption."

"This Order is in need, because of you and your whims. I ask you respectfully, Archlord, to reconsider Lachlan's offer."

"A most curious form of respect," Marsais mused, and then he leaned forward, coins chiming with the sway of his goatee. His next words contained no trace of amusement. "You forget who I am, Tharios, so allow me to remind you. I am a seer of no small talent, and I tire of your masquerade. Let us get to the root of the matter."

His gaze flickered down the hall to the nameless chamber beyond. There was nothing there, save the ornate gate that separated this hall from the next.

Tharios smirked at the seer's lapse. But then Marsais continued to speak, eyes still fixed on the beyond as if he were occupying two places at once. "I know your desires. I know what lies in your heart and fills your dreams."

"It's no secret. Everyone knows I plan to cast my name for your throne."

"I speak of your other desire," Marsais whispered, his voice echoing from all corners as his eyes shifted, piercing the Wise One.

Tharios took a step back, hesitating, but the effect was lost when Marsais glanced back down the long hall. This time, there was someone there. Tulipin Tuddleberry floated towards the throne.

Tharios glanced over his shoulder at Tulipin, and then whirled, issuing an ultimatum. "Don't get too comfortable."

"You will not find what you seek."

Tharios blinked, clearly taken aback. His smooth mask slipped and a smirk twisted his lips. Without waiting to be dismissed, Tharios turned on his heel and stalked from the throne room.

CHAPTER 20

Marsais stared straight ahead, stroking his braided goatee as Tulipin drifted closer. The gnome stopped before his throne.

Isiilde frowned at a familiar-looking scroll in his hand. Perhaps Tulipin had been so impressed by her report that he'd come to praise her?

He cleared his throat. But either Marsais didn't notice, or he did, and simply didn't acknowledge him.

After two more noisome throat clearings and a muttered "Archlord," Tulipin finally bellowed Marsais' name.

Marsais raised a hand, demanding silence, as he sat with eyes turned inward and lost in thought. Time ticked onwards. And Tulipin waited, twisting the scroll in his hands.

Marsais finally shifted his attention to the gnome. "Hmm?"

Tulipin exploded with rage, shaking the scroll. "That insolent—" his face turned the same color as his hair, which made him look like a floating beet. "—brat you call an apprentice!" He stuttered to a halt, too furious to speak.

Isiilde's optimism deflated.

Marsais arched a brow. "I don't have an apprentice who is insolent or a brat, but since I only have one apprentice, I'm assuming you're referring to Isiilde."

"Yes," Tulipin spat. "That faerie was mucking about in class the other day. She insulted the Blessed Order, so I cast her out and ordered her to write a report for penance."

"And did she write it?"

"Yes."

"Indeed?" Marsais looked surprised. "I don't see the problem—"

"Read this." Tulipin thrust the scroll at Marsais.

He unrolled it and began reading. During the long minutes of uncomfortable silence that followed, Isiilde sank against the stone column, chewing on her fingernails until Marsais finally handed the scroll back to Tulipin.

"Well?" the gnome fumed, transforming from a beet to a boiling teapot.

"She has the ruling of 1101 A.S. dated wrongly, and she misspelled "deceitful"," he noted.

"It's utter blasphemy!"

Isiilde cringed.

"Certainly not from a faerie's viewpoint."

"The words speak for themselves, no matter whose viewpoint. She states that the only reason the paladins passed the laws regarding nymphs was so they'd have leave to rape them!" Tulipin bit off each word, tightening his grip on the scroll until his knuckles were white.

"Master Tulipin," Marsais said calmly, in contrast to the gnome's anger. "The paladins did do so, and they continue to rape them—as does everyone else."

"Bah, outrageous! They're *nymphs*. They're happy as long as someone is bedding them. Nymphs have crude instincts at best—little more than animals whose sole purpose is to tempt and destroy the will of decent men. The Blessed Order passed the laws to stop men from slaughtering one another over them. As soon as the creatures were put in their place, the wars stopped. But this... *temptress* scoffs at the noblest of Orders! The Chapterhouse in Drivel is already fuming over her desecration of the temple, and when they hear of this—"

"And who is going to deliver it?" Marsais asked, rising from his throne, cutting Tulipin's tirade off. "How easily you forget the state of your own race in Vaylin and Kiln. I believe gnomes are still enslaved there—a class of *creatures* who are happy as long as they're toiling in the mines. I wonder what a Vaylinish slave lord would say about a gnome's report on his land?"

"Vaylin is full of Void-worshiping heathens. That's hardly a comparison for the ruling of an Order that speaks for the gods. It's unforgivable for a mere *animal* to pen such blasphemous claims," Tulipin huffed.

"What do you propose, then? Surely you don't plan on putting an animal on trial for sacrilege? Hmm, if that were the case then we should be more diligent in capturing the seagulls that relieve themselves on the temple roofs," Marsais mused, holding out his hand to Tulipin, palm up, fingers commanding. "I think that sounds like a splendid waste of *your* time, Master Tulipin, wouldn't you agree?"

Tulipin hesitated. Then placed the scroll in his waiting hand.

"Your bluntness has been insightful," Marsais continued, once the scroll was safely tucked away. "I assure you that my apprentice will never grace your lectures again."

A chill entered the throne room.

Tulipin blinked, swallowing. He opened his mouth to say more, but one look at the crimson figure stilled his tongue. Instead, he floated from the chamber as fast as his enchantment would allow.

When he'd passed over the threshold, Marsais gestured sharply, and the heavy gate at the end of the throne room obeyed his command, slamming shut with a deafening thud.

Isiilde sank to the stone floor, tears running down her cheeks.

Tulipin's words kept echoing in her ears until she thought they'd haunt her forever. She had no idea he loathed her so.

Eventually, her silent tears ran dry. And she lay on the stone with her palms pressed against her eyes, feeling ill and hopeless.

A presence, more than any sound, finally roused her. She peeked through her fingers. A pair of worn boots and the crimson hem of a familiar robe greeted her, telling her all she needed to know.

"That doesn't look comfortable, my dear."

Isiilde stirred, lowering her hands to hug her shivering body. Her eyes followed robes, moving ever upwards, until she found the warm eyes of her only friend.

"I didn't think you noticed me," she sniffed.

"I always notice you, Isiilde." His gentle voice soothed her ears. He sat on his haunches, regarding her patiently.

Isiilde accepted his proffered handkerchief, noting the lone *M* embroidered on its cloth before bringing it to her nose. "I hate being a nymph," she confided.

When Marsais didn't answer right away, she thought he must have blanked out, but when she sought his eyes again, she found him studying her, a look of fondness softening his sharp features.

"I don't like being a seer," he whispered. "But I am who I am. Just as you're a nymph. We have no say in the blood we are born to. So trust me when I say that there is little use in us feeling sorry for ourselves."

"I'm not feeling sorry for myself." She swallowed back her tears. "I just... I thought Master Tulipin was at least tolerant of me. I would rather be disliked for *who* I am, not *what* I am, because I cannot change it, no matter how I wish to."

Each hateful word had been like a slap to her face.

"If it makes any difference, I am largely disliked for both who and what I am. Seers make dreadful guests at celebrations," Marsais admitted.

"Then those who dislike you are fools."

"Oh, I don't know about that, for I am vexing more often than not."

"And I love you all the more for it."

"Ah, love," Marsais said, with feeling. "A word so little spoken in this ill place. Your innocence brings light to the grimmest shadows."

"You are the only one who thinks so, Marsais."

"Because I see what others do not."

"A red-eyed, big-eared, puffy-nosed nymph?"

"A rare and privileged sight for these ancient eyes of mine."

"Only as ancient as the sun," she said. "Your eyes are more alive than any I've seen."

"A mirror of your soul, and no more," he replied.

This last compliment was too much for the nymph. She reached out to take his hand, but it disappeared beneath his long sleeve before she could grasp it. Her hand strayed to his robe instead, resting on the supple fabric that covered his forearm.

"But is what Master Tulipin said true? Am I an animal?" She could face the truth if it came from a friend.

"Far, far, from it. Compared to you, my dear, *we* are the animals." He placed a covered hand over hers.

"Then what am I that you cringe to touch me?" Her voice was full of hurt.

If he thought she hadn't noticed his avoidance of her touch, then he was sorely mistaken.

A gentle smile curved his lips. "You are a goddess whom I have no right to touch," he whispered like the prayer of a devout.

Isiilde stared at him in wonder, confusion, and finally a delicate blush graced her unearthly skin.

"We should get you into some sunlight. I think you'll feel better."

CHAPTER 21

Isiilde basked in the sunlight streaming through the crystal window. Bliss, pure and simple.

Marsais was not so relaxed. He'd been a whirlwind since they'd entered his study. He wove a series of messages, sending them off with a flick of his fingers to whisper in someone's ears. Then he turned to the shelves, attacking them like a madman, until stacks of ancient tomes tottered on his desk.

Isiilde watched him while she ate. It was all very entertaining. Several times she started to ask him what he was about, but then stopped herself—she didn't want to be rude and interrupt the conversation he was having. With himself.

A knock at the door heralded Isek's arrival. He walked over the threshold, performing an impressive balancing act with an armful of scrolls and books.

"As requested, Arch—" Isek dropped half the scrolls on the floor as he caught sight of the sunbathing nymph.

Isiilde offered a greeting. But he just kept staring.

Marsais looked up in surprise, his gaze darting from Isek to the shimmering dream lounging in his study.

"Thank you." Marsais stepped into Isek's line of sight, blocking his view. "Are you quite done?"

Isek shook himself. "Do you need anything more from me?"

"Tell me, has Tharios traveled recently?"

"He's always coming and going," Isek replied, weaving a Kilnish crown between his fingers. It was a mesmerizing habit of his.

"I need to know where he's traveled in the past year—no matter how trivial it may seem."

"Should be easy enough. Tharios has a ship and crew."

"Splendid. While you're wheedling information out of his crew, you have my permission to get soused, as long as you bring something back for me."

"I'll do my best." Isek leaned to the side, stealing one last peek at the nymph. "And Marsais?"

"Hmm."

"I don't know how you do it, old friend."

Marsais did not reply and Isek said no more. After he left, Isiilde rested her hands on her chin (which still hurt), and stared at the closed door.

"What did he mean by that?"

"By what, my dear?" Marsais asked, as he studied one of the newly delivered manuscripts.

"By what he just said."

Marsais gestured toward the disorder on his desk. "Perhaps he was referring to this mess I've gotten myself into."

"What exactly have you gotten yourself into?" Isiilde grabbed a handful of strawberries and joined him at his desk.

"Hmm, weren't you listening in the throne room?"

"Yes, but I don't understand. If you already know what Tharios wants, then what are you looking for?" She poked at a few scrolls, noting that they were dated maps of long forgotten borders and kingdoms.

"Right to the point. Have I ever told you what a sharp mind you have?" Many times, but she never tired of hearing it. "To put it simply, I bluffed and he took my bait."

"So..." She mulled over what she'd overheard, along with his interest in Tharios' recent travels. "...you suspected he was searching for some-thing, but you don't know what he wants, and now you know whatever it was, he's already found it."

His grin told her she was on the right track.

"But if he's found it, then why does he desire it?" She bit into a berry while she puzzled through this conundrum.

"The gap between knowledge and possession can be infinite. For example: a man might see a woman and desire that woman, but it certainly doesn't mean he possesses her."

Isiilde chewed thoughtfully. "But Marsais, can a man really possess a woman without ruining her? I should think, though I am no expert, when a person desires someone or something, it ends up possessing them."

"Excellent!" His eyes twinkled down at her. "Therein lies the cycle of power that I spoke of in the throne room. You, my dear, have grasped what Tharios could not. And they wonder why I made you my apprentice."

"It sounds as if they have their own ideas," she said, waggling her eyebrows.

Marsais grunted.

"Would you like a strawberry?" she offered.

His grey eyes flickered to the bright red fruit, narrowing on the inno-cent berry as if it were poison. "You've been to the kitchens again."

Her cheeky smile faded. "Am I not allowed to eat?"

"Isiilde—" He closed his eyes, a shudder sweeping down his body. She'd rarely seen him so affected.

When he recovered, he thanked her and took the offered strawberry, balancing the near perfect specimen on his fingertips. She waited beside him as he studied the berry.

"Do you trust me?" he asked, looking at her.

"You're the only one I trust, except for Oen and Morigan, but that's obvious."

"If I ask you to do something for me, will you do it without question?"

That did require a great deal of trust. But it was Marsais, so she nodded. "I will."

"Please don't go to any of the kitchens. Swear to me you won't go near them."

Isiilde tilted her head. "May I ask one question that doesn't involve specifics?"

"Hmm."

"If I can't go to the kitchens, how will I eat? Starving doesn't seem like a good way to die."

"Few ways are," he said dryly. "But you need not fear starvation. A platter fit for a queen will be delivered to your door, morning, midday, and eve. I will personally see to it—*if* you keep up your end of the bargain."

"You would do that for me?"

"There is very little in this realm that I would *not* do for you. But first, swear to me that you won't set foot in the kitchens again."

"I swear it, Marsais," she promised.

He studied her for a few moments before nodding and turned back to his books, forgetting her entirely.

Isiilde watched him for a time, puzzling over his request. When he began scouring the dusty tomes, she returned to her rug, sprawling on the warm pelt.

Marsais rarely requested anything of her. The other Wise Ones were taskmasters who trained apprentices in exchange for their servitude. Their work was grueling; hers was not. She mostly lounged around, talked with Marsais, or played King's Folly with him. But when he did give her a task, it was always intriguing—he focused on whatever sparked her interest.

So why was he worried about the kitchens of all places? An answer came when she looked at the remains of her lunch.

"Marsais?"

"Hmm."

"Is it because of Stievin?" After eavesdropping in the throne room, she'd forgotten all about her recent encounter with the cook.

"I thought we agreed on no questions," he mumbled from the depths of his book.

"But I'm confused. Oen forbade me to visit Coyle, and you have just forbidden me to go to the kitchens—where Stievin is."

"I've asked you not to go to any of the kitchens," he said.

Isiilde rolled onto her stomach. "Well, since you didn't want me to ask any questions, I'm assuming you just said that so I wouldn't get suspicious. Did Oen put you up to this?"

"No," he muttered. "You've far exceeded your allotment of questions."

"I snuck away to have lunch with Coyle."

Marsais glanced up from his reading. "You know, my dear, you probably shouldn't tell me things like that."

"Why?"

Marsais seemed on the verge of saying something, then glanced back down at his book. He sighed. And with a small growl, slapped it closed. Dust flew in his face, and he quickly wove an air rune before she started sneezing. A sudden breeze carried the dust away from her.

"How was it?" he asked.

"How was what?"

"Your illicit lunch."

"It was all right. I brought sandwiches—seed bread and cucumbers..."

"Strawberries?"

"No berries," she sighed. "I didn't feel like sharing."

Marsais reached into a nearby fruit bowl and tossed her a grape. It hit her head and she laughed.

"You're supposed to catch it with your mouth."

"I don't think that's a rule, Marsais."

"It is," he insisted. And demonstrated by tossing a grape high into the air, catching it in his open mouth and gulping it down. "Try again."

Three grapes later, and she finally caught one. Then bowed as he clapped, and settled back down on the rug.

"Did you make grape tossing part of Isle law?" she asked.

"I tried to," he sniffed. "Isek wouldn't let me propose it to the Nine."

"A pity."

"You're the only one who agrees with me," he admitted.

Marsais walked around his desk to perch on its edge. There was a smile in his eyes and one on her lips, and Isiilde basked under his gaze.

"Why is everything so easy with you, Marsais?"

"Because I'm a madman."

"Shouldn't that make things difficult?"

"It makes it easier to throw me off course and avoid answering questions," he pointed out. Then arched a brow, waiting.

She sighed. "All Coyle talked about was forging swords. He's good at it. And he's nice to look at, too. But then so are you."

"Have you been drinking?"

Isiilde threw a grape at him. But he caught it in his mouth and gulped it down. "You'll end up choking one of these days."

"Then hit me in the back."

"Does that work?" she asked.

"You may have to kick me. Nymphs aren't known for their strength."

"You'd probably dodge my kick," she muttered.

"So now I'm good looking *and* agile."

Isiilde snorted. Then waved a hand between them. "See!"

"Yes, I see you."

"No, I mean *this*," she said. "We can't even have a proper conversation without diverging off topic."

"Isn't this a conversation? Conversing. Exchanging words."

She gave him a look. "You know what I mean."

"But it's so amusing to skip off topic with you. I never know where a conversation will lead. Who wants to stay on one?"

"Coyle doesn't want to travel. He hasn't even been to the south side of the island."

"So he's not your prince."

"I don't get one."

"Actually, you might," Marsais mused.

"It's not the same when a prince *buys* me."

"You're probably right," he admitted. "It certainly takes the romanticism out of a meeting. I wonder if a prince can return you if he doesn't like you..."

"*Marsais.*"

"Isiilde."

"You'd likely be returned in a day."

Marsais spread his hands. "Feigning madness is an option you might consider. No one wants to sleep with a madman."

"Is it contagious like Blight?" she wondered.

"More like 'birds of a feather flock together,' I should think. You're one of the few who can tolerate me for any length of time."

"Sanity is overrated," she said. "When I mentioned my impending enslavement to Coyle, he said his apprenticeship was the same. He was more interested in hardening steel."

"I hope it wasn't an innuendo."

"It might have made things more interesting. He called King's Folly a *game*. I suspect he's terrible at it."

"He could just be average," Marsais pointed out. "You are brilliant at it."

"So are you."

"I know." Marsais looked at his nails. "But don't compare other men to me. They can't compete with madness, my dear."

"He wanted my piss."

Marsais barked out a laugh.

"It's not funny," she said, glaring.

He chortled.

She pelted him with another grape. This time he caught it, and popped it into his mouth.

"I told you other men can't compete with me."

"I already knew that."

Marsais sobered. "I suppose our steel-obsessed young human has heard of the legend."

She tilted her head.

"Steel quenched in the piss of a virgin nymph will imbue it with uncanny power."

"Is there any truth to it?" she asked.

Marsais stroked his goatee in thought, the coins woven in his hair chiming in response. "Perhaps," he drawled. "I don't really know. I find swords to be crude weapons. But I suspect it has more to do with the price of a nymph's urine."

She wrinkled her nose.

"Only the most gifted bladesmiths can afford it, therefore the swords are always of the best make."

Isiilde fell back on the carpet with a sigh. "Sometimes I think you are the only sane person I know, Marsais."

"By the gods, what a terrifying thought."

After a stretch of silence, Marsais stirred, and came over to sit cross-legged on the rug. But as always, he kept his distance.

"He sounds like a kind man, at least."

"Yes, and that's the problem. Most men seem kind. But apparently I'm some sort of..." she gestured helplessly at the rafters, "...of a walking euphoric truthsayer that 'tempts and destroys the will of decent men.'"

"In all fairness, most men find the majority of women tempting—look no further than Oenghus for proof of that. But nymphs are enticing by nature; they can't help being what they are. No more than a bird can keep from flying."

"I don't feel enticing," she said, turning over and propping her head on a hand.

"Neither do I."

"Zianna certainly thinks you are."

"She's after my perceived power."

"I don't think that's all she's after, Marsais."

"Ah well." He spread his hands. "I shall remain unreachable. Humans are far too young."

"Some humans are long-lived—I've heard of ones who are close to a thousand."

"It's their blood," he said. "They *feel* young. To me, at any rate."

"That must be lonely," she said softly.

The edge of his lip raised ruefully. "You always get me to reveal more about myself than intended."

"I'm a walking truthsayer, remember?"

Beneath his thoughtful eyes, a surge of warmth flooded through her, and she plucked up a strawberry to savor its sweetness.

"I'm sorry, Isiilde," he whispered. "In another time... in another age..." He trailed off.

"What?" she demanded.

Marsais retreated to his desk. "As an Awakened nymph, you would have chosen a druid and bonded with him. It was a special time for a nymph. Not the terrifying one you experienced."

"If I can't get off this island, I'll never be able to make my own choices," she bit out, then pulled Binding and Baiting from her knapsack.

She knew about a nymph's Bond, but since she had never been with a man, she had no idea what she might expect.

Oenghus had told her once that the man and nymph merged; their spirits became one, but he was the only one who spoke of it in such a way. Everyone else whispered of the unimaginable pleasures that the nymph bestowed on the man, making no mention of the nymph.

Isiilde told Marsais as much. "Even as things were... It doesn't sound like a 'special time' for the nymph. With the way you've explained history, it was more likely that some druid plucked up an Awakened nymph and bedded her."

"It did happen," he admitted. "But it was a rare thing. The first bonding was of spirit and the nymph remained untouched. It kept her safe from other men, because a bonded nymph is not near as potent as an unbonded one."

"You mean the druid and his nymph didn't—they weren't intimate?" She tilted her head in puzzlement.

"Not until her blood began to stir."

"What does that mean?"

"It means," he said, leveling his gaze on her, "that the nymph begins to take note of men."

"Oh." A creeping blush spread to the tips of her ears. "I suppose I skipped to that part, didn't I?"

"Hmm. Another reason for the druids. It could be... overpowering for the nymph."

"Is that what happened with my fire in the hallway? We never talked about it. It was... it felt..."

Just thinking of what she and her fire had done with the coin made her skin tingle and her heart flutter.

"I've never felt like that before," she admitted, and then a sudden thought came to her. She *had* felt it before, in the pleasure house when she'd touched Marsais.

"It's part of what's happening to you," he said. "But to be honest, I've never heard of a nymph with such an affinity to fire. Regardless, without a druid as your guide, your Awakening won't get any easier. I can't stress how cautious you must be."

Marsais was not very reassuring.

"How long does an Awakening last?" she asked.

"Until a nymph matures," he sighed, settling at his desk again.

"Which is?"

"When does a nymph do anything, my dear?" His eyes twinkled with mirth before answering his own question. "When she feels like it."

BAITING and Binding was a meandering thesis penned by a writer in love with his own words.

She reached the end and stared at the splotchy page in dismay. The bloodstains were probably the writer's—someone had surely killed him to keep him from writing any more.

Through the tedious exposition, she'd learned about different imps, their diets, cultural structure, and even mating habits (she would have preferred pictures).

But she was no closer to figuring out how to get the imp back *into* the rune-etched flagon.

Isiilde flipped through the book, searching for the chapter on baiting. There'd been a word she didn't understand.

Marsais was standing in front of the crystal window with hands clasped behind his back. She knew him well enough to know he was deep in thought. And rather than interrupt him, she wandered over to his desk, settling in the high-backed chair to peruse his notes.

Through the years, she'd learned to decipher his hurried handwriting and chaotic thought process. Today, it was mostly notations of names that she didn't recognize. But a few stood out: the Kingdom of Vaylin (far to the East), along with the jumbled names of Thanes (in the South), which often changed from month to month.

Marsais was also interested in Lachlan's heritage. He had traced his lineage through the ages.

Many of the names were neither people nor kingdoms, but by the sound of them, artifacts of legend: the Dawn's Dead Scythe, the draught of Salisthane, and Soisskeli's Stave. The last was circled.

Marsais began to pace.

"Marsais?"

Startled, he whirled around, searching for the owner of the voice until he spotted her at his desk. "I didn't see you behind all those books," he said. "My keen observation whispers to me that you have a question."

"What's a fetish?"

"Hmm." He stroked his goatee. "I should ask what the context is before delving into this subject."

Isiilde hopped up and went over to her book to read. "It says, *It is common for Imps to have fetishes. These often direct their course of action.*" She looked up at him in question. "Is there more than one meaning?"

Marsais nodded and picked up his braid, shaking the coins in front of her eyes.

"These are fetishes, or talismans—trinkets if you will—that are most commonly associated with enchantments."

She took his braid in hand, studying the coins, surprised to find the hair soft and lightly scented with oils. The coins were ancient, tinged with green and faded with time, each carefully woven into his hair.

Isiilde narrowed her eyes. "Are these the same trinkets that you showed Witman?"

"Why ever would you think that?"

"These three coins are the same size as the strange discs you showed Witman. You just started wearing these. They look different, but they *feel* familiar."

"How do they feel?"

Isiilde rubbed one coin between her fingertips. "Like a... broken whisper of something greater." Her words made no sense.

"Hmm."

She looked up into his eyes. But his face was impassive. "You had Witman disguise them, didn't you?"

"You seem to think so."

"Why?"

"Why do you think?"

"They are likely something that you should not have."

His brows lifted. "Ever suspicious of your master."

"Curious, perhaps, but never suspicious. What do these trinkets do?"

Grey eyes twinkled. "It would be far easier for me to explain what they do *not* do."

"And what is that?"

"Deter you from asking questions."

"Questions are the stepping stones to wisdom," she quoted.

"*The Sacred Texts Of Oshimi?*"

"*A Study In Vagueness: A Work In Progress*, by the Archlord of the Isle."

"Sounds tedious."

"Diverting, more like."

"Better diverting than dull, I suppose." Marsais sighed wistfully. "I'd prefer captivating."

"You may prove to be if you answer my questions."

"Hmm, coerced with flattery. You have me cornered—do your worst."

Determined not to be sidetracked by another circular line of questioning, she knocked him back on topic. "So what kind of talisman does the imp have?"

"Well, both meanings can apply to these creatures."

"The other being?"

"Why is Oenghus never around when you ask these questions?" he muttered. "It has to do with desire—what gets your blood pumping."

"Mine would be fire?" she asked, staring up at him expectantly.

"Erm... I suppose," he said, slowly, eyeing her warily. "It's usually of a more intimate nature and slightly less dangerous."

"You mean like what arouses a man?"

"Nicely put."

"You know, I do have a basic understanding of how that sort of thing works. I learned a lot at the pleasure house."

Marsais closed his eyes and rubbed the bridge of his nose.

"Does your head hurt?" she asked.

"Now it does."

"Marsais?"

"Hmm."

"Is that why the woman was putting her foot in the man's mouth?"

Marsais groaned, and began massaging his temples.

"I could ask Oen," she offered, brightly.

His eyes widened in alarm.

"I'm only jesting, Marsais," she said with a grin. "By the gods, where is your sense of humor today?"

"Gone with the vision of my death. It wouldn't be much of a jest after Oen beat me to a bloody pulp." His tone was grave, but his face relaxed, and a hint of a smile played at the corner of his long lips. "I suppose the woman is one example, although everything becomes muddled when you throw Primrose spirits into the mix. That particular wine has some very potent side effects," he confided with a roguish grin.

"May I try some?"

"Absolutely not," he said. "I shudder to think how it would affect a nymph."

"You're a man," she blurted out.

"That's very observant of you."

"What arouses you?"

Marsais blinked at her question, completely caught off guard. His mouth worked silently for a long moment before he found his tongue again. "That's not something one asks in casual conversation."

"I wouldn't call any of our conversations casual," she replied.

"You have a point, but your question will go unanswered."

She opened her mouth to ask another, but he held up a halting hand. "Come, my dear, I think it time I escort you home before you wheedle any more unscrupulous information from me." He stuffed her book into her knapsack and slung it over his shoulder. "Perhaps Oenghus will have something for my headache."

ALE WAS OENGHUS' cure for most things—including headaches. He had his feet propped up on a table, and was leaning back with pipe in hand as he and Marsais roared out a drinking song.

Isiilde felt lightheaded with laughter. The room was swaying, too.

Oenghus leaned back. Too far. His chair tipped, and he fell backwards. But he turned it into a drunken roll and hopped to his feet.

Marsais applauded, sloshing ale all over his disheveled shirt. "That was drunk luck," he said.

Oenghus snorted. "The Void it wasn't. I'll wager you five silver that I can weave a Rune of Holding around your mug before it hits the floor."

The pair were as fond of wagering as they were drinking together.

"My friend, you can't weave that rune when you're sober." Marsais slammed his mug down in challenge.

And Oenghus gathered himself with all the wobbly dignity of the truly inebriated. "Ready?" he asked, cracking his fingers.

Marsais chugged down his ale in one long swallow and then tossed the cup in the air. Oenghus slurred the Lore, his fingers a sloppy blur. When the cup was a pace from the floor, it shattered, bursting apart.

"Aha!" Marsais slapped his hand on the table.

"That was bloody successful," Oenghus defended.

"Your hand was too heavy; the mug is broken. That's five silver, but I'll give you a chance to win it back. I'll wager that I can stop a full mug with the same weave, without spilling a drop, and what's more—you can throw it at me."

Oenghus bared his teeth. "Make it fifteen, you fool."

Marsais stood up, bowed to Isiilde, and stoically brushed the crumbs from his shirt. Swaying from side to side, he squinted at Oenghus, then took a long step back. Satisfied, he shook out his arms, and held his hands at the ready, fingers poised.

With a satisfied grunt, Oenghus brought back his arm. Isiilde closed one eye. And the heavy mug sped towards Marsais, slamming into his face, knocking him off his feet in a wash of ale.

Oenghus roared with laughter.

Despite the swaying walls, Isiilde hurried over to Marsais. He was sprawled on his back, bleeding from a gash on his forehead.

"That was foolish of you," she said, kneeling beside him to press a handkerchief to the wound.

"My dear, all men are pathetic fools," he said, taking her hand in his, and to her amazement, he brushed his lips against her knuckles.

"I'm up twenty silver!" Oenghus staggered over. "He's an old bastard, Sprite. He'll live." He helpfully kicked Marsais in the ribs to show his living state.

"Blast you, Oen!" Marsais let her hand slide from his grasp. "I never said ready."

CHAPTER 22

Isiilde's skull throbbed. She moaned and rolled over, then fell off her bed. "Bollocks," she groaned.

Daylight hurt like needles in her eyeballs, so she lay curled on the floor for a time, still dressed in yesterday's clothes.

She finally picked herself up and stumbled towards Oenghus' bedchamber, where she found him snoring loudly.

"Oen," she said, poking his shoulder.

He scratched at his chest. How he could sleep without a blanket or shirt was beyond her. All the windows were open, and it was freezing.

"Oen!" Isiilde tugged on one of his braids and he jerked awake, reaching for his war hammer. She batted his hand away before he could grab the weapon.

"What?" he growled.

"My head hurts." And her throat felt like sand.

"That's what happens when you drink too much."

"Can I have some of that potion you and Marsais drink all the time?"

Oenghus snorted in answer.

"Why not?"

"I had eight hundred years' worth of hangovers before I discovered the potion. I'm not about to give it to you after your first rough night.

Maybe you'll think twice before stealing a man's grog. Take a bath, drink some water, and let me sleep."

Isiilde narrowed her eyes. But he was already snoring again.

The bath helped. While Isiilde soaked in her copper tub, she stared out the window, watching a silvery drizzle collect on the glass.

Autumn was fast fading. Another summer gone, and the sun had barely graced the isle's shores. She did not know if she could bear another winter.

A fire blazed in the hearth. She closed her eyes, soaking up the warmth. Heat caressed her skin with a delicious flicker of flame.

Her gaze drifted to a tray sitting on a table by her tub. It brought a smile to her lips.

Just as Marsais promised, a tray fit for a queen had been waiting in front of her bedchamber door, laden with cheese, grapes, fresh biscuits and honey, and best of all, a bowl of strawberries topped with whipped cream. A mug of apple cider sat steaming on a Heat Stone.

The previous evening was mostly a blur of singing and laughter, but she remembered one thing clearly: the feel of Marsais' lips on the back of her hand.

She studied the spot where he'd kissed her. How could such a little thing feel so wonderful?

Coyle's kiss had felt like nothing, while Stievin's touch had been disturbing, but Marsais… his touch had felt like the sun's caress.

The memory tingled up her spine and swept past her lips in a moan —a feeling so powerful that fire roared from its hearth, sending a wave of heat rippling into her bedchamber.

Isiilde screamed and scrambled over the side of her tub. Fire raced across the rug, climbing her bed curtains with unnatural fury. In desperation, she batted uselessly at the flames.

Oenghus charged into her bedroom, took stock of the situation, and ripped the curtains down, tossing the burning fabric onto the rug.

Angry heat licked at his arms. He gripped the copper tub and heaved it over, sending a wave of water crashing onto the fire. It sizzled, spitting angrily, until it was robbed of its fury.

"What in the Nine Halls happened?" Oenghus demanded.

Isiilde stared at the drenched fireplace in shock. "I didn't do anything, Oen. I swear it. The fire—it just exploded." The excuse sounded pathetic. But she didn't have anything else to offer.

Oenghus wrapped her in a robe and pulled her into an embrace. "It's all right, Sprite," he whispered.

"I wasn't even singing to it!"

"There's no harm done," he soothed. "Everything can be replaced."

But he was wrong—there was harm done. Oenghus' hands and forearms were red with blisters.

Isiilde watched as Morigan bandaged his arms, and she began to feel better. The burns weren't serious. At least nothing Morigan couldn't fix with one of her salves.

It would have been quicker to use the Gift to heal his wounds, but healing took a toll on the patient's body, demanding sleep afterwards.

There were too many patients in the infirmary for Oenghus to rest. The imp had been busy.

Isiilde went from patient to patient, trying to determine what happened to each. Where had they been when attacked? What had they been doing? Did they notice anything?

A pattern emerged—no matter what prank the imp played, each victim had at least one tooth ripped out.

Isiilde recalled its grin of mismatched teeth in the temple, and a theory took shape, one that brightened by the second, until it blossomed into a plan.

...common for Imps to have fetishes... The words came to memory, unbidden. Yes, she thought. That was it.

"Where's Oen?" she asked Morigan.

"In one of the private rooms—with a woman suffering from the Keening."

Isiilde hurried down a hallway. A candle-shrouded shrine to Chaim, Guardian of Life, watched over a quiet ward. She glanced up at the statue's cowled head. His face was serene. And she wondered if the god was as compassionate as everyone claimed.

Of late, she felt as though she had been given a new pair of eyes. The realm was decidedly grim now.

Isiilde found Oenghus kneeling beside a narrow bed. A woman lay there. She looked ever so worn, like an old garment, threadbare and used. Despite her young age, she was fading—in the grips of the Keening.

Oenghus spoke softly to her, smoothing back her auburn hair. "Have some water," he was saying. "Some food. Wine if you like."

But the woman only shook her head. And then tears came unbidden, silent and full of misery. She clutched her stomach beneath the heavy blankets.

"Where is she, m'lord?" the woman whispered.

"Gone to the Spirit River. Safe and sound."

"I will join her soon." At this prophecy of death, hope entered her eyes.

"Why would you want that, lass? There's a lot of life you haven't lived and a lot of hearts that haven't been broken by those eyes of yours."

"I'm tired. Please, just let me go."

"You'll do as you wish, but I'll be back to bother you later," he replied. "Sweet dreams, lass." Oenghus bent forward and placed a fatherly kiss on her forehead.

She did not respond, but stared dimly at the stone wall. Her chest moved steadily with breath, but there wasn't any life in her eyes. A shadow hung in the room, a canopy of death shrouding the woman in silence.

After they left the room, Isiilde asked, "What's wrong with her?"

"Gwen lost her baby in childbirth, and then her Oathbound up and left. She's in the last stages of the Keening."

Inhabitants of Fyrsta did not die of old age, they died when the will to live left them, and not before. Their spirit slowly faded, drifting back to the Spirit River. Nearly everyone felt the Keening's sting from time to time. And some never even made it to the prime of their lives.

"Where's her other family?"

"She doesn't have any, Sprite. It's been near a month. A traveler brought her in when he found her lying in a ditch on the side of a road."

Isiilde's ears wilted. "Why doesn't she just... tell herself to get better?"

"You've never felt the Keening's touch." He gave her shoulders a squeeze. "It's not as simple as that. Life's not always fair and sometimes death seems an easier path."

Isiilde frowned. It was difficult to understand something she couldn't fathom. Besides, the Spirit River sounded cold, wet, and lonely. The last place Isiilde wanted to go.

The thought of the woman lying all alone twisted her heart. Imp or no, she had to do *something*. "Can I sit with her?" she asked. "If it wouldn't be a bother."

"You can't do any harm to her at this point."

Isiilde slipped into the room again and sat by the woman's side. She hesitated, then took Gwen's hand in her own. It was as cold as the sea. No wonder the woman wanted to leave this place.

Gwen should feel the sun before she drifted away, so Isiilde sang in a pure, lilting voice. Her voice soared, weaving emotion rather than words. She sang of the sun, the warmth of its touch, and its lazy caress. Of trickling streams, and swaying hillsides draped in wildflowers.

Her song drifted from the room like a breeze rustling through leaves, traveling along hallways to whisper in every ear. Healers paused, babes calmed, and the injured quieted, listening to a voice of life.

Oenghus glanced around the infirmary. Time seemed to slow, and people moved in a dream. He leaned against a wall and closed his eyes. The ache, the pain, and the worry lifted from his heart. And he smiled at the memory of her mother.

A caress whispered across the back of his neck.

"Light of my life," he whispered. "What will become of our daughter?"

CHAPTER 23

"Oᴇɴ?" She found him leaning against a wall with his pipe in hand. "Do you have any teeth?"

"What in the blazes are you talking about? Of course I have teeth." He bared said teeth.

"No, I mean extra—like in a jar, or something."

Oenghus narrowed his eyes.

"It's for an experiment," she explained.

"I don't bloody keep spare teeth around. Rashk might. Seems like something a Rahuatl might do."

"Why would they keep teeth?"

"You're the one who's asking for them."

"Oh." It *was* an odd request. "I suppose I'll go check with her then."

"Wait now," he growled. "What's this experiment of yours?"

"It's uhm..." she shifted nervously. "...for Marsais."

Isiilde disliked lying, but in a roundabout way the teeth *were* for her master. Before Oenghus could question her further, she hugged him and hurried down the hallway.

Rashk lived on the topmost floor of the second highest tower in the castle. Rahuatl either liked to be up high or slinking in shadows. Isiilde was glad her friend preferred heights—the darkness and press of stone terrified her.

She suspected Rashk had chosen to live as far as she could from N'Jalss. He lived on the same floor as the dungeons. The two Rahuatl loathed each other.

Halfway up the stairwell, she stopped to peek through an arrow loop. Far below, in the outer bailey, the Isle Guard trained in a gloomy drizzle. They looked like little wooden soldiers. Their grunts and clash of wooden sparring swords echoed in the courtyard as a steady stream of horse-drawn carts, messengers, and robed Wise Ones hurried about their business.

Isiilde was about to move on when a bellow pierced the drone of activity. The soldiers in the bailey quickly formed ranks, and Kreem Wyrmbane, the Isle's sharp-tongued quartermaster, marched up the line. After his inspection, he fell in with his troops.

A moment later, the gates were pulled open, and a river of horses and riders flowed into the castle.

Standards bearing the red and gold Phoenix of Xaio glistened like gems in the mist. Two cloaked figures rode in the center with an escort of bodyguards. Their golden helms bristled with steel feathers and beaked visors.

Mearcentian Ship Lords, clad in flowing fabrics of grey, blues, and deep greens, rode in on their heels, their standards billowing like sails.

A terrifying group thundered in after, bearing the black standard of Kiln. Their armor bristled, and their mounts looked set to trample anything in their path.

Hooves stamped, armor settled, and harnesses jingled as the groups dismounted in the inner bailey. Stablehands bolted forward to take the reins.

Lord General Ielequithe of the Isle Guard strode down the steps of the Keep to greet them, her black cape billowing like a storm cloud behind her.

Words were spoken, bows exchanged, and Ielequithe turned on her heel. The diplomats followed, disappearing into the Keep.

It was common for emissaries to visit the Isle, but she'd never seen so many at once. Something to do with the political maneuvering in the South? It seemed every kingdom had a stake in the outcome.

Isiilde knocked on the door at the top of the landing, and Rashk opened it, baring her pointed teeth in greeting.

"Sorry to bother you," Isiilde said, noting the grease on her hands.

Rashk wasn't wearing her finger caps, and she looked naked without the long, curving claws her people favored.

"You are always welcome, fierce one. I was just tinkering. The sun is hidden and Mother Gyrrn sleeps." Rashk urged her in and closed the door, slinking back to her worktable with a sway of wide hips.

Mother Gyrrn was the Rahuatl's mother Goddess who was often represented as a wild, bronzed woman with ten breasts, four arms, pointed teeth, wielding an array of deadly weapons. Isiilde was not sure why Gyrrn's slumber was significant, but she'd learned not to ask about the Rahuatl Goddess, because the answers always made her sick.

Rashk was a collector of oddities and had been amassing a hoard of unlikely treasure for years. Feathers, skulls, insects pinned to cork boards, and everything and anything Isiilde could imagine. Rashk was also a rune enchanter.

A sleek steel helm sat on the table, along with a pile of gems that were scattered around a bowl of clotted blood.

"What are you working on?"

"A paladin of Zahra hired me to craft a helm that will identify a Void-tainted. Perhaps she won't dam the river to catch one fish when this is finished."

Isiilde poked at the helm.

"Do not touch!" Rashk hissed in warning. "Curiosity kills foolish faeries."

Isiilde stuck her hands in her pockets. "Have you ever seen Voidspawn?"

"I have," Rashk replied, sniffing the air with her flat nose. "The Reapers have many lairs in Rraal—nests in the shadow; lairs in the dark."

Isiilde hoped to never meet a Reaper. They were shadow and claw, feasting on the blood of the living.

There was another knock at the door. Rashk growled from the back of her throat.

"I'll get it," Isiilde offered.

Tharios stood at the threshold, his eyes narrowing on the nymph. He wore a wide leather belt of buckles, and a Xaionian half robe of crimson that flared at the waist, leaving his chest bare. A twisting maze of artwork covered his pale skin.

One tattoo moved, and she took a hasty step back. But the reality was far worse than shifting ink—it was a black snake, slithering over his shoulder and twining around his arm. Its lidless eyes watched her with an intelligence a serpent should not possess.

Tharios brushed past her without a second glance. "Rashk, I would speak to you in private." He held a scroll in hand, sealed with a heavy circle of wax.

"I have already told you I do not care what you humans do with your kingdoms."

"This concerns another matter. I require your expertise."

"Isiilde was here first," Rashk said.

Tharios spun on Isiilde, eyes flashing with annoyance.

"Erm…" She faltered. "I was wondering if you had any extra teeth lying around? Unattached ones."

Accustomed to bizarre requests, Rashk walked over to a shelf and plucked a grisly jar from the clutter. In another life, the jar had been a small dog's skull. Clay plugged the openings, sealing the eye sockets, mouth, and nostrils.

"Why do you need teeth, nymph?" Tharios asked, twisting the last word like a curse.

"An errand for the Archlord."

Tharios narrowed his eyes. And she quickly retreated.

With prize in hand, Isiilde sprinted down the stairwell, taking two steps at a time.

Now, only one question remained—where to place the bait? The imp could be anywhere in the castle. She stood at a junction of hallways, poking at the jar full of bloody teeth while she considered her options.

If she were an imp, where would she go? The answer came in a flash:

a place where no one wanted her to go—somewhere with priceless objects. The Hall of Artifacts.

Isiilde cracked the door open and crept into a long, narrow chamber. It was cluttered with priceless objects from before the Shattering. Faded tapestries, pieces of pottery, delicate figurines, and broken swords and melted armor.

She thought of Marsais, of his lost kingdom and his dead people. It saddened her, this tomb of fading memories.

Halfway into the chamber, Isiilde upended the grisly jar. She crouched to study the pile of assorted teeth like a shaman searching for portents. And her stomach flipped. Rashk had not cleaned the teeth.

Before her breakfast joined the bait, she scattered them across the floor with her boot and squeezed behind a nearby tapestry to wait.

Isiilde studied her nails, adjusted her bodice, and started counting to a hundred. But she only got to five before inhaling a layer of dust. She bolted from her hiding place.

Three quick puffs of flame burst from her ears as she sneezed. When her body had finished with her, she whirled around to check the tattered cloth and sighed with relief. The tapestry wasn't on fire.

This time, she chose her concealment with more care, scrambling beneath a table free of flammable materials. She rested her back against stone, and waited.

Long minutes stretched. And she was about to give up on this fool's errand when she heard tuneless humming. The imp appeared, skipping down the hall and picking up a single tooth at a time. It paused with each, holding up its prize to the light and chittering with approval, before moving on to the next.

Isiilde's heart skipped. Her bait had worked—teeth *were* fetishes to the fiend. She'd figured out more than a castle full of Wise Ones. But the book had been vague about the binding part. What in the Nine Halls was she going to do?

When the imp reached the pile of teeth, it squealed with glee, and began dancing merrily around the hoard of ivory treasure.

Isiilde had a dagger, but the thought of stabbing something twisted her heart. Besides, hardened soldiers hadn't been able to kill the fiend.

Without taking her eyes off the imp, she eased the flagon out of her knapsack. The Rune Bind. It was her only option.

The Lore sprang to her lips and her fingers flashed, tracing an intricate series of runes. When the weave was complete, she flicked her wrist towards the imp. It shot off like an arrow, knocking the creature clean off its feet. But her triumph was short-lived. The air around the imp rippled and spread outwards in gentle vibrations. Stone heaved, shifting with a groan; the walls warped inwards, knocking pottery to the floor.

Then everything in the hall moved, caught in a vortex of power, swirling towards the focal point of her weave.

Tapestries were ripped from the walls, and the table covering her was yanked from the floor. It slammed into a chair, smashing the wood to splinters.

As the vortex tugged at her hair, she snatched her things and fled the chaotic weave, the panicked imp matching her stride for stride. They reached the doors together when thunder struck.

A blast hit Isiilde from behind. It hurled her through the doors and into a wall. The castle shook, then settled back on its foundations.

Silence hummed in her ears. The inside of her skull throbbed, pressing against the back of her eyes. She tried to move, but could only curl into a ball of pain.

By the time she cracked an eye open, the dust had settled. A thin figure marched through the ruin, robes flapping in her wake. A small puffball pranced at her side.

Terror breathed life into her. She tried to flee. But she only fell to her knees, coughing with pain.

Thira shook with rage. "You stupid, pathetic, insolent nymph."

Crumpet snarled in agreement.

"I will have you ousted for this!" Thira plucked the flagon from the floor, grabbed Isiilde by an ear, and dragged her past a sea of faces. No one dared challenge the woman.

CHAPTER 24

MARSAIS STOOD in his chamber in front of the crystal window, peering into its complexities. A bellow of flame cut across the misty sky, hitting the tower and cracking the window. It splintered and fell away into a myriad of shards frozen in time.

Marsais tapped a floating fragment, freeing it from time's grip. It fell to the ground and crunched underfoot as he moved to the edge of the opening. The city below burned.

The seer blinked, the bubble of time burst, and a heartbeat later, the crystal window snapped back into focus. Another vision.

It was difficult for him to tell the past from present and future. He drifted in and out of time, battered by its currents like a piece of drift-wood. The driftwood had stopped struggling years before.

His thoughts churned as he sifted through the ages, sorting an expanse of memory in search of the single piece needed to complete his puzzle.

"Marsais."

He snapped back to the present.

Isek stood to the side, looking hungover. "I've been knocking for a while," his assistant said by way of apology.

There was a smudge of lip paint on top of Isek's bald head.

"I hope you had an eventful evening at the pleasure house."

Isek's eyes flashed with surprise.

"I'm a seer." Marsais shrugged, wondering how long it would take his friend to discover the lip paint.

"You also owe me ninety silver. The crew was a tight-lipped bunch, even after four kegs."

"Hmm." The conclusion was obvious. "So you were forced to bed one of their women, who, as it conveniently turned out, knew their deepest secrets."

"Wooed her fair, I did." Isek flashed a charming grin. "So, you ready to hear what I learned? Yes? Right, then. Earlier this year, Tharios' crew harbored in Nefir for a fortnight. The crew was instructed to remain on board. Tharios took a band of twenty mercenaries with him, but only eight returned, and Tharios came back injured. He carried a long box, about yea big—" Isek held his arms apart. "It was a plain box, unadorned and narrow."

"Made of wood or metal?"

"It was blackish, sickly like. I'm thinking witchwood, maybe even ironwood."

Marsais stroked his goatee, coins clinking together like whispering chimes.

"Do you know what it is?"

"Know?" Marsais asked, amused by the question. "I dread what it is, but I need to see it."

"Now look here... Getting a few men soused is one thing, but I'm not about to sneak into Tharios' private chambers. I'm not suicidal."

"I'm glad to hear."

Isek shifted under his stare. "I'll do it if you really want."

"An exceedingly foolish idea. Even for a spy," Marsais said, clucking his tongue in reproof. "As it turns out, I have another idea. Tell me, does Tharios still keep an estate on the outskirts of Drivel?"

"He stays there more than here."

Marsais nodded. It confirmed a suspicion. "Thank you, Isek. You know where I keep my coin. Help yourself to whatever you like."

"Oh, and I haven't forgotten my end of the bargain." Isek pulled a small flask from beneath his coat. "Primrose wine. I thought you could use a few moments of peace."

Marsais brightened, half tempted to indulge on the spot, but he gestured for Isek to place it on his desk. "Ever thoughtful."

Isek turned to leave, but another thought brought him up short. "I passed a flock of emissaries on my way here."

Marsais' heart lurched. No amount of Primrose wine could erase the pain he felt. "I've just come from an audience with them. They'll... inspect her tomorrow."

"Does she know yet?"

Marsais shook his head. "They arrived three days earlier than we expected. *Fair winds*," he said, twisting the words.

"It won't be so bad if Mearcentia wins the bid for her. But Kiln will break her. And you well know what Xaio would do with her. Their bloody Sultan rents out his own harem."

"Isiilde will be broken no matter who buys her," Marsais said with a finality that sealed her fate. At his prophetic words, the castle shuddered.

Isek's eyes widened in alarm. Not a vision, Marsais decided. The two men locked eyes before Isek rushed out of the room to investigate.

It was probably another one of Timmon's miscalculations. Marsais walked over to his desk to search through the tottering pile of books, scrolls, and parchments until he found what he sought: a tattered grimoire with no name. He flipped through its pages until he found a sketch.

"Why this?" he whispered.

The yellowed page of human skin displayed a staff with ornate and nearly identical end caps, each with the symbol of the Nine Halls: the Scorching Sun, a tangle of wicked spikes. Abyssal runes swirled up the staff's surface, too faint to make out, so he studied the notations hastily scrawled onto the skin: *The staff is hot to the touch, charred, yet strong as steel, and covered with thorns.*

A powerful artifact that would have to be carried in a case made from witchwood. Soisskeli's Stave—thought to be lost to time and ruin —was crafted by a powerful Bloodmagus who was tainted by the Void.

An artifact with infinite binding capabilities, so legend went. Its last known location was in Kiln, near Vaylin's border. And Nefir was a perfect launching point for an expedition into Kiln.

Marsais' visions of the future had hinted at Tharios' ambition. Threads of past and present confirmed his knowledge of forbidden arts, but what would binding a fiend from realms beyond accomplish—other than to expose the ambitious young Wise One? What was his interest in Lachlan? *Why* did he need Soisskeli's Stave, and why did he insist on having the Isle's support?

Marsais' eyes widened as the missing piece thudded into place. The Isle *was* the key. Tharios was after something here, in the Order, for the same reason he desired the Archlord's throne: the knowledge of secrets long buried and better off forgotten. But how could he possibly have discovered what lay beneath the Spine, and the true purpose of the Order?

An icy trickle crawled down his spine. "The young fool," he muttered, gently closing the book with a weary sigh.

A stir of air interrupted his thoughts. '*You better get down to your throne room,*' Isek's voice whispered in his ear. '*Trouble has found your apprentice again.*'

Marsais sat on the obsidian throne like a hawk, imperious and all seeing. No sooner had his long fingers curled over the armrests when a trio of figures appeared.

Isek stepped aside at the gate, and Thira marched towards the dais, dragging a terrified nymph by her ear while that dog nipped at her heels.

"*Take your hand from her!*" Marsais' voice crashed over the throne room, echoed by a thousand stone faces, booming from corners above and beyond. One did not ignore a command issued through the Voiceless—not even Thira. A thousand tongues had been sacrificed for the Archlord's power, and another could easily be added.

The Mistress of Novices propelled the nymph forward with a hard shove, and the slip of a faerie stumbled, falling at the foot of his dais.

Isiilde was pale and trembling, bleeding from a gash on her forehead. Despite her distress, she was still a shimmering dream—skin as soft as a petal, lips ripe and red, breasts pushing against the confines of her bodice. She clutched her bruised ear, clearly in pain, but she was alive. More so than any other.

Marsais ached to comfort her. Instead, he focused on Thira. Steel clashed with steel, the cross guards of their eyes locked in a battle of wills, each as unyielding as the other.

"No one may touch my apprentice—not even *you*, Thira." His voice was as hard as the stone at his back.

"I'm a woman, Marsais. It doesn't matter," Thira snapped. "*Your* apprentice has destroyed the Relic Hall. There's nothing left of it."

Marsais arched a brow. He glanced at Isiilde for confirmation, but she wouldn't look at him. She'd flinched at the fury in his voice. And now shook from it.

"I found this in her hand." Thira tossed the rune-etched flagon towards him, and he caught it. "She's to blame for the imp. I want her ousted from the Order."

"What imp?"

"The one causing havoc in the castle."

"Oh, yes, now I remember." He rapped his knuckles on the flagon, listening to the hollow ring that followed. "I'm not sure why you'd oust her when I was the one who opened it."

"You opened it?"

"Didn't I just say that?"

Thira's eyes narrowed on him. "And why would *you* open it?"

"I forgot what was in there."

Thira opened her mouth, but said nothing before closing it with an audible click.

Marsais met her gaze. "Hmm?"

Silence deepened, along with Thira's suspicion. "Why was she carrying the flagon?"

"I asked her to capture the imp. A fiend from the lowest caste of the Nine Halls is hardly worth my time. Or yours, it would seem. You are, after all, a gifted binder."

"And you, after all, are the *Archlord*. It's your responsibility."

"It's a *rat*, Thira. If our guards and fellow Wise Ones can't catch a single rat, then I despair for this Order. Consider it a military exercise. A little damage is expected."

"Damage?" Thira repeated. "The *entire* Relic Hall was destroyed, including priceless artifacts from before the Shattering."

"Artifacts that *were* priceless," he pointed out.

Thira huffed.

"I always thought that hall could be put to better use," he mused.

"You're not going to do anything about this, are you?"

"I will punish her as I see fit," he said calmly, ignoring the fury in her eyes. "She is *my* apprentice."

"She is useless, Marsais. There is only one reason you keep her here. Why else would a man tolerate so much? She's a nymph. You indulge her every whim. But this time she has gone too far." And with a dangerous hiss, she added. "*You* have gone too far."

"Isiilde is my apprentice because she is brilliant. She is also one of the few people I can tolerate. As for my indulgence... Well, I must give you that. After all, she is faerie, and their kind are meant to be indulged."

"Your indulgence borders on blind devotion."

"You may leave now," Marsais ordered, silencing any further arguments.

Thira and her beast stalked out of the throne room. Isek followed on their heels. With a sharp gesture, Marsais ordered the gates to close. They slammed shut with a deafening clang.

Isiilde wept at his feet. Softly. The mournful sound echoed in the vast chamber. "I'm so sorry, Marsais. I can't do anything right."

Marsais watched the trembling nymph. He did not trust himself with her today. Too much of his heart ached to comfort her—to wrap her in his arms and take her from this Isle, far away from the path that awaited.

But this realm would pay for his weakness. And all the realms would suffer.

The nymph was a single, seemingly insignificant thread in the tangle, yet so much was bound to her Fate. This beautiful, innocent, and brilliant creature shivering at his feet was the catalyst that could send the lands spiraling into chaos.

No matter how he ached, Marsais could not see a way to extract her thread from the rest. Of all the creatures who ever drew breath, of all the good and evil that walked the lands—why Isiilde?

Damn the gods, Fate, and the imbecile who wrought them.

Marsais forced himself to focus on the present—on every breath, every heartbeat, because the future would come too soon.

He went to her, sitting down on the edge of the dais, feeling drained. "Let me see your forehead."

Isiilde raised her eyes to him, as deep as the seas and full of sadness. Marsais couldn't face those eyes today, so he focused on her injury.

Taking care not to touch her, he dabbed at the cut with the long sleeve of his robe, and then fished around his pocket for a handkerchief, pressing the clean linen to her wound.

"Head wounds always bleed profusely, but I believe you will live." He smiled down at her.

"I think she broke my ear."

Marsais studied the slender, swept back ear that rose from her copper curls, climaxing in an enticing crescendo. *By all that breathed, she was distracting today.*

"Hmm, bruised, but not broken, I think. Some ice will help."

Marsais stood abruptly and paced on the dais, balancing carefully along its edge. "So what happened?" he asked.

Talking brightened her mood, and he listened with interest to her account. He drew up short when she told him about the binding rune.

"What an interesting side effect—if dangerous. You're lucky to be alive, my dear. I believe you bound the imp, but you forgot to tether him to the flagon."

"Oh." Her ears wilted. "Are you angry with me?"

"No more than last time I was angry with you."

"But, Marsais, you've never been angry with me." A smile curved her lips, and he nearly fell off the dais.

"Exactly, but I *am* relieved you're not seriously hurt. And if you feel up to it, I require your assistance."

"But what's my punishment?"

"Spending your afternoon with an insane old man."

"You're not old, Marsais," she said, climbing to her feet.

"You see, my dear, I was hoping you'd say I wasn't insane, because the fact is, I am rather old. Ancient, in fact."

"If you're insane, then maybe you haven't lived as long as you think."

"Are you an expert on matters of insanity?"

"I don't think you could be an expert unless you were insane. Your qualifications would be suspect."

"But if I'm insane and I believe myself old, isn't that the same as the reverse?" he asked, eyes twinkling with mirth.

"What I meant," she said, crossing her arms, "is you don't look old. In fact, compared to Tharios, you are much nicer to look at."

"Aha! Here I thought you were spying; instead, I discover you were comparing men."

"I was doing both," she said. "I'm talented like that."

"Yes, you are. More so than you know."

Isiilde blushed. "You're quite beautiful, you know."

"Just what a man wants to hear," he said dryly.

"Oen *does* call you a dandy all the time."

"Well, I prefer your term of beautiful. Not, I should add, if Oen used it. And..." he gave her a gracious bow, "thank you."

"Marsais?"

"Hmm."

"Will there be food involved in this punishment?"

CHAPTER 25

BECAUSE A PROPER PUNISHMENT should always involve food, they stopped at a small kitchen. Then they strode through the castle, eating like a pair of barbarians. Marsais noticed that every man they passed gawked at the oblivious nymph, and he moved to obstruct the men's open-mouthed stares. Her hips might be slender, but their sway was hypnotic.

Isiilde was beautiful. But not the mere beauty of flesh. It was beauty of the kind only nature could create—a sunset, the wash of waves, an endless sky, and an untouched glade. It was beauty that moved one to tears and cut to the bone.

Primrose wine was an apt comparison to an Awakened nymph. Her blood was ancient, and it called to him. Her touch from the pleasure house lingered still. She'd been on the verge of bonding with him, but he'd stopped it.

Every vision warned him away from that path. Every such road led to destruction.

She loved him. And he loved her. But Marsais could not abandon the realm to ruin. He would not. No matter how it ravaged his heart.

"Marsais." Isiilde stopped so suddenly he nearly ran into her. "Where are we going?"

Marsais scratched at the raw scar beneath his robes, pondering that very question. "We're looking for that blasted imp." He pulled the flagon from her knapsack. Unfortunately, when he touched it, nothing came to mind. His *gift* of foresight was rarely useful when he needed it.

"Where would you go to find him?"

"The armory," she replied.

"Hmm, any reason?"

"I'm not allowed there."

It had a certain... logic to it. "As good a place as any. Lead on, my dear."

At his gesture, Isiilde continued walking. But after a time, she glanced over her shoulder. "Marsais?"

"Hmm."

"Why are you behind me?"

"Because your trousers are too tight and every man we pass is staring at your backside," he told her bluntly.

Isiilde stopped again (though he had expected it). "That's ridiculous, Marsais. I'm far too—how did you put it in Coven—*slight*?"

"I was attempting to be optimistic. And you may think it ridiculous, but if you're a man, your figure is exceptionally nice to look at."

Isiilde twisted around, trying to glimpse that portion of her anatomy. "I thought they were staring at my funny ears."

"They're not funny. You have lovely ears, Isiilde."

Mist shimmered in her eyes. "Thank you."

She will not think so well of me tomorrow, he thought grimly. A moment later, Marsais ran into the nymph whose feet had faltered once again. She stumbled forward, and he nearly reached out to steady her, but brought himself up short, tucking his hands into his sleeves instead.

"You should keep walking."

"Are *you* staring at my backside?"

"No."

She narrowed her eyes at that single, clipped reply, but said nothing more.

Isiilde led him to a long chamber filled with suits of armor—a library of warfare. The displays gleamed eerily beneath torches of everlight.

"Why aren't you allowed in here?" He'd assumed she meant the armory in the barracks wing.

"The Seneschal kicked me out last year." Isiilde didn't expound; he didn't ask.

"Do you have those teeth?"

Her ears wilted. "I left them in the Relic Hall."

"I suppose you had no time to retrieve them. Wise of you."

Isiilde brightened, and slipped her hand into one of her trouser pockets, working her fingers into the tight fit to produce a blood-caked molar.

"Thedus gave this to me," she explained, dropping it into his palm.

Marsais studied the tooth with a wary eye as she cleaned her hands on his robe.

"Is Thedus really dangerous?"

"People fear what they don't understand."

"That doesn't answer my question."

"No, it doesn't," he agreed.

After determining that the tooth was harmless, he placed it on the floor. Then stepped back beside a suit of Kilnish steel—blued and bristling with spikes.

The air rippled, and a horde of soldiers in crimson and black livery snapped into view. They turned on each other; the battle raged across the chamber, filling with screams and howls as blood and bowels spilled over the floor.

Marsais blinked. Time shifted, and all was quiet. Not even an echo lingered. The hall stood empty, and the nymph stood staring up at him.

"Ah, my dear." Marsais smiled, pleased to watch her instead of men being disemboweled.

"Are you all right?" Her lilting voice soothed his mind.

"Likely not," he muttered. His gaze settled on the lone tooth in the center of the floor. "Ah, yes, the imp."

"How are you going to catch him?"

"I'm not."

"But I don't think he can be killed," she pointed out, studying the bristling set of armor.

"You're correct. Why else would I bind an imp to a flagon?"

"Marsais," she hissed. "You said you didn't know what was in the flagon! That's why I opened it. I couldn't stop wondering what was in there."

"That's understandable. Faerie, myself included, have insatiable curiosity."

"Then why didn't you tell me what was in there?" Isiilde crossed her arms, which drew attention to her breasts.

Marsais closed his eyes briefly, wishing for another vision to distract him. None was forthcoming, so he looked everywhere else.

"I had forgotten about the little fiend, which brings me to another dilemma. I can't remember the imp's name."

"Why do you need its name?"

"We're not here to recapture him. I have something else in mind."

"Which is?"

"I'm not at liberty to say."

Isiilde bristled, emerald eyes flashing, and he could not help but look at her. *By the gods, she was breathtaking when she was angry.*

"Does it have to do with the emissaries who arrived earlier today?"

"No," he replied curtly, and began pacing before she could ask another question. "I think it starts with a *B*."

"What?"

"The imps name. Do try to pay attention, my dear. I need to remember it before he shows up."

"How about Bjorn, Bolvine, Bazrin—" she began.

"No, no, imps aren't noble by nature. They usually have ridiculous names such as Blimp or Bip."

Isiilde pondered this for a moment, then launched into a sing-song stream of names beginning with *B*.

Marsais listened with half an ear while he searched his faulty memory, trying to recall when he had bound the little devil. Where had it been? Somewhere in the Bastardlands, terrorizing a village, long before he trained Oenghus as an apprentice. So over eight hundred years ago.

He stopped to regard his current apprentice, who was still busy listing a myriad of mostly made-up names, while she studied her backside in a mirrored greave. His attention was drawn elsewhere when he spotted the imp crouching over the tooth.

The currents shifted, time rippled, and a heartbeat later it vanished. "Our little friend is coming."

Isiilde blushed in surprise, abandoning her self-inspection to take cover behind him. Minutes passed, and the name still eluded him.

Isiilde prodded the suit of armor, sniffing at the breastplate. "Marsais?" she whispered, sliding her hand into a dangling gauntlet.

"Hmm."

"Have you ever been in a battle?"

"Yes," he replied, softly.

A surprised face with wide eyes poked around to stare up at him. "Did you wear one of these?" She wiggled her fingers in the gauntlet.

"My thin frame was never intended for such casing." He arched a brow down at her. "Why do you ask?"

"They are like monsters waiting for a spirit to enter them." She snatched her hand from the metal, inching closer to him. He could feel her trembling. "I don't think the man who died in this ever left."

Further questioning on this remarkable bit of insight was cut short when a little greasy creature came skipping in.

"Have you remembered?" she whispered. He gave a slight shake of his head.

The imp skipped up to the molar, plucked it from the ground, and began a maniacal dance of glee.

Blast it, what in the Nine Halls was its name?

Prize in hand, the imp turned to leave. But before it could escape, Marsais wove a quick enchantment, and with a careless flick of his hand, the doors slammed shut.

The imp straightened in alarm, then took flight, bolting for a shuttered window.

"Isiilde, go distract him."

"What?" She looked up at him as if he weren't already insane.

"Imps love faerie," Marsais said, waving a languid hand towards the fiend. "Keep him occupied."

The imp caught sight of the pair and began chattering angrily.

Isiilde took a few timid steps towards the center of the chamber, glancing nervously at the flapping imp overhead. It screeched, whipped its tail, and flew straight for her. She threw up her arms, and ducked.

Marsais grabbed a spiked helm off its stand and hurled it at the fiend. It hit a wing, sending the creature spiraling out of control and skidding along the floor. When the imp recovered, it zipped straight for Isiilde. She retreated in panic and tripped, falling.

"Luccub!" Marsais snapped his fingers in triumph.

The imp scampered to a halt.

"Stay where you are," Marsais ordered in the Abyssal tongue. "Or I will put you back in this flagon without your collection of teeth."

The imp's beady eyes flashed with threat.

"Don't you dare try it, Luccub," he warned. "I have a simple task for you. You'll enjoy it. And you can steal all the teeth you desire."

Luccub straightened with a flutter of wings, tail swishing back and forth.

By nature, imps were cunning creatures—when they felt like it. As Marsais explained what he required, the imp bared its misshapen teeth, offended by the meager use of its talents. For a fiend who could not be killed by usual means, sneaking into Tharios' private estate offered little challenge.

But Marsais needed to confirm his theories before accusing the traitorous Wise One (or soon to be traitorous, at any rate). A delicate touch was called for—one of risk and timing. A show of strength too soon could prove disastrous.

Marsais dismissed Luccub, who flapped dutifully out, and turned to find an agitated nymph glaring up at him.

"What?" He snatched the helm turned missile from the floor and set it carefully back on its stand.

"You said his name started with a *B*," Isiilde said, slowly. "Luccub does not start with a *B*."

"How very perceptive of you."

"So you're not going to tell me what all that was about?"

"Perhaps you should learn Abyssal," he suggested.

She frowned, spun around, and stalked away. Marsais watched her departing form, admiring the sway of her hips. When he realized what he was doing, he shook the vision from his mind.

After two thousand years, one would think I'd be immune, he thought irritably.

"Isiilde," he called, hurrying after her. She waited for him to catch up. "I'm not going to tell you because it's dangerous."

"It has to do with Tharios," she stated.

"Correct, but the less you know the better."

"You've discovered what you thought he found."

"Hmm."

"And now you've sent the imp to investigate."

"I haven't told you a single thing, so if Oenghus asks why I've dragged you into this—I haven't."

"Well, I'm not sure if it matters, but Tharios paid a visit to Rashk this morning. He said he needed her expertise."

Marsais stroked his goatee at this bit of information. It confirmed his hope that Tharios still had questions about the stave.

"Marsais?"

"Hmm."

"Can I spend the rest of my punishment napping?"

"Whatever you deem proper, my dear."

"In that case, a foot rub would be near torture." Her smile was hopeful, and her eyes large and entrancing. The effect was stunning.

Marsais tore his gaze from those eyes, because he doubted he could deny her if he lingered a moment longer. He strode briskly away, leaving the nymph to catch up.

CHAPTER 26

Tharios paused, quill poised, to study his notes, the echo of his past lives whispering in his ear, urging him onwards.

We will be remembered. You will be remembered. And feared.

At first, those voices had come in dreams. But secrets grew in the dark, the veils between rebirth had dropped, and light had dawned.

"So close, so soon, my Lord," he whispered.

A secret dwelt beneath this tower. And Tharios would be the one to set it free—the Chosen One.

A loud knock shattered his past, and he inhaled deeply, calming his thoughts. Tharios sheathed his quill, draped a silk robe over his bare shoulders, and closed his writing desk before rising to meet his unexpected visitors.

Unexpected, but not unforeseen.

"Master Tulipin and Mistress Thira, to what do I owe this pleasure?" Tharios purred, noting the gnome's extreme agitation and the dangerous glint in the woman's eye. Neither of these surprised him, considering the recent destruction of the Relic Hall. Thira was ever the stickler for order.

"We're sorry to disturb you at such a late hour, but there is a delicate matter we wish to discuss," Thira said.

Delicate. The word was music to his ears. At his invitation, Thira marched inside with the vermin on her heels.

Next came Tulipin, eyes darting nervously around the chamber. Tharios offered them seats, but neither accepted, so he settled into his chair, and waited patiently for them to utter the first words of rebellion.

He did not have to wait long. Thira immediately dragged the matter into the open.

"The nymph must be ousted. She has brought nothing but trouble to this Order."

"The destruction of the Relic Hall is a grave loss, but this Order is rife with accidents," Tharios reasoned. "We dabble with dangerous forces. One expects it in our line of research."

"Most have sense enough to take precautions," Thira snapped. "The nymph is utterly devoid of common sense."

"It's not a simple matter of accidents," Tulipin said. "She has desecrated a shrine to Zahra and accused the Blessed Order of blasphemous deeds."

"The nymph's list of misconduct grows by the day," Thira said. "I will not stand for it a moment longer. You have the Order's support, Tharios. You're well respected and your voice carries weight. Do something about this... this *thing*!"

"I'm afraid I'm not the Archlord," Tharios said. "I believe we've tried to cast her out before. But Marsais has always used his position to overrule us."

"Marsais is mad," Thira hissed. "There is no other word for it. He defends that creature's every action."

"The seer's cycle is nearly up. A new vote will be cast and we're confident you will win the majority," Tulipin said.

"The vote won't be for another year."

"That's why we've come," Tulipin said.

Tharios leaned forward with interest. Let them think this was their idea. The immortal fool would lose his throne with or without Tharios' meddling. But he needed to speed things along, and the nymph was proving a useful tool with which to hang her master.

CHAPTER 27

A KNOCK PULLED Isiilde from slumber. She cracked open an eye, blinking at the dim light of her room. The knock sounded again. It was not on her bedroom door, but on an outer one that opened to the tower.

She yawned, pulling a blanket over her head. Oenghus would answer it.

And that was true. He did. She heard the door open, hushed voices, her guardian's rumbling. It sounded like a muted roar.

Who would visit so early? Marsais?

The thought got her out of bed, and she was tugging on a robe when someone did knock on her door. "Tell Marsais I'll be right there."

"Sprite…" Oenghus sounded exhausted. Wounded.

Isiilde opened the door, and froze. It was not Marsais, but Lord General Ielequithe standing in their main room. Her raven hair was pulled into a topknot, the hair shorn on the sides. She held a helm under her arm, and her face was a determined mask.

There were others, too. Isle Guards waiting in the outer hallway.

Isiilde looked to her guardian, startled. He was dressed in his kilt and best shirt, with his hair pulled back and beard neatly trimmed. "What's going on, Oen?"

Oenghus ran a hand over his haggard face, then turned to the Lord General. "Give us a moment."

"A moment, Grimstorm, that's all."

Oenghus led Isiilde back to her room. "A message arrived from the Emperor last week."

Her heart skipped a beat.

"I didn't want you to—I didn't tell you. I wanted you to have a peaceful few days."

Isiilde could hardly breathe.

"Emissaries from Kiln, Xaio, and Mearcentia arrived yesterday morning. They've come to meet you."

Isiilde shook her head in disbelief. She shivered, her skin crawled, and her heart fought to free itself from her breast.

"They will not take you," he growled, cupping her face in his massive hands. He held her eyes with his own. "*Not yet.*"

"I don't want to see them, Oen." Her voice sounded distant in her own ears. "Have Marsais send them away."

"He can't do that, Sprite. The order comes straight from your—from the emperor. These are emissaries from powerful kingdoms. Marsais can't send them away without risking war. Do you understand?"

Isiilde looked into his eyes. They shone like sapphires, deep blue and glittering with pain. She did not understand. Not at all. And she told him so. "But I'll meet them," she heard herself saying.

LORD GENERAL IELEQUITHE and her soldiers escorted Isiilde to a barren room in the tower. A pedestal sat in the room's center, bathed in light from a row of windows.

Isiilde focused on the blustery garden outside, where emerald leaves dripped with rain.

"You're looking well, nymph."

The woman's voice made her shudder. Caitlyn Whitehand stood in the window's light, as far away as she could get from another occupant in the room. Caitlyn's blonde hair was severely pulled back in its customary chignon. She wore an austere green dress with a crisp white apron.

Isiilde ignored the woman, looking to Marsais, who stood resplendent in his crimson robes. He did not turn to greet her, but kept his eyes fixed on the garden.

"There is a robe for you. I'll inspect you shortly." Caitlyn gestured to a small room off to the side.

Isiilde bristled. "You inspected me six months ago. I'm not of age yet." The lie was convincing, because she wanted to believe it with all her heart.

"The only thing your buyers are concerned with is your virginity. Don't prolong this, nymph. If need be, I'll have my assistants hold you down."

Oenghus stood in the doorway, glaring at the healer with baleful eyes.

Isiilde could feel her guardian trembling with barely controlled rage. What would happen if he lost control? Would Oenghus kill the emissaries?

She glanced at Ielequithe and the waiting escort of veteran guards. Those guards, she realized, were not for her—they were for Oenghus. And he was not the only formidable warrior on the isle.

Morigan was right: there *is* always a choice. But that didn't mean one was better than the other.

Isiilde made her choice, and walked into the side room.

The waiting robe was different than usual. Nearly sheer Kilnish silk slid over her skin. It felt divine, and yet repulsive for what it represented.

Caitlyn wasted no time; her inspection was as humiliating as ever. When the healer had finished, Isiilde stood to redress, untying the robe with trembling fingers.

"That won't be necessary," Caitlyn said. "Leave the robe on and come with me."

Isiilde froze as Caitlyn opened the door. Oenghus and Marsais were still there, heads bent together in quiet conversation.

She took a slow breath, hugging the robe to her, and walked back into the room. As she rejoined them, Oenghus looked over at her, eyes narrowing.

"Get your clothes on," Oenghus ordered, and Isiilde eagerly started to obey, but Caitlyn blocked her path, closing the door.

"The robe is perfectly suitable. You may both leave now," Caitlyn said, nodding curtly to the men.

Neither of the men left.

"What are you getting at?" Oenghus growled, taking a threatening step towards the woman.

In reply, Caitlyn produced a sealed scroll. Oenghus snatched the scroll and ripped the seal off. Marsais moved over to his side, brows climbing ever higher as he read the missive in Oenghus' hands.

While the men were occupied, Caitlyn began brushing Isiilde's hair, fussing over her bruised ear and the gash on her forehead.

Confused, near to panic, Isiilde watched Marsais and Oenghus, searching for answers.

One came when Oenghus crushed the scroll in his hand, and turned on Caitlyn. "I'll not stand for this!" he roared.

Lord General Ielequithe stepped forward. Not in threat, but as a reminder of one. Shouldn't the Lord General serve the Archlord?

Isiilde's confusion seemed a small thing compared to the tension in the air.

"Then accept the consequences of treason, Oenghus Saevaldr. What did you expect would happen? Would you buy a horse without examining it? Oh, don't start crying, nymph, you'll look a wreck."

"Isiilde is not a horse," Oenghus growled, taking another step forward.

"You're correct, she's a nymph," Caitlyn replied, as if that were all the explanation needed.

"Oenghus," Ielequithe warned. "Would you really risk it with an innocent in the room?"

The berserker looked to the Lord General with all the wildness of his kind. The woman did not even flinch.

Marsais quickly stepped forward and placed a hand on his arm. "I'll stay with her."

"*Both* of you must leave," Caitlyn said, firmly. "I'll not suffer any distractions. The potential buyers have each paid fifty thousand crowns for the privilege of viewing her."

Isiilde's eyes widened, but the exorbitant price was far from flattering; instead, the cold knot in her chest tightened and began to spread to her limbs.

"I am Archlord of this Isle," Marsais said, stepping forward. "You are a guest in my house, and I will have the final say."

"Then I will take her back to Kambe," Caitlyn threatened. "His Majesty's orders were explicit in this matter."

"Hmm." Marsais stroked his goatee, eyes flickering to Isiilde for the first time. "One does wonder why she wasn't taken to Whitemount. Perhaps the seas are a bit more turbulent than the emperor would currently like." His voice was soft and suggestive. "No one is safe with the Bastard Prince roaming the seas, especially a treasure such as she."

Caitlyn's mouth clicked shut.

"Very well, as Archlord, you may stay." She surrendered with a respectful nod.

Isiilde's knees went weak with relief.

"How magnanimous of you," Marsais said dryly.

"I'll be right outside, Sprite." Oenghus squeezed her shoulder, leaning down to whisper in her ear. "I'm sorry."

When her guardian left, along with Ielequithe, Caitlyn ordered Isiilde to stand on the pedestal. Caitlyn placed a supporting hand on her elbow, but Isiilde shook it off with a glare, stepping on top of the cushioned pedestal unassisted.

She felt like a vase on display as Caitlyn stepped back to appraise her.

Marsais appeared impassive as ever. Serene in power, aloof from others. But Isiilde *knew* him—she could read his turmoil from the set of his shoulders and spine. And his anger, from the restlessness in his fingers.

"You will not speak, nymph, unless I tell you to do so. Keep still and do not meet their eyes. Look straight ahead, or down at the floor if you must. Otherwise the Kilnish emissaries will claim you aren't properly submissive."

"May I sit? My legs are shaking." She barely recognized her own voice.

"You must stand and do as you're told. This won't take long." Caitlyn paused to primp the nymph one last time, tilting her chin just so, and fluffing her robe before striding out.

"*Marsais,*" Isiilde pleaded. But he said nothing, looking as pale as his white hair. He gave her a slight shake of his head, stirring the coins on his goatee with a soft chime.

The door opened and her body went numb as six men, dressed in the finery of their respective kingdoms, entered the room.

First came the Kilnish lord—ebony skin, broad-shouldered, and firm of jaw. His chest was bare, his muscles rippling with power. Chin raised proudly, his pale eyes appraised her. An assistant followed closely on his heels, his position apparent from his lighter skin tone and the ring that pierced his nose. He carried a ledger and a quill in hand.

Xaionian officials entered, garbed in bizarre trappings of leather and buckles with silver piercings linked by thin chains. They appraised the nymph with the cool disinterest of merchants, acting bored and convincing no one.

The Mearcentian lords were last. They were dressed in high-collared robes of embroidered fabric that resembled a gleaming sea. Trinkets and charms were woven into their long black hair. They paused to bow respectfully to the Archlord before turning their gazes to the nymph.

The room felt small, their eyes too close, as the men moved slowly around their desired prize.

"Her name is Isiilde Jaal'Yasine, and her blood is pure, a daughter of Emperor Soataen Jaal III," Caitlyn said without offering introductions.

The men's eyes were fixed on her—studying, assessing, greedy for possession. She did not like their stares. Isiilde cast about for Marsais, who stood silently off to the side, watching the men.

After a single circuit, the Xaionian officials stopped directly in front of her and one gestured languidly towards her robe. "Let us see what this creature has to offer."

Caitlyn stepped forward, reaching for the sparse robe. Isiilde clutched at the front of the garment as it began to slide from her shoulders.

"I will not!"

The Xaionians gave a sickening smile.

"She will need to learn obedience," the Kilnish emissary told his scribe, who made a note in his ledger.

Marsais stepped next to the Xaionian, ignoring the man to look into her eyes. Standing on the pedestal as she was, they were nearly of the same height.

"My dear," his gentle voice soothed her heart. "I want you to look at me, and focus as you would on your fire."

"But Marsais, please—" A tear broke free, shimmering down her cheek.

"Look into my eyes," he whispered for her alone, standing tall and proud in her line of sight. "I am the only man here."

Caitlyn tugged the robe free, and it slid from her shoulders. Cold air whispered against her bare flesh as the silk pooled at her feet.

Sounds of appreciation traveled the room. The air was thick with lust as they circled her like vultures. But Isiilde paid them no mind. She was drawn into a pair of calm grey eyes.

"I have seen boys more shapely than this nymph," remarked the Kilnish lord.

"Some clients find that appealing," the Xaionian mused.

"Does she not eat?" the Mearcentian asked with concern.

"She is so frail," his companion agreed.

"Too willful."

Their voices droned on, and Isiilde did not care. They were ever so far away, distant flutters of blustery air and nothing more. Marsais' lips twitched with the slightest of smiles.

"She will need a proper diet."

"How old is she?"

"Her breasts are too small—"

"My assistant will check her claim to innocence."

"You will not touch her!" Marsais snapped, breaking the spell he'd woven for her.

Isiilde jerked at the harshness in his tone. The connection was broken, and it left her cold and rigid with a heart that thundered like a waterfall.

The emissaries took a hasty step away from the Archlord, eyeing him warily.

"I have already established her innocence," Caitlyn said into the tense silence.

"You represent the interests of Kambe," the Xaionian pointed out. "We wouldn't know she had been sullied until after payment was received. It is in your best interest to make that claim."

Marsais stepped directly in front of Isiilde, blocking her body with his own as he turned to face the emissaries. His long hair brushed her bare skin. She could feel the heat of his body beneath his robes.

"I will vouch for the nymph. I give you my word as Archlord that no man has ever touched her."

The Kilnish lord started to object, but Marsais silenced him with a sharp gesture.

"Anyone with half a brain knows there's no such thing as a *virginity test*. But a nymph's mark does not lie. There is no mark. Therefore, she has never bonded with a man, or as you say, she is still innocent."

His words were calm, but there was an undercurrent of quiet threat that stilled the other men in the room.

"You must hear the nymph sing," Caitlyn said, trying to diffuse the tension. "Sing for them, nymph."

Isiilde's eyes flashed with fury. "My voice is my own and I will *not* be ordered about." She stared defiantly at the men.

But the emissaries took no offense; instead, their eyes went wide, drinking her in with thirsty gazes.

"You have seen enough," Marsais said. "Leave. *Now*."

There was more command in his steely voice than a roar. One by one, the men tore their eyes from the vision and filed out, casting furtive glances as they left.

When the door shut, Isiilde's legs gave out, and she collapsed in a trembling heap.

CHAPTER 28

Marsais watched a vision of Tharios pacing in front of the crystal window. He wore the crimson robe of an Archlord.

The study was changed, too. More impressive than Marsais' current one. The frost bear pelt had been replaced by a circle of blue runes. Portal Magic. And not of a common sort: it lacked the gruesome style of the Bloodmagi and looked nothing like the golden Portals of Iilenshar. This was something ancient, similar to the Gateways hidden beneath the Spine.

Marsais did not recognize the rune pattern. But that meant little—there were gaps in his memories. Knowledge was a beautiful thing; it came to one when it chose and not before.

As if to underscore his thoughts, the vision vanished, or perhaps it shifted (he could never really tell).

"Dare I ask?"

Marsais twitched in surprise. Another vision. He turned, searching the room, but relaxed when he spotted Isek standing behind a cluttered desk. "Ask what?"

"What you were staring at?"

"Not unless it's what we were talking about," Marsais snapped.

Undaunted, Isek pointed to a stack of reports. "I was sharing news from the Thanes in the South. In short, Lachlan united the Thanes without swinging a blade. The newly united kingdom is having a joyous festival, and he's sent greetings of 'peace and goodwill' to all his neighbors."

"Hmm, didn't Ramashan do the same when he liberated that cursed island in the name of peace?"

"Aren't we cynical today," Isek muttered, shifting to another report. "He's named his new kingdom 'Lachland'."

Marsais snorted. "By the gods, what an unimaginative absurdity."

"Yes, imagine a ruler naming his lands after himself, such as—Marsais *zar'Vaylin*."

"You're not supposed to know that."

"Well, you shouldn't get drunk and tell me."

Marsais yanked on his goatee in irritation.

"Oenghus is being 'questioned' by the Blessed Order concerning his desecration of Zahra's temple. The Circle conveniently called an emergency council, and since he was absent, Thira agreed to sit in his place until he returns. One gold crown says they're going to reassess our position in the South."

"You'd make an excellent seer," Marsais replied dryly.

"Of a more delicate nature, the bidding for Isiilde is in high swing. They've been communicating with Kambe through Whisperers for the past four days. Xaio is on top at the moment. They threw in exclusive trade rights and free passage for Kambe—as long as Isiilde lives. Although Mearcentia could do the same, and we all know how Kiln feels about losing to them, so I wouldn't count them out yet."

Marsais scratched at the burning scar on his chest as he gazed at the plush pelt. A vision of Isiilde was there, broken and battered, dressed in the trappings of a Xaionian bed slave, staring at something unseen.

How she had faded.

Marsais surged to his feet. He dunked his head in a washbasin, scrubbing at his eyes as if something so simple could wipe the vision from his mind. Just as quickly, he pushed the hair out of his face. Water dripped down his robes as he clutched the side of the table, trying not to be sick.

Isek watched him carefully. "When did you last sleep, Marsais?"

"I do not need a nursemaid," he snarled.

"You can't go to the council looking like that."

"Then you go." He paced his study, closing his eyes against the shifting sands of time.

"Why don't *you* buy Isiilde?"

"I can't."

"The bidding is up to four hundred thousand crowns, but if you empty your coffers and throw in a few 'trinkets' from that vault of yours, I'm sure you could match it."

"Do not tempt me!" Marsais shouted.

Isek's brows shot up.

Marsais shuddered and took a calming breath. It did not loosen the ache in his heart.

"I went to the pleasure house some months back. I needed a respite, a bit of the seed for my mind. You can't imagine the visions plaguing me of late," he confided. "I had a true vision, a dreaming daze atop my perch, like a bird of prey watching the byways of time. It all stretched out so clearly. In one, I walked down that path, but in our happiness this realm suffered. I am not meant for her. I *cannot* choose her!"

Isek answered this outburst with silence. And finally, when Isek spoke, he chose his words carefully. "For as long as I've known you, I've never seen you in love—until now."

"My heart perished too long ago for that," he whispered. "I cannot love Isiilde as she deserves. I only wish her happiness—to protect her until a more deserving man arrives."

"That sounds a lot like love to me, old friend."

"There is but one path—one death." He swallowed back the words like bile rising in his throat. "I can't do it. I couldn't before, and I can't now. Oenghus will, if it comes to that."

"You're not making any sense. What are you talking about?"

"Never mind." Marsais waved a dismissive hand. "I'm a raving madman, remember?"

"If you're going to the council, then you should get cleaned up."

"Stand for me. Say what you like. I care not if they take my throne." Marsais spared one last look at the empty rug before stalking out of his study.

CHAPTER 29

Isiilde narrowed her eyes at a guard. The stern-faced woman stood ten feet away on the King's Walk. She glanced uneasily at her charge, half-concealed behind a statue.

The unit of guards had begun as four, but through misdirection, twisting corridors, and secret passages, Isiilde had shaken the others off her trail.

This one was persistent, though. And nervous. The guard couldn't leave Isiilde to get reinforcements, so she stood in the flickering torchlight, watching and hoping the others would catch up.

Isiilde ducked back behind the statue. She rested her head against the faerie queen's thighs, and poked sullenly at the sheathed dagger on her hip. How could she hope to escape the island when an entire army was keeping an eye on her?

She'd tried to sneak out through a gate. Several times. But there were eyes in every corridor. And early this morning, the Blessed Order had come for Oenghus. He'd been charged with sacrilege, for destroying a temple of Zahra, and taken away for questioning.

People were executed for sacrilege. And it was her fault—she'd loosed the imp. Her tears had dried up. They were useless anyway.

"I've always wondered if you were related to her," a familiar voice mused.

Isiilde clenched her teeth, keeping her eyes firmly on the back wall of the alcove where she hid.

"You missed three of your lessons."

Marsais had come by every day. But Isiilde either made sure she was gone, or didn't answer the door. She didn't want to speak with him—he'd left her on the floor. In that room. The men's eyes had gleamed so brightly it made her skin crawl.

There was a long silence, filled only by the clinking of the guard's mail and the soft chiming of Marsais' coins.

"Well..." He sighed. "If you change your mind, you know where to find me."

"What's the point?" she seethed.

"The point of what, Isiilde?"

"Lessons! Lore books, reading, wielding the Gift?" Isiilde hopped to her feet, and stepped from behind the statue to face the man. Torches flared along with her anger, and Marsais took a hasty step backwards.

"The point? Why to learn, of course."

"Why should I learn? I am to be *sold*." Isiilde bristled, hot tears hissing on her skin. "Do you think they will let me stay here?"

Isiilde advanced, but Marsais stood his ground.

"Do you think Oenghus will be able to come? Will they let either of you visit? I will never see you again, because I am nothing more than a man's plaything! What use is a *nymph* who can read and write? What good will that do in my slave master's bed?"

Torchlight surged three feet in the air to singe stone.

"Calm down, my dear," Marsais urged. "It may not be as bad as you believe. They are rich kingdoms. You'll have every luxury."

"So am I to be the king's prize steed?"

The embodiment of fury flared to life in front of Marsais and he stiffened, fingers twitching nervously.

"To be groomed as my owner sees fit."

The words burned down her throat.

"To be fed what he wishes and exercised when he deems it proper. To be mounted whenever my owner has an urge—do not speak to me of luxury!"

With the final lash of her tongue, fire filled the tunnel, seeking something to sate its hunger.

Marsais gathered the flame into a rolling ball with a quick flash of his fingers and hurled it into a wall. Sparks flew, stone blackened, and the tunnel went dark.

"Stop it!" Isiilde screamed.

"Stop what?" Marsais snapped back. With a flash of fingers, he wove a Light Rune, and it pulsed to life in the dim.

The guard had drawn her sword, but Marsais held up a halting hand.

"I hate it when you do that," Isiilde fumed.

"Do what?"

"Stop answering my questions with more questions," she growled.

"I didn't realize you asked one," he said, hastily. "Truly, I didn't know you felt so strongly on the matter."

"I hate it when you take *my* fire!"

There was power in her voice and wrath in her eyes, but both sputtered out, leaving her empty. Isiilde collapsed, quivering with weakness. She slapped her fist uselessly on the floor.

"It's all I have." It was barely a whisper.

The silence was absolute. The guard stood stricken, afraid to move.

Marsais blinked, stunned. And suddenly the weight of ages settled on his shoulders. He leaned against the wall, took a ragged breath, and finally slid down, slumping beside the nymph on the floor.

"I'm sorry, my dear," he whispered.

At the agony in his voice, Isiilde raised her head. His grey eyes glistened like mist. And for the first time since she had known him, he looked defeated.

"I am so sorry for all of this."

"Why did you let them look at me?"

"Forgive me if I annoy you, but my answer requires another question." His voice was thin and faded. "What would have happened if I *had not* allowed them to view you? How would your mind have settled things?"

"Oen would have ripped off their heads," she stated without hesitation. "And then we would all have gone somewhere warm to live our lives as we see fit."

"What I wouldn't give to walk down that path." He chuckled bitterly. "I wish such lovely visions would grace my eyes. Shall I tell your virgin ears what I see in my waking dreams?"

Isiilde swallowed down a lump in her throat. His voice was like iron. Marsais had never spoken of his visions before.

"Beyond a doubt, Oen would have killed the emissaries. Now he becomes a treasonous traitor, hunted by not one, but by *four* kingdoms. He would have taken you and fled, but where, my dear?"

Marsais glanced over at her in question.

"The Bastardlands," she said at once.

"Hmm, let's follow that thread. I'll even skip the tricky parts of sneaking through the Western Gates undetected with the Blessed Order after you. I ask you, Isiilde, what becomes of a lone nymph in the Void-infested wilds after the Widow's Own have hunted down Oenghus and slit his throat in the night? What will you do, then?"

Marsais gestured sharply, as if erasing a slate.

"Another path! I refuse to let the emissaries see you. Caitlyn White-hand takes you back to Kambe, only you never arrive on those shores. Pirates can't resist a prize like you," he said, searching her face with haunted eyes.

Isiilde put a hand to her lips. Marsais had lived these visions, she realized. He had seen each path to its conclusion. He'd been forced to endure every single one.

"Are you too innocent to see that Fate? A nymph as beautiful as you on a ship full of scoundrels?"

She shivered at the anguish in his voice.

"Shall I go on?" he whispered. "What would happen if I kept you locked away in my tower? Oh, to be sure, no man would ever touch you, Isiilde. But what of the price that comes with such a dream? A war that destroys the Isle and kills every breathing thing on it before rippling through the rest of the realm?"

"Stop it, please," she whispered, not for her own sake, but for his. How could he live like this? How could he bear so much suffering and death?

"This realm is a cruel and twisted place. Sometimes you must choose the lesser of two evils. That is why I allowed them to inspect you, and I do not regret it. I *cannot* regret it."

Isiilde forced herself to meet his gaze. "They were laughing at me, Marsais."

"I assure you they were not."

"But I heard them—I don't look like other nymphs. My breasts are small, I have no meat, no curves. My ears are big. *Why* do they desire me?"

"You are a living myth, my dear. A dream come alive—a respite from the cruelty of this realm. And that dream is beautiful. *You* are beautiful."

"You didn't even look at me." There was pain beneath her accusation. "Why not?"

"It would not be gentlemanly, for one."

"And the other?" she demanded.

Marsais hesitated, struggling with a decision.

"Tell me."

"I cannot bond with you, Isiilde." The ache in his voice tore at her heart. "There is... too much at stake. So I have never encouraged you. Though I sensed you tried to forge a bond with me in the pleasure house."

"Yes," she realized. She'd acted on instinct. Who else would she bond with but a faerie? A man she trusted; a man she loved.

"It's why I never touch your skin. We simply cannot be."

Isiilde reached for his hand, but he snatched it away with a shuddering breath. "Please, Isiilde, do not." His rejection caused her more pain than the leering emissaries.

She stood to stare down at the man. "You say one thing, and yet do another. *Always.* You reject me. And yet you have no qualms with kissing my hand when you're drunk."

His eyes flickered with surprise. He didn't even remember.

Infuriated, she lashed out with words that cut him to the bone. "You are no gentleman, Marsais."

Isiilde turned and stalked down the tunnel. And the guard of the First Watch hurried after her, leaving the seer slumped against the wall in defeat.

CHAPTER 30

"I thought this was supposed to be a bloody inquiry?" Oenghus growled.

A pale blonde woman sat behind a desk. She looked up from her notes and arched a thin eyebrow.

"Oh, a thousand apologies. Cursing is part of my bloody vocabulary. A savage like me can't much help it." He bared his teeth at her.

The woman showed no reaction, so Oenghus turned to a golden-robed Inquisitor. He was laying his instruments on a table.

Oenghus itched for his pipe. He'd been kept in this windowless interrogation room for four hours.

The woman behind the desk called it a *room of reflection*. But the only thing he'd reflected on was who he was going to bash over the head first.

His patience was running thin; he had to get back to Isiilde.

A massive golden statue of Zahra dominated the room, its serene face looking down in judgment. He offered a crude gesture in return.

When the Inquisitor's tools were perfectly arranged, he left, pausing to bow at the statue's feet.

The tools were mostly for show—to intimidate. All they really needed to do was check him for signs of a Void taint, then weave an Orb of Truth, and question him. But the bloody Blessed Order liked their rituals.

Oenghus shifted in his chair, trying to lean back, but the armrests were in the way. With a growl, he gripped the wood, yanked the armrests clear off, and dropped them on the floor.

The woman frowned from behind her desk. She waited to see if he planned on doing anything else, then returned to her writing.

Oenghus turned to his thoughts, as grim as they were, of Isiilde's impending sale. He should be with her now; not in this gods-forsaken temple.

He wanted to rip off heads. To bash skulls. To break bodies, and carve a path of carnage through the realms to keep his daughter safe. His need was near to overwhelming. But he'd sworn to Isiilde's mother to stand aside and let their daughter find her own path.

And now he was forced to watch as their daughter was sold.

Oenghus let his head fall back and glared at the ceiling. "How many times will you tear my heart in two?" he muttered. But she could not hear him here—not in a temple of stone without a window.

Oenghus raised his head to find the woman behind the desk staring at him. The slight point to her ears and her upturned eyes and pale blonde hair marked her as Kamberian. She had the hard physique of a warrior and might be attractive if she ever relaxed.

Two Inquisitors glided in, bowing at the enormous feet of the ridiculous statue before taking their places beside the table. The woman pushed back her chair and stood with a clink of mail. She walked to the center of the room, clasped her hands, and studied Oenghus for a silent minute.

"I am Acacia Mael, Knight Captain of the Chapterhouse here in Drivel."

"Oenghus Saevaldr, my lady, or should I call you 'your holiness'?" He flashed his most charming grin.

"You may call me Captain Mael."

"And you may call me Oenghus."

Acacia ignored him. "This was to be a mere inquiry until I discovered this isn't your first offense."

"Can we skip the flirting and get on with it?" he growled.

"I had not realized you were in a hurry, Oenghus."

"Aye, a bit of one."

"Then perhaps you will think twice before destroying a temple dedicated to Zahra."

Oenghus lifted a shoulder. "I wasn't much thinking at all. Should I have stood by and let the fiend piss all over Zahra's head?"

The Inquisitors jerked, eyes blazing, but Acacia quickly cut off their anger with a gesture.

"I would rather you use more sense," Acacia replied, then nodded to the Inquisitors. "Proceed."

The Inquisitors began their complicated ritual of prayers, which was their equivalent of the Wise One's Lore, only bloody irritating. Their droning seemed to last forever.

"Finally," he muttered when they fell silent.

"I assume you know the drill, since this is not your first inquiry?"

Oenghus only grunted, then offered his hand, palm up. Acacia stepped forward and gripped his wrist.

"You have nice hands."

Acacia ignored him and began chanting in the tongue of her Order. When she had completed the ritual, a pure light flared to life, hovering over the palm of his hand, revealing the essence of his spirit.

Surprise flickered across her eyes, but she recovered quickly, studying the swirling orb of gold until it dissipated.

"Can't get further from Void-tainted than that, aye?" Oenghus smirked.

Acacia met his gaze with a cool appraisal.

"Let me guess—you've never seen its like before. It's because I'm blessed."

"I *have* seen it before."

It was Oenghus' turn for surprise. "You served on Iilenshar?"

"Yes, I did, but I doubt a 'blessed man' would be caught urinating on our temple wall." Acacia walked over to her desk, selecting a stack of reports.

"I was drunk and got lost," he defended. "Don't tell me you've never had one too many."

Acacia ignored his question, shuffling through the papers.

He wagered she was buying time so she could decide how to proceed with the inquiry. A pure essence like his was rare. Most were so shocked they let him leave.

But not this Knight Captain.

"Your grievances are many. Drunkenness, disorderly conduct, destruction of property... Well, I could continue, but it's safe to say you've started fights in just about every tavern on the Isle. Three of which were with paladins."

"They got in my bloody way."

"Six paladins and a shrine to Asmara 'got in your way'? The details of that fight are rather obscure," she noted with a disapproving quirk of her lips.

"I had a good reason for that."

"Let me guess—you were drunk?"

"Aye, and a bloody good reason, that is," he grunted, tugging on one of his braids. "That, and I was bored." It sounded a lot like something his daughter would say.

"You will find, Oenghus Saevaldr, that I am not as lenient as the former captain. With your reckless and uncivilized record, this inquiry will be far more thorough than those of my predecessor."

CHAPTER 31

ISIILDE POUNDED ON A DOOR. Its echo filled the stairwell and shook the hinges. No one answered. Rashk was not at home.

Isiilde was suffocating. Her blood boiled, and she felt like a dam about to burst.

We simply cannot be.

Isiilde slammed her fist against the wood. Her knuckles split.

Marsais wanted nothing to do with her.

An Isle Guard eyed her as torches flickered restlessly in their sconces. She licked her lips, fingers curling around a sword hilt. "Lass," the guard said slowly. "Just calm down now. Why don't we head to the infirmary? Morigan can help you."

Isiilde looked at the guard. And saw fear. She nearly laughed at the absurdity of it—afraid of a *nymph*? But the guard was right. With Oenghus gone, busy or not, Morigan would help.

Isiilde raced down the stairs. She couldn't bring herself to take the shortcut through the gardens—they evoked too many memories of Marsais. So she stalked down a maze of hallways with barely a thought, ignoring the curious glances, whispered comments, and blatant leers that followed her path.

Let them look, she thought. She had nothing else to lose.

Rage urged her onwards at a reckless pace. She quivered with tension, and her vision blurred, narrowing to a long, dark tunnel of sight.

A part of her embraced the rage, but another cowered from it. In her desperation to reach Morigan, she took a shortcut through the main library and was forced to slow down to navigate the apprentices and desks.

All eyes turned to the nymph. Including Zianna's.

"Why, there she is now. Come and join us, Isiilde," Zianna said with a flash of eyes.

The hated voice pounded in her ears. Isiilde kept walking, but the woman blocked her path.

"Won't you stop to talk with us? You're quite famous now."

"Leave me alone," Isiilde warned through clenched teeth.

"What's the matter, dear?" Zianna purred. For a moment, the woman almost sounded kind. "You should be flattered."

"Why?" Isiilde snapped, slipping past the apprentice. But Zianna grabbed her arm, keeping her in place. She tried to break free, but the woman's grip was like iron. Fingernails dug into flesh.

"Haven't you heard?"

Everyone in the library stopped to watch the confrontation.

"A friend of mine is a Whisperer. He told me that the bidding for you is up to four hundred thousand gold crowns. You'll be the most expensive whore ever sold."

Isiilde went still with rage. "I am not a whore."

"What are you then—a high-priced animal?"

The words cut deep, like a length of cold steel twisting in her insides. The last shreds of her self-control caught like brittle tinder. "I am not an *animal*!"

The fury in her voice was answered by fire. It surged, breaking free from warded lanterns with an explosion of searing glass.

Screams, panic, terror. Fire raced along shelves with ravenous hunger and a flame leapt onto Zianna's skirt, swirling up her body to nip at her lips with glee.

Fire rolled up the timbers in hypnotic waves, and rafters glowed with heat. Terror-stricken apprentices fled for their lives as Zianna thrashed on the floor and the knowledge of ages curled to ash.

History was burning. And Isiilde stood in rapture.

Heat licked her skin, her lips parted, and on the verge of release, she moaned. But the ached-for moment never came.

A blizzard washed over the library, and ice took root in her bones. Her flames were snuffed in an instant. But as fast as it had appeared, the blizzard died, blanketing the ruin in a shroud of white.

Thira stood, wide-eyed with rage, as scorched pages fluttered around her head. Zianna twisted in agony at her feet.

"You," Thira snapped at Isiilde's stunned guard. "Get this woman to the infirmary now!"

The soldier hurried to obey, issuing orders to nearby apprentices. They rushed forward, picking up Zianna as she screamed in agony.

Isiilde tried to flee, but Thira was quicker. She spat out a harsh word, gesturing sharply. A Weave of Silence slammed into the nymph, pushing past her lips, seizing her tongue in a vise-like grip. Isiilde collapsed, clawing at her throat in panic. She tried to scream, to beg for mercy, but no sound emerged. Not even a whimper.

"*You*—" Thira wrenched her up by an ear. "Your master can't save you now."

Thira dragged the nymph from the ruins, past guards, Wise Ones, and servants who were racing to aid the wounded and fighting to salvage their treasured books.

Familiar with Thira's disciplinary methods, no one paid the pair any mind. Not even the kitchen staff, who barely glanced from their duties as Thira brought in another errant novice.

"Got another one, I see. She'll be in there for days." The Ogre chuckled before returning to his pie crusts.

Thira ignored the cook, propelling the nymph into a washroom and chasing out the scullery maids.

The washroom was a dark, moldy place that smelled of rotten meat. A dingy fountain sputtered in the center. Cauldrons and dishes were piled up, one atop the other, full of grime and grease that had no end.

"Wash everything," Thira ordered. "I'll fetch you when you've finished, and not before. This will give me time to think of a more fitting punishment."

Thira yanked Isiilde closer, so she was forced to stand on her toes.

"You can ponder what your life will be like in Xaio while you slave away in here, *nymph*," Thira hissed before slamming the heavy door shut.

Isiilde collapsed onto the slick stones. Tears swelled in her eyes as she clawed at her throat. The weave was a cruel, torturous bit of work that made her throat burn and her tongue swell. It was an invasion, every bit as humiliating as Caitlyn's probing fingers.

But without her voice, she couldn't hope to unravel the weave.

Exhausted from the fire's rage, she crawled to a pool of silver moonlight shining from a single window set high in the ceiling. She looked to the Sylph's moon and climbed to her feet, breathing in fresh air.

It calmed her, and she breathed easier. The memory of rage and fire felt like a dream. Of Zianna's screams...

Isiilde shivered. And to distract herself, she turned to the dishes and rolled up her sleeves. She might as well get to work.

She picked up an abandoned scrub brush, and the door behind opened. Relief washed over her. Someone had come for her—Morigan, perhaps. But hope was replaced by an icy trickle as the door closed with a whisper of air.

A figure stood in front of the door. His perfect teeth gleamed in the dark.

"I've missed you," Stievin said softly, slick as the stones beneath her feet.

The icy trickle spread through her body.

"Don't worry, Isiilde, I'll help you get all this cleaned up." He turned to the side, gripped a large cauldron, and rolled it in front of the door, wedging it beneath the handle.

Isiilde stiffened like a startled deer. She thought he said more. His lips were moving as he approached, but all she could hear was the thunder of blood in her ears.

Suddenly, she realized she had a lot to lose. And step by step, she backed towards the pool of moonlight as Stievin came forward.

Her fingers brushed the knife at her hip.

"Get back," she tried to say, but the words got stuck on the weave burning her throat.

Isiilde drew her knife. And Stievin laughed as he unbuckled his belt.

"Come now, Isiilde. It's only me. I won't hurt you. This will be enjoyable for you." Nearly within arm's reach, he stopped and spread his arms.

Isiilde wanted to scream at the man. To rage. But Thira's weave held her tongue in a vise. Cold sweat trickled down her spine. Her legs were unsteady, but her fingers tightened on the dagger's hilt.

Stievin cupped a hand to his ear. "What was that? I didn't hear a no." He unlaced his trousers. "I'll get you strawberries afterwards. You won't even have to wash all this when I'm done. Just put the knife down and get on your back like a good nymph."

Isiilde thrust the blade at him in warning.

Stievin lunged for her. Moonlight flashed on steel, hitting his eyes, and Isiilde ducked under his reach. She struck, slicing a rib under his arm.

The man hissed and staggered back. "I was going to be gentle. But not anymore," he growled.

The scent of blood filled her senses. She glanced at her blade, and wavered. Her fingers spasmed, every instinct screamed at her to drop the weapon. But she ignored her nature. Clenching her jaw, she tightened her grip and fell into a fighting stance that Morigan had taught her.

He came again. But he was quick and strong and ignored the blade slicing through his thigh. Blows came, one after another, to her face, her jaw, and ribs. She lashed out blindly. The blade caught on flesh. A grunt. And she staggered back, stunned.

Stievin slammed her to the ground. Dishes smashed, cutting into her back. Her head hit the stone with a smack.

His weight crushed her. His breath close.

Stievin grabbed her wrist, and cracked her arm with a snap. The knife fell from her fingertips. With his other hand, he clawed at her shirt, ripping it open.

Silently, she screamed. And drove her knee upwards into his groin. He cursed. But it only seemed to anger him.

Stievin covered her mouth with his own. And another intrusion was forced down her throat. Isiilde bit his tongue. And he reeled back, then cracked his forehead against her nose. A knee slammed her rib. But like a panicked animal, pain was a distant thing. She twisted, struggling, turning beneath the man.

Stievin grabbed her hair, wrenched back her head, and slammed her face into the stone. He roughly rolled her onto her back. One hand pinned her to the ground, while the other worked at her belt and laces.

His eyes were crazed. He panted with need. And her trousers were yanked down around her knees.

Isiilde clawed at his arms. But he was so strong. One large hand grabbed her by the neck and squeezed while he shoved his left between her legs. She arched, trying to break free, even as her vision narrowed and her lungs burned.

She could go limp. She could stop. Give up and let him be done. Isiilde looked to the moon instead of his leering eyes. Light glinted off a blade. And then she did go limp.

Stievin released her neck and spread her legs with a knee. Isiilde edged her broken arm up along the floor, pawing at the grimy stones. Her fingers wrapped around a slick hilt.

She stabbed at his chest. Steel pierced flesh to the hilt, and Stievin screamed. She rolled away, or tried to, but pain washed over her, and all went black.

CHAPTER 32

A DOOR WAS CRACKED, and the imp pressed a bulbous eye to the gap. The room beyond was shrouded in silver moonlight, and a crimson-robed figure was picking his way carefully over a maze of books spread on the floor.

The imp shuddered. It sensed layers of wards and illusion, of ancient power barely contained within the figure—a faerie of the highest hall.

Sensing the imp, Marsais whirled towards the door. "Luccub, come here," he ordered in Abyssal.

The imp was bound to the faerie who held its name, so it landed on a stack of books, folding its leather wings around its body.

"Did you see it?"

Luccub chattered back, palming a glittering object from the desk. The high faerie did not seem to notice.

"Draw it for me, here." Marsais unfurled a roll of parchment and handed the imp a stub of charcoal.

Luccub chattered on as it added a few personal touches to its sketch.

While the imp worked, Marsais returned to the circle of books on the floor, bending at the waist, squinting at the swirl of words.

Two questions plagued him: How did Tharios know what was

hidden beneath the Spine, and what was he planning to do with that knowledge?

Marsais ran his fingers through his hair, clutching his scalp in frustration. By the gods, he could not think straight.

His visions were colliding.

The Sea of Time churned beneath his eyes, a great whirlpool of threads gathering around the Isle—to a single pinpoint shrouded in chaos. Had he charted the wrong path from one point to the next? But impossible—his visions had been clear. Beyond a doubt, Tharios had knowledge of Portal Magic. But before or after? And more important, after what?

Luccub chattered, pointing a claw at the sketch. It was finished.

Marsais picked his way over books to study the sketch. "Are you sure this is all?" he hissed.

Luccub straightened, tilting its pointy chin with wounded pride.

Marsais muttered an apology to the fiend, and turned to study the charcoal rod, the source of his confusion. The rune-etched rod before him was just that, a rod—without the symbols of the Scorching Sun decorating its tips. Both end caps were missing, and with that realization, another piece of the puzzle clicked neatly into place.

Tharios had a *part* of Soisskeli's Stave, but not all of it. A powerful artifact like this would have been dismantled and its parts scattered to the far corners of the realm.

"Thank you, Luccub. I may have use of you again, so stay close. Continue whatever you were doing, *but*—" he held up a finger, "try not to kill anyone. These humans are fragile. The gods only know what they'd do if a Greater Fiend appeared on their doorsteps. And give that back to me."

The imp hurled the stolen trinket at a wall, and flapped out the door.

Marsais sat in a chair, but the moment he sat, he surged to his feet, his fingers twitching as visions danced in front of his eyes: Oenghus lay in a pool of blood. The crystal shifted and a solid door of blue flame illuminated the circle. A figure, just on the other side, stood waiting. The flagon on his desk tipped, and an elemental from Isiikle surged forth in icy glory.

All of Time shifted and churned as his heart convulsed from one moment to the next.

A horde of Wedamen swept below him, charging across the pages of history as the gleaming palace of Whitemount burned black in the corner of his study. The Spine crumbled beneath his feet, the crystal shattered, and a Balor fiend roared through the gaping wreckage. The Scorched Sun hovered overhead, and an agonizing heartbeat later, Oenghus stood with his hands wrapped lovingly around his daughter's neck. Three heartbeats later, the berserker snapped her neck with an effortless twist.

The nymph crumpled lifelessly to the floor.

Marsais squeezed his eyes shut. But the visions still came. If this was not madness, then what was?

He stormed over to a draped mirror on the wall and ripped off the covering.

The breath in his throat caught in pure wonder. He saw himself as he was—haggard, afraid, with a haunted gaze. And there she was, peering over his shoulder, bright-eyed and curious. Isiilde's lips whispered against his cheek. He spun, but the nymph wasn't there.

Another message brushed his ear. It was Morigan's voice. *'Marsais, where's Isiilde? There was a fire in the main library. An apprentice was injured. Is she with you?'*

His grey eyes widened with alarm. And as he stormed from his study, the visions collapsed around him, wonder giving way to dread.

Marsais strode into the ruined library, taking in the destruction with a sweep of his steely gaze. Without a doubt, this was Isiilde's doing.

"Thira," he barked. "Where is Isiilde?"

The Wise One was shouting orders to a small army of servants, but turned at his question. "You're a seer, Marsais. You figure it out."

"I am in no mood, woman!" He seized her arm and the entire room froze.

"I treated her as I would treat any other novice. Compared to what she did to Zianna, a Weave of Silence and a few days scrubbing pots is small penitence."

His eyes flashed silver. "Damn you, Thira. You've taken away her only defense." His voice thrummed with furious power.

Thira paled at what she saw, and took a hasty step back. Only his hand held her in place.

"Come with me," he ordered.

Servants and scribes dropped their wounded books, backing away in fear as he raced out of the library. Thira was forced into a run, and so was her runt of a dog.

Marsais charged into the kitchens, scattering servants like frightened chickens. He skidded to a stop in front of an unguarded washroom door, cursing sharply when he found it barred.

With a gesture and a growl, Marsais ripped the door from its hinges and strode in with Thira on his heels, fearing and knowing what he would find.

Isiilde sucked in a sharp breath. Pain. It nearly shoved her back down into oblivion. She blinked past blood, and coughed, her ribs sending sharp stabs through her side. A pool of silver moonlight called to her.

Dazed, she searched the dim.

Stievin.

The scent of blood made her gag. But she had to get away.

Stievin was on his knees. He stared down at the knife protruding from his shoulder. Blood seeped from the wound. His breath was ragged.

Isiilde crawled forward, towards the moonlight, away from him. Bones ground together. Her trousers around her knees. She dragged herself forward into the light.

Her world blurred. A haze of blood. The floor tilted, and a wave knocked her over.

Stievin staggered to his feet. He lunged closer, eyes burning into her.

Isiilde curled a fist, trying to focus. But her vision was narrowing—the tunnel closing in again.

Then the world exploded. The door splintered with a smash of iron and wood. The cauldron rolled like a child's top, and a tall, red-robed figure radiating power strode in.

Silver eyes flashed in the dim. With a cold chant and quick fingers, Marsais thrust his hand at Stievin, fingers splayed. Runes converged into an ethereal hand, and with a sharp gesture, Stievin was plucked off the floor.

She heard him howling. But the sound was far away. Isiilde fumbled with her trousers, trying to pull them back up. It seemed the only thing that mattered, but her fingers refused to work.

THIRA'S EYES widened in shock. A battered, half-clothed woman lay on the filthy floor in a pool of moonlight.

Stievin howled, pinned to the wall fifteen feet from the floor by a Runehand. The laces of his trousers gaped for all the world to see.

Marsais switched focus, but Thira gripped his arm. "Don't go too far," she warned.

With a snarl, Marsais dropped his Runehand, and rushed to Isiilde. She lay on her side, one arm bent at an unnatural angle, trying to tug her trousers back into place.

"Isiilde." At the sound of his strained voice, her eyes darted to his with relief. And pain.

Marsais reached for her. But the moment his hand entered the moonlight, his skin burned. He retreated with a hiss, then looked to the Sylph's moon through the window.

His eyes widened a fraction.

"Come now," he murmured to the moon. "Would I hurt her?" Marsais knew who would be listening. He could imagine the Sylph now—kneeling at her pool of scrying in an ethereal garden.

Marsais took a breath, then tried again. This time, his hand entered the light unscathed. He knelt to help Isiilde with her clothes, blocking Thira's view, but her buttons had been ripped off.

He passed a hand over Isiilde's lips, dispelling the weave in an instant.

"Marsais," she croaked. Throat raw and burning, she clutched her neck.

Carefully, he peeled her fingers away to inspect the injury. No bonding mark. But bruises from a near strangling.

"Can you stand?"

With his aid, she stood on shaking legs. Thira offered her cloak, and Marsais wrapped it around the nymph.

"I'll get you somewhere safe."

Isiilde trembled from head to toe, but she walked with the support of his arm. And then her knees buckled.

Marsais gently lifted her in his arms. Bone ground against bone, and despite his care, the shift of position sent her eyes rolling.

"Send Morigan to my tower," he said to Thira. "Find Oenghus and bring him at once."

"What about *him*?" Thira gestured to the gasping man pinned to the wall.

"Leave Stievin where he is," Marsais warned. "If anyone touches him, they will answer to me."

Thira nodded.

Marsais cast one last look at Isiilde's attacker, and paused, turning to study the man with surprise. There were cuts along Stievin's face and arms, deep ones made by a blade. The blade's hilt protruded from Stievin's shoulder, its steel lost in his flesh.

The significance of that dagger was not lost on Marsais. Isiilde had fought. And fiercely.

This path was unforeseen.

CHAPTER 33

MARSAIS STEPPED out of a teleportation rune and hurried down the hallway to his study. Silver moonlight shone through the crystal window. He hastily kicked his books out of the way, and laid Isiilde on the frost bear pelt. It would keep her warm.

Isiilde curled onto her side, arms held protectively around her ribs. The moonlight deepened, shrouding her like a cloak. He knelt to smooth the hair back from her bloodied face.

"You're safe, Isiilde," he whispered. "Morigan will be here shortly."

She stared at nothing.

"I'll be back."

Marsais returned with basin and cloth. With care, he traced a heat rune over the water, then dipped his finger in to test the temperature. Satisfied it wouldn't burn, he set about wiping her face and hands clean of blood. He took care of her broken nose and arm. But her silence was concerning.

"Isiilde?"

Frozen with shock.

Marsais warmed her hands in his own. At his touch, her eyes flickered to his. She stirred, long enough to rise, then slump against him, broken ribs shifting with every ragged breath.

Marsais cradled her close as she shivered in his embrace. She felt hollow.

"I stabbed him," she whispered.

"With good reason."

"It only made him angry."

"But you tried."

"I couldn't even scream."

Marsais stroked her hair. "You had no choice."

"Yes, I did. If I hadn't—" she cut off. "I burned Zianna."

Her voice was void of emotion. Far away, and flat. Lifeless.

Isiilde had rebelled against her nature—nymphs did not fight back. But she had. And it was breaking her. Twisting her into something else.

"Many paths lead to the same end," he murmured.

Fate. That was the word. But not this time.

The threads of endless time had shown her as a timid thing, frightened and limp, too afraid to move. But that dagger protruding from Stievin's shoulder changed everything.

Isiilde had steered the realm into uncharted seas.

"Did you intend to burn her?" There was no judgment in his question.

"No..." she hesitated. "Yes. I don't know. She wouldn't let go, and... Does it matter?"

Marsais looked to the crystal window. He could *feel* the goddess, the Sylph, watching—her rage and her despair. But not directed at Marsais, for once.

"Yes, I think it matters," he whispered. "Your fire is both weapon and guardian."

"I did nothing to provoke Zianna. Or Stievin. *Nothing*."

"Cruelty needs no reason."

"I hate humans," she admitted.

A chill burned the scar on his chest. "There are days like today," he closed his eyes to savage memories, "when I do, too."

"They are worse than animals."

Marsais swallowed. Her spirit was slipping into shadow—like the Fey so long ago. "Do you remember this last summer, nearly four months back? The sun was bright and the ocean was calm."

"No."

"You were lying on the beach soaking up the heat."

"It feels like a dream."

"It isn't." He spoke gently in her ear, leading her to brighter days. "Remember the sun beating on your skin and the lull of the tide. The coarse sand against your body and the whisper of breeze brushing your hair. Do you remember the way it made you feel, and how happy you were that day?"

"I don't think I'll ever feel like that again."

"Do you trust me?"

"Always," she breathed.

"Then believe me when I say you will."

When Morigan arrived, she looked set to commit murder. A muscle in her jaw twitched. Marsais knew that muscle well; he'd seen it on rare occasions.

Morigan busied herself with a satchel of supplies as she reined in her emotions. "Who did this?" she asked.

"Cook's Steward Stievin."

Morigan met his gaze. "Alive?"

"Yes, with her knife in his shoulder."

Morigan raised her brows.

"He's pinned to a wall in the kitchen washroom." Marsais would not be surprised if she reached for an axe and went to finish the job.

Instead, Morigan touched Isiilde's chin and tilted it to look at her neck, then into her eyes. "You have a fine set of bruises."

"It doesn't hurt anymore," Isiilde said.

Morigan glanced at moonlight blanketing the nymph's skin. Marsais did not miss that knowing look in the healer's eyes.

"That's a good thing." Morigan did not ask Isiilde to leave his arms, only ran her hands over the nymph, searching for injuries.

"I'll need plenty of hot water, Marsais. Lie down, Isiilde. He'll be back. Yes, that's it. Careful with her." Morigan helped him ease Isiilde onto the pelt.

Morigan was a formidable healer. But she was more cautious than Oenghus. With his godlike constitution, he could take tremendous pain upon himself. Whereas Oenghus healed a body in one fell swoop, Morigan healed each injury separately: a broken nose, swollen eye, split lip, and bitten tongue; a collar of bruises around her neck and windpipe; broken elbow, wrist, and ribs; and deep scratches between her thighs.

Water fetched, Marsais stood on the edge of moonlight. His body was present, but his mind was elsewhere as he searched the pathways of time and possibility. But there was no path, only shadow. The seer was blind to this future.

After injuries were healed with the Gift, the body demanded rest. Isiilde sank into a deep, merciful sleep. The only outward signs of her trauma were faint bruises.

Morigan set about washing the blood from Isiilde's body. "I have seen everything there is to see in my lifetime, but I will never understand *this*."

It took a moment for Marsais to realize the woman had spoken. He focused on her as she sat back on her haunches. Isiilde lay pale and ethereal in the silver light. She was clothed in one of his shirts.

"I came across a village on the borderlands of the Fell Wastes once." Morigan's voice trembled with memory. "Wedamen attacked it. Set upon the women, girls and boys, and even babes like animals. Most were killed. Many taken." Morigan looked at him. "Her mother was raped, you know. By a 'good' man, just like Stievin. Only it was an emperor."

"But Soataen isn't her father," Marsais noted.

"No, he's not."

He wasn't surprised Morigan knew. She and Oenghus might not be currently bound by an Oath, but they were bound by a lifetime.

"What else is going on here, Morigan? Oen first told me that Isiilde's best chance was to be sold to a more powerful kingdom. And if she were a typical nymph, I would agree. But I have never known him to stand aside as he has. I expected him to take her away *long* before this."

That path in his visions had not ended well.

Morigan sighed. She paused, seeming to listen to something. A voice, perhaps. She didn't answer until after she'd carried Isiilde to his bed. "Oen swore an oath to her mother, to not interfere with her life."

Marsais paused with growing dread. "The moonlight... it burned me when I first tried to reach her in the washroom."

Morigan pulled the blankets over Isiilde and sat on the bed to smooth her hair.

"I thought her power came from Oenghus," he said, slowly. "It didn't, did it?"

Morigan chuckled. "I'm sure it does. I've always thought her affinity for fire had something to do with his brimgrog, only it manifested differently in a faerie. He drinks far too much of the stuff."

"And her mother?" he pressed. "She wasn't a nymph, was she?"

"It's not my place to say."

That was answer enough.

Marsais clenched his jaw. To give himself something to do, he turned to the hearth and started flinging wood into it. "So Oenghus brings her here, to me, to *my* doorstep—a direct link to the essence of *life*," he hissed, whirling to face her. "Do you have any idea what he has done?"

Morigan met his gaze without flinching. With his slip of control, his illusion weaves wavered, and she saw the silver eyes beneath the surface.

"I don't know for sure who, *or what,* you really are, Marsais, but I have my suspicions," she said evenly. "You need to have this conversation with Oen. Not here. *Not* in front of a girl who's just been savaged. And not with me."

His shoulders sagged. "I apologize."

"Don't," she said. "I *know* who Oen is. He's pure chaos like his daughter. He's also maddening and stubborn. I'm well used to it."

The edge of his lip twitched in rueful acknowledgement. He nodded towards a shuttered window. "*She* does not like me."

"Oh, I know it," Morigan said. "Unfortunately, her daughter loves you."

Feeling suddenly ill, Marsais sat on the hearthrug and slumped against the cold stone. "I did not encourage Isiilde's affections, only her friendship," he whispered.

"I would have castrated you if you had."

The woman wasn't jesting. But then he hadn't thought she was—he was only surprised she'd admitted it.

"She tried to bond with me some months ago," he confided. "Not physically, but a nymph's first bonding of spirit. I don't believe she knew what she was doing—it was pure instinct. Regardless, I stopped it."

"Why the bloody void did you do that?"

Marsais jerked his head off the wall. "What?"

"Stop her from bonding with you." Morigan narrowed her eyes. "Are you... Do you mean Oen's not joking when he calls you a dandy?"

"He wishes I was."

Morigan bit back a laugh.

"There's certainly rumor aplenty about me," he said wryly.

"I like the one about how you're a white dragon sitting atop your treasure hoard up here."

"Along with a harem of young men."

"And you don't eat or sleep, and you bathe in moonlight to get your hair so white."

"Close to the truth," he mused. "Though I believe I also feast on the souls of those condemned to an ill fate."

They shared a small smile before Morigan turned back to the original topic. "So you're not a dandy. Why did you refuse her?"

"I'm not meant for her."

Morigan's eyes dimmed with sympathy at the pain in his voice. "And why is that?"

Marsais waved a vague hand. "Visions."

Morigan frowned at him. "I'll ask you one more time. *Why?*"

Marsais searched his visions. He'd never stopped to think on the why, only the end of each vision—disaster.

"I don't know for a certain," he admitted. "But I suspect it has something to do with the Eldritch. You know something of them, of course."

"I do. The elder druids who bonded with nymphs. Tell me your reasoning all the same."

Marsais took time to gather his tattered thoughts. "A druid did not choose a nymph; a nymph chose her druid. But as the druids were hunted, their numbers dwindled, and younger men were allowed into the Circle—even half-elves. It corrupted the Circle of Druids, clearing a path for Ramashan and his ilk.

"The younger Eldritch were not as patient with their nymphs. Some took them before they were ready. And others saw their bonded nymphs as their very own. A druid is a nymph's first, but he is never her last. And slighted love is a dangerous thing."

"So you think you'd become a jealous lover?"

"No... At least I can't imagine behaving in such a way."

"I can't either. So what then?"

"My visions—"

"I don't give a Void about your visions, Marsais. Isiilde is Nuthaanian. We make our own fate."

He could hardly argue, considering the dagger stuck in Stievin's shoulder.

Marsais rested his elbows on his knees, and studied his hands. "It's not just that," he said without looking up. "You have heard the whispers, I suppose, of Dagenir and his nymph?"

There were texts, ancient and forbidden, that suggested a nymph had sparked Dagenir's betrayal and his subsequent theft of the Orb. But Iilenshar and the Blessed Order squashed such heresy with a vengeance.

"What does that have to do with you?"

"Every vision I've had of our future ends in destruction. The realm burns—worse than the Shattering. And considering the Sylph's dislike of me... Well, it's hard not to believe. Isiilde is meant for another—a man who stalks the shadows of Time, a man as yet vague and undefined."

Marsais' vision of the future, on this single point, had been clear: he must not meddle with Isiilde's Fate.

Morigan stared down at the nymph for a time, stroking her head with the affection of a mother. "Oenghus swore an oath to not interfere. To let Isiilde choose her own path. It's not for *you* to decide her path, either. She chose her path—you. And unless you were not willing to bond with her, you should have allowed it."

He looked up, surprised. "Oen would have killed me."

Morigan snorted. "Aye, he would've tried. But after Isiilde's mother died, I nursed her as a babe, and by Nuthaanian law that makes me her mother. I'd have had my say first."

"And what do you say?"

"She could do worse."

CHAPTER 34

"I NEED TO CLEAN UP. Can you sit with her?" Morigan asked.

"Of course."

Isiilde was twitching and murmuring in her sleep, so Marsais pulled a chair beside the bed and took her hand. She stilled at his touch.

Morigan returned to light a fire. She glanced at the pair, but said nothing as she worked. A knock sounded.

"Come."

Isek strode into the room, weaving a gold coin over his knuckles. "How is she?"

"Sleeping," Morigan said.

Isek shifted, glancing from Isiilde to Marsais, who stared blankly at some undefined point on a wall.

"I have some news. Should we step outside?"

"Just keep your voice low," she said, and walked over to touch Marsais' shoulder. He jerked in surprise, then followed her nod to Isek. Taking her hint, he untangled his hand and tucked Isiilde's back beneath the covers.

"Are you ready for all this?" Isek asked when they were all gathered by the fire.

Marsais braced himself against the mantel.

"Since the ranting fellow stuck to a wall in the washroom is hard to miss, everyone in the Order knows about the assault, including the emissaries."

"What is Stievin ranting about?" Morigan asked.

"That the nymph seduced him, and she's rightfully his. And that the Archlord attacked him."

"And what is Thira saying?" Marsais asked.

"Nothing. She seems pensive. If I didn't know better, I'd say she was disturbed by the assault."

Morigan frowned at the comment. "The woman does have a heart."

"Cold, brittle, and pumping ice through her veins," Isek said. "Regardless, Kiln promptly removed their bid because of Isiilde's... spoiled state. Xaio and Mearcentia have requested an audience with the Archlord."

Morigan glanced at Marsais, but he was staring into the fire. Neither one corrected the spy.

"There's been no word from the emperor, but with all the eyes and ears he has in the Order, I'm sure it won't be long. Several Wise Ones, along with the Ogre, are angry you left Stievin pinned to a wall. It's affecting dinner. But no one is suicidal enough to unravel one of your wards. Thira could manage it, but she seems content to follow your orders. She had a healer see to him, though."

"And Oenghus?" Morigan asked.

"Thira sent a message by Whisperer, but the Blessed Order refused to release him until their inquiry is finished. I've sent a messenger with a scroll bearing the Archlord's mark. It's a few hours to Drivel, so I imagine Oenghus should be along shortly, one way or another."

"It's well you didn't send a message directly—he'd go into full berserk and slaughter his way free," Morigan said. "There's nothing he can do here, anyway."

"True," Isek agreed. "Except tear Stievin from the wall. The kitchen staff would be happy about that."

"As much as I'd like to..." Morigan took a steadying breath. "I think we should leave him for the Blessed Order. They'll no doubt come, too."

Marsais glanced at her, and the two shared a silent look before Morigan nodded in agreement.

"Right, then: leave rapist on wall." Isek made an unnecessary notation in his notebook. "The council was a piece of work earlier today. They took advantage of Thira sitting in for Oenghus, and voted for a re-vote. I voted no in your place, but we were outnumbered—the Order now supports Lachlan."

Marsais was on familiar ground again—he'd foreseen this section of the path.

"I suppose you have the final say, Marsais, but you're not exactly popular right now. You've been ruffling the council's feathers and they've turned to Tharios. He's poised to take your throne in the next cycle. I can't say I blame them, old fellow. Tharios is focused, energetic, and diplomatic while you're a madman and a recluse."

"Thank you for your bluntness."

"Yes, well, what I wasn't expecting was their decision to oust Isiilde from the Order."

"Bastards," Morigan cursed.

"I agree," Isek said. "But she destroyed the Relic Hall, and it pushed everyone over the edge. I reasoned she was going to be sold anyway, so there was no use kicking her out, but they cast her out with a sweeping vote, minus one."

That was unexpected.

"They weren't going to make it official until after the bidding, since Eiji had a wager with N'Jalss regarding the final price. They were worried her removal from the Order would affect the bidding. But now that she's burnt Zianna to a crisp... Well, I suspect that will change."

"Zianna will probably live," Morigan said. "I was late getting here because I was healing her."

"That's some good news," Isek said. "I questioned the witnesses. No one is really sure what happened in the library. It seems Zianna grabbed Isiilde and wouldn't let go. The two exchanged heated words, and the next thing anyone knew, all the warded lanterns exploded at once."

"So they can't pin it on Isiilde?" Morigan asked.

"No one can explain what happened. I can't even explain it. An explosion from *inside* a warded lantern... It should be impossible. And apparently they all exploded at once, which makes it even more improbable."

Marsais felt vaguely angry, but mostly queasy. He cleared his throat, forcing himself to focus, and changed the subject. "What do you know of Soisskeli's Stave?"

His sudden question took both Wise Ones by surprise.

Isek whistled softly, rocking back and forth on his heels in thought. "If memory serves, the stave was crafted by Soisskeli, who was a Void-tainted Bloodmagus. He was one of the Chaos Lords who worshipped Karbonek, a greater fiend from the Nine Halls—the god of the Fomorri. Or the Unspoken. Soisskeli created the artifact to control the dragons. But The Serene One, Oshimi, finally defeated him."

"So legend claims." Marsais was ever doubtful of recorded history. At the questioning look from his assistant, he dismissed the subject with a gesture, moving on to the next question. "What do you know about Portal Magic?"

"It's a bloody mess if you're a Bloodmagus."

"Spare me your puns, Isek. I'm in no mood."

"You probably know as much as I do."

"Indulge me."

"What's there to say about the Portals on Iilenshar? They're secretive. I sometimes wonder if the Guardians even know what's behind their power."

"I'm asking after the rune variety, as in Rune Portals."

Isek gave a low whistle. "That knowledge was scarce long before the Shattering, even before we forgot how to use those Gateways beneath the Spine."

Although Isek had simply confirmed what Marsais already knew, it helped to listen to others. Sometimes, it nudged a piece of his memory back into place.

"Thank you, Isek. If anything develops, let us know."

Isek nodded, then hesitated, placing a hand on his shoulder. "You need some sleep, old friend. You look awful."

"You should have seen Isiilde a few hours back."

"You'll be no use to her passed out." Isek left with those final words, closing the door softly behind him.

"He's right, you know," Morigan said.

"I could say the same to you."

Morigan tucked a tendril of hair back into her bun. "I'm headed to Oen's rooms to catch some sleep. Healing Zianna nearly did me in." She hesitated. "You'll stay with her?"

"Yes."

Morigan edged closer to whisper. "You didn't correct Isek about what happened to her."

"I did not."

"What do you have in mind—other than this buying her time?"

Marsais stroked his goatee as his mind raced with possibilities. "I don't know yet," he admitted.

"I'm surprised Thira hasn't corrected the others about her not being raped."

"After I tore off the door and walked inside, I feared she had been. It looked like it." He grimaced at the memory. "I... When I knelt to help her, I blocked Thira's view to spare her further humiliation."

"With Isiilde's injuries, by Nuthaanian law, even an attempted rape would give her the right to gouge out her attacker's eyes or castrate him. And by Kilnish law she *is* spoiled goods. But the Blessed Order isn't so straightforward. It will depend on the paladin handling the case. They might very well hand her over to Stievin."

"Hmm, yes.... I need to consult with an expert in the law."

"A loophole?"

"Assurance," he said.

"That business about the stave... Is there something I should know?"

He waved a dismissive hand. "Tharios is easy to plot. I've foreseen his path. I'm simply waiting for the *right* time to do something about it."

"Don't get cocky, Marsais. Remember what I said—Oen and Isiilde are pure chaos. And as you know, Oen wreaks havoc on plans and battle strategies. I've found it best to wait until the blood dries to see what he's left me to work with. It's what I was planning to do with Isiilde. Though..." She sighed with regret. "Perhaps I should have acted sooner."

"Wouldn't that be interfering, Morigan?"

"I swore no oath."

He grunted. And she left.

CHAPTER 35

Marsais slumped in a chair, asleep. His chin on his chest, his hand resting over Isiilde's, a finger on her pulse.

Movement woke him as Isiilde threaded her fingers through his own, pressing her palm to his. He opened his eyes and looked at the nymph in the firelight.

She stared back. Quiet.

Marsais straightened in his chair, rubbing at the scar on his chest. "Can I get you water?"

She nodded.

He squeezed her hand, and left to fetch food and water. When he returned, she was sitting upright, propped against a mound of pillows.

She drank, but refused the food.

"Where are Oen and Morigan?"

"Oen is on his way. Morigan is sleeping in his room. I can get her..."

"No."

Marsais poured more water from a jug. But she only stared down at the cup in her hands. "It feels more like a nightmare than anything real."

"Are you in any pain?" he asked.

"Some. But... I think it's more memory."

"Healing can be disorienting," he said. "It will pass."

Isiilde shivered, and quickly set her cup aside to pull up the blanket. She looked around the dimly lit room in a daze. "Where are we?"

"My bedchambers."

She frowned.

The room was a study in disorder: odd trinkets, glass vials on shelves, weapons leaning in corners, clothes flung over furniture, and gems being used as paperweights. The sole oasis of order was the canopy bed she lay in.

"I've never been in here."

"I should think not," he said. "I would advise against opening anything you come across."

Isiilde sighed. "I've learned my lesson."

"You know it's fortunate you freed Luccub, considering I'd forgotten about him. He's quite helpful."

"He's a fiend, Marsais."

"Fiends have feelings, too."

"Did Luccub come through here?"

Marsais looked around, startled. "No, why do you ask?"

"Your bed is comfortable, but your room is a mess."

A smile twitched his lips. "So Isek tells me."

"He shares your bed?"

The humor in her voice gave him hope, even if it didn't touch her eyes. "It is large enough," he noted.

She tilted her head. "I didn't think you slept."

"Not well," he admitted.

"Your visions?"

Marsais hesitated. "My memories."

A shadow dulled her eyes. "I can see that now. Do they ever go away?"

"No," he said, then cleared the grit from his throat. "But they do get easier to carry."

Isiilde fell silent with thought. "What will happen to me now?" she finally asked.

"I don't know."

"You're a seer."

"I..." Marsais paused to gather his thoughts. She thought he had slipped into another vision. But then he looked up from his hands, searching her eyes. "What do *you* want, Isiilde?"

"What I want has never mattered. Why should it now?"

"It *does* matter," he insisted. "And I was a fool for not seeing it before."

"I can't have what I want."

"Tell me what it is."

"I do not want to be sold."

"You will not be sold."

The conviction in his voice stunned her. It was some minutes before she ventured another request.

"I want to leave this island."

"I shall arrange it."

"But only with you," she whispered.

"Still?"

"You fool, Marsais. Do you think my heart is so fickle? I love you. And damn your visions."

"It's who I am. I can't change the blood that runs through my veins any more than you can."

"I want to go back. To before."

"Would you, truly?" he asked. "I've often wondered..."

"Wondered what?"

"If only innocence and wisdom dwelled together. One cannot have both."

"Wisdom hurts."

"And madness softens the pain."

The fire popped, logs shifted, and Marsais offered his hand to her, palm up. Her eyes flickered to his in surprise.

"What of your visions?" she asked.

"Damn them."

Her brows drew together. "You said we cannot be."

"It's not my choice. But it is *yours*."

Without hesitation, Isiilde placed her hand in his, and he bowed over it, brushing her knuckles with his lips. "I'm so sorry. If I had not angered you—"

"Please don't," she cut in. "You said it yourself; one cannot pluck at a single thread to fix a mistake."

He looked up into her eyes.

"There is one more thing I'd like, Marsais."

"Name it."

"I am cold. And you are tired." Isiilde shifted to make room for him.

Marsais hesitated, uncertain, fearful, and dreading he was about to set the realm onto a path of destruction. But he went. And when he'd settled on top of the blankets beside her, she clung to him. And he to her.

Marsais was awoken by a rough shake. His eyes snapped open, alarm giving way to confusion. Clarity came when he felt a warm weight snuggled against his chest.

He looked up to find Oenghus glowering. But the baleful gaze wasn't directed at him. Oenghus brushed back his daughter's hair with a shaking hand, surveying her neck. He shuddered with relief.

A nymph's bond usually manifested as a collar around her neck. But there were only faded bruises. Bad enough.

"What happened?" Oenghus asked through clenched teeth.

Marsais held up a halting hand, then carefully untangled himself from the nymph. He pulled the covers over her and gestured Oenghus towards his study.

"Are you sure you want to know?" Marsais asked when they were alone.

Oenghus grunted, gripping the mantel as if bracing himself for a flogging.

Long after Marsais finished relating the details of the attack, Oenghus remained still, head bowed, dark hair obscuring his face, hiding his eyes but not his shaking shoulders.

Marsais shed what remained of his robes, giving his friend time to collect himself.

"Where's the bastard?" Oenghus growled.

Marsais' fingers faltered on the laces of his trousers. Here it comes, a crossroads, a divergence in time. Would Oenghus go right or would he go left?

"He's where I left him," Marsais said. "Pinned to the washroom wall."

Oenghus straightened and made to leave.

"You can't kill Stievin," Marsais called, cinching the ties with a sharp tug.

"And why not?"

"Because he may be useful."

Oenghus' eyes flared with rage. "*Useful?*" he growled.

"Morigan agrees. Hear me out."

"Where is Mori?"

"Sleeping in your rooms. Although..." Marsais wove a quick message, and sent it fluttering to Morigan's ears. She was the only one who could keep Oenghus from flying into a berserker's rage. Sometimes.

"You bastard."

"Yes, terrible of me," Marsais said dryly. "Asking a profoundly wise and level-headed woman to talk some sense into you."

"By Nuthaanian law, I have the right to kill that coward."

"To challenge him; not murder him."

"I don't care."

"But what if there is another way—a way that would sever Isiilde's ties with Kambe?"

"There *is* another way," Oenghus snapped, stepping towards him. "I'll kill that bastard, and I'll take her off this island. Kambe can kiss my arse."

"So you kill him! Fine, go ahead, get your revenge. And then what? The paladins will hang you for murdering a helpless man over some damaged property, because that is *exactly* how they will see it. And if you resist, you'll end up dragging Nuthaan into a war. Isiilde will be sold to Xaio, because Mearcentia won't touch this political powder keg."

"Those sniveling cans of tin couldn't get near enough to put a rope 'round my neck."

"Perhaps not, but you are still one man in a realm of powerful men.

Do not think yourself invincible, because your daughter won't benefit from your arrogance."

Oenghus growled dangerously.

Marsais pressed on, undaunted. "Listen to me. Isiilde has a fierce will. She fought back—a *nymph* fought! This was no vision of mine. She's forged a new path. This may very well be—do not get angry at this —a blessing in disguise."

The berserker's hands curled into fists.

"*Oenghus.*"

Morigan's voice brought him up short. His eyes burned into Marsais, and then he spun to face her.

Morigan stood in the doorway. Her black hair was loose, spilling around her shoulders, her blouse hastily donned along with a rumpled skirt.

"I have a right to kill him," he bit out.

"No, you don't," she said. "It's Isiilde's right by *our* laws. She's been bloodied in battle. She's a warrior now. It's her choice."

"You expect her to gouge out his eyes?" he snapped.

Morigan stepped up to the quivering berserker. He was on the edge, run ragged with restraint for years and aching to snap. She held his eyes and slid a hand under his shirt, over his heart. "The entire tower thinks Stievin raped her."

"By our laws, he did."

"I agree, but her nymph's bond is intact. Something the Order doesn't know, because Stievin's claiming her."

"What of it, woman?"

"*Think*, Oen. By the Blessed Order's own laws, Stievin stole her from Kambe and he must answer for that theft. He alone. If we stand back and allow a trial, then there's a possibility that the emperor will lose his claim to her. And you can drop this ruse. Your daughter will no longer be backed by the might of Kambe. She'll belong to Stievin."

Oenghus shook off his bloodlust with a shudder of control. "He doesn't hold her bond."

Morigan ran a soothing hand over his chest. "But he's claiming it."

"What you're getting at is a loophole in the law. It might not hold with this Chapterhouse. The blasted Captain took my brimgrog and said I couldn't drink in public."

Marsais snorted, but quickly covered it with a cough.

"Keep your mouth shut, Scarecrow."

"She sounds like a wise woman," Morigan said, drawing attention back to her eyes.

"What if this cook admits they aren't bonded?" he growled.

Morigan glanced at Marsais. "I don't think that will be an issue," she said.

"What do you mean?"

Marsais quickly cut in. "Just give me a few hours. I need to consult with a friend who is well-versed in the law."

"It's not up to your *friend*. It's up to the bloody Chapterhouse, and that Void-spawned woman," Oenghus said.

Morigan raised her brows. "Sounds like you've found yourself a future Oathbound."

Oenghus looked down at her, his beard twitching, but in the end, he only placed a hand over hers.

Morigan sighed. "I want to kill the bastard, too," she whispered. Then leaned forward to rest her forehead against his chest.

Oenghus wrapped his arms around her and held her close. The pair fit easily together. And Marsais busied himself with clearing a space in the detritus of his study. He tried not to overhear the words of comfort Oenghus murmured. It stirred up too many memories—an old pain, a sharp ache, another scar on his torn heart.

Eventually Oenghus pulled away, and went off to sit with his daughter.

Marsais was staring at the cleared floor, scratching at his chest, and Morigan took advantage of his distraction to compose herself. She had to call his name several times to pull him from his thoughts.

"Is your friend who I think he is?" she asked.

"Hmm," he confirmed.

She moved closer so their voices wouldn't carry. "Why doesn't the Sylph like you?"

Marsais glanced uneasily at the moonlit window.

"I don't care if she overhears."

"Spoken like a true Nuthaanian." The race did not scrape and bow before gods. They were more likely to spit in their faces. "The simplest answer is, long acquaintance."

"Don't be vague."

"It might be easier on your mind."

"You're still being vague, Marsais."

"Do you know the legend of the three Sylphs?"

Few did anymore. The Blessed Order made sure of that due to it being a Vaylinish legend and the blasphemous belief that there had originally been three Sylphs: Life, Death, and Chaos.

Morigan nodded. She was, after all, Nuthaanian.

"It's a pretty little tale. One far removed from the truth for those of us who were there."

Morigan put a hand to her temple. "That *does* hurt."

"I warned you," he said. "Matters of Time are never comfortable. And people wonder why I'm insane..."

Morigan shivered. "Not reassuring."

"I rarely am."

Morigan glanced towards the hallway, then pinned him with a dark glare. "You'll need to be, Marsais. For her. Isiilde's just been brutally assaulted. Her wounds are healed, but... don't dare rush her."

Marsais placed a hand over his heart. "On my honor."

She nodded, satisfied. "I don't pretend to know a thing about the deeper mysteries of this realm, or the bloody tapestry of time, but every bone in my body says your visions are wrong."

Surprise flickered over his eyes. "Why do you say that?"

"I can't say," she said.

"Morigan..."

She held up a halting hand. "I've already said too much. Ask Oen." She quickly changed the subject. "You realize you'll have to fight whoever they send?"

"I know."

"Oen still might kill you."

His lips twitched. "Not the first time he's tried."

"No... it's not. And you may want to put this on before you speak with your friend." She held out a white bundle of cloth.

He stared at it, perplexed.

"It's a shirt," she said.

Marsais glanced down his body and realized he'd only gotten as far as his trousers. Still with bare feet, too.

"Ah."

Morigan was sizing him up as he slipped the shirt over his head—hopefully not for a burial mound. "Well, at least you're easy on the eyes. If a woman likes her men pretty," she muttered.

"I'm *sleek!*" he called to her back.

CHAPTER 36

Marsais chanted the Lore under his breath, linking himself to the powerful currents of energy that pulsed with the essence of All. Weaving thought to action, stirring the waters as his fingers traced a complicated pattern over the floor, coaxing runes of glowing ice to life with a delicate touch.

One could not master such a power; rather he gave himself over to it, like a bird caught in a current of wind, skillfully maneuvering, soaring and drifting, but never seeking to control the Gift—no more than a bird might control the skies.

When his masterpiece was complete, he stepped back to appreciate the pulsing beauty of his art: a circle of flowing runes and flawless lines.

A heartbeat later, he stepped inside the circle.

Marsais had spent a lifetime in constant disorientation. While most would find the sensation unsettling, he did not blink an eye as his mind left his body as easily as one might set off for a stroll. He always liked where he ended up, which was nowhere, neither dark nor light, up nor down; it simply was, and he waited.

A white-robed figure materialized from nothing, joining Marsais in nowhere. The man pushed back his cowl, revealing a mop of unruly white hair, light brown skin, an aquiline nose, and bright silver eyes as reassuring as the stars. Neither young nor old, he was apart from time, like Marsais.

Chaim, the Guardian of Life, smiled warmly. "It's good to see you, Marsais. Though you don't look well." His voice was deep and full of compassion.

"Still full of compliments, I see."

"Only for you."

"I'm sure I'm blushing," Marsais said dryly.

"*Do* you blush?"

"I'm sure I did once upon a time." He gave the god a lopsided grin. "Thank you for meeting me."

"There is little that I would not abandon for you, my friend." Chaim crossed his arms, slipping his hands inside the voluminous sleeves of his robe.

Marsais envied his serenity, but as the god had pointed out in the past, he did not have Marsais' curse of foresight.

"More visions?"

Marsais sighed. "In part. I have questions of matters which are wisely not penned, let alone answered. I was hoping to pick your brain."

"Ask away."

"What do you know of Soisskeli's Stave?"

"I know I don't like hearing mention of it."

"So the legends are true? It has the power to bind virtually anything?"

"Anything not born of this realm, yes. Soisskeli wanted to make sure no one used it against him."

"Ah, well then. What if I told you that an ambitious Wise One has possession of the haft?"

Chaim frowned. "Only the haft?"

"I think he knows the location of at least one segment, and an end cap, perhaps both. Am I correct in thinking the artifact was separated and scattered to distant parts of the realm? The haft was placed somewhere near Vaylin. One of the end caps was hidden in the South along the Spotted Coast. And the other? I can't remember."

A troubling ailment of his fractured mind.

"The other is hidden," Chaim answered. "And although I don't question your motives, I hesitate to tell you for obvious reasons."

"Allow me to paint a suggestive picture for you. This Wise One, Tharios, has been pushing for the Order to support a new Thane gaining power in the South. And Tharios has gotten what he wanted. The Order of Wise Ones has thrown their power behind this upstart—against my recommendation."

"Ah, yes. Lachlan. He's uniting the Thanes."

"The very one," Marsais said. "But I've had visions of war. I believe Lachlan possessed one of the end caps or had knowledge of its location. In exchange for it, Tharios peddled our Order like a whoremonger. Regardless, a flame will rise from the South and the West will burn. Death howls in the sky, Chaim, which leads me to believe that Tharios may know where the third piece is."

Chaim shook his head. "Not necessarily."

"Why do you say that?"

"The Stave can be used with only one end cap."

Marsais muttered a curse. "Then what's the second one for?"

"One end has the power to bind anything not of this realm, and the other can open a Runic Gateway between realms. What good is a binding enchantment if you have nothing to bind?"

Marsais' fingers twitched. "That complicates things."

"Dare I ask?"

"What do you know of the passages beneath this tower?"

Chaim frowned. "You can't tell me this Tharios knows about the tomb? Only Archlords are supposed to know."

"And apparently the Guardians," he noted. "Tharios is ambitious. Capable of wearing any mask he chooses. I suspect he is more aware of memories beyond the River than he has a right to be. Tharios will be Archlord. I've foreseen it, and so has everyone else for that matter. I'm unpopular at the moment."

"Then make yourself agreeable."

"It wouldn't change anything. Tharios *will* be Archlord."

"Then kill him," Chaim said. "Or this realm will be lost."

"Hmm." Marsais stroked his braided goatee. "You forget the Tapestry of Time, my friend. A path begins at one spot and ends at the next crossroads. It's too late to turn back. The sands have already begun to slide, and the rocks will follow, one way or another. In my attempt to kill him, I would only quicken the end."

"I didn't say attempt, and you're confusing me again."

"No more than I confuse myself," Marsais said with a dry chuckle. "We must wait for a crossroads in the byways of Time. *Then* choose a direction."

"In that case, I might as well tell you of the third piece. The end cap in the South is the Gateway enchantment—by far the more dangerous of the two, considering what lies beneath the Spine. The binding part was hidden right under their noses in Fomorri. Do you remember the Finnow Spire?"

"The Unicorn's Horn?"

Chaim nodded. "It's well protected."

"That's always relative."

"I'll see who I have nearby to help," Chaim offered. "We've had our hands full with other matters of late. If Tharios succeeds in what you think he's after, I fear it will stretch this realm to its limit."

"Hmm, and here I thought you've been lounging around Iilenshar bedding Zahra's Valkryies."

Chaim grinned. "It's the other way around. I have little choice where they're concerned."

"Oh, you poor bastard."

"I'm not sure how I've survived all these years," Chaim agreed, but then the god turned serious again. "Keep me informed, will you?"

"Of course." Marsais hesitated. "I have a few questions of a more personal nature."

"Your wound?"

"No, not that." Marsais dismissed it with a wave of his hand. "My apprentice was brutally beaten and assaulted—"

Chaim choked in surprise. "The giant berserker?"

"No... I've had a new apprentice for the past two years, who happens to be the berserker's daughter. She's also a nymph."

"You have a nymph for an apprentice?" Chaim asked carefully.

"Has your hearing gone? Didn't I just say that?"

Chaim shook his head. "Your choice of apprentices never ceases to amaze, Marsais. I thought you were insane—"

"I am."

"—when you dragged that crazed berserker from the gutters. To say nothing of the dragon, or Nereus' daughter, and I try to forget the fiend all together—what was her name?"

"Saavedra."

"Didn't she try to kill you in the end?"

Marsais shrugged a shoulder. "They all try to at some point in their apprenticeship."

"Has the nymph?"

"Not intentionally."

"How much have you taught her in two years?" Chaim asked. "Can she even weave the Gift?"

"It depends if she feels like it." At the thought of Isiilde, a smile spread across his lips. "And when she does—it's flawless. She's as hot-headed as her father, and possesses a strange affinity with fire."

Marsais quickly skimmed over the events surrounding Isiilde, the complications of her ties with Kambe, and her impending sale.

"She *stabbed* her attacker?" Chaim asked, surprised.

"Yes. Considering her size and diminutive strength, she fought fiercely. She and Yvesa would get along splendidly."

Chaim raised his eyes to the nothingness above. "Why Yvesa ever got the title of Guardian of Peace, I'll never know. She misses you, by the way."

Marsais smiled at the thought of the Guardian sprite. "Give her my warm regards."

"Not as you would, but I will," Chaim said. "You know this nymph of yours... I've never heard of one like her. There have been 'nymphs of power' as they are called, but their affinity is for water or earth and their powers subtle and unobtrusive. There's nothing destructive about them."

Marsais kept her true heritage to himself. He couldn't risk telling Chaim—not until he'd spoken with Oenghus.

"I suspect it has something to do with her father," he said, shading the truth.

"Yes, very likely," Chaim mused.

"What of the Blessed Order? Will they proceed with a sanctioned duel?"

"They'll check her for a nymph's mark. But it's not there, so they won't proceed with the Right of Challenge, and she'll still belong to Soataen." Chaim began to pace in thought, hands folded behind his back. "Although…"

"Yes?"

Chaim stopped, tilting his head. "The nymph… Isiilde… was attacked while her guardian was being detained by the Blessed Order. So they bear some blame."

"Her guardian was being detained for desecrating your mother's temple. He shot her statue's head off with a lightning bolt. In his defense, he was aiming at a fiend."

Chaim snorted. "That might complicate things, but one never knows. I'll whisper a word in the Knight Captain's ear, but I can't guarantee anything. So-called gods we may be, but we're still bound by our own laws."

"With good reason," Marsais said, feeling his heart sink. "We've both seen what happens when the powerful ignore their own laws."

"Yes…" Chaim said, sighing. "Though your own boundaries are rather shady. What will you do?"

"Something very unwise."

"*Marsais*," the younger god warned.

"Stievin is claiming Isiilde wanted him. And that I unjustly attacked him. He thinks he has the Blessed Order on his side. But once he realizes what his claim involves, I suspect he'll try to back out."

"The knights won't believe him."

"I thought as much, too."

"But again, with no mark present—" Chaim cut off, eyes narrowing. "You can't tell me a nymph who has been Awakened for three months hasn't had her eye on at least *one* man, especially if she's as fierce as you claim."

"Hmm."

"Hmm, indeed," Chaim said, with a knowing glint in his eye. "Stuck in a tower with a nymph. You poor bastard."

"We're not talking about Valkryies here."

"Considering who you are, I'm surprised she hasn't thrown herself at you already."

"I've tried to keep my distance."

"And yet you love her," Chaim noted.

Marsais pressed his lips together. There was no denying it. The two had known each other for far too long.

"It *is* probably unwise," Chaim agreed. "Your visions aside, the bond of spirit is intimate. You'll have trouble masking yourself from her."

Marsais mulled this over. Intricate illusion weaves masked his true nature. Yet occasionally Isiilde saw through the illusion. She would eventually figure it out.

"Do you know precisely how the Eldritch bonded a nymph's spirit? I can't seem to recall."

"I was too young to enter the Eldritch Circle," Chaim said. "But from what I've heard, aside from the physical act, a bonding of spirit is pure instinct on the nymph's part."

"That would be fine if Kambe wasn't involved. But I fear we have little time."

"With her attachments to Kambe, likely only a few days," Chaim agreed. "But you're right about the law. Why do you think I didn't fight it? It serves its purpose. The law stopped the wars. But the law also gives the nymph an opening, one that's not apparent to many.

"Stievin has already claimed ownership. As long as there's a nymph's mark on her when she's inspected, the paladins will assume he took her—no matter if he tries to claim otherwise. The Blessed Order will hold Stievin responsible. Right of Ownership will be from Kambe, to Stievin, and then to… whomever she bonds with."

Chaim gave him a pointed look.

"The emperor will have no claim—she is no longer his stolen property. Soataen *cannot* hold you responsible. The Right of Challenge will be observed. If it isn't, send word. You will have Iilenshar's full support. Even the emperor is not fool enough to defy us."

"Gods, what a complicated mess," Marsais muttered, scratching at his chest.

"Politics or love?"

"Humans."

Chaim grunted, and pulled up his hood. "It's only complicated because we're trying to prevent them from slaughtering each other and destroying this realm."

"Sometimes I wonder if we shouldn't just let them."

Chaim grimaced. "My mother would. But our hearts aren't so calloused to suffering."

"One does tire though…"

"No doubt," Chaim said gently. "But come now, Ancient One, you're supposed to be *my* pillar."

Marsais gave him a sad smile. "A rather ruined one, aren't I?"

"Still standing."

"Hmm."

"Keep me posted. And… I hope all goes well for you and your nymph. At the very least, you might sleep better."

Chaim smiled beneath his hood and faded, leaving Marsais alone in the middle of nowhere.

CHAPTER 37

A PLAGUE VIPER lay coiled in a basket. It was the color of death, of funeral wrappings and dried bone, and its eyes were milky white.

N'Jalss took a step back as Tharios picked up the viper by its tail. The viper hissed, tasting the air with a forked tongue. And then it whipped its head around, seeking prey.

As casually as could be, Tharios placed his forearm in front of death. The viper struck, sinking its fangs into the human, pumping venom into flesh.

Tharios arched his neck like a man in the throes of passion.

Humans were strange creatures, N'Jalss mused. Torture them, and they howled like infants. Yet for their pleasures, they freely subjected themselves to pain.

"Have you ever taken ethervenom directly from its source?" Tharios asked, his voice a near moan.

N'Jalss was Rahuatl. His race did several odd things, but only a madman would risk ethervenom.

"Pure ethervenom, if one survives, affects the mind," Tharios continued. "But contrary to legend, it doesn't cause madness; it enlightens."

Tharios carefully pulled the plague viper's fangs from his forearm, and wrapped a bandage around the bleeding wound. "What progress have you made?"

"None, m'lord."

Tharios' lips pressed into a line. But that was all the displeasure he betrayed. Without a word, the sleek Wise One walked over to a large window overlooking the turbulent sea. He stood for long minutes, quiet and contemplating.

N'Jalss sensed danger and smelled aggression in the air. Tharios was not a man to be crossed.

"The Shadowed Dawn approaches," Tharios said at length, stroking the viper slithering over his naked shoulders.

"I am searching day and night, m'lord."

"My plans will be useless if we can't locate the entrance of the tomb."

N'Jalss relaxed at the inclusion of 'we'. Tharios did not hold him entirely responsible for the failure.

"What of Tulipin?" N'Jalss asked. "Did he hold up his end of the bargain?"

"He recreated the scroll—a simple matter for a mind like his. As we speak, it's being shown to the Blessed Order. But I'm afraid it won't be enough to have Marsais prematurely disrobed."

"A toad may bring down a giant," N'Jalss said, quoting a proverb of his race. "Our *esteemed* Archlord digs his own grave with the help of that whining creature."

"True," Tharios admitted. "She's done most of the work for us. It's almost *too* easy. If time were not a factor, I'd let events run their course and take his throne when the names are drawn. Still..." Tharios trailed off in thought, turning back to the window, where he stood for a silent time.

N'Jalss rubbed his split tongue along the insides of his pointed teeth, cutting the flesh, and wetting his palate for his dinner below the castle. He was so distracted by the scent of blood that he nearly missed Tharios' next words.

"Tell me, N'Jalss. If you saw your death coming—would you run from it or fight?"

"Fight it," he hissed.

"A sane man would fight it and a wise man would run, but what of a madman?" Tharios mused, turning to regard him with a tilt of his brow.

Slow realization crept over N'Jalss, and at its conclusion he dug his claws into the palm of his hand. "Embrace it," he spat.

Marsais was playing his own game while they played theirs.

But what was Marsais planning? What was he waiting for?

"Our plans have changed," Tharios said. "We must strike before he sees us coming."

"How?"

"We strike at his blind spot."

N'Jalss bared his fangs. "The ruined nymph?"

"Precisely."

CHAPTER 38

Marsais plunged back to his body with a frisson of shock. He shivered, and began rubbing his arms briskly as he stepped out of the dissipating rune circle.

Oenghus sat brooding by the fireplace, sucking on his long pipe and plotting murder.

Isek had his boots propped on the cluttered desk, snoozing in Marsais' chair. A quick gesture from Marsais sent a jolt of energy hurling into his assistant's shoulder.

Isek bolted awake. "Just resting my eyes." He hopped to his feet and wiped mud off the desk. "What were you doing?"

"Consulting a friend who is well-versed in the law. What time is it?"

"Past the tenth bell."

"What news?" Marsais asked.

"The emperor is furious, but not out of any concern for Isiilde. This will hit his coffers hard. The bidding was up to four hundred thousand crowns and now that Kiln's pulled out, he can't hope to get that much. The terms have changed, so the slate will be wiped clean for the bidding to begin again."

"Hmm."

"Oenghus has been exiled from Kambe. If he sets foot within the borders, he's to be executed for treason. Or at least they'll try."

"Point out to Kambe that the Blessed Order was detaining Oenghus, so they're to blame for his failure to protect Isiilde."

"With pleasure." Isek flashed a grin. "The emperor summoned the Hound from the Fell Wastes as his champion. He'll take Isiilde to Kambe after the duel with Stievin."

"My arse he will," Oenghus growled.

Marsais muttered an oath. "I was hoping Soataen would keep her here until Mearcentia and Xaio renegotiated. When will the Hound arrive?"

"If the winds favor his mount, he could be here tomorrow morning. But with the storms this season, his griffin will have a hard time of it. If we're lucky, tomorrow afternoon."

"Void," Marsais muttered. "That doesn't give us much time."

"For what?" Isek asked.

Silence answered. And Isek thought he'd fallen into one of his visions again. But Marsais stirred, looking to the men. "What would you do if you abruptly lost your vision? Here, now, in the middle of this room?"

Through long association, Isek and Oenghus were used to odd questions.

"Kill whoever is closest," Oenghus grunted.

Isek rolled his eyes at the berserker. Then, noting his proximity, took a hasty step to the side. "As imaginative as that is, I'd cling to my last moment of sight, reconstruct the layout of the room and try to get to the bloody infirmary without breaking my neck."

"Hmm, I never much cared for stumbling around in the dark. I believe it's best to stand and wait."

"Until you starve?" Oenghus snorted. "That's bloody useful, Scarecrow. Do you have any other words of wisdom?"

"Never stand next to a berserker."

The door opened, and Morigan walked in carrying a tray and her herbalist's satchel. Her hair was in place, and her bodice and skirts were back in order.

Her gaze swept over the grim faces in the study, before landing on Oenghus.

"Bath," he grunted in answer to her silent question.

Morigan nodded with approval. And Isek quickly hopped forward to clear a space on a table for her tray.

"What did your friend say, Marsais?" she asked.

"They'll need proof of a nymph's mark to proceed with the trial by combat. But... as long as one is present, then they'll believe that Stievin took her bond."

Isek nearly dropped the tray he took from her hands. "What do you mean... *believe*?"

Marsais raised his brows at the long-time spy.

Isek narrowed his eyes. "Oh, that's bloody good. I like it."

What Isek grasped, Oenghus did not. He stirred with a grumble. "She doesn't have a bloody mark."

"No, she doesn't, Oen," Morigan agreed, sitting down to prepare some herbal concoction.

Oenghus knocked his pipe bowl into the fire until it was empty, and stood. "Right, then. We'll leave tonight. Don't you have that strawberry ship in port?"

"Hmm?"

"The one you charter to ship in strawberries for Isiilde."

Isek laughed. "Is that your plan?"

Oenghus turned on the man. "My plan," he said through clenched teeth. "Is to get Isiilde off this island."

"On a ship? From one of the docks? You, fighting a fleet of Kamberians from a ship's deck? From what I remember, you don't do so well fighting at sea. In fact, the last sea battle ended when you sunk your own ship by accident."

Oenghus took a step towards the man, but Isek held his ground. "And have you forgotten that Marsais pissed off the sea god?"

Before Oenghus could pummel the man, Morigan cut in. "Oen, he's antagonizing you."

"That'll stop when I rip out his tongue."

Morigan gave a shake of her head and went back to her mixing.

"Anyway, to get back to the topic at hand, and away from Oen and his strawberry ship—"

Oenghus clenched a fist, snapping his pipe in half.

"—Caitlyn Whitehand wants to see her," Isek said. "Kambe doesn't believe Isiilde was attacked. They're convinced Oenghus didn't rein her in tight enough, and she went to Stievin of her own free will. And High Inquisitor Multist and the new Knight Captain, Acacia Mael—"

Oenghus growled.

"—are here to investigate. They've requested an audience with you, Marsais, but wish to inspect her first."

"Since they have requested an audience, I deny them one. And they can wish all they like. I refuse to subject Isiilde to an interrogation," Marsais said.

"So, what are you going to do?" Isek asked. "Hide up here until the Hound shoots a lightning bolt through the window?"

Marsais stroked his goatee, coins chiming, as he considered the option. It was appealing.

"Marsais, you *have* to see them."

"I don't want to see them." It sounded petulant, but he was too immortal to care. "I have more important things to do."

Isek flicked a coin in the air. And kept doing it, because he knew it annoyed the seer. "Now's not the time to get on their bad side, old fellow."

"An appearance of cooperation, short of subjecting Isiilde to their inspection, would not be a bad idea," Morigan said.

"I swear you're the only one with sense in this tower." Isek flicked her a coin in gratitude.

Morigan paused her mixing long enough to catch it and drop it on the floor.

Oenghus bent to retrieve the coin, and tucked it under his belt. "Try to get it back now, weasel."

Another gold coin appeared in Isek's hand, and he smugly started weaving it between his fingers.

Oenghus grunted.

"Fine, a brief audience," Marsais relented. "Tell the Inquisitor and Knight Captain I'll see them as soon as I'm presentable."

Isek blinked.

"I can hardly speak with the illustrious Inquisitor of the Blessed Order dressed as I am."

"Marsais," Isek said dryly. "You've met with dignitaries while wearing patched trousers and sandals."

"At least I was partially clothed." Marsais shrugged. "Have them wait for me outside of the throne room."

Isek smirked. "Plan to make an entrance?"

"Hmm."

"Bloody dandy," Oenghus muttered.

CHAPTER 39

STEAM FILLED THE CHAMBER, swirling over mosaics that flowed to the circular bath in its center. It was more of a fountain than a tub. Water splashed from a smaller basin into the larger, stirring the frothy waters with a gentle touch.

Isiilde felt lost in the bath chamber. Why did anyone need a bath this large? Not that she was complaining.

She shivered despite the heat and hugged her body, keeping her shoulders below the water. She wanted to hide from the world—from leering eyes and cruel hands.

Something inside felt broken. Numb. In what seemed like another lifetime, she would have relished the bath chamber, soaked in its opulence, and tested the acoustics. Now she was only hollow inside.

Marsais' words came back to her.

"I don't think I'll ever feel like that again."

"Do you trust me?"

"Always."

"Then believe me when I say you will."

But did she even *want* to feel again? The woman, Gwen, deep in the Keening, came back to her. And now Isiilde understood. It seemed too great an effort to drag herself out of the bath. But she did.

She wrapped herself in a robe that belonged to Marsais. It smelled of him and it enveloped her with comfort.

The Archlord's private suite was larger than the cottage by the beach that she'd burned down. She walked down a short hallway, and paused at an open door.

Marsais stood in a dressing room. He was wrapping a wide sash over austere robes the color of night. He was freshly shaven (aside from his braided goatee), and his white hair looked luminous in the everlight.

The robe emphasized his leanness to the point of severity. From his noble brow to his hawkish nose and the three hollow coins chiming at the end of his goatee, he was every bit the famed Archlord of the Isle.

Marsais looked up to find her leaning, with arms crossed, in the doorway. A warm smile transformed him from regal power to roguish charm.

"How did you find the bath?" he asked, shaking out his sleeves.

"It makes me wonder about the previous Archlords."

Marsais chuckled. "Definitely not to my taste, either."

"What's going on?"

He told her about the laws, the Right of Challenge, and the promise of freedom. Her heart twisted with dread.

"I have the entire entourage waiting in the nameless chamber. Let them sweat in there for a time—" He cut off when he saw the look on her face. "What is it?"

She swayed unsteadily on her feet and he took her face in his hands. His touch warmed her ears and his eyes drew her away from fear. But he felt distant. "You do not have to bond with me, Isiilde. I'll find another way to—"

Isiilde swallowed down her fear. "That's not it... You'll have to fight the emperor's champion for me."

"As I once told you, there is very little in this realm that I would *not* do for you."

"But you can't use a weapon."

"Can't I?"

"The only weapon I've seen you hold is your eating knife."

"You *did* say I have the body of a duelist."

But she found no humor in his quip. "My freedom doesn't matter if you're dead, Marsais."

"It matters to me."

Isiilde arched her body against his, and pulled him down by his goatee to kiss him. The touch of his lips made her body come alive. It burned away the fog in her mind, and she felt the carpet under her toes, his soft hair brushing her neck, and the gentleness of his lips.

She rocked back down to her feet and stared up into his eyes as he caressed the curve of her ear.

"I've never kissed a man until now."

"I've never kissed one either," he murmured in a daze.

Isiilde snorted, burying her face in his robes. When she looked back up, he was grinning like a fool, eyes glittering.

She toyed with the coins woven into his braid. "I've wanted to do that since I saw you in the pleasure house."

"You mean when you ran your hands all over me?"

"Not *all* over you."

"Your touch lingers still."

"So does yours," she whispered.

His caress trailed down her neck.

"How long will you keep them waiting?"

"Hmm?"

"The paladins."

Marsais narrowed his eyes.

"The ones waiting in the nameless room for you," she reminded.

"Right," he said slowly. "Not the first thing on my mind at the moment."

"What is?"

"You."

"Go, Marsais. I will be waiting here."

Reluctantly, he left, and Isiilde settled herself in front of the fire in his bedchamber to dry and brush her hair. She stared at the flames, but despite the heat she felt cold again.

The rattle of crockery jerked her around. But it was only Morigan bringing in a tray. Isiilde relaxed her grip on the brush's handle. Morigan held out a cup. "Drink this. You'll feel better."

Without even a wrinkle of her nose, Isiilde drank the herbal concoction.

"Eat this."

Isiilde frowned at the bowl of strawberries. She felt something, then. The urge to be sick. She turned back to the fire. "I'm not hungry."

Morigan pulled over a footstool and took the brush from her hand. Without a word, she began brushing out Isiilde's hair. It was familiar, and soothing, and Isiilde let herself be lulled by the woman's touch.

After a time, Isiilde turned slightly to look at her. "Can Marsais fight?"

"So you've talked with him?"

"Yes. But will it work? Using the Right of Challenge?"

Morigan met her eyes. "We think so. There's no guarantee. And just so you know, there are other options, but most would put us on the run and we'd be hunted."

"And Nuthaan would be dragged into war."

Morigan's eyes flickered with surprise.

"I understand some of it now," Isiilde admitted. "The kingdoms are like a runic ward—runes woven together in a tight knot. One slip will trigger the trap."

"An apt observation," Morigan agreed, impressed. "But you don't have to bond with Marsais. We could try an illusion weave to mimic a nymph's bond, or—"

"I want him, Morigan."

The woman raised her brows.

"I mean to bond. I've wanted to for some time now. Though I did not realize it..." Isiilde frowned. "I feel like I have new eyes. But they are not bright ones anymore."

"Brutality will do that to you." Morigan set aside the brush and took Isiilde's hands, warming them in her own. "You fought fiercely."

"I *lost*. If Marsais hadn't come in..."

"That's not what matters, Isiilde," Morigan whispered. "Whether you win or lose, or even if you rolled into a ball and endured what Stievin had in mind... it's the getting back up part that matters."

"Why do I feel like it's my fault?"

"Because it makes the realm seem like a safer place." A shadow of a smile played in Morigan's dark eyes. "It'll get better. I know. I've been where you are."

"Truly?"

Morigan nodded.

"But you're..."

"Strong? A formidable fighter?" Morigan chuckled bitterly. "It doesn't matter, Isiilde. Not when you're overwhelmed. It happens to men, too."

Isiilde paled, feeling ill again.

Morigan touched her chin, and drew her eyes to her own. "But I got up. As you did. And as you will continue to do. So hold your chin up with pride, like the true Nuthaanian that you are."

"But I'm a nymph, Morigan."

"Aye, but you're my daughter, too. I nursed you, and in Nuthaan that makes you kin. You've earned your place as a warrior in Clan Freyr. So never mind this bloody Order."

"It can kiss my faerie arse," she agreed.

Morigan smiled and tucked a stray tendril behind the nymph's ear, looking down on her with pride. "All my girls grow up too quickly and before I know it, they're bringing men home. But I never imagined one would bring Marsais home."

"How long have you known him?"

"As long as I've known Oen. Those two are intertwined."

Isiilde grimaced. "Oen is going to kill him."

"Probably."

"But *can* Marsais fight? What if he's killed during the duel?"

Morigan laughed at the thought. But Isiilde saw nothing amusing about it.

"I wouldn't worry, child," Morigan finally said when she caught her breath. "He *could* be killed, true, but there's a reason Oen calls the man *Scarecrow*."

CHAPTER 40

Knight Captain Acacia Mael shifted in the nameless room. The place made her skin crawl and her fingers itch for her sword.

Shadowy forms drifted in the obsidian stone. Under the surface of stone? Impossible. But she did not think it was a trick of the eye.

High Inquisitor Multist and his nervous scribe crowded around her. Round-faced and bedecked in ceremonial armor, Multist would be useless in a fight.

"How long must we wait here?" Multist demanded of the Archlord's assistant.

The man had no eyebrows, which made him look even balder than he already was. He rocked back and forth on his feet, weaving a gold coin over his knuckles, completely at ease in the room—or at least pretending to be.

"Until the gates open," Isek said.

The scribe clutched his book closer to his breast. Acacia hoped he didn't piss his trousers.

"Does the Archlord generally keep you waiting, Inquisitor?" Acacia asked.

"No," Multist said through clenched teeth. He was sweating in his golden plate, and the metal at his knees knocked together from his shaking.

Acacia looked to Isek. "Open the gate."

"I apologize, Knight Captain, but only the Archlord can open the gate. He commands the Voiceless."

She'd heard of the Voiceless—the stone faces encircling monolithic columns in the throne room. But she had never set eyes on them. This was her first time to the Spine.

It was said that a thousand tongues had been sacrificed for the Archlord's power. Acacia had thought the rumors about the Spine were all just whispers and fear, but after waiting in this nameless room she was willing to believe anything.

The ornate gates opened, and Isek bowed them forward with a flourish. The throne room was vast, and the light that shone through stained glass windows deepened shadows rather than illuminated.

Acacia's fingers twitched. Darkness made her uneasy; Reapers dwelled in shadow, and she'd fought too many of the Voidspawn in her lifetime.

Their heels clicked on stone as they marched to the end of the immense hall. She frowned at the mutilation of stone faces that ringed the columns.

They were too lifelike.

Her gaze was drawn to a figure perched on an obsidian throne at the far end of the hall. His long white hair shimmered in shadow, his ears rose to a sharp point, and his long fingers were curled over the armrests.

Acacia's breath caught, her step faltered, and her hesitation drew the man's attention. He focused on her with eyes that gleamed like stars.

This was no man. No Kamberian. He was an elf, and his resemblance to the Guardians of Iilenshar was striking—graceful yet hardened like a deadly blade.

It took effort to step up to the dais.

The Archlord tapped a finger rhythmically on the glassy stone. "High Inquisitor Multist." His words were sinuous, repeated a thousand times by a thousand whispering voices.

Acacia glanced at the mutilated faces on the stone. The Voiceless had a voice after all.

The full weight of the Archlord's gaze settled on Acacia, and she had to clench her jaw to keep from taking a step back. It took all her will to meet those eyes.

"I have not been introduced to your companion."

"May I present, Acacia Mael, our new Knight Captain of the Chapterhouse in Drivel." Multist turned unnecessarily to her. "This is the Archlord."

The Archlord inclined his head, and Multist forged on without giving her a chance to speak.

"Emperor Jaal has asked the Blessed Order to take the nymph into custody until his champion arrives."

"Oh, well, that seems reasonable," the Archlord agreed amiably. "May I see the Emperor's orders?" He held out an expectant hand.

"It was relayed by Whisperers," Multist explained.

"Hmm." The Archlord stroked his braided goatee, coins chiming in the vast chamber. "A Whisperer, you say? I'm afraid that won't do. A message can be intercepted and altered. It's like snatching a feather from the wind." An elegant hand rose, swiping the air like a viper. "Not very hard to accomplish with a quick hand. You should hear some of the things I pluck from the winds."

Multist's eyes narrowed. "You refuse to hand over the nymph?"

"No, I refuse to hand over the nymph without orders bearing the emperor's seal. I assure you the nymph is quite safe where she is."

"What of the young man? I suppose you won't hand him over either?"

"You can remove him from the wall as long as you don't execute him. I left him up there as proof. Thira can also testify."

On familiar ground, Acacia stepped forward. "As a witness to events, Archlord, I would like to hear your account."

The pinched-faced scribe fumbled with his implements, and she waited until he was ready.

The Archlord related the facts without emotion. Thankfully, the Voiceless did not repeat his words.

Trapped in a washroom, gagged with a weave, left to fend for herself, and unable to even scream—Acacia swallowed down rising anger. And now the battered nymph was locked in a tower with this formidable elf. She must be terrified.

"Morigan, the Master Healer, will testify to her injuries," the Archlord finished at length.

His face was impassive, but his hands betrayed him—his knuckles were white from gripping the armrests.

"Did Isiilde have prior contact with Stievin?" Acacia asked.

"Only when picking up food from the kitchens."

"And how did the guards lose sight of her?"

"You will have to question the guards."

Multist grew impatient with her questioning. "There is another matter, Archlord."

Acacia glanced at the Inquisitor. His eyes were fevered with righteousness as he shook a scroll at the Archlord.

"You are charged with heresy and summoning. You must present yourself for questioning."

"On what grounds?"

"Your apprentice handed in a blasphemous manuscript. Since she's a nymph, we hold you responsible." Multist paused dramatically.

The Archlord looked bored.

"It's also come to our attention that you loosed a fiend on the isle. You broke the Laws of Summoning."

"Did I?" The Archlord sounded amused by the thought.

"You don't deny it?"

"I freely admit to opening the flagon. I was casting about for something to drink and saw it on my desk. So yes, I opened it. I forgot he was in there."

"You forgot that there was a bound fiend in a flagon?" Multist asked.

"It's been near fifteen hundred years since I bound the imp," the Archlord purred. "I can't be expected to remember every petty detail of a lifetime spent fighting fiends."

As impassive as the elf might be, Acacia watched his expressive fingers, which were tapping the armrest with impatience now.

"A trial will decide that," Multist announced.

Acacia wondered how the Inquisitor expected to drag this elf to trial.

"Don't get too comfortable in that chair. Your treatment of the cook Stievin was barbaric. Law demands that you answer for the damages inflicted on his person."

"*My* treatment of Stievin?" His voice was like a ring of steel.

"By your own admission, you attacked an unarmed man and humiliated him."

The Archlord bounded to his feet in disgust, robes billowing around him with restless anticipation. "He was raping my apprentice!" A thousand voices rose in fury. "I suppose you would have watched and waited while he finished up!"

Acacia tensed, her hand straying to the sword on her hip while the scribe pissed his pants. But Multist stood his ground with an air of triumph. He'd burrowed under the Archlord's skin.

"The creature in question is a nymph—not worth the damage caused," Multist stated.

"Get out of my tower," the Archlord ordered, fingers twitching at his side.

Isek quickly stepped forward. "The audience is over."

As they were escorted out, Acacia glanced over her shoulder in time to see the Archlord touch something on the throne's armrest. With a flash of light, he vanished through a teleportation rune. But not before she glimpsed the pain etched on his face.

CHAPTER 41

THE MOMENT MARSAIS landed in his desk chair, he surged to his feet. Isiilde jerked in surprise, Morigan unsheathed a dagger at her belt, and Oenghus glowered.

"Do I want to know?" he grumbled.

Marsais shook his head. It would only provoke the berserker.

The white pelt had been restored to the center of the room, and Isiilde sat in the sunlight, its warmth blanketing her face. She was still wrapped in his robe.

Marsais fought to control his rage. He turned to the window, and clasped his hands behind his back to keep them from twitching.

Morigan sheathed her knife.

It was well past midday. Light was fading to twilight—time was slipping through their fingers. Isiilde's bruises hadn't even fully faded.

A stir of cold air signaled Isek's arrival, but unlike Marsais, he sat back in a chair and exhaled with a low whistle.

"You know, for a moment there, I thought you would turn Multist into a pig."

"He's well on his way," Marsais growled.

"He was smug enough when you dismissed him," Isek mused. "I

think he actually believes those charges will stand. You could see it in his eyes—he wants the privilege of gutting you himself."

Isiilde rose to her feet. "What happened?"

"The Blessed Order charged me with summoning and heresy."

"*Summoning*?" Morigan asked.

"The fiend."

Isiilde went to his side. "Will the charges hold up in a trial?"

"I don't know," he admitted, turning to her. "It depends how much I've pissed off the powers that be."

"This is my fault," she breathed. "Isn't it?"

"Gods, Sprite," Oenghus growled. "Don't be dramatic. The Scarecrow has done a lot worse than heresy and summoning."

Marsais reached for Isiilde's hand. "I won't let them execute me."

Isiilde twined her fingers with his own, and Oenghus narrowed his eyes at the pair. Morigan watched him curiously, wondering when he would put two and two together.

"So," Isek said cheerfully. "Shall we just leave now so you two can get on with the bonding?"

Isiilde blushed furiously.

Before anyone could react, Oenghus surged forward, grabbing the wiry man around the neck with one hand to wrench him three paces off the floor.

Isek's eyes bulged, and every futile second of struggle turned his face another unnatural shade.

"What the Void are you talking about?" Oenghus demanded.

"*Oen*," Morigan said. "Put him down."

Oenghus glared at her. She gave him a look. Isek was dropped to the floor.

"Get out before he kills you," Morigan ordered.

Isek half crawled, then lurched to his feet and stumbled out the door. Oenghus turned his rage on Marsais, but Isiilde stepped between the men, bringing Oenghus up short.

His beard twitched. "Is this what you all were planning?" He glanced at Morigan. "You *knew* about this?"

Isiilde's eyes flashed in defiance. "Don't blame her. It's *my* choice."

Oenghus spluttered, then jabbed a finger over her head at Marsais. "You can't bond with that bag of bones."

Isiilde crossed her arms. "Why not?"

"Because *I* said so."

Morigan sighed at his answer.

"I'm not leaving you alone with that..." His face turned red with rage. "Scoundrel!"

"I love that scoundrel."

"Marsais practically raised you."

Isiilde snorted. "*You* and Morigan raised me. I barely saw him. We only became friends a few years ago."

Marsais was very careful not to move. But Oenghus pinned him with a glare. "*You* planned this all along."

"Oenghus—" Marsais held up his hands.

"You said we could be at each other's throats over her. This entire time you've been plotting to have your chance at a nymph, you whore's son of a swine!"

"Stop it," Isiilde pleaded.

"You don't know him like I do. Marsais has a... thing for exotic women. You'll just be another notch in his belt."

"You're only making this harder for her," Marsais said calmly. But his old friend had reached the limits of his self-control. Truth be told, Marsais was surprised Oenghus had held it together this long.

"Ask him why he trembles every time he sets foot on a ship," Oenghus growled.

"Curse you!" Marsais snapped, stepping forward. "I did not foresee *this*. I swear on my children's graves."

Those final words rang in the silence. The two men stood toe to toe, the berserker looming over the elf, fists flexing, beard twitching.

"Oenghus," a gentle voice finally pierced his rage. He turned away from Marsais to find the eyes of his daughter. "I'm asking you to leave. Please. This is my choice, not yours."

Oenghus hesitated, his eyes darting between Marsais and Isiilde. Finally, she mimicked Morigan's earlier stance—a defiant tilting of her chin and crossed arms.

It did the trick.

"Are you sure you want this sack of bones?"

Isiilde nodded.

Oenghus grunted, then grabbed Marsais by the front of his robes, yanking him off the floor. "Treat her good or I'll have your head, Scarecrow." He released Marsais, who landed easily on his feet.

Then, with a growl at Morigan, he stalked out of the room.

Morigan bent to gather her satchel. "Well, no one is dead. The ceiling and walls are still intact, and he didn't fly into a berserker's rage. That went better than I expected."

"Hmm," Marsais agreed, as he straightened his robes.

"Will he be angry with you?" Isiilde asked.

Morigan snorted as she shouldered the satchel. "Don't worry about me. I've been dealing with that mule-brained man for far too long. Goodnight, you two." And with barely a glance, Morigan shut the door firmly behind her.

CHAPTER 42

"Well, that was embarrassing."

Marsais sat back on his desk and stretched out his long legs. "Not if you've lived as long as I have."

"Has this happened to you before?" Isiilde asked.

"Hmm." Marsais paused in thought. "Something close to it. Did you know some cultures require a couple to consummate an Oath in full public view?"

"That sounds like something Nuthaanians would require."

"Oh, it's not required... They just don't care who watches."

She arched a brow. "What did Oen mean when he said I'd be another notch in your belt?"

Although the lilt to her voice was gone, her curiosity was there.

"Oenghus was accusing me of keeping count. Although his belt far surpasses mine," he said dryly.

"Keeping count of what?"

"Women." He waved a dismissive hand. "For some odd reason, womanly creatures tend to throw themselves at me."

Isiilde eyed him. "I'm not surprised. Does it have something to do with your fear of ships?"

"I'm not afraid of ships. I've spent a fair amount of time sailing the seas, but I pissed off the sea god."

The coins at the end of his braid chimed, and she drifted closer to rub them between her fingers. "What did you do?"

"I found a female washed ashore one day. She had the most beautiful scales..."

"Scales?"

"Hmm, she was rather taken with me. It was only afterwards I discovered she was the sea god's daughter. Nereus wasn't happy."

"You made love to a woman covered in scales?" she asked slowly.

"It has been known."

"What happened?"

"Whether or not you think me a gentleman, I will not go into details."

"I meant what happened with her father. Not your... scaly love making." She wrinkled her nose. "Did she smell like fish?"

"Do *you* smell like nymph?"

She sniffed at her wrist. "Do I?"

Marsais took her hand, and the sleeve of her robe fell back, exposing a slender arm. The pale skin was marred with fading bruises. He inhaled her scent, then brushed his lips against the sensitive skin of her wrist. "You smell intoxicating. So yes... like a nymph."

Isiilde smiled. "What did the sea god do?"

"Perhaps another night?" He drew her into the circle of his arms. "I find myself pleasantly distracted."

"I'll hold you to that," she warned. "I suppose we should 'get on with the bonding.'"

"I do apologize for Isek. That was... indelicate of him."

"I was wondering when everyone would leave. I suppose he sped things up."

"There is that," Marsais sighed.

"He's right, though..." She frowned. "We *do* have to bond tonight, don't we?"

"Before the Hound arrives. But *only* if you desire it."

Isiilde traced the subtle embroidery of his dark robe. "I don't know how to."

Marsais lifted a shoulder. "You're a nymph. Trust your instincts."

"I think they're broken," she whispered. "I don't feel the same."

"How do you feel?"

"Empty. Except when you touch me."

Marsais slid his fingers along her neck. "Like this?"

"Yes."

"What does it feel like?"

"Like..." She closed her eyes, sinking into his hands, and his body. "Your touch feels like the sun's caress. It burns away the shadows."

"Shadows?"

There were no words to explain, so she took his hand and placed it over her heart. "In here, Marsais. I don't feel like singing. I don't hear music anymore."

"Maybe not now," he whispered. "But at some future time you will."

"That's a long time."

"Time is eternal." A shadow flickered across his eyes.

Isiilde raised his hand to her lips, kissing his palm. Then she led him from the study into his bedchamber.

"Did your instinct lead you here?" he asked, gazing around his room.

"Yes."

"Anything else?"

"In the pleasure house... I wanted to feel you. So I think I need to get that robe off you."

"I'll not argue with that," he muttered, tugging at the collar.

"Do I speak some sort of words?" she asked, unwinding his sash. "Did the druids have a ceremony of some sort?"

Marsais considered this as she helped him shed his robes. When he'd stripped down to trousers, he sat to remove his boots, still lost in thought.

"I don't think so," he finally said.

"Would you know?"

"I feel as if I *should*."

Her eyes fell on his back—long and lean, with a myriad of scars crisscrossing the muscles. She traced the whip scars with a pang of sympathy.

"More instinct?" Marsais asked.

"Do you mind?"

"Not at all."

Isiilde trailed her fingers along his ear as she moved around to stand between his legs. "I like your ears, Marsais." She stared down into his eyes. And he was entranced. Hers glittered like emeralds in the firelight.

"Ears," he said, suddenly.

"Ears are the key to bonding?"

"It seems to be a factor," he admitted. "But no, I was referring to the afternoon in my study when you asked what arouses me. I happen to find a woman's ears particularly alluring."

Marsais caressed the curve of one ear, and for the first time, he let himself linger over her beauty. "Yours are exquisite."

"I can tell you're not lying," she said with a smile.

"Obvious?"

"Hard not to miss."

Isiilde untied her robe and let it slip from her shoulders. His breath caught. Heart quickened. And he did look at the nymph then—lithe and ethereal. Her skin shimmered like a dream.

Isiilde tilted up his chin and brought her lips down on his. The world fell away. Somewhere in that kiss he stood, and she melted into his arms, moaning as he caressed her spine.

Isiilde ached to explore him. But when she reached for his trousers, the fire shifted with a pop, and Marsais gently gripped her shoulders, and pushed her back a step.

"What is it?"

Marsais glanced at the fire. "I need protection." His voice was hoarse with desire.

"Morigan gave me some root to chew."

Marsais cocked his head. "No... I mean for me. So I don't die."

"Why would you die while bonding with me?"

"Call it a hunch," he said.

Reluctantly, he tore his eyes off her and went to search the shelves. "I have high expectations of... Shall we say, my performance."

"Your what?" she asked, sliding under the bedcovers.

"I plan to leave you breathless with pleasure," he said over his shoulder.

"I don't think that's how a nymph's bond works," she said, settling against the pillows. "Everything I read only mentioned the boundless pleasures that a nymph's bond bestows on a man."

Marsais snorted. "Written by selfish fools." He walked over and held out two vials. "Smell them both, then pick one."

Puzzled, she did so. Then she tapped a vial that smelled like ashes. Marsais upended the one she'd selected, and gagged.

"Was that the wrong one?"

"Hmm, no, it's the right one, thank you."

The potion took a few moments to work its way through his veins before the frisson of frozen needles subsided.

Still shivering, he traced a Ward of Protection over the hearth.

"Is that a Ward?"

"Yes." Marsais turned to face her in bed, and hesitated, wondering if he should Ward the entire room.

Isiilde narrowed her eyes. "Are you nervous?"

"A little."

"Why?"

"I'm never quite sure what your instincts will have you do."

Isiilde laughed, the fire surged, and Marsais hopped away from the spout of flame.

"Get in here. I'm cold."

Marsais stripped and slid under the covers, gathering her close. She pressed against him, alive with the feel of his body—the beat of his heart and the breath of his lungs.

Marsais caressed the curve of her neck, then explored the intricacies of her spine with a featherlight touch. But when Isiilde placed a hand over the raw scar that cut across his chest, he sucked in a sharp breath.

The pain of that scar vanished beneath her fingertips, bringing a flood of lost memories. As they surged to the surface of his mind, he froze in shock.

Isiilde snatched her hand away. "Did I hurt you?"

"No, not at all," he breathed, pressing her hand back against his chest. "It... Your touch feels like a balm."

"You feel like my fire." And with that, she smiled and kissed him.

Past, present, and future faded. The nymph consumed his world.

She tasted of innocence and passion, of fire and ice. She was as potent as a drug.

Warmth flooded her body, chasing away nerves and chills and any unease. Isiilde gave herself to him, relishing the surprising intimacy of unexpected things: the brush of air on bare skin; the jolt of her stomach touching his; flesh to flesh, bone to bone, heart to heart.

Soft sheets sliding over legs. His strong, gentle hands sliding over her. The pauses, where he would search out her eyes, silently asking for permission.

Their bodies intertwined; their scents mingling. Marsais' ragged breath in her ear. His quiet voice enquiring after her comfort. And laughter, too.

As he covered her body with lingering kisses, her eyes flashed with hunger and her moans were music to his ears.

When her breasts were heaving and toes curling, she eased herself down the length of him. And at that blissful moment, Marsais discovered he had never truly lived. Power shuddered through his body. He gasped in shock, overwhelmed, thrusting his hips with more force than intended.

Isiilde cried out with pain, surprise, but mostly pleasure as her neck arched and her lips parted. Through the blur of ecstasy, he watched as a serpentine dragon of fire slithered over her shoulder, and wound itself down his arm, merging two spirits into one.

All her fear, pain, love and pleasure settled in his heart as if it were his own. His breath was hers, and her heart thundered in his chest. Each filled the other.

Marsais growled, low and urgent. Her fingernails dug into his chest. Their panting breath rose in the room, and her desire echoed in his blood, amplified a hundredfold.

Time stilled. A brush of skin, slick bodies, hearts beating as one. Then it surged forward, and the nymph arched, threw back her head with a cry, and burst into flame.

Fire licked along their twining bodies. Marsais was lost, beyond the point of stopping, beyond the place of thought. And as he gazed up into her face, he felt awe. And fear. Isiilde's eyes blazed with an emerald fire.

CHAPTER 43

THE HEARTH WAS COLD, and the salty bite of the sea drifted through a window. A dream of softness and warmth draped his limp bones. Marsais stirred, exploring this new, sublime world, gliding over a waterfall of silken fire.

I must have drunk an entire bottle of Primrose wine, Marsais thought in the haze between sleep and consciousness. A knock at the door tore him from perfection, and he jerked awake as Isek brought in a breakfast tray.

Marsais became aware of a supple weight over his body. He tensed in surprise. He had not been dreaming. Isiilde was stretched out on top of him, her head nestled on his chest, sleeping deeply and peacefully.

All around them, the bedclothes were scorched and brittle. The bed curtains hung in tatters, and the hearth was blackened by an intense explosion of heat. He snatched a robe from the floor to cover her body.

Isek pretended not to notice as he placed the tray on the bedside table. "I hope you remember you have a duel today."

"What time is it?"

"Midday."

Marsais winced. "Has the Hound arrived?"

"Not yet, but you already look spent, my friend. You two look like you had... a blast," Isek said, warily eyeing the scorched room.

Marsais ignored the pun. "Where's Oenghus?"

"Far as I know, he's in his rooms."

"Let me know when the Hound arrives. In the meantime…" Marsais raised a brow towards the door.

"Of course," Isek said, stealing one last look at the nymph before leaving with a low whistle.

Marsais frowned at the door. He would need to ward his chambers from now on.

Taking care not to wake her, he slid to the side and propped himself on an elbow, pulling down the robe to study her slender back.

A graceful, dragon-like creature was wrapped around the length of her spine, twining in and out of view. It was a sleek thing with wings of swept flame and slitted eyes. The whole long length of it was wreathed in flame—or was it entirely made of fire?

It was a physical manifestation of her spirit. A nymph's mark. But like none he'd ever seen.

The mark shared her emerald eye color, and the slitted pupils suddenly blinked at him. Marsais jerked upright in shock. Cautiously he leaned closer, gazing at the angular face and the watching eyes. Some minutes passed, and he wondered if he had imagined the movement.

An identical mark curled around his own arm. The creature's head rested in the palm of his hand—a fiery brand of immense power. He could *feel* her exhaustion and the shadow that lingered in her heart.

It threatened to consume her.

Isiilde groaned about the cold, before turning to him for warmth.

"Good morning, my dear."

"It can't be morning," she murmured against his chest. The night's passion came to mind and her eyes snapped open. She pulled away to study him, clearly concerned.

"You're not burned, are you?"

"No, I had an inkling of what might happen." He picked up his braid, studying the end. "Just a bit singed, and feeling rather used."

She grinned. "I'll take that as a compliment."

"And you? Am I tolerable?"

"I can *feel* you, Marsais," she purred, running her hand along the mark that wound its way up his arm. "You feel like the sun glowing inside me—although I feel like I've been trampled by a horse."

"Hmm, I'll take that as a compliment."

"But..." Her smile faded, and she sank back into his arms. "I don't think I will ever sing again."

"Give it time, my dear. It can do wonders."

Marsais held her for a time, caressing the small of her back in slow, soothing circles, until she stopped shivering.

"Although it's rude of me," he whispered in her ear. "I'm afraid I must leave you here while I speak with someone."

"Who?"

"Oenghus."

"Is that wise?"

"Probably not, but it needs doing."

MARSAIS LEFT Isiilde lounging in a steaming bath, devouring her breakfast and most of his. Even as he walked down the stairway to Oenghus' rooms, he could feel her *inside* him—an echo of calm warmth, telling him she was content and safe.

For once, legend was living up to fact: a nymph's bond was a remarkable thing. The world was sharper, vivid, and he felt reborn. But this particular nymph was set far apart from the rest, which fueled his unease.

Marsais had spent a good deal of his life avoiding needless conflict, using his head over the baser instincts of his body. But occasionally confrontation was unavoidable.

With a steadying breath, Marsais raised his fist to knock on Oenghus' door. But the moment before fist touched wood, the world spun, time unraveled, and a deluge of memory was unleashed, dropping him brutally to the floor. His mind was overwhelmed.

Marsais clutched his head, pressed his forehead to the stone, and tried not to scream as the scar across his chest flared with heat. And pain—sharp and searing as a brand.

He fought for breath and sanity, clinging to the remnants of his current life. The stone floor was his anchor, and he focused on that point of contact, letting the flood of memory wash over and through him, until it settled into a churning pool of thought.

Long minutes passed, filled with ragged breath and the frantic gallop of his heart. When the tide finally ebbed, he dragged himself over to a wall. Resting his elbows on knees, he held his head, sifting through the bits and pieces that had washed up on the shores of his mind—ages upon ages of past lives.

He dared not explore them now.

With a grimace of pain, he climbed to his feet, leaning against the wall for support.

When the floor stopped spinning and he was grounded in the present once again, he straightened and stood unaided in the empty hallway. Despite recent revelations, his errand had not changed.

Marsais knocked. No one answered. He pressed his hand to the wood, unraveling the protective ward with a murmur of Lore before walking in uninvited.

Oenghus was working at his alchemy table, grinding a toad into mash with pestle and mortar and far more force than necessary.

Marsais cleared his throat from the doorway. "I need to speak with you, Oen."

The kilted berserker kept grinding away.

"It's about Isiilde's mother."

The grinding stopped.

Oenghus turned slightly to eye him before returning to his work.

Marsais glared at the man's back. "Fine! I'll give you *one* bloody shot, but anything after and I'll fight back."

Oenghus turned. "Where's her mark?"

"On her back, where it should be—do you actually think I'd do anything less for her?"

Marsais rolled back his sleeve to expose his own mark. "Happy?"

Oenghus snorted and stepped up to him. "You can keep her at a distance. That way she won't feel your pain."

Marsais turned his attention inwards. Yes, he remembered now.

With a shift of focus, he dropped a curtain between their spirits. "If you knock out a tooth, I'll take it personally."

"Oh, I wouldn't worry 'bout your teeth," Oenghus growled an instant before he yanked Marsais forward by the shirtfront. The fist never came. But a knee did—right between his legs.

Soundlessly, Marsais dropped to his knees, doubling over and curling into a wheezing ball.

Oenghus resumed his work.

Some time passed before Marsais managed to groan, and even longer before he dared move.

Oenghus muttered the Lore, tracing a sharp rune over a basin and freezing the water within. He broke it into chunks with a knife, then stuffed the ice into a pouch before hoisting Marsais into a chair and dropping it onto his lap.

"Thank you," Marsais puffed.

"You're ugly enough without a broken nose. Figured I'd save what looks you have for my sprite."

Marsais readjusted the ice. "How thoughtful."

Oenghus snatched a twig from the fire and put it to his pipe before settling into the chair opposite. Both men puffed for a time—one with pain and the other with thought.

"Isiilde's mother..." Marsais finally broke the silence. "She wasn't a nymph, was she?"

Oenghus regarded him through a haze of smoke. "You're just figuring that out now, ol'bastard?"

Marsais clenched his teeth. "I took your word for what it was... that Isiilde was a nymph."

Oenghus jabbed his pipe stem towards him. "No, you said she wasn't a sprite, then called her a nymphling. *You* put words into my mouth."

Marsais glared while Oenghus smugly smoked.

"Did you know before you bonded with her?"

"Of course I bloody knew." Oenghus stared at the fire, but his eyes were faraway. "I'd know her spirit in any form. We're always connected—a part of our Bond lingers. It's stronger than life and death."

"You should have told me."

"I gave you a bloody hint."

Marsais arched a brow.

"Isiilde Jaal'*Yasine*," Oenghus bit out.

The emphasis on Yasine knocked loose a memory. Yasine—the Sylph's true name.

"I've forgotten my own bloody name for a good hundred years," Marsais snapped.

Oenghus shrugged. "Not my fault."

"Shrug all you like, but my spirit is far, *far* older than yours."

"And my cock is bigger."

Marsais bit back a rude comment. Instead, he let his head fall back on the chair and pondered the rafters.

"In order for Yasine to give birth to a child in this realm... she'd need to be reborn. Into the body of a nymph?"

Marsais took his silence as confirmation.

"Why did she risk it?"

"She missed my cock."

"Yes, of course," Marsais said dryly. "Yasine risked losing the Everwar because she missed you."

Oenghus flashed a grin.

"Then let herself die after a mere year or so..." Marsais tapped a finger on the armrest. "What's her aim?"

"She wanted to have a child with me."

Marsais eyed him. But there was no boast in his words, only flat truth. "But why? And why would Yasine make you swear to stand aside?"

Oenghus grumbled. "You've been talking with Morigan."

"That's all she said. Then she told me to speak with you. Although... when I told Morigan about the visions—"

"I don't bloody care about your visions."

"—I had of bonding with Isiilde and the ensuing destruction, she told me the visions were wrong. Why would Morigan be so certain?"

Oenghus shifted. "Yasine told me this realm was already lost. That it's broken. So maybe Mori figures it doesn't matter if it gets broken some more."

Marsais frowned. It wasn't a comforting thought.

"Can we stop talking about this?" Oenghus asked.

"Why?"

"All this bloody talk about realms and rebirth makes my head hurt. I don't like to think about my past lives. It's bad luck."

"The past has a way of creeping up on the present. We can't afford to ignore it. Not if this realm has any chance of surviving." With every passing year, the veil thinned between lives, and memory whispered in dreams.

"I'm not bloody ignoring anything. I know *who* you are, and I know what you're capable of, so don't think I'm all right with this, you manipulating bastard!"

"What *I'm* capable of?" Marsais asked. "Says the brute who once abducted the Sylph."

"Good to see you finally remember, but your memory still has holes in it. Yasine came with me of her own free will."

"You hit her over the head and tossed her over a shoulder."

"It was for her own bloody good," Oenghus defended. "And besides, she stayed with me afterwards."

"As does Isiilde with me." Marsais pronounced each word with biting precision.

"Bollocks," Oenghus grumbled under his breath. But he finally settled back in his chair. "Fine, we're even, but don't think I'll let you take my daughter on one of your romps through the realms."

"I won't be romping anywhere... Curse it! I have a duel today, and I can barely stand."

As the air cooled between the men, Oenghus finally shifted in his chair, nearly looking ashamed of himself. Shocking.

"You don't need me to tell you that Isiilde is a direct link to the essence of life. If anyone with an inkling of knowledge got a hold of her..." Marsais blew out a breath. "Do you realize the power a man would have if he took her by force?"

"My bloody hands were tied," Oenghus growled. "I swore an oath."

"And yet you brought Isiilde to my doorstep. Wasn't that interfering?"

Oenghus scowled at the rug. "I'm not perfect," he murmured. "I couldn't..." His massive shoulders slumped.

Marsais almost felt sympathy for the man. "You should have told me."

"What difference would it have made?"

"A great deal of difference," Marsais said, sharply. "It would have explained a few things. Though looking back, it seems so obvious. Still, I can't believe the Sylph took such a risk—especially now."

"What's done is done. I could've taken her to Iilenshar. But I figured I'd have a better chance of hiding her here. Trust me, if I'd known you'd end up bedding her, I'd have taken her to the Guardians. I don't exactly trust you with the well-being of my daughter."

"You are, and always have been, utterly narrow-sighted. The scales have tipped, Oen. They favor the Void. If this realm is lost, then the others will follow. I wish I wasn't the one to make the choices forced on me. But someone has to. And I make them for the good of all."

"I know you do, and always have, but some things shouldn't be sacrificed, Scarecrow."

"Isiilde lies at the center of this tangled mess. I can't change that. Believe me, I would if I could, but I no longer know what her future holds. Or ours, for that matter."

"And that's just it. That's what I'm afraid of—your meddling. All your deeds, all your manipulating runs together, until you can't even recall the threads of life you weave and snip. You probably don't even remember why I left the Isle and didn't speak to you for ten years, do you?"

Marsais' brows furrowed as he tried to dredge up the memory.

"That town on the border of the Fell Wastes," Oenghus reminded. "You knew it was going to be attacked by Wedamen, and yet you said nothing. Instead, you tricked me into leaving, knowing that I'd change the tide of the battle. That I'd interfere with the course you'd plotted through your sea of visions. Afterwards, while we were sifting through the tortured remains of the massacred, you told me that all of it was done because one child needed to die—*one* out of thousands!"

The stones shifted in answer to his bellow. When the tremors stopped, Oenghus continued, keeping a tight rein on his voice.

"And you wonder why I didn't tell you about Isiilde's mother. It's why I'm less than pleased that my daughter is bound to you. I've seen what you'll sacrifice for your schemes, and I've never been able to stomach it."

"I don't expect you to," Marsais whispered. "The ocean of blood on my hands is mine to bear, and mine alone. But I *do* remember. I do." His voice was worn with endless time and boundless grief. "I would do anything to safeguard Fyrsta. You must at least believe that of me. If this realm falls to the Void, then the Sylph will perish, and that includes her daughter—*your* daughter."

Oenghus stared long and hard at the immortal, searching for any signs of deception or trickery. In the end, he nodded, satisfied.

"Fine, I'll accept that, but stop talkin' about it. I don't like to think about the past—not *my* past, but farther, beyond the ol'River. My head is throbbing now."

"Not to worry, you were never much of a thinker in any life. I have no intention of overtaxing your brain."

"And you've always been an annoying bastard, so don't think I'm apologizing for the—" Oenghus gestured towards the bag of ice.

"Lack of an apology accepted."

Silence fell over the two men. Marsais slumped in his chair with a sigh, running a weary hand over his face as if he could erase the past.

If only he could wipe the slate clean and begin anew. But there was no going back, only forward, and if the stakes were not high enough already, they had just gone up considerably.

"How did you survive after Yasine died?" Marsais asked, breaching the silence. "Until last night, I feel as if I've been dead all these years."

"For the same reason you'll be fighting the Hound—for Isiilde. I've stayed alive for my little sprite."

"Speaking of your little sprite." Marsais cleared his throat. "I'd appreciate it if you brewed an ample supply of fire ward potions for me. The more potent the better."

"Why?"

"You know what happens when she sneezes..."

"Aye, but it's easy enough to dodge."

"Hmm, well, the rest of your little sprite is just as flammable."

"What do you—" Oenghus cut off, beard twitching with mirth. "And you're gonna bloody trust me to mix up some protection?" His laughter rumbled through the room like thunder.

CHAPTER 44

Guthre Dragonbone. The name sent a shiver of fear through Isiilde. And fear was justified. The emperor's champion bore an impressive list of titles earned on the battlefield: Champion of Kambe, Right Hand to the Emperor, Devout of the Blessed Order, and the highest of honors, Knight of the Sylph. Guthre Dragonbane was feared by his enemies, and rightly so.

Legend claimed that he lost his eyes while battling Indrazor, Guardian of War, and as a reward for his fearless stand against a god, the Sylph blessed him with sight keener than any living creature.

Isiilde's stomach twisted as she sat on the bed watching Marsais get ready for his duel, because at the moment her champion did not look very fear-inspiring.

Marsais was rangy rather than powerful, and his ribs showed through tanned flesh. He reminded her of a winter wolf who was half starved—all bone and sinewy muscle without an ounce of fat on him.

At that moment her wolf was rummaging through the clutter, muttering under his breath as he searched for something to wear. So far, he had located boots and trousers, but was having difficulty selecting a suitable shirt.

"Have you checked in your armoire?"

He started in surprise. "I have an armoire?"

It was odd, considering he had a dressing room. But then he wasn't searching for clothes in his dressing room.

Isiilde pointed to an elegant piece of furniture in the corner of his bedchamber. He eyed it suspiciously.

"I don't think I'll find what I'm looking for in there..."

"What's in there, if not clothes?"

"An excellent question." His gaze fell on a chest at the foot of his bed, and he brightened, flinging the top open to rifle through its contents.

Isiilde stared at the mysterious armoire. A few days before, she would have thrown herself at it for curiosity's sake. But not today. The realm was not so friendly a place anymore.

"Can't we just stay up here so you won't have to fight the Hound?"

"As tempting as that is—I believe we would eventually get hungry." He gave her a lopsided grin before lifting a bundle of dark green cloth from a tangle of clothes.

Isiilde could hardly breathe. Her stomach was in knots, and she feared she'd be sick. She hurried over to Marsais, and he opened his arms to her. She took refuge in his embrace, burying her face against his chest.

"I can feel you, and you're afraid." It had never occurred to her that Marsais or Oenghus might be afraid of anything.

"I fear only what my failure would mean for you. So with that said— I *cannot* fail." He lifted her chin, kissing her softly before stepping back to slip the garment over his head.

The dark tunic fit him perfectly. Runes, the color of autumn, swirled up his arms like leaves. She helped him lace the sleeves. Each tapered to the back of a hand and was secured by a ring that slipped around a middle finger.

She stood back to survey the foreign garment. The effect was impressive. It emphasized his leanness, making his arms seem impossibly long. He looked like a snake poised to strike.

Marsais thanked her and then limped gingerly over to his mirror. A swath of velvet concealed the glass—all of his mirrors were covered. He squared his shoulders, reaching up with a hesitant hand to touch the fabric. A moment later, he steeled himself and snatched off the covering, letting it drop to the floor, forgotten as he stood gazing at his reflection.

Isiilde joined him, standing on the footstool to peer over his shoulder. With his gleaming white hair and steely eyes, she thought perhaps he stood a chance against the Hound after all.

"What do you see?" she whispered in his ear.

His reflection grinned roguishly. "A beautiful woman staring at me with eyes that could stop a heart." At his words, a blush spread to the tips of her ears and a smile danced in her eyes.

CHAPTER 45

THE THRONE ROOM made Isiilde uneasy at the best of times, and this was not the best of times—far from it. This was the last place she wanted to be.

Marsais sat on his throne, tapping rhythmically against the stone armrest. She wanted to be closer to him, but she stood off to the side on the dais with Oenghus.

Isiilde huddled in her cloak and backed against the bear of a man behind her. Oenghus wore his kilt in battle fashion, along with a breastplate of banded leather and greaves strapped to his shins. A spiked shield was slung over one shoulder along with a brace of knives crossing his chest. The rune-etched war hammer, *Gurthang*, hung at his side.

The gate at the end of the hall opened, and Isek led a procession inside. A squad of Isle Guards had fallen in behind him, followed by paladins of the Blessed Order whose armor echoed with the grate of duty. The emissaries, officials, and Wise Ones came next, followed by what appeared to be every apprentice and novice within the Order. The latter whispered in hushed voices, their gazes darting to the nymph.

Isiilde wanted to flee, but the Laws of Challenge demanded her presence. Even if she had the choice, would she allow Marsais to fight in her absence? The thought was unthinkable—she would stand with him and face what lay ahead.

The Isle Guards fanned out, and turned towards the audience, watching the crowd as they jostled one another for better positions.

She spotted Morigan in the crowd of Wise Ones, standing off to the side. But the distance seemed small as she met the woman's eyes. *Focus on me.* And Isiilde did, feeling a little stronger and not so afraid. Morigan gave her a nod of approval.

Isek stepped into the space before the dais and bowed deeply towards the throne. "Archlord, I present High Inquisitor Multist of the Blessed Order."

Multist clanked forward, inclining his head, more to the audience than Marsais.

"Knight Captain Mael of the Blessed Order," Isek announced, gesturing towards the severe woman, who stepped forward lightly despite her armor.

"Lord Champion Guthre Dragonbane of Kambe."

The man who stepped forward was more fearsome than Isiilde could ever have imagined. He was nearly as tall as Marsais, though his broad shoulders made him seem the taller of the two. Along with his height, he wore armor crafted from dragon scales.

His pale blond hair was trimmed close, displaying the pointed ears of a Kamberian, while his square jaw whispered of Nuthaanian blood. And his eyes—his eyes, or lack of them—drew her in. A jagged scar sliced across the bridge of his nose, beginning and ending in his eye sockets. Silver liquid filled the fleshy basins, shifting like pools of mercury.

Guthre's nostrils flared, sniffing the air like the hound for which he had been named. His presence was formidable, a warrior who had been honed for battle and stripped of all else.

"And Stievin Maxwell of Coven." The name rolled off Isek's tongue like a curse.

Two paladins marched Stievin forward, and he eyed her with a look of disgust. At the sight of him, she went numb. Marsais' spirit stirred inside of her, wrapping around her heart, glowing with warm reassurance.

"All parties are present," Isek announced, inclining his head to a paladin. "You may proceed, Inquisitor."

"By the Blessed Order's ruling and declaration regarding nymphs," Multist began, unfurling an official-looking scroll. "The said property, being referred to as Isiilde, was stolen and seized by Stievin Maxwell of Coven on the twenty-third day of the Reddened month. By order and law, Emperor Soataen Jaal III has Right of Challenge. By his request, Knight of the Sylph Guthre Dragonbane will stand in His Majesty's stead as champion."

Guthre Dragonbane stepped forward, handing a sealed scroll to the Inquisitor. "The victor will claim the property and no other challenges will be recognized as written in the Law and Decree of Damien Caal."

"That *creature* seduced me!" Stievin spat. "I went into the washroom to help her, and she came at me. When I rejected her, she attacked me. Everyone knows she's a murderer!"

Murmurs traveled through the throne room.

Thira stepped into the clearing. "I saw what you did to her, Stievin. I saw her wounds."

"She did it to herself! To make it look like I attacked her. I have an Oathbound and a child, for gods' sake. That creature is a temptress." Stievin thrust a finger at Isiilde, and she flinched as if she'd been struck with his fist. "The Archlord attacked *me* for defending myself."

The Knight Captain stepped forward. "You were questioned under an Orb of Truth. We have two witnesses, the Archlord and Mistress Thira, as well as the healer's testimony. My investigation confirmed the charges laid against you. It's too late for your defense."

"I have no bond with that thing. How do you explain that?" Stievin said with a note of desperation.

A ripple of shocked confusion traveled through the crowd. Seeing that his accusation had struck a chord, Stievin smirked at Isiilde. She swallowed down bile, and her knees went weak.

"*Silence!*"

Every mutilated face decorating the pillars cried out the single word in unison, cutting off speech, and even breath.

All eyes turned to the Archlord as he rose with purpose; a single, clear chime issued from the coins weighing down his goatee.

"I hold the nymph's Bond." Marsais held up his hand and the crowd's eyes widened in shock—the head of a fiery dragon was nestled in his palm. "You attacked a nymph, Stievin. You waited until she was defenseless, locked in a room and alone, her guardian detained by the Blessed Order. You took Emperor Jaal's property. If she were a scullery maid, you'd answer for your crime by the Isle's laws, but—"

"I didn't bond with her!"

"—Oenghus has the right to challenge you. It is a matter of honor."

Stievin's face drained of blood. And Oenghus glowered down at the man. "Don't worry," he purred. "I'll give you more of a fighting chance than you gave her."

"Unacceptable!" Multist stepped forward. "The barbarian is not involved in this matter."

"Lord Saevaldr has the right," a harsh, damaged voice interrupted. It was the Hound who spoke up, blatantly overruling the Inquisitor. "He was her appointed guardian when she was stolen. Justice will be upheld."

Multist opened his mouth to argue, then decided against it, taking a step back and bowing to the knight's interpretation of the law.

The Hound's liquid gaze focused on Marsais. "I was ordered to fight the one who holds her Bond. Although I'm saddened it's you, old friend, it will be a great honor to face you in battle."

Marsais stepped off the dais to grip the Hound's forearm in greeting. "It would have been a greater honor to stand beside you against the Void once again, Guthre."

"May our spirits drift side by side in peace when we meet in the great River." Guthre stepped back to clench a fist to his heart in salute. "If you're ready, I would like to get this over with. I was pulled from the Fell Wastes for this errand."

"Oh, by all means," Marsais mused. "I don't like waiting for my death to come, either. Hmm, the hours before are spent in useless contemplation."

"To the arena!" Isek's voice boomed in the throne room.

CHAPTER 46

The arena was packed. The prospect of a duel between the Hound and an apprentice cook hadn't caused much of a stir. It was more akin to an execution. But a duel with the reclusive Archlord, who had never fought in the arena, was quite another matter. It seemed the entire castle was present.

"I didn't think it would be today," Isiilde whispered from her chair. She sat in a private balcony reserved for the Archlord. The spacious seats were only ten feet from the meticulously groomed sand. Across the arena, on the edge of the ring, Stievin readied himself for the duel.

"Better to be done with," Morigan said, giving her shoulder a squeeze. "I need to be in the healer's tent."

"I thought these duels were to the death?"

"Sometimes the victor is close to death."

Isiilde swallowed. "Are you worried about Oen?"

Morigan looked to where Oenghus had planted himself beside the arena pit. "Anyone can be killed, Isiilde."

That was not reassuring.

"But I'm more worried about you having to watch this."

That also was not reassuring.

Morigan slapped Marsais on the shoulder. "Piss in the ol'River."

"I would never," he said, primly.

Morigan clucked her tongue at him. "You don't even have a shield to be carried home on."

"Precisely why I don't have one."

The two shared a smile before Morigan left, leaving Isiilde sick with worry.

Nuthaanians had an odd sense of humor about death.

The arena was mainly used for experiments involving dangerous runes or explosive mixtures. The circular basin in the center was filled with sand. Smooth stone walls etched with protective wards created a barrier of shimmering greenish light that extended forty feet above the sand. The arena ward protected the audience from runic backlash.

Once in a while, like today, the arena was used to settle differences in blood.

Some people stood on their seats for a better view, stable boys perched on walls, and a few Wise Ones floated above the audience. Even the battlements were packed, offering a bird's-eye view of the fighting pit. A chorus of voices rose in excitement. Wagers were shouted, and everywhere there was jostling in the crowd.

The festive atmosphere sickened her. She looked past the banners and streamers, the waving arms and sea of faces, to the sky overhead.

Why were humans so bloodthirsty?

The sun had burned away the morning fog, leaving a crisp blue sky and autumn breeze. The cold tickled her nose, and made her sneeze. Fire puffed from her ears.

The two paladins guarding her, one heavily scarred and the other too young to grow a proper beard, shifted uneasily at the burst of flame. Knight Captain Mael gestured for them to be at ease, while her own pale gaze focused thoughtfully on the nymph.

The paladin had insisted on an inspection. But instead of performing one in the middle of the crowded throne room, she'd taken Isiilde to a side room along with Marsais and the Hound, and refused entry to anyone else. Much to Isiilde's relief, the paladin hadn't ordered her to strip. Isiilde only had to unlace her shirt partway, enough to allow Marsais to expose her shoulder blades and the mark on her back.

No one else had touched her. Caitlyn Whitehand had subjected her to years of humiliating inspections when all that was needed was a look at her back.

"Piss and wind," Isek cursed. "They're not even accepting bets for Oenghus' fight. Oh, and Marsais, I think I should let you know—the odds are against you for your duel."

Isek was rocking back and forth on his heels with merry good cheer.

"And who have you wagered on?"

"Haven't decided yet."

Isek flashed Isiilde a grin, but there was nothing amusing about the situation. She glanced down at her hands, where they trembled in her lap. Marsais encompassed her hands in one of his own, sending a flood of reassurance through their Bond.

An energized hush fell over the crowd as Inquisitor Multist walked into the arena, striking a commanding pose in the center.

"Oenghus Saevaldr of Nuthaan has issued challenge to Stievin Maxwell of Coven. A duel of honor to the death for Stievin's theft of the nymph."

Isiilde frowned at the Inquisitor: she didn't even have a name; even a dog had a name.

The two combatants stepped onto the sands to thunderous applause. Stievin wore the chain mail of the Isle Guard. He was crouched and ready, shield and sword in hand, but he looked terrified.

Isiilde grabbed Marsais' hand in alarm. "Oen forgot his weapons."

"I wouldn't worry, my dear."

Oenghus strode forward. Stievin retreated to the edge, but Oenghus stopped in the center, planting his feet. He cracked his knuckles.

The Inquisitor shuffled out of the circle, and before Stievin could retreat to the sidelines, the runes activated with a rush of energy that created a greenish wall of protection around the fighting pit.

Stievin backed into the shield. A zap of energy singed him, and he hopped away. No one could get in, and no one could get out.

Oenghus spread his arms. He'd shed armor, shield, and weapons. He stood only in his kilt. "What's the matter, Stievin?" he asked in a low, dangerous voice. "I'm defenseless. I can't escape. I won't even use the Lore. Isn't that how you like it?"

"I don't want to fight you," Stievin hissed.

"Because I'm not half your size? Should I get on my knees? Will that give you courage?"

"I shouldn't be here!" Stievin looked desperately to the Archlord's balcony, while the audience booed and jeered, urging the man to fight.

"But you are. You're trapped. Just like you trapped her. With no escape." Oenghus slowly walked forward.

Stievin focused on her. "Isiilde," he said hoarsely. "Tell them the truth. We were friends."

Isiilde stared back. She'd thought of him as a friend; she'd believed it—right up until he attacked her. And now all she saw were his fevered eyes and felt his unwanted body against her own. She shook with the memory of it.

"Do not speak to her!" Oenghus bellowed, shaking the arena. Sand shifted, stones cracked, and his roar clutched at hearts.

Stievin cowered in fear. Then, like a terror-stricken animal, he charged the berserker with a frenzied howl, his sword raised to strike. Isiilde jerked as the sword swept through the air. Oenghus stepped into the blow, catching Stievin's wrist, and drove his head into the shorter man's face.

The crowd roared with excitement.

Stievin reeled, bringing his shield around, but Oenghus absorbed the blow and twisted Stievin's sword arm. A second later, Oenghus brought his elbow down, breaking Stievin's arm at the elbow with a snapping crack and a protrusion of jagged bone.

Stievin howled in pain. His sword fell to the ground with a dull thud.

Frantically, Stievin pounded his shield against Oenghus, trying to break free. But Oenghus would not let go. The berserker heaved upwards with a roar, ripping the arm clean from Stievin's shoulder with a sickening pop.

The crowd went silent with shock.

Isiilde buried her face against Marsais as Stievin's screams became frantic. The berserker continued his gruesome work, even as the audience shied away from the slaughter.

Stievin was pleading for mercy now, whimpering like an animal with unnatural, impossible sounds tearing from his throat. Another bone-breaking pop echoed in the stillness, followed by fist meeting flesh in a savage flurry of hammering blows.

Marsais covered Isiilde's ears with his hands, but she could still hear the howling pleas of Stievin. Finally, a single crack echoed in the arena, and a lifeless body crumpled to the ground.

The bloody mess polluting the sand was barely recognizable. In the hush that followed, Oenghus tossed aside a dismembered arm, and spat on the corpse before stalking out of the arena.

"And he wasn't even berserking," Isek whispered in horror.

A weeping woman ran out on the sand with the litter bearers, sobbing over the mutilated corpse.

"Who is that, Marsais?" Isiilde swallowed down the bile that rose in her throat as stray pieces of Stievin were tossed onto the stretcher.

Marsais didn't answer until the body was carried out of the arena and the woman disappeared from view.

"That was Stievin's Oathbound."

Isiilde studied her hands with revulsion, remembering Marsais' words: *faerie have an intoxicating effect on humans, especially nymphs. It has something to do with a nymph's scent—it's like a potent drug.*

But she had never touched Stievin; it was he who reached for her. The thought brought little comfort. And a small part of her thought that perhaps her kind might be better off locked away in a dungeon, separate from the rest of the world.

CHAPTER 47

Soldiers ran out to remove the blood-saturated sand. They smoothed the rest, erasing the slate to begin anew.

The next battle's outcome was not so clear-cut. The audience sat in restless anticipation.

Oenghus stomped into the private balcony and took the vacant seat beside Isiilde. Thankfully, he had washed Stievin's blood from his face and hands, changed his shirt, and donned his armor.

"You'll never have to think about that bastard again," he growled, keeping his gaze on the arena.

Isiilde was glad he was looking away, because she feared what she might see smoldering in his eyes. It was difficult to connect this man with the one who used to sing her to sleep at night.

"I must leave you now, my dear," Marsais said, squeezing her hands. "Don't worry, I have a weapon." With a twinkle in his eyes, he brandished his little hunting knife.

Isiilde glared at his dark humor. But before he could rise, she grabbed his goatee and yanked him closer. She pressed her lips to his. The single, aching kiss conveyed everything that words could not.

When Marsais finally recovered from her kiss, he steeled his shoulders, and left.

"Could you not kiss that bastard when I'm around?" Oenghus grumbled.

"I'll kiss him whenever I like," she said, tugging her cloak closer.

When Marsais said he had to leave, he meant it in a complete sense. The warm presence that had filled her since they'd bonded left. Isiilde could still feel him, knew the direction she could walk to find him, but compared to the blaze of his presence, what remained was a flickering candle that left her cold—as if he were holding her at arm's length.

Alone with her confusion and fear, silent tears came unbidden, trailing down her cheeks.

"Sprite," Oenghus whispered, leaning close. "When you're bonded —your feelings, including *fear*, affect him. For his sake, have courage and he'll fare better for it."

"How do you know?" She had not considered that their Bond might go both ways.

What did she feel like to Marsais?

"Common sense." Oenghus shrugged. "Isek, go put the whole pouch on the Scarecrow. I might as well make some coin off this." He tossed a heavy pouch at the man and settled back in his chair, making himself comfortable.

Acacia looked over at the berserker with obvious disapproval. He returned her look with his most charming smile.

The wager bolstered Isiilde's spirit. The odds couldn't be all that bad if Oenghus was putting coin on Marsais. Unfortunately, her spirits fell when the Hound came soaring into the arena on his griffin.

The beast pounded into the sand with a galloping gait of clawed talons. Its wings were lined with razor-sharp feathers, and the beast folded them inwards, shielding its body. It snapped its powerful beak and tasted the air with a forked tongue. Large, slitted eyes scanned the cheering crowd with frightful intelligence. The griffin inhaled, its mighty chest expanding a moment before it let loose an earth-shattering screech.

The Hound straddled its back. He was no less impressive than he had been in the throne room. But now he wore a fearsome helm of scales, which completed his transformation into some nightmare combination of half dragon and half man.

How could Marsais ever hope to face both of them?

In the fading echo of the griffin's battle cry, her champion strolled calmly onto the sands. The crowd quieted. And a thrill of silent anticipation pulsed in the air as the Inquisitor marched into the arena.

"Lord Champion Guthre Dragonbane of Kambe issues challenge to Marsais—" There was a slight pause as the Inquisitor realized the Archlord didn't have a surname. "—of the Isle, for ownership of the nymph. May the Law preserve us all."

Marsais bowed to his opponent, who returned the gesture of respect with a salute of his gleaming spear. In contrast to his challenger, Marsais wore no armor or weapons. He looked naked, standing on the sands, wearing only a tunic and trousers. He plucked a pebble from the ground and balanced it on the tips of his fingers.

The Inquisitor left the ring; one heartbeat passed into two, and the long seconds before the shield sprang to life were agony. The griffin stomped, digging its talons restlessly into the sands with a shift of armor, and all the while, Marsais stood with calm poise, dwelling in the moment and not beyond.

Fyrsta held its breath.

The runes around the arena flared, the shield shimmered to life, and the griffin charged. Marsais tossed the pebble towards the center, weaving a bind to the stone in midair.

Guthre's spear pulsed with crackling energy. He heaved the weapon at his opponent, but the sands had already begun to stir around the pebble. A whirlwind of force seized the spear, halting its momentum. The tip stopped inches from Marsais' chest. As one, the crowd gasped, and then the weapon was sucked backwards into the gathering whirlwind.

Ignoring the charging griffin, Marsais snaked through a complicated weave, so swiftly that she couldn't follow a single rune in the pattern. Guthre shouted an order, and the spear returned to his outstretched hand. He lowered it like a lance at his opponent, who stood at the edge of the barrier.

With a final sweep of his hand, Marsais shimmered, his coins chiming above the biting sands. Ten mirror images of Marsais sprang to life.

Blinded by the sand, the griffin barreled into the line of identical enemies, passing through illusion and slamming into the rune barrier. Burnt feathers flew into the air with a lash of energy. In fury and pain, the creature spun, raking the illusions with bristling talons.

The real Marsais reappeared on the opposite side of the arena, tracing a series of runes. Guthre tugged at the reins, spinning his mount around to hurl a blackish bolt of raw energy. It slammed into Marsais' shoulder but didn't break his concentration.

Guthre raised his spear with a shout, and a blue aura surrounded him like a shield, deflecting the sandstorm and clearing his vision.

Marsais' hair flapped wildly in the wind as its fury increased. With a sharp clap of his hands and a commanding word, his weave flashed, and a creature appeared in front of him.

It was another griffin. A female.

Guthre's mount reared with excitement. He caught the female's scent and charged through the sandstorm at her. The vortex intensified; the binding rune on the pebble backfired, and the air exploded with a deafening boom.

Marsais threw up an arm. His griffin reared with panic and took flight. The male griffin shot after the female and Guthre was forced to abandon his saddle. He landed and rolled, regaining his feet.

"Charge!" Guthre bellowed, thrusting his shield towards Marsais.

Before Marsais could react, a spectral bull materialized from thin air and slammed into him with a muffled thud. The impact hurled Marsais against the shimmering shield. He bounced off in a crackling daze.

Guthre took two quick steps forward, hurling his charged spear across the arena. Isiilde gave a cry, but Marsais rolled beneath the blade. The deadly tip sped harmlessly past his head.

With a sharp command, Guthre ordered his weapon to return. The spear spun in midair, reversing directions, leaping to its master's hand.

Marsais sprang to his feet. He thrust his hands toward the charging knight, and a stream of lightning shot from his splayed fingertips. It blasted into Guthre, but failed to stop the knight. Coins chimed, echoing in the arena. Guthre jabbed, and Marsais blurred, becoming indistinct, like a wavering mirage. He twisted to the side as the tip of the spear stabbed the blurry edges of his snaking form—again and again until steel came back with blood.

Marsais faltered, but only for a heartbeat, rallying with an intricate weave. When it was complete, he tapped the ground. The sands rippled, and the ground beneath the knight shifted, sinking and opening to swallow him whole. Guthre threw himself towards the edge of the sinkhole, fighting against a waterfall of sand.

Marsais stumbled away, clutching his side.

Guthre raised his spear heavenward. "In the Sylph's name, I smite this foe!" he shouted.

A column of silver fire roared from the sky to wash over Marsais, and Isiilde screamed as he vanished beneath the mercurial deluge.

The onslaught continued long enough for Guthre to pull himself from the pit. It was apparent by the knight's relaxed stance that he fully expected Marsais to perish in the divine fire.

When the column of silver dissipated, there was a universal gasp of shock. Marsais stood unharmed.

"Looks like the Sylph doesn't favor this fight," Oenghus muttered.

Marsais moved with a serpent-like quickness, his fingers flashing. Isiilde tried to follow the complex weave, but his hands were a blur. As quick as he had begun, Marsais thrust his arms out, wrists crossed, fingers curled inwards. Raw energy burst from his palms, glowing brighter than the sun.

Guthre threw up his shield, bracing against the attack. He chanted a thundering prayer, fighting against the power battering at his shield, then thrust his spear point towards Marsais. A bolt of lightning slammed into his chest. Coins chimed discordantly. Marsais grunted, but stood his ground, muscles straining, brows furrowed in concentration.

Time slowed, and then stopped, gathering like water behind a dam. The arena pulsed, pressure built, and the air snapped. Time surged forward.

Guthre's shield shattered with a rush of violent energy that knocked both men to the ground. He climbed to his feet, dazed, his shield arm hanging limply at his side. Blood ran in rivulets down his scaled armor, dripping onto the sands.

Marsais stayed on his back, fingers flying, lips moving. Guthre lurched forward, hurling his spear as Marsais scuttled backwards. The steely spike sank into the sand between Marsais' legs, and the audience groaned in collective sympathy. But before Guthre could summon his spear, Marsais touched the haft. He jerked in pain and cried out as a surge of energy traveled up his arm.

The spear was away and returning to its master when Marsais hissed out a command, thrusting his hand towards Guthre. At the very last moment, the spear spun in midair. The haft never reached Guthre's outstretched hand. Two feet of crackling steel plunged through jade scales, impaling Guthre through the heart.

The Hound staggered backwards. He ripped off his helm, let it slip from his fingers, and gazed at the haft protruding from his chest. He took one step, and fell forward into the sand with a dull clunk.

CHAPTER 48

Isiilde sat in stunned disbelief with the rest of the crowd until realization settled. An eternity later, the arena erupted with wild cheers.

Marsais lay on his back, breathing harshly. He rolled onto his knees, tried to stand, but fell forward, catching himself with one hand while clutching his side with the other. Blood seeped through his fingers.

"Oen, he's hurt!" Isiilde said, rushing to the balustrade.

"Stay here." Oenghus vaulted over the low wall, landing with a thud in the arena pit.

Isiilde started towards the stairs, intending to follow, but an iron hand clamped down on her shoulder, bringing her up short. Fear fluttered in her breast.

"You should stay here, nymph. There's too many people." The hand and voice belonged to Knight Captain Acacia Mael. Concern rather than malice shone from her eyes.

Remembering that Oenghus had asked the same of her, Isiilde remained. Acacia kept one hand on the nymph and the other on her sword hilt as she scanned the overcrowded arena.

Oenghus knelt beside Marsais, a supporting hand on his shoulder as he leaned forward and spoke in his ear.

Isiilde could not hear what he said, but Marsais shook his head in answer. Oenghus pressed a hand to his side, caught sight of Morigan heading onto the sand with two stretcher bearers, and shook his head. Morigan stopped with a slight raise of a brow. Whatever silent conversation passed between the two, the woman turned on her heel and gestured the stretcher bearers back to their places.

Oenghus helped Marsais to his feet, and the two strode back to the balcony, surrounded by the thunderous applause of an audience who knew they had just witnessed something legendary.

Isle Guards cleared the way, keeping the crowds at bay as Marsais returned to his private balcony. The moment he walked through the curtain—his knees buckled. Oenghus caught him, hoisting Marsais' arm over his own shoulder to keep him upright.

"Heal him, Oen," Isiilde urged, looking Marsais over with concern. He was coated head to toe with a layer of sand that had masked his wounds from the audience, but up close the extent of his injuries was apparent. His clothes were saturated with blood, and the skin beneath was raw with burns.

"Not here," Marsais croaked. "It's too dangerous." His voice was brittle and cracked with pain.

"We'll escort you to the Keep." Acacia signaled a group of paladins to clear a path through the crowd, then looked to the pair who'd guarded Isiilde during the fight. "Lucas and Rivan, with me."

Oenghus quickly wrapped a bandage around Marsais' ribs, the linen soaking through with blood before he cinched the knot. Isiilde moved under his arm, and with clenched teeth, Marsais straightened, putting much of his weight on her.

"You need a stretcher," she said.

"We can't risk a show of weakness. Not with our enemies close."

Isiilde frowned at the sea of faces. For once in her life, she couldn't wait to feel the press of stone on her shoulders. Soon, they'd be safe.

As the paladins cleared a path, Marsais nodded to the cheering crowd. Isiilde was tucked against his side to conceal the bloody bandage, and to all outward appearances, he looked uninjured. She might have believed the ruse if she couldn't feel his quivering body. Oenghus stayed close, ready with a hand in case he collapsed.

Isek broke free of the pressing crowd to fall in step beside them. He tossed a heavy pouch to Oenghus. "Not bad, Marsais. You made us all a small fortune."

Oenghus hefted the pouch with a satisfied grunt before tucking it into his belt.

"Guthre worked you over, though. I thought I'd wagered on the wrong man." Isek moved beside Isiilde, weaving the ever-present coin between his fingers.

The crowds thinned and the knot at the back of her neck eased. As they climbed the steps into the Keep's main hall, the knot unwound completely.

Safety was a quick teleportation rune away. And it made her light-headed with relief. She was free, and bonded to the man she loved. But when they entered the Keep, her dreams shattered.

The Storm Gate slammed shut, Marsais' coins chimed, and Isiilde was ripped from his side by none other than Isek Beirnuckle.

CHAPTER 49

Several things happened at once: Eiji materialized with a blowpipe already raised to her lips. Her dart nailed Oenghus in the neck, who ripped it out with a jerk. The paladins drew their swords with a rasp of steel, and another pair of hands grabbed Isiilde, pressing something cold to her throat as Isek stuffed a gag between her lips.

"Stop or the nymph dies!" a voice hissed from behind her.

"Do as he says!" Marsais shouted, dropping his offensive weave. His eyes were wide with dread, fixed on the blade pressed to her throat.

Oenghus wavered, his eyes unfocused, sweat beading on his sallow skin.

"Put your weapons down," the voice of Tharios ordered, and as if by some prearranged cue, ten cowled Wise Ones dropped their Weave of Invisibility, materializing along with a host of Isle Guards.

Isek quickly retreated, moving behind N'Jalss, who had Isiilde by the throat.

"Do it!" Oenghus bellowed.

At his command, the paladins dropped their swords and shields with a clatter of metal on marble.

"I see you're both familiar with this dagger," Tharios said, stepping to the forefront and lowering his hood. "A Devourer of the Spirit. One prick from the blade will leave your nymph drifting the realms for all time as a Forsaken." The immaculate Wise One walked slowly over to Isiilde, keeping his eyes focused on Marsais. "Never to be reborn, offering her an existence of endless torture."

But Marsais ignored Tharios, looking to Isek instead. "*Why?*" The sting of betrayal clouded his grey eyes.

"You're the seer. You should have foreseen it. They would have done it anyway, Marsais. This way I've guaranteed Isiilde's safety, but you have to do what you're told."

"Ah! So you get the nymph. You're right, I should have foreseen it."

"And you should have warded your conversations. I've always warned you about that."

Marsais flinched with realization. Isek Beirnuckle, former spy, had been doing what he did best: listening to conversations. Particularly the one Marsais had this morning with Oenghus.

Isek knew exactly what ran through Isiilde's veins: the power of a goddess.

Tears rolled down Isiilde's cheeks as she struggled to escape. But N'Jalss put a quick stop to her futile attempts by yanking her back by the hair, nearly lifting her off her feet.

"Enough," Tharios cut in. "Get down on your knees, hands on stone. All of you—*now!*"

"I'm surprised Grimstorm's still standing," Eiji said with morbid excitement. "Stone adder venom could drop a bull."

"My Order will investigate," Acacia said.

"Do I look worried?" Tharios asked. "On your knees, hands down, or N'Jalss will bleed her."

Oenghus fought for air, his muscles seizing a moment before he collapsed to his knees, falling forward with a thud.

"He's sturdier than a bull, but it still works," Eiji said, kicking his ribs.

A guard stepped forward to clout Marsais on the back of the head, then shoved him to the floor and pressed a foot to the side of his face. Marsais struggled as his wrists were bound and then yanked forward by a rope, stretching his arms to hold his hands in place.

Shimei Al'eeth stepped forward. He wrapped both hands around his mace, brought it up, and brought it down on Marsais' hands with ruthless force, crushing bone and flesh.

Marsais howled in agony.

Again, he swung his mace with enough force to crack the floor. Isiilde thrashed, but it was useless. N'Jalss had her by the hair like a dangling fish.

"How could you serve him, Shimei?" Marsais screamed. The guard let go of the rope, and Marsais jerked his arms in with a whimper, cradling his mangled hands against his chest.

"Your friend Isek let your name slip, Marsais *zar'Vaylin*. You're the first king of my people's greatest enemy." The Kilnish lord spat in his face. "You hid like the coward you are."

"Bind them and bring them," Tharios ordered.

"Not your greatest enemy, Shimei. Do you know what he plans?" Marsais wheezed. His face was twisted with pain, and he had to force every word past his lips. "Ask him about his plans to summon Karbonek."

"You were always a raving lunatic. Did you have another vision?" Tharios was all poise and confidence. "They know my plans. That was always your problem—no one could ever fathom how your mind worked."

The cowled Wise Ones gagged the prisoners, and the guards bound their wrists, dragging them forward. But the guards didn't bother with Oenghus, because every muscle in his body was convulsing and spittle dripped from his lips. He was struggling to draw each breath.

N'Jalss sniffed at Isiilde, before running a grating tongue up her ear.

"She's mine," Isek hissed, stepping forward.

N'Jalss sneered at the little man before shoving the nymph into Isek's arms. He bound her hands, ignoring the desperate plea in her eyes. Isek had been Marsais' trusted friend for hundreds of years. How could he betray him so completely?

"I won't hurt you," Isek whispered. "You're safe with me."

Isiilde brought her knee up, and Isek jumped back with a grin, then moved forward and hoisted the kicking nymph over a shoulder.

She could see little from her awkward vantage point as Isek

followed the group of betrayers. Oenghus' feet dragged on the stone floor as two muscular soldiers struggled with his body.

Shimei and N'Jalss had Marsais by the arms. He glanced over his shoulder at her. There was fear in his eyes. She called out to him through their Bond, but there was no reassuring answer, only the distance he'd kept her at since the beginning of his duel.

Acacia and her two paladins were being prodded with spears. The captain seemed calm, eyeing her captors like pigs about to be slaughtered. Isiilde could only hope the paladin had something in mind.

The group walked for a time—long enough for Isek's shoulder to become uncomfortable. She struggled for breath, squirming to lessen the pressure on her stomach, but found little relief.

The party entered a narrow stairwell that plunged into the earth. The passage was dank and smelled of mold, with torches fluttering fitfully in their rusty sconces. She tried to call her flame, to summon it to her aid, but she was gagged. And without the power of her voice, the fire only sputtered weakly.

Isiilde did not recognize this part of the castle. She'd been forbidden to enter the lower levels. But then she'd never wanted to—the press of stone was suffocating.

Mold tickled her nose. She sneezed painfully around her gag, and Isek cursed, setting her down to pat out the flames that had caught on his cloak.

"You said a gag would take care of that," N'Jalss hissed.

"It's just an involuntary reaction. She can't help it," Isek said, grabbing her by the arm and pulling her forward.

"We can't afford any surprises."

"And you'll have none."

The narrow stairwell ended, flowing into a passage that sloped downwards. They were led through a series of twisting chambers. A spider's web of passages branched off into darkness. The muffled noises of turning cogs and hissing steam filled the air with the dull hum of activity.

There were rooms filled with alchemy equipment, giant cauldrons, and walls of shelves packed with herbs and other dubious ingredients.

One room held the remains of a monstrous animal, its bleached bones propped against the walls like fallen timber.

Another stairway, and they went deeper still, the weight of stone crushing her chest. She tried to bolt back up the stairwell, tugging against her captor, but Isek hoisted her over his shoulder again.

"Be still," Isek ordered, squeezing her thigh in warning.

Isiilde was at his mercy. Without a knife, without her voice, trapped again. Only this time it was far worse—Marsais and Oenghus were here, too. Both badly wounded. Was Oenghus still alive?

From her uncomfortable position, she could only see N'Jalss' boots in the narrow corridor. Isiilde tried to think of something—anything. She eyed Isek's belt. Unfortunately, he'd moved his knife to the front. Carefully, so no one would notice, she started working her wrists, trying to slip free of the rope while she silently prayed to the Sylph for help.

THEY WERE TAKEN to a large chamber. Its rafters were lost in shadows, the corners obscured in darkness. The prisoners were shackled to chains looped over beams, and then hoisted off their feet with a cruel winch.

Marsais' eyes rolled back in his head as he was wrenched off his feet. Fresh blood gushed from his wounded side, dripping onto the floor.

Tharios gestured towards the seer, and one of their captors stepped forward, lowering his cowl. It was Zander, a Xaionian Wise One. He removed Marsais' gag and pressed a vial to his lips, forcing him to drink its contents.

Oenghus hung limply from his chains. His broad chest rose with a shudder and deflated with a rattle.

The room made her skin crawl. It contained strange devices bristling with blades, screws, and leather straps. A row of rusted cages sat in filthy ichor to one side. Shadowed, vaguely human lumps languished behind the bars. Coals smoldered in a rusty brazier in the center, an array of instruments resting on the edge, their tips nestled beneath the coals, glowing red in the dark.

Most of the traitorous soldiers had been left at key points along the way to discourage unwanted visitors. Only six soldiers remained with Zander, Shimei, N'Jalss, Eiji, and Tharios.

Isek pulled her back so she had a view of Marsais—or perhaps so he could see her.

Tharios strolled over to a cruel wooden chair with metal buckles and clamps, and sat down. The pale Wise One lounged, letting his prisoners ponder their fate as he studied his lacquered nails.

Eiji poked curiously at Oenghus, surprised every time he managed another breath.

Acacia watched from her hanging position. And her scarred comrade, Lucas, glared at their captors. The young paladin, Rivan, was sweating with fear.

Whatever they had forced down Marsais' throat seemed to revive him, because he lifted his head. And in one fluid motion, Tharios rose, drew his dagger with a hiss of steel, and swept the blade towards Marsais.

Isiilde jerked, but the blade fell short of his throat, slicing through his goatee instead. Braid and coins clattered to the floor.

"We mustn't forget about those little trinkets." Tharios kicked the severed braid away. "You look more alert, Marsais, though perhaps not comfortable. But we hardly want that. N'Jalss is skilled at finding the perfect balance between life and death—that finite line between agony and unconscious. It's a fascinating study. We certainly don't want you passing out."

Marsais remained tight-lipped, blood dripping from his mangled hands onto his face as he watched Tharios pace slowly around him.

"I'll get to the point, and if you're in a talkative mood, we can skip the nasty bits. Allow me to paint a picture for you: the Archlord is suddenly attacked by Oenghus Saevaldr for his... indiscretion with his charge."

Tharios nodded towards Isek. "We even have a trustworthy witness willing to testify. Oenghus, his honor slighted, flies into a rage and tears the Archlord to pieces. And our noble paladins here foolishly try to stop a berserker. They're quickly slaughtered for their gallant efforts, at which point Eiji is forced to kill Oenghus.

"Oh, there will be the skeptical, the doubting, but in the end the

Wise Ones will do what they always do: argue, debate, investigate, argue some more and finally—nothing at all."

Isiilde continued loosening her ropes, her wrists slick with blood, but she had to keep her movements to a minimum.

"You will be a scratch on that useless table in the Hall of Judgment, and I will be Archlord in the wake of your unfortunate, but not widely mourned, death."

Tharios lifted Marsais' chin to look him in the eyes. "You already know what I want. I have never questioned your foresight, although it seems to do you little good, so let me narrow down your options. I doubt torture will work, but I'll give N'Jalss the satisfaction, anyway. The same goes for your barbarian friend, although by the looks of him, I doubt he'll last much longer."

The man's voice chilled her blood. If ever a realm existed where no sun shone, his voice would whisper to all ears in the dark. He spoke of torture as someone might remark on the weather.

"I know what will cut to your heart. She's standing over there like a terrified rabbit."

Isek tensed, hugging her closer as Tharios walked behind Marsais, whispering in his ear. "Look at those eyes. Wide and innocent. Do you think she can even imagine what horrors the body can endure?"

"You swore she wouldn't be harmed," Isek said. "That was our agreement."

"And I honor my agreements, Isek. You will have the nymph. I assure you she will not be harmed any more than you would harm her."

Isiilde could feel Isek's heart quicken against her back.

"I leave the choice to you, Marsais zar'Vaylin. Tell me how to reach the tomb, and I will send her off to live in safety with Isek. He's not such a bad fellow, is he? She wouldn't be the first nymph to set two friends at each other's throat."

Marsais remained still. But Oenghus stirred, a low rumble rising from his chest as he sucked in another unbelievable breath.

"Now the first option isn't so bad," Tharios purred. "Let me give you the second: you will have the privilege of watching my men pleasure themselves with your nymph. I've always wondered what would become of a nymph who changed hands so quickly."

N'Jalss moved towards Isiilde. The Lore sprang to Isek's lips, but Tharios was faster. An ethereal hand materialized, lashing out at Isek and seizing him by the throat. Tharios gestured, and the traitor was lifted off his feet.

Isiilde grabbed the knife from his belt and plunged it double-fisted at N'Jalss, but the tip only pierced his muscled chest an inch. The warrior had stopped her short, catching her bound wrists before she could finish her attack. She tried with all her strength to overcome his one-handed grip, but he only laughed.

"Pathetic," he hissed, wrenching the knife from her bloodied hands and tossing it aside.

Tharios released the hand, and Isek crumpled to the dingy stone, gasping for air. "It's unwise for a turncoat to turn again," Tharios warned. "I swore you'd have her, and you will. But keep silent or I will rip out your tongue."

N'Jalss dragged Isiilde over to a slanted table.

"No," Oenghus rasped, stirring weakly against his chains. Eiji jumped backwards in shock.

"I don't know where the tomb is!" Marsais shouted. "If I knew, don't you think I would have investigated it myself?"

"I think you're lying," Tharios said.

N'Jalss slammed her onto the table and shackled her wrists. As the chains were pulled tight, she fought to slip free, ignoring the rusty metal digging into her flesh. She kicked at N'Jalss, but he caught her ankles in one strong hand.

Isiilde fought, she raged, and it was useless. All the heroic tales about the weak overpowering the strong with some mystical force of will were absolute drivel. She didn't stand a chance against his strength. But she still tried.

N'Jalss shackled one ankle, and then the other, spreading her legs to opposite corners of the table. Isiilde struggled like a trapped animal until blood trickled down her arms and feet.

"I know you're lying." Tharios gestured to the soldiers, who lined up eagerly, jostling to be the first. "Think back to before you were even born, to the founding of this Isle—over three thousand years ago. Legend claims that Hengist Heartfang, the first Archlord of the Isle, raised the Spine. But I know the truth." Tharios lowered his voice to a whisper. "And I know what lies beneath this rock."

Marsais gazed at Tharios with new understanding—and fear.

"So you see, Marsais zar'Vaylin, you can either save your nymph some agony, or not. It doesn't really matter because I will eventually find what I seek."

"I swear I don't know where it is, you fool."

"Well," Tharios said, clapping his hands. "It looks like we'll have a show after all. Would you like to get things started, N'Jalss? And, Isek, since I'm a man of my word, you can get in line, too. At the end. She'll be nice and ready for you."

Isek stood frozen in place. He looked like he might be sick.

"Do it!"

"Don't touch her!" Oenghus roared, straining against his chains, but his feet dangled and there was nothing for him to brace against.

"I'm told a Rahuatl's barbs are particularly painful to women," Tharios said, ignoring the berserker. He strolled back to his chair, and steepled his fingers to watch.

N'Jalss moved in front of the nymph, running his tongue over his fangs. Isiilde squeezed her eyes shut, pulling at the shackles with all her strength.

"Oh, look, even Thedus wants to watch."

Hope entered her heart for the first time, and she opened her eyes. Everyone watched the sun-scorched Wise One wander aimlessly over to the grim tableau.

N'Jalss hissed at him and tensed to strike, but Eiji shouted a warning. "Don't provoke him!"

N'Jalss halted.

"I've heard... rumors about him," Eiji said uneasily.

"Cowardly Wise Ones, and their aimless talk," N'Jalss spat, flexing his claws, but he withheld his strike, warily watching the half-naked man approach.

"Maybe he wants a turn," one soldier snickered.

Thedus, as much a permanent fixture of the Isle as its stones, placed a small tooth on the table beside Isiilde's ear. He turned and shuffled out of the chamber as silently as he had arrived.

Hope died.

Tharios applauded with slow amusement, and N'Jalss sneered, ripping her shirt with a swipe of his claws.

"Wait, stop it—I'll tell you!" Marsais pleaded. "I remember." The truly frightening thing of it was—he probably *had* forgotten.

Isiilde trembled from the tips of her fingers to her toes. It didn't mean a thing. Marsais would still be murdered, and so would Oenghus. She no longer cared what happened to her.

"Yes?" Tharios raised a halting hand, and N'Jalss pulled back, growling impatiently.

"In my bedchamber... there's a warded flask," Marsais wheezed, struggling to form words through the haze of pain.

"Where is the tomb? I want direction!"

"The flask is handed down from Archlord to Archlord. There's supposed to be a map inside, but I've never seen it."

"You've never opened it?" Eiji asked.

"I may be a lunatic, but I'm no fool. It's warded with a powerful binding." Tharios stepped up to Marsais, searching for a hint of deception. "That's all I know. *Please*, I beg you, just let her go."

During the unbearable silence that followed, Marsais met her gaze, his eyes shimmering like mist.

"N'Jalss, Eiji, come with me—you too, Isek. You can show me how to reach my new quarters."

Isek started for the nymph. "Leave her," Tharios snapped. "She'll draw attention."

"I'm no guard, Tharios," Shimei said, stepping proudly forward.

"Very well. Zander will remain with the guards. Do not touch the nymph, or I will make sure you never plow another whore as long as you draw breath."

N'Jalss snaked forward, and Isiilde thrashed in pain as his teeth sliced into her neck. When he withdrew, his pointed teeth dripped red with her blood. He licked his lips with a forked tongue, and left.

CHAPTER 50

The guards leered at the prone nymph, and Zander moved closer, drinking up the sight of her.

"Crazed fool should have kept his mouth shut," one guard muttered.

"Do you know what he's planning, Zander? What did Tharios promise you?" Marsais asked, trying to divert the man's attention.

"Shut your mouth."

Oenghus was huffing like a wounded bear, eyes burning into the leering men. His arms strained against the chains, flexing and testing their make.

A guard hurried over, driving the blunt end of his spear into Oenghus' gut. "Stop that!"

Oenghus growled back. It seemed to aid him rather than hinder.

"I doubt life will be what you imagined when Tharios releases Karbonek," Marsais said, forcing some strength into his voice.

"Put their gags back on," Zander ordered, running a hand over his slick hair, trying and failing to take his eyes off the helpless nymph.

The guards rushed to obey, and Oenghus heaved against his chains, lifting his legs. He caught one guard by surprise, wrapping his legs around the guard's neck and twisting violently. The soldier dropped to the floor in a motionless heap.

"Brainless fools!" Zander spat.

The five remaining guards rushed forward, pummeling the berserker with a barrage of blunted blows that were meant to beat him into submission.

And while Oenghus was grunting with pain, Zander's resistance shattered. He moved on top of Isiilde, eyes alight with lust, his hands moving up her thighs as she struggled beneath him. Consumed with desire, Zander struggled to loosen his belt, fumbling with the buckle.

Marsais was speaking in a harsh tongue, Oenghus was roaring, and Zander was groping her when a grinning imp with grotesque teeth appeared above her.

The imp stood on the table, studying her upside down. Zander bunched up her skirts, and was on the verge of claiming her when the imp ripped the gag from her mouth.

Isiilde screamed with rage.

Fire surged from the brazier with a roar. It hit Zander, igniting his robes like dry grass. He howled in terror and reeled backwards.

The unnatural flames exploded outwards, roiling with a life of their own. Marsais gave the imp a sharp order, and it hopped off the table.

Flames devoured the chamber, racing along wooden devices and climbing up chains to consume the rafters overhead.

Isiilde continued to scream, blind with fury, seeking to erase Zander's touch. She wanted every one of them to burn.

Flames burst from her flesh, consumed her tattered clothing, and stirred her hair. She moaned at the fire's touch. But her pleasure was short-lived—the manacles around her wrists and ankles glowed. Isiilde realized her mistake too late. The metal seared flesh, blistering skin, and her rage quickly turned to panic.

Marsais ripped the veil between their spirits, and their Bond flared to life, bringing all his injuries, too. The shock of pain stunned her to silence. Her fire sputtered, and he quickly dropped the veil back in place.

Freed by the imp, Oenghus waded into the middle of the soldiers, and the newly liberated paladins rushed to assist.

Marsais gave Luccub another order, and the imp skittered up his body to unlock his shackles with a curved claw.

The shackles popped open, and Marsais fell to the ground. As he struggled to stand, the imp flapped over to Isiilde, dug its claw into her own shackles, and quickly popped all four.

Marsais staggered against the table. "We need to leave. Can you walk?"

The chamber glowed with heat, and he eyed the burning rafters overhead. But Isiilde barely heard his question. She was staring at the charred body of Zander. She'd killed him. On purpose.

"Isiilde!"

His sharp command got her moving. Isiilde tried to stand, but her legs gave out. The unnatural fire had fed off her power and left her drained. Her body refused to move.

Marsais hoisted her over a shoulder despite his crushed hands, and nearby, Oenghus snapped the last guard's neck, then recovered his shield and hammer.

A store of potions went up in flames. Marsais ran for the nearest passage, and the others were close on his heels when an explosion rocked the stone. A fireball engulfed the chamber. Stone and timber caved in, and an inferno of heat roared after them, licking at their backs.

The fire warmed her empty bones, and for a moment she could feel her fingers again. Then the heat was sucked back in a vortex of air, and she felt a mind-numbing ache of cold before a wave of blackness washed over her.

CHAPTER 51

THE BATTERED group hurried down a rough passage of natural rock. Smoke swirled at their backs and darkness beckoned them into a honeycomb of tunnels that burrowed under the stronghold.

"Tell me you have my grog," Oenghus growled at the captain when they stopped to catch their breath.

Acacia handed over his flask, and he took a life-saving swig of the divine liquid. It burned through his veins, devouring the stone adder venom. He drove his fist into the stone with a roar, then shook himself.

"You weren't joking when you said she's flammable." He quickly removed his breastplate and shirt and took his daughter. Naked and ethereal in the near dark, her eyes fluttered open as he slipped the shirt over her head. "It's all right, Sprite. You're safe."

The fire hadn't harmed her, but the shackles had left her skin raw and blistered. She stared vacantly at the thick smoke inching towards them, but at least her mark was still coiled around her spine.

It had been close—too bloody close for his liking, and they weren't out of danger yet.

"How many stand with Tharios?" Acacia asked.

"Too many," Oenghus grunted. "And the Scarecrow can't hope to weave with those hands."

"Bandage his hands," Acacia ordered, and the younger paladin snapped to obey.

"We won't be able to go back that way," Lucas said. "Where does this passage lead?"

"I don't bloody know. Down?" Oenghus shrugged, looking to Marsais. He was slumped against the wall, his arms crossed over his chest, trying to stay conscious as Rivan bandaged his hands.

"Give me a moment." Marsais took a shuddering breath and closed his eyes, retreating into the complicated web of memories that twisted through his mind.

After some minutes, a chiming noise echoed in the corridor. Acacia moved to the forefront with her sword raised as an imp flew from the smoke—one half of a severed goatee clutched in its clawed feet.

"Hold!" Marsais ordered. "Ah, thank you, Luccub." The imp dropped the braid in his bandaged hands before chattering angrily at the paladins.

"You command this fiend?" Lucas demanded.

"I didn't hear you complaining when he freed you." Marsais pushed himself off the wall with some effort. "I know where we are." He caught Oenghus' eye, and the two shared a silent conversation. Namely, that their location wasn't encouraging.

"I'll take Isiilde. I won't be any use in a fight and you'll need your hands free."

There was no use arguing; he was right. And Marsais was a lot sturdier than he looked. Oenghus draped Isiilde over the wounded man's shoulder, then cinched on his breastplate and beat his hammer against his shield in warning: Death was coming.

Oenghus took the lead, while Marsais gave him directions through a twisting maze of tunnels. When they reached a crossroads that looked identical to the last, Marsais ordered them left. Again.

"This will be our *fourth* left," Oenghus growled.

"I know where we are."

"You always go left when you're lost."

"Obviously, I don't remain lost for long, or I'd still be wandering the Great Expanse."

"Because I rescued your bony arse."

"I would have been perfectly fine," Marsais muttered.

Oenghus grunted and took the passage to the left.

They filed down a tunnel, and after some time heard the first signs of pursuit, or rather an attempt to cut them off farther ahead.

"Hurry or you'll have no room to fight!" Marsais hissed at his back.

Oenghus surged blindly forward. The narrow tunnel opened into a bloated crossroads, and Oenghus barreled into the wider passage before enemy soldiers could claim the strategic ground.

Charging feet, grating armor, and the labored breath of fear filled the tunnel. Oenghus turned towards the echoes, hefting his war hammer.

Death awaited the first enemy soldier. With nowhere to go, he was forced to charge the waiting berserker. The soldier swung his sword in terror.

Oenghus easily diverted the chopping swing with his shield, and slammed his war hammer into the wide-eyed man. The guard flew against the wall with a crack of bone.

The second soldier had no more choice than the first. Oenghus caught his spear jab between hip and shield, and snapped the haft. He brought his war hammer up, and drove it down onto the soldier's head. It exploded like a melon.

Oenghus stepped over the oozing skull, and roared a challenge.

The six soldiers who remained trapped in the narrow passage skittered to a stop. The soldier in front tried to retreat, but pounding footsteps signaled reinforcements from another passage, and his comrades shoved him forward.

Their sacrificial lamb met Oenghus' war hammer. The third soldier crumpled with a spray of blood.

"Hold the side passages, then follow after!" Marsais ordered.

The paladins spilled into the crossroads, moving to defend against the second tunnel that was about to disgorge another group of guards.

Oenghus picked at his own line of attackers. But they kept backing up, away from his reach, trying to draw him into their tunnel. Frustrated with their cowardice, he bellowed the Lore and his war hammer crackled to life with raw energy. The charged air gathered, and he hurled a bolt of lightning into the line of soldiers. The bolt blasted through all save the last. Oenghus bared his teeth at the sole survivor. He dropped his weapons and ran.

"Lucas will bring up the rear—go!" Acacia shouted.

Oenghus left the rear defense to Lucas, whose smaller size allowed more maneuverability in the narrow space. Oenghus charged after Marsais, leaving Rivan and Acacia to follow.

Lucas Cutter sliced a soldier open from shoulder to hip, and kicked the man back into his comrades. It slowed the knot of soldiers trying to push their way into the wider passage. Lucas took advantage of the distraction and raced after the gleam of his captain's mail, the soldiers charging on his heels.

The tunnel soon widened, and Acacia held off a third group of soldiers as Marsais limped past, carrying his nymph.

A frustrated line of soldiers, trapped like fish in a barrel, could only wait their turn to engage the captain at the mouth of their grave.

"I'll bring up the rear, Lucas!" Acacia shouted to her lieutenant as he emerged from the dark. He obeyed her without question, and continued on.

Acacia's smaller size was an advantage in the narrowing passages. But it wasn't until Lucas heard her lighter footsteps approaching that he fully applied himself to an all-out retreat.

As they moved deeper into the maze, Oenghus lost track of the twisting turns. Soldiers continued to nip at their heels, but no one challenged them at the intersections they came to.

Oenghus risked a backwards glance, looking past the fearful face of the younger paladin and the grim visage of the older, to spot the quick, efficient blade of their captain flashing in the dark. As one soldier fell beneath her blade, another took his place. With the skill of a veteran, she kept pace, shuffling backwards as she fought.

A doorway loomed at the end of the tunnel. Oenghus ducked under the lintel, Rivan, Lucas and Acacia following on his heels. Then Rivan threw his weight against the door. The iron squealed in protest, gained momentum, and a moment before it slammed shut, a flapping shadow darted through the gap.

Oenghus skidded to a stop, reversing direction. The Lore sprang to his lips, and he slapped his palm against the door, spreading his fingers over the iron.

While the paladins wedged a rotting beam into place, he chanted, tracing crude runes of warding. His runes flared to life on the iron, dimmed, then glowed with faint power.

The imp chortled at the shoddy work, swishing its tail in mockery. Oenghus glared at the pest. "It will do for now." But in truth, an apprentice could unravel one of his wards.

The faint green glow of ancient everlight flickered in rusty sconces, casting sickly shadows in the deep dark. Far overhead, stalactites poked through the blackness, reaching towards their counterparts on the cavern floor. The gaping maw of stone twisted sounds, throwing voices and footsteps hollowly against the cavern's walls.

Oenghus had heard of this place; every Wise One had, but few had been here. A ring of fifty standing stones sat in the cavern's basin, the air between the stones shimmering like a rippling pond. It was the circle of Runic Gateways.

CHAPTER 52

"There's no way out," Acacia said. The only sign of disapproval was a slight narrowing of her eyes.

"Hold the door," Oenghus ordered.

A set of steps hewn in stone led down to the cavern's basin. Oenghus took the stairs two at a time.

Acacia sprinted after him, leaving her men to guard the door. As they approached the ring of stones, they slowed, warily eyeing the shimmering circle of energy.

There was a gap, like a doorway, between the standing stones. Marsais was on his knees and Isiilde was slumped against his chest, staring vacantly at the stones.

"Tell me you've remembered how to navigate the Pathways," Oenghus growled at Marsais.

"We need to get her off the island."

Acacia glanced uneasily at the pair. "You mean you don't know where they lead?"

The Gateways of the Isle had not been used by anyone who valued their life since the Shattering—no one could read the mysterious runes. Some had tried. And likely died.

"It's Portal Magic," Oenghus said. "The Gateways are easy to activate, but no one bothered to write down how to read the runes—it was common knowledge before the Shattering. Without direction, the Pathways shift, changing locations from one minute to the next."

Acacia frowned at the monument to lost knowledge. "So we could end up a thousand feet above the ground, or in the Nine Halls."

"At least you'd have plenty of fiends to take that righteous anger of yours out on."

Acacia ignored the berserker. And Marsais ignored them both. "I need you to pick one, my dear."

Her eyes sought his own. "I can't…"

"You must."

"What if I choose wrong?"

"I've always trusted your instincts," he said, kissing her softly. "Now trust yourself. Oenghus, take her around the circle. Let her look at them—"

The iron door shuddered on its hinges.

"Quickly now."

Oenghus gently lifted her, and walked over to the first set of standing stones. At their approach, the runes swirled to life, moving like blue fireflies beneath the stone's surface.

Isiilde said nothing, so he moved on to the next. When they had traversed half the circle, he stopped to make sure she was looking at the stones. It was difficult to tell—her eyes were wide with shock. Oenghus had seen that faraway look in hardened warriors and brutalized women and children who'd suffered too much. And in his own eyes, too.

The noises behind the door became more urgent and forceful. Reinforcements had arrived.

Marsais was right. They had to get her out of here. If the Sylph's daughter fell into the wrong hands… Oenghus shuddered at the thought.

"This one," she said.

Her confidence brought him up short. These stones looked no different from the rest—the same unknown runes swirled below the surface.

"Why this one?"

"I like these runes. They feel… familiar."

Marsais staggered over to join them.

"Don't you want to look at the rest?" Oenghus asked, frowning at the Gateway. She shrugged in reply. On principle, he completed the circuit with her.

Marsais remained at the chosen Gateway, studying the runes with a critical eye. Familiarity tickled the back of his mind. He turned and called the paladins down.

"I'll stay and hold them off as long as I can, sir," Rivan called to his captain.

"My dear young man," Marsais spoke before Acacia could answer, "bravery is overrated. Leave the heroics to the door."

The two paladins looked to their captain, who nodded. At her silent command, Lucas and Rivan abandoned the door and hurried into the circle of stones.

"Where does it go?" Acacia asked Marsais.

"Probably somewhere."

A muscle in the captain's jaw twitched.

"Wait, Oen." Isiilde's ears perked up when they stopped in front of another Gateway. "I like this one better."

Marsais hobbled over to investigate. "Why this one?"

"It's hot."

Marsais cleared his throat, caught Oenghus' eye, and with an arch of his brow, gestured towards her first choice. Oenghus took the hint. Neither of them wanted to end up in Firˇdum.

Lucas scowled at the Gateway. "We're trusting a nymph?"

"I won't laugh if you piss your pants," Oenghus said.

"It's remarkable where a single step can take you."

"Oh, shut up, you dandy bastard," Oenghus growled, shoving Marsais through the portal.

He vanished as silently as a wraith.

"Is he still alive, Sprite?"

Isiilde gawked at Oenghus.

"I'm guessing that's a yes." He tossed his daughter over a broad shoulder and hefted his war hammer. "Into the bloody unknown and all that."

Oenghus Saevaldr stepped through, leaving the paladins and an imp to follow or not.

It turned out they did follow, a moment before the chamber's door burst open, spewing out a flood of treacherous Wise Ones and soldiers. They rushed into an empty cavern with no exit, save forty-nine Gateways leading to realms unknown.

READ THE NEXT IN THE SERIES:

FLAME OF RUIN

BOOK TWO

If you enjoyed *Spark of Chaos*, and would like to see more of Isiilde and Marsais, please consider leaving a review. Reviews help authors keep writing.

Keep up to date with the latest news, releases, and giveaways.
It's quick and easy and spam free.
Sign up at www.sabrinaflynn.com/news

About the Author

Sabrina Flynn is the author of the ***Ravenwood Mysteries*** set in Victorian San Francisco. When she's not exploring the seedy alleyways of the Barbary Coast, she dabbles in fantasy and steampunk, and has a habit of throwing herself into wild oceans and gator-infested lakes.

Although she's currently lost in South Carolina, she's lived most of her life in perpetual fog and sunshine with a rock troll and two crazy imps. She spent her youth trailing after insanity, jumping off bridges, climbing towers, and riding down waterfalls in barrels. After spending fifteen years wrestling giant hounds and battling pint-sized tigers, she now travels everywhere via watery portals leading to anywhere.

You can connect with her at any of the social media platforms below or at www.sabrinaflynn.com

APPENDIX

Acacia Mael (ah·kay·shaa may·el) - Knight Captain of the Blessed Order on the Isle of the Wise Ones.

Afarim - Winged race of the Isle of Winds

Ardmoor - Void-worshipping barbarians in Vaylin.

Asmara - A Guardian of Iilenshar, or the Guardian of Love, also known as the Everchild. Asmara was six when the Orb shattered, and has not aged a day since. Daughter of Zahra, sister of Chaim.

Assumer - A race that can assume any shape.

Auroch - A massive bull-type creature found in Nuthaan and the Fell Wastes

Bastardlands - The continent that lies between the west and east. Separated by two chasms on either side, it's believed that the Keeper erected the Gates (chasms) to trap the Guardians of Morchaint.

Berserker's Rite - Some Nuthaanian warriors risk drinking Brim-grog on the eve of the Reddened Month. Most warriors die. The ones who survive have a reputation for being volatile and lethal.

Blessed Order - An Order that worships the Guardians of Iilenshar.

Blood Moon - A day and a night of light. All three moons are visible in the summer sky. The Dark One's moon is closest, playing havoc on coastal areas.

Brimgrog - Nuthaan's sacred brew. Few dare drink the burning brew, and of those few, most die. The rare Nuthaanians who survive the Rite are known (and feared) as Berserkers.

Brinehilde (brin·hillda) - A Nuthaanian Priestess of the Sylph who runs an orphanage in Drivel.

Carpinvale - A small fishing town in the south that exiled Oenghus.

Chaim (high·em) - A Guardian of Iilenshar, also known as the Guardian of Life and the River God. Son of Zahra, older brother to Asmara.

Circle of Nine - The ruling council of the Wise Ones.

Coven - A harbor town that sits directly beneath the stronghold of the Wise Ones.

Da'len - A barbarian tribe in Vaylin.

Dagenir (day·jen·near) - A Guardian of Morchaint, also known as the Dark One. He tried to steal the Orb, and battled with Zahra. The Orb shattered during their struggle.

Drivel - A large city on the Isle of Wise Ones.

Easthaven - The east side of the city of Haven, separated by the Gate and chasm.

Eiji (ee·Gee)- a gnome Wise One.

Ethervenom - An addicting drug made from harvested Plague Viper venom.

Everwar - The endless struggle between light and oblivion.

Fell Wastes - A harsh, mountainous region to the north of Nuthaan, populated by Wedamen.

Fey - Lindale (a race of elves) who rebelled against their nature and were twisted by their dark deeds.

Fomorri (fah·moor·ee) - A race created and twisted by the Fey's foul experiments.

Fyrsta (fears·tah) - The Sylph's favored realm.

Galvier Longstride - A legendary wanderer whose feet never stop moving.

Grawl - The Dark One's Own. Monstrous Voidspawn with void-like eyes.

Guardians of Iilenshar (ill·en·shar) - Six Guardians who survived the Shattering and were blessed with the Orb's power: Zahra, Chaim, Asmara, Zemoch, Oshimi, and Yvesa.

Guardians of Morchaint - Six Guardians who sided with the Void: Dagenir, Shade, Indrazor, Pazia, Mourn, and Silvanthe.

Gwaith - A Merchant kingdom along the Golden Road.

Haimon Goodfellow - Owner of the Glass Goblet.

Harsbane - A poisonous herb. The leaves contain an hallucinogen when smoked.

Hengist Heartfang - First Archlord of the Isle of Wise Ones.

Ielequithe (ill · ay · quith) - Lord General of the Isle of Wise Ones.

Iilenshar- Floating Isle of the Guardians. Coat of arms: the Sacred Sun caught in a maze-like circle.

Isiilde Jaal'Yasine (is · seal · dee jawl · yah · seen) - A combustible nymph with an affinity for fire.

Isek Beirnuckle - Spymaster to Marsais.

Isle of Blight - An island to the south of the Bastardlands that was ravaged when Ramashan, a druid, opened a Portal to the Nine Halls.

Isle of Winds - A grouping of islands off the Spotted Coast.

Isle of Wise Ones - An island off the Fell Coast where the Wise Ones Order is located.

Kambe (cam · bee) - A powerful kingdom ruled by Emperor Soataen Jaal III in the West.

Karbonek (car · bah · neck) - A Greater Fiend from the Nine Halls. A god revered by the Fomorri.

Keeper - A favored servant of the Sylph who was tasked with protecting Fyrsta.

Keening - The inhabitants of Fyrsta do not age like others. They only die of old age when the will to live fades. Someone who has lost the will to live is said to be in the Keening. As a result, many die in their twenties and thirties.

Kiln - A powerful kingdom to the East.

King's Folly - A game of runes that involves two hundred stones, and a cycle of ever-changing power.

Lindale - A race of elves (faerie) who were wiped out during the Shattering.

Lispen's Folly - A whirlpool of chaotic energy churning on the ceiling of the outer sanctum of the main hall, just outside of the Council Chambers of the Nine. Lispen was a Wise One who tried to open a Runic Portal, and disappeared.

Lome (low · meh) - A barbarian tribe in Vaylin.

Lucas Cutter - Paladin of the Blessed Order.

Luccub - An Imp with a tooth fetish.

Marsais (mar · say · es) - A sexy elf immortal.

Medwin - A barbarian tribe in Vaylin.

Miera Malzeen - A Wise One teacher who tried to link with Isiilde and was subsequently burned to a crisp.

Morigan Freyr (more · eh · gen fray · er) - Master Healer on the Isle of Wise Ones. Matriarch of the ruling Nuthaanian tribe. On and off Oathbound to Oenghus. Adopted mother of Isiilde. Savior of Nuthaan.

N'Jalss (nah · jaal · ss) - A Rahuatl Wise One.

Nereus (near · rose) - God of the seas.

Nine Halls - A realm that was overrun by the Void.

Oathbound - Inhabitants of Fyrsta take oaths, vowing to remain together as a couple for a specified amount of time determined by the couple.

Oenghus Saevaldr (oh · won · gus say · val · der) - A formidable Nuthaanian Berserker. Also known as: Wise One of the Isle, Bone Mender, Skull Crusher, the Bloody Berserker of Nuthaan and the Grimstorm of the Fell Wastes.

Oshimi (oh · shim · mee) - Guardian of Wisdom, also known as The Serene One.

Pip - A street urchin from the Dock Districts of Drivel. Brother to Zoshi and Tuck.

Pits o'Mourn - A deep chasm in Kiln. Criminals are lowered into the gorge and none ever emerge.

Pyrderi Har'Feydd (pie · deer · rhee haar · fade) - The first fey.

Rahuatl (raw · tule) - A race of humanoids who live in the Jungles of Rraal. Their culture is steeped in ritual and pain.

Rashk (rash · ka) - A Rahuatl Wise One who has a knack for enchanting.

Reapers - Voidspawn with a taste for fresh blood. Sometimes called Death's children.

Rivan (riv · en) - A young paladin of the Blessed Order.

Shattering - A powerful artifact that the Sylph imbued with her power to fight the Void. When Dagenir, its own guardian, attempted to steal the Orb for himself, Zahra tried to stop him. During their fight, the Orb was shattered, releasing a cataclysmic wave of power that nearly extinguished life on Fyrsta.

Shimei Al'eeth (shim · mee awl · eeth) - A Kilnish Wise One

Sidonie (sid · own · ee) - A Mearcentian Wise One

Soisskeli (soice · kill · ee) - The Chaos Lord who crafted a stave capable of opening Runic Gateways and binding any creature not of Fyrsta. Oshimi, the Serene One, defeated him in battle.

Somnial's Realm (salm · knee · el) - The Realm of Dreams, where all realms touch.

Spine - A tall, naturally formed spire that towers over the Wise Ones' stronghold.

Suevi (sweh · vee) - A barbarian tribe in Vaylin.

Sylph - The Goddess of All.

Tharios - A Wise One from Xaio.

Thedus - A sunburnt man who wanders around the Wise Ones' tower naked.

Thira Olander - Wise One of the Isle, Mistress of Novices, and High Alchemist.

Tuck - Urchin from the dock district in Drivel. Brothers: Pip and Zoshi.

Ulfhidhin (ulf · fid · hin) - The wild god who once abducted the Sylph and fought Karbonek.

Unspoken - or Disciples of Karbonek. A group of devout Bloodmagi who worship the Greater Fiend.

Void - Everything opposite of life.

Weeping Mark - A venomous spider.

Westhaven - The west side of the city of Haven, separated by the Gate and chasm.

Wisps - Tiny faeries who are often captured, put in jars, and used as a light source until they die.

Witchwood - A rare wood that has a natural resistance to enchantments.

Xiao (zow) - A merchant kingdom in the Bastardlands known for their pleasures.

Yvesa (yeh·veh·saa) - A Guardian of Iilenshar. A sprite who is revered by jesters and bards. She has a reputation for being a prankster.

Zahra (zah·rah) - A Guardian of Iilenshar, also known as the Radiant One, Goddess Of All That Was Just, Guardian of Good, and the Divine Savior. She battled with Dagenir when he tried to steal the Orb.

Zander - A Wise One who served Tharios, attacked Isiilde, and was burnt to a crisp.

Zianna (zee·anna) - A gifted Wise One's Apprentice.

Zoshi (zo·shee) - Urchin from Dock districts in Drivel. Brothers: Pip and Tuck.

CALENDAR OF FYRSTA

350 days in a year
10 Months in a year
35 days in a month

MONTHS
Wintertide
Thawing
Greentide
Sowing
Summertide
Faded
Harvest
Reddened
Carvers
Frostmarch

FESTIVALS

The Shadowed Dawn: 35th of Frostmarch to the 1st of Wintertide. Marks the new year with a night and a day of darkness, when all three moons align and the Dark One's own moon smothers the sun.

The Lightened Dusk: 17th-18th of Summertide. A day and a night of silver light when all three moons align and the Sylph's moon shines bright.

The Sylph's Fortnight: 10-24th Summertide. Fourteen days of Festivities dedicated to the Sylph.

Feast of Fools: 1-7th of Greentide. A week of costumed festivities that celebrate the end of winter.